ELIAS. COME. IT IS TIME. . . .

"Time for what?" Dr. Rax called before he realized the voice he answered was in his head.

Elias. Come.

He turned and faced the door, unable to stop himself. From a distance, he felt his hand go into his pocket for his keys, saw them turn in the lock, heard the quiet movement of air as the door opened, smelled the cedar that had been filling the room with its scent since they'd opened the coffin, tasted fear.

The coffin was empty save for a pile of linen wrappings already beginning to decay. A man stooped with age, eyes deep sunk over ax blade cheekbones, flesh clinging to bone and skin stretched tight, walked out of the shadows. Somehow, Elias Rax had known it would come to this. From the moment he had first seen the unbroken seal on the sarcophagus, he had felt this moment approaching.

"Des . . . troy those." The voice creaked like two pieces of old wood rubbing together.

"Do what?" Dr. Rax asked, looking down at the linen wrappings and then up at the man who had so recently worn them.

"There must be . . . no evi . . . dence."

"Evidence. Of what?"

"Of me. . . ."

BLOOD LINES

TANYA HUFF

DAW BOOKS, INC.

DONALD A. WOLLHEIM, FOUNDER

375 Hudson Street, New York, NY 10014

ELIZABETH R. WOLLHEIM
SHEILA E. GILBERT
PUBLISHERS

First Printing, January 1993

2 3 4 5 6 7 8 9

DAW TRADEMARK REGISTERED
U.S. PAT. OFF. AND FOREIGN COUNTRIES
—MARCA REGISTRADA
HECHO EN U.S.A.

Printed in Canada

For Mother Bowen, who taught me that a book lasts because it touches the heart and soul. She not only gave me ancient Greece but Middle Earth as well and while I might have found Tolkien without her, I would've been the poorer for Homer's loss. She also put up with more spelling mistakes in a single semester than one woman should have to deal with in a lifetime. For both of these, for Christmas sherry and gingerbread, for Adeste Fideles and wine-dark seas, thank you. (Oh, and by the way: "Ab, cum, de, ex, in, pro, sina, sub, all take the ablative case. All others take accusative. Go team!")

I'd also like to take this time to thank Ms. Roberta Shane, Curatorial Assistant, Egyptology, at the Royal Ontario Museum for taking the time to show me around behind the scenes and for helping me to work out just how an undiscovered mummy could be, well, discovered. For those interested, the Egyptology Exhibit at the ROM is fantastic.

One

He had been almost aware for some time. Nothingness had shattered when they removed him from the chamber long concealed behind the centuries empty tomb of a forgotten priest. The final layer of the binding spell had been written on the rock wall smashed to gain access and, with that gone, the spell itself had begun to fray.

Every movement frayed it further. The surrounding ka, more souls than had been near him in millennia, called him to feed. Slowly, he reached for memory.

Then, just as he brushed against self and had only to reach out and grasp it and draw home the key to his freedom, the movement stopped and the lives went away. But the nothingness didn't quite return.

And that was the worst of all.

Sixteenth Dynasty, thought Dr. Rax running his finger lightly along the upper surface of the plain, unadorned rectangle of black basalt. Strange, when the rest of the collection was Eighteenth. He could now, however, understand why the British were willing to let the artifact go; although it was a splendid example of its type, it was neither going to bring new visitors flocking to the galleries nor was it likely to shed much light on the past.

Besides, thanks to the acquisitiveness of aristocracy with more money than brains, Great Britain has all the Egyptian antiquities it can hope to use. Dr. Rax was careful not to let that thought show on his face, as a member of said aristocracy, albeit of a more recent vintage, fidgeted at his shoulder.

Too well bred to actually ask, the fourteenth Baron Montclair leaned forward, hands shoved into the pockets of his crested blazer.

Dr. Rax, unsure if the younger man was looking worried or merely vacant, attempted to ignore him. *And I thought Monty Python created the concept of the upper-class twit,* he mused as he continued his inspection. *How foolish of me.*

Unlike most sarcophagi, the artifact Dr. Rax examined had no lid but rather a sliding stone panel in one narrow end. Briefly, he wondered why that feature alone hadn't been enough to interest the British museums. As far as he knew the design survived on only one other sarcophagus, an alabaster beauty found by Zakaria Goneim in the unfinished step pyramid of Sekhem-khet.

Behind him, the fourteenth baron cleared his throat.

Dr. Rax continued to ignore him.

Although one corner had been chipped, the sarcophagus was in very good condition. Tucked away in one of the lower cellars of the Monclairs' ancestral home for almost a hundred years, it seemed to have been ignored by everything including time.

And excluding spiders. He brushed aside a dusty curtain of webbing, frowned, and with fingers that wanted to tremble, pulled a penlight out of his suit pocket.

"I say, is something wrong?" The fourteenth baron had an excuse for sounding a little frantic. The very exclusive remodeling firm would be arriving in a little under a month to turn the ancestral pile into a very exclusive health club and that great bloody stone box was sitting right where he'd planned to put the women's sauna.

The thudding of Dr. Rax's heart almost drowned out the question. He managed to mutter, "Nothing." Then he knelt and very carefully played the narrow beam of light over the lower edge of the sliding plate. Centered on the mortared seam, six inches above the base of the sarcophagus, was an oval of clay—a nearly perfect intact clay seal stamped with, as far as Dr. Rax could tell through the dust and the spiderwebs, the cartouche of Thoth, the ancient Egyptian god of wisdom.

Just for a moment, he forgot to breathe.

An intact seal could mean only one thing.

The sarcophagus wasn't—as everyone had assumed—empty.

For a dozen heartbeats, he stared at the seal and struggled

with his conscience. The Brits had already said they didn't want the artifact. He was under no obligation to let them know what they were giving away. On the other hand . . .

He sighed, switched off the penlight, and stood. "I need to make a call," he told the anxious peer. "If you could show me to a phone."

"Dr. Rax, what a pleasant surprise. Still out at Haversted Hall are you? Get a look at his lordship's 'bloody-great-black-stone-box'?"

"As a matter of fact, yes. And that's why I've called." He took a deep breath; best to get it over with quickly, the loss might hurt less. "Dr. Davis, did you actually send one of your people out here to look at the sarcophagus."

"Why?" The British Egyptologist snorted. "Need some help identifying it?"

Abruptly, Dr. Rax remembered why, and how much, he disliked the other man. "I think I can manage to classify it, thank you. I was just wondering if any of your people had seen the artifact."

"No need. We saw the rest of the junk Montclair dragged out of his nooks and crannies. You'd think that with all the precious bits and pieces leaving Egypt at the time, his Lordship's ancestor could have brought home something worthwhile, even by accident, wouldn't you?"

Professional ethics warred with desire. Ethics won. "About the sarcophagus . . ."

"Look, Dr. Rax . . ." On the other end of the line, Dr. Davis sighed explosively. ". . . this sarcophagus might be a big thing for you, but trust me, we've got all we need. We have storerooms of important, historically significant artifacts we may never have time to study." *And you don't,* was the not too subtly implied message. "I think we can allow one unadorned hunk of basalt to go to the colonies."

"So I can send for my preparators and start packing it up?" Dr. Rax asked quietly, his tone in severe contrast to the white-knuckled grip that twisted the phone cord.

"If you're sure you don't want to use a couple of my people . . ."

Not if my only other option was to carry the sarcophagus on my lap all the way home. "No, thank you. I'm sure all your people have plenty of historically significant things to do.''

"Well, if that's the way you want it, be my guest. I'll have the paperwork done up and sent down to you at the Hall. You'll be able to get your artifact out of the country as easily as if it were a plaster statue of Big Ben.'' *Which,* his tone said clearly, *is about its equivalent value.*

"Thank you, Dr. Davis.'' *You pompous, egocentric asshole,* Dr. Rax added silently as he hung up. *Oh, well,* he soothed his lacerated conscience, *no one can say I didn't try.*

He straightened his jacket and turned to face the hovering baron, smiling reassuringly. "I believe you said that 50,000 pounds was your asking price . . . ?''

"Uh, Dr. Rax . . .'' Karen Lahey stood and dusted off her knees. "Are you sure the Brits don't want this?''

"Positive.'' Dr. Rax touched his breast and listened for a second to the comforting rustle of papers in his suit pocket. Dr. Davis had been as good as his word. The sarcophagus could leave England as soon as it was packed and insurance had been arranged.

Karen glanced down at the seal. That it held the cartouche of Thoth and not one of the necropolis symbols was rare enough. What the seal implied was rarer still. "They knew about . . .'' She waved a hand at the clay disk.

"I called Dr. Davis right after I discovered it.'' Which was true, as far as it went.

She frowned and glanced over at the other preparator. His expression matched hers. Something was wrong. No one in his right mind would give up a sealed sarcophagus and the promise that represented. "And Dr. Davis said . . . ?'' she prodded.

"Dr. Davis said, and I quote, 'This sarcophagus might be a big thing for you, but we've got all we need. *We* have storerooms of important, historically significant artifacts we may never have time to study.' '' Dr. Rax hid a smile at the developing scowls. "And then he added, 'I think we can let one unadorned hunk of basalt go to the colonies.' ''

"You didn't tell him about the seal, did you, Doctor?''

He shrugged. "After that, would you?''

Karen's scowl deepened. "I wouldn't tell that patronizing

son of a bitch, excuse my French, the time of day. You leave this with us, Dr. Rax, and we'll pack it up so that even the spiderwebs arrive intact.''

Her companion nodded. "Colonies," he snorted. "Just who the hell does he think he is?''

Dr. Rax had to stop himself from skipping as he left the room. The Curator of Egyptology, Royal Ontario Museum, did not skip. It wasn't dignified. But *no one* mortared, then sealed, an empty coffin.

''Yes!'' He allowed himself one jubilant punch at the air in the privacy of the deserted upper cellar. ''We've got ourselves a mummy!''

The movement had begun again and the memories strengthened. Sand and sun. Heat. Light. He had no need to remember darkness; darkness had been his companion for too long.

As the weight of the sarcophagus made flying out of the question, a leisurely trip back across the Atlantic on the grand old lady of luxury ocean liners, the QE II, would have been nice. Unfortunately, the acquisitions budget had been stretched almost to the breaking point with the purchase and the packing and the insurance and the best the museum could afford was a Danish freighter heading out of Liverpool for Halifax. The ship left England on October 2nd. God and the North Atlantic willing, she'd reach Canada in ten days.

Dr. Rax sent the two preparators back by plane and he himself traveled with the artifact. It was foolish, he knew, but he didn't want to be parted from it. Although the ship occasionally carried passengers, the accommodations were spartan and the meals, while nourishing, were plain. Dr. Rax didn't notice. Refused access to the cargo hold where he could be near the sarcophagus and the mummy he was sure it contained, he stayed as close as he could, caught up on paperwork, and at night lay in his narrow bunk and visualized the opening of the coffin.

Sometimes, he removed the seal and slid the end panel up in the full glare of the media; the find of the century, on every news program and front page in the world. There'd be book contracts, and speaking tours, and years of research as the contents were studied, then removed to be studied further.

Sometimes, it was just him and his staff, working slowly and meticulously. Pure science. Pure discovery. And still the years of research.

He imagined the contents in every possible form or combination of forms. Some nights expanding on the descriptions, some nights simplifying. It wouldn't be a royal mummy—more likely a priest or an official of the court—and so hopefully would have missed the anointing with aromatic oils that had partially destroyed the mummy of Tutankhamen.

He grew so aware of it that he felt he could go into the hold and pick its container out of hundreds of identical containers. His thoughts became filled with it to the exclusion of all else; of the sea, of the ship, of the sailors. One of the Portuguese sailors began making the sign against the evil eye whenever he approached.

He started to speak to it each night before he slept.

"Soon," he told it. "Soon."

He remembered a face, thin and worried, bending over him and constantly muttering. He remembered a hand, the soft skin damp with sweat as it brushed his eyes closed. He remembered terror as he felt the fabric laid across his face. He remembered pain as the strip of linen that held the spell was wrapped around him and secured.

But he couldn't remember self.

He could sense only one ka, and that at such a distance he knew it must be reaching for him as he reached for it.

"Soon," it told him. "Soon."

He could wait.

The air at the museum loading dock was so charged with suppressed excitement that even the driver of the van, a man laconic to the point of legend, became infected. He pulled the keys out of his pocket like he was pulling a rabbit out of a hat and opened the van doors with a flourish that added a silent *Tah dah* to the proceedings.

The plywood packing crate, reinforced with two by twos and strapping, looked no different from any number of other crates that the Royal Ontario Museum had received over the years, but the entire Egyptology Department—none of whom had a reason to be down in Receiving—surged forward and Dr. Rax beamed like the Madonna must have beamed into the manger.

Preparators did not usually unload trucks. They unloaded this one. And as much as he single-handedly wanted to carry the crate up to the workroom, Dr. Rax stood aside and let them get on with it. His mummy deserved the best.

"Hail the conquering hero comes." Dr. Rachel Shane, the assistant curator, walked over to stand beside him. "Welcome back, Elias. You look a little tired."

"I haven't been sleeping well," Dr. Rax admitted, rubbing eyes already rimmed with red.

"Guilty conscience?"

He snorted, recognizing she was teasing. "Strange dreams about being tied down and slowly suffocating."

"Maybe you're being possessed." She nodded at the crate.

He snorted again. "Maybe the Board of Directors has been trying to contact me." Glancing around, he scowled at the rest of his staff. "Don't you lot have anything better to do than stand around watching a wooden box come off a truck?"

Only the newest grad student looked nervous, the others merely grinned and collectively shook their heads.

Dr. Rax grinned as well; he couldn't help himself. He was exhausted and badly in need of something more sustaining than the coffee and fast food they'd consumed at every stop between Halifax and Toronto, but he'd also never felt this elated. This artifact had the potential to put the Royal Ontario Museum, already an internationally respected institution, on the scientific map and everyone in the room knew it. "As much as I'd like to believe that all this excitement is directed at my return, I know damned well it isn't." No one bothered to protest. "And as you can now see there's nothing to see, why don't the lot of you head back up to the workroom where we can all jump about and enthuse in the privacy of our own department?"

Behind him, Dr. Shane added her own silent but emphatic endorsement to that suggestion.

It took more than a few last, lingering looks at the crate, but, finally, Receiving emptied.

"I suppose the whole building knows what we've got?" Dr. Rax asked as he and Dr. Shane followed the crate and the preparators onto the freight elevator.

Dr. Shane shook her head. "Surprisingly enough, considering the way gossip usually travels in this rabbit warren, no. All of our people have been very closemouthed." Dark brows drew down. "Just in case." *Just in case it does turn out to be empty, the less people know, the less our professional reputations will suffer. There hasn't been a new mummy uncovered in decades.*

Dr. Rax chose to ignore the subtext. "So Von Thorne doesn't know?" While the Department of Egyptology didn't really resent the Far East's beautiful new temple wing, they did resent its curator's more-antiquarian-than-thou attitude concerning it.

"If he does," Dr. Shane said emphatically, "he hasn't heard about it from us."

As one, the two Egyptologists turned to the preparators who worked, not just for them, but for the museum at large.

One hand resting lightly on the top of the crate, Karen Lahey drew herself up to her full height. "Well he hasn't heard about it from *us*. Not after accusing us of creating a nonexistent crack in that porcelain Buddha."

Her companion grunted agreement.

The freight elevator stopped on five, the doors opened, and Dr. Van Thorne beamed genially in at them.

"So, you're back from your shopping trip, Elias. Pick up anything interesting?"

Dr. Rax managed a not very polite smile. "Just the *usual* sorts of things, Alex."

Stepping nimbly out of the way as the preparators rolled the crate from the elevator, Dr. Von Thorne patted the wood as it passed; a kind of careless benediction. "Ah," he said. "More broken bits of pottery, eh?"

"Something like that." Dr. Rax's smile had begun to show more teeth. Dr. Shane grabbed his arm and propelled him down the hall.

"We've just received a new Buddha," the curator of the Far East Department called after them. "Second century

BC. A beautiful little thing in alabaster and jade without a mark on it. You must come and see it soon.''

''Soon,'' Dr. Shane agreed, her hand still firmly holding her superior's arm. Not until they were almost at the workroom did she let go.

''A new Buddha,'' he muttered, flexing his arm and watching the preparators maneuver the crate through the double doors of the workroom. ''Of what historical significance is that? People are still *worshiping* Buddha. Just wait, just wait until we get this sarcophagus open and we'll wipe that smug temple-dog smile off his face.''

As the doors of the workroom swung closed behind him, the weight of responsibility for the sarcophagus lifted off his shoulders. There was still a lot to do, and any number of things that could yet go wrong, but the journey at least had been safely completed. He felt like a modern day Anubis, escorting the dead to eternal life in the Underworld, and wondered how the ancient god had managed to bear such an exhausting burden.

He rested both hands on the crate, aware through the wood and the packing and the stone and whatever interior coffin the stone concealed, of the body that lay at its heart. ''We're here,'' he told it softly. ''Welcome home.''

The ka that had been so constant was now joined by others. He could feel them outside the binding, calling, being, driving him into a frenzy with their nearness and their inaccessibility. If he could only remember . . .

And then, suddenly, the surrounding ka began to fade. Near panic, he reached for the one he knew and felt it moving away. He hung onto it as long as he could, then he hung onto the sense of it, then the memory.

Not alone. Please, not alone again.

When it returned, he would have wept if he'd remembered how.

Refreshed by a shower and a good night's sleep plagued by nothing more than a vague sense of loss, Dr. Rax stared down at the sarcophagus. It had been cataloged—measured, described, given the card number 991.862.1—and now existed as an official possession of the Royal Ontario Museum. The time had come.

"Is the video camera ready?" he asked pulling on a pair of new cotton gloves.

"Ready, Doctor." Doris Bercarich, who took care of most of the departmental photography, squinted through the view finder. She'd already taken two films of still photography—one black and white, one color—and her camera now hung around the neck of the more mechanically competent of the two grad students. He'd continue to take photographs while she shot tape. If she had anything to say about it, and she did, this was going to be one well documented mummy.

"Ready, Dr. Shane?"

"Ready, Dr. Rax." She tugged at the cuffs of her gloves, then picked up the sterile cotton pad that would catch the removed seal. "You can start any time."

He nodded, took a deep breath, and knelt. With the sterile pad in place, he slid the flexible blade of the palette knife behind the seal and carefully worked at the centuries old clay. Although his hands were sure, his stomach tied itself in knots, tighter and tighter as the seconds passed and his fear grew that the seal, in spite of the preservatives, could be removed only as a featureless handful of red clay. While he worked, he kept up a low-voiced commentary of the physical sensations he was receiving through the handle of the knife.

Then he felt something give and a hairline crack appeared diagonally across the outer surface of the seal.

For a heartbeat the only sound in the room was the soft whir of the video camera.

A heartbeat later, the seal, broken cleanly in two, halves held in place by the preservative, lay on the cotton pad.

As one, the Department of Egyptology remembered how to breathe.

He felt the seal break, heard the fracture resonate throughout the ages.

He remembered who he was. What he was. What they had done to him.

He remembered anger.

He drew on the anger for strength, then he threw himself against his bonds. Too much of the spell remained; he was now aware but still as bound as he had been. His ka howled in silent frustration.

I will be free!

"Soon," *came the quiet answer.* "Soon."

It took the rest of the day to clear the mortar. In spite of mounting paperwork, Dr. Rax remained in the workroom.

"Well, whatever they sealed up in here, they certainly didn't make it easy to get to." Dr. Shane straightened, one hand rubbing the small of her back. "You're sure that his lordship had no idea of where the venerable ancestor picked this up?"

Dr. Rax ran one finger along the joint. "No, none." He had expected to be elated once work finally began but he found he was only impatient. Everything moved so slowly— a fact he was well aware of and shouldn't even be considering as a problem. He scrubbed at his eyes and tried to banish the disquieting vision of taking a sledge to the stone.

Dr. Shane sighed and bent back to the mortar. "What I wouldn't give for some contextual information."

"We'll know everything we need to when we get the sarcophagus open."

She glanced up at him, one raised brow disappearing under a curl of dark hair. "You seem very sure of that."

"I am." And he was, very sure. In fact he *knew* that they would have all the answers they needed when the sarcophagus was finally opened although he had no idea where that knowledge came from. He wiped suddenly sweaty palms on his trousers. No idea . . .

By the time they finished removing the mortar, it was too late to do any further work that day—or more exactly, that night. They would see what their stone box contained in the morning.

That night, Dr. Rax dreamed of a griffinlike animal with the body of an antelope and the head of a bird. It peered down at him with too-bright eyes and laughed. He got up, barely rested, at dawn and was at the museum hours before the rest of the department arrived. He intended to avoid the workroom, to use the extra time for the administrative paperwork that threatened to bury his desk, but his key was in the lock and his hand was pushing open the door before his conscious mind registered the action.

"I almost did it," he said as Dr. Shane came in some

time later. He was sitting in an orange plastic chair, hands
clasped so tightly that the knuckles were white.

She didn't have to ask what he meant. "Good thing you're
too much of a scientist to give way to impulse," she told
him lightly, privately thinking that he looked like shit. "As
soon as the others get here, we'll get this over with."

"Over with," he echoed.

Dr. Shane frowned, then shook her head, deciding not to
speak. After all, what could she say? That just for a moment
the Curator of the Department of Egyptology had neither
sounded nor looked like himself? Maybe he wasn't the only
one not getting enough sleep.

Five hours and seven rolls of film later, the inner coffin
lay on padded wooden supports, free of its encasing stone
for the first time in millennia.

"Well," Dr. Shane frowned down at the painted wood,
"that's the damnedest thing I've ever seen."

The rest of the department nodded in agreement; except
for Dr. Rax who fought not to step forward and throw off
the lid.

The coffin was anthropomorphic but only vaguely. There
were no features either carved into or painted on the wood,
nor any symbols of Anubis or Osiris as might be expected.
Instead, a mighty serpent coiled its length around the coffin, its head, marked with the cartouche of Thoth, resting
above the breast of the mummy. At the head of the coffin
was a representation of Setu, a minor god who stood guard
in the tenth hour of Tuat, the underworld, and used a javelin
to help Ra slay his enemies. At the foot of the coffin was a
representation of Shemerthi, identical in all ways to the other
guardian save that he used a bow. Small snakes, coiled and
watchful, filled in the spaces that the great serpent left bare.

In Egyptian mythology, serpents were the guardians of
the underworld.

As a work of art, it was beautiful; the colors so rich and
vibrant that the artist might have finished work three hours
instead of three millennia ago. As a window on history, the
glass was cloudy at best.

"If I have to hazard a guess," Dr. Shane said thoughtfully, "I'd say, based on the cartouche and the workman-

ship, that this is Eighteenth Dynasty, not Sixteenth. In spite of the sarcophagus.''

Dr. Rax had to agree with her even though he seemed incapable of forming a coherent observation of his own.

It took them the rest of the day to photograph it, catalog it, and remove the seal of cedar gum that held the lid tightly in place.

"Why this stuff hasn't dried to a nice, easily removable powder, I have no idea.'' Dr. Shane shook the kinks out of one stiff leg, and then the other. This had been the second day she'd spent mostly on her knees and, while it *was* a favored position of archaeologists, she'd never been a great believer in crippling herself for science.

"It looks,'' she added slowly, her hand stretching out but not quite touching one of the small serpents, "like something interred in this coffin was not supposed to get out.''

One of the graduate students laughed, a high-pitched giggle quickly cut off.

"Open it,'' Dr. Rax commanded, through lips suddenly dry.

In the silence that followed, the soft whir of the video camera sounded intrusively loud.

Dr. Rax was not completely unaware of his subordinates' shocked glances, both at each other and at him. He spread his hands and managed a smile. "Will any of us sleep tonight if we don't?''

Will any of us sleep tonight if we do? Dr. Shane found herself thinking, and wondered where the thought came from. "It's late. We've all been working hard and now we've got a whole weekend ahead of us; why don't we start fresh on Monday.''

"We'll only lift the lid.'' He was using the voice he used to get funds out of the museum board, guaranteed to charm. Dr. Shane didn't appreciate it being used on her. "And I think all that hard work deserves a look inside.''

"What about Xrays?''

"Later.'' He pulled on a clean pair of gloves as he spoke, the action serving to hide the trembling of his hands. "As the handles that were used to lower the lid into place appear to have been removed, I will take the head. Ray,'' he motioned to the largest of the researchers, "you will take the feet.''

It could have stopped there, but when it came down to it, they *were* all anxious to see what the artifact held. As the assistant curator offered no further objections, Ray shrugged, pulled on a pair of gloves, and went to his place.

"On three. One, two, three!"

The lid lifted cleanly, heavier than it looked.

"Ahhh." The sound came involuntarily from half a dozen throats. Placing the lid carefully on another padded trestle, Dr. Rax, heart slamming painfully against his ribs, turned to see what might lie revealed.

The mummy lay thickly swathed in ancient linen and the smell of cedar was almost overpowering—the inside of the casket had been lined with the aromatic wood. Someone sneezed although no one noticed who. A long strip of fabric, closely covered in scarlet hieroglyphs was wrapped around the body following the path the serpent had taken around the coffin. The mummy wore no death mask, but features were visible in relief through the cloth.

The dry air of Egypt was good to the dead, preserving them for the future to study by leeching all the moisture from even protected tissue. Embalming was only the first step and, as sites that predated the pharaohs proved, not even the most necessary one.

Desiccated was the only word to describe the face beneath the linen, although other, more flattering words might have been used once, for the cheekbones were high and sharp, the chin determined, and the overall impression one of strength.

Dr. Rax let out a long breath he hadn't been aware of holding and the tension visibly left his shoulders.

"You were expecting maybe Bela Lugosi?" Dr. Shane asked dryly, pitched for his ears alone. The look he turned on her—half horror, half exhaustion—made her regret the words almost instantly. "Can we go home now?" she asked in a tone deliberately light. "Or did you want to cram another two years of research into this evening?"

He did. He saw his hand reach out and hover over the strip of hieroglyphs. He snatched it back.

"Pack it up," he said, straightening, forcing his voice to show no sign of how he had to fight to form the words. "We'll deal with it Monday." Then he turned and, before he could change his mind, strode from the workroom.

* * *

He would have laughed aloud had it been possible, unable to contain the rush of exaltation. His body might still be bound, but with the opening of his prison his ka was free.

Free . . . freed . . . feed.

Two

"My name is Ozymandias, King of Kings: Look on my works, ye Mighty, and despair!"

Detective-Sergeant Michael Celluci frowned at his companion. "What the hell are you babbling about?"

"Babbling? I was not babbling. I was ruminating on the monuments that man builds to man." Pushing her glasses securely into place, Vicki Nelson bent, stiff-legged, and laid both palms against the concrete at her feet.

Celluci snorted at this blatant display of flexibility—obviously intended to remind him of his limitations—tilted his head back and gazed up the side of the CN Tower. From their position at its base, foreshortening made it appear simultaneously infinite and squat, the radio antennae that extended its height, hidden behind the bulge of the restaurants and observation deck. "Cows ruminate," he grunted. "And I assume you mean man in the racial sense rather than the genetic."

Vicki shrugged, the motion almost lost in her position. "Maybe." She straightened and grinned. "But they don't call it the world's tallest free-standing phallic symbol for nothing."

"Dream on." He sighed as she grasped her left ankle and lifted the leg up until it rose into the air at a better than forty-five-degree angle. "And quit showing off. You ready to climb this thing yet?"

"Just waiting for you to finish warming up."

Celluci smiled. "Then get ready to eat my dust."

A number of charitable organizations used the one thousand, seven hundred and ninety steps of the CN Tower as a means of raising money, climbers collecting pledges per step from friends and business associates. The Heart Fund was sponsoring the current climb; as well as a starting time, both Vicki and Celluci had starting pulses measured.

"You'll find the run pretty clear," the volunteer told them as he wrote Vicki's heart rate down on a slip of paper. "You're like the six and seventh up and the others have been serious racers."

"What makes you think we aren't?" Celluci asked belligerently. With his last birthday, he'd started on the downhill run to forty and was finding himself a little sensitive about it.

"Well . . ." The younger man swallowed nervously—very few people do belligerent as well as the police. ". . . you're like both wearing sweats and normal running shoes. Climbers one to five were seriously aerodynamic."

Vicki snickered, knowing full well what had prompted Celluci's question. He glared but, recognizing he'd probably come out the worse for any comment, kept his mouth shut. With their time stamped, they ran for the stairs.

The volunteer had been both right and wrong. Neither of them cared about racing the other climbers or the tower itself, but they couldn't have been more serious about racing each other. Competition had been the basis of their relationship from the day they first met, two very intense young police constables both certain that they were the answer regardless of the question. Michael Celluci, with four years' seniority, an accelerated promotion, and a citation, had some reason for believing that. Vicki Nelson, just out of the academy, took it on faith. Four years later, Vicki had become known as "Victory" around the force, they'd discovered a number of mutual interests, and the competition had become so much a part of the way they operated that their superiors used it to the force's advantage. Four years after that, when Vicki's deteriorating eyesight compelled her to choose between a desk or leaving, the system broke down. She couldn't stay and become less than what she was, so she left. He couldn't just let her go. Words were said. It took months for the wounds left by those words to heal and more months where pride on both sides refused to make the first move. Then a threat to the city they'd both sworn to serve threw them together and a new relationship had to be forged out of the ruins of the old.

"Blocking me is cheating, you long-armed bastard!"

It turned out not to be significantly different.

The yellow metal steps switchbacking up the side of the CN Tower were no more than three and a half feet wide— easy enough for a tall man to keep one hand on each banister and use his arms to take some of the strain on the muscles of his upper body. And, incidentally, make it impossible for anyone behind to pass.

Six landings up, Vicki put on a burst of speed and slid between Celluci and the inner wall, the damp concrete scraping against her shoulder blades. She pulled out ahead, two stairs at a time, feeling Celluci climbing right on her heels. At five ten it was almost easier for her to climb taking double strides. Unfortunately, it was definitely easier for Celluci at six four.

Neither of them paused at the first water station.

The lead switched back and forth twice more, the sound of high tech rubber soles pounding down on the metal stairs reverberating throughout the enclosed space like distant thunder. Later in the day, the plexiglass sheets that separated the climbers from the view would begin to cloud over with the accumulated moisture panted out of hundreds of pairs of lungs, but this early in the morning, the skyline of Toronto fell away beside them with vertigo-inducing clarity.

Giving thanks in this one instance that she had almost no peripheral vision and therefore no idea of how high they actually were from the ground, Vicki charged past the second water station. Three hundred feet to go. No problem. Her calves were beginning to protest, her lungs to burn, but she'd be damned if she'd slow and give Celluci a chance to get past.

The stairs turned from yellow to gray, although the original color showed through where countless feet had rubbed off the second coat of paint. They were into the emergency exit stairs for the restaurant level.

Almost there . . . Celluci was so close she could feel his breath hot against her back. He hit the last landing seconds behind her. One, two strides to the open door. On level ground, his longer legs brought them even. Vicki made a desperate grab at the edge of the doorway and exploded out into the carpeted hall.

"Nine minutes, fifty-four seconds. Nine minutes, fifty-five seconds."

As soon as I have enough breath, I'll rub it in. For the moment, Vicki leaned against the wall, panting, heart pounding with enough force to vibrate her entire body, sweat collecting and dripping off her chin.

Celluci collapsed against the wall beside her.

One of the Heart Fund volunteers approached, stopwatch in hand. "Now then, I'll just get your finishing heart rates. . . ."

Vicki and Celluci exchanged identical glances.

"I don't think," Vicki managed to gasp, "that we really want . . . to know."

Although the timed portion of the climb was over, they had another four flights to go up before they reached the observation deck and were officially finished.

"Nine minutes and fifty-four seconds." Celluci scrubbed at his face with the lower edge of his T-shirt as they moved back into the stairwell. "Not bad for an old broad."

"Who are you calling old, asshole? Let's just keep in mind that I can give you five years."

"Fine." He held out his hand. "I'll take them now."

Vicki pulled herself up another step, quadriceps visibly trembling under the fleece of her sweatpants. "I want to spend the rest of the day submerged in hot water."

"Sounds good to me."

"Mike?"

"Yeah?"

"Next time I suggest we climb the CN Tower, remind me of how I feel right now."

"Next time . . ."

His kind never dreamed, or so he'd always believed—they lost dreaming as they lost the day—but in spite of this, for the first time in over four hundred and fifty years, he came to awareness with a memory that had no connection to his waking life.

Sunlight. He hadn't seen the sun since 1539 and he had *never* seen it as a golden disk in an azure sky, heat spreading a shimmering shield around it.

Henry Fitzroy, bastard son of Henry VIII, romance writer, vampire, lay in the darkness, stared at nothing, and wondered what the hell was going on. Was he losing his mind? It had happened to others of his kind. They grew so

that they couldn't stand the night and finally they gave themselves to the sun and death. Was this *memory*, then, the
beginning of the end?

He didn't think so. He felt sane. But would a madman
recognize his condition?

"This is going nowhere." Lips tight, he swung his legs
off the bed and stood. He certainly had no conscious wish
to die. If his subconscious had other ideas, it would be in
for a fight.

But the memory lingered. It lingered in the shower. It
lingered as he dressed. A blazing circle of fire. When he
closed his eyes, he could see the image on his lids.

His hand was on the phone before he remembered; she
was with *him* tonight.

"Damn!"

In the last few months Vicki Nelson had become a necessary part of his life. He fed from her as often as it was
safe, and blood and sex had pulled them closer into friendship if not something stronger. At least on his side of the
relationship.

"Relationship, Jesu! Now *that's* a word for the nineties."
Tonight, he only wanted to talk to her, to discuss the
dream—if that's what it was—and the fears that came with
it.

Running pale fingers through short, sandy-blond hair, he
walked across the condo to look out at the lights of Toronto.
Vampires hunted alone, prowled the darkness alone, but
they had been human once and perhaps at heart were human
still, for every now and then, over the long years of their
lives, they searched for a companion they could trust with
the truth of what they were. He had found Vicki in the midst
of violence and death, given her his truth, and waited for
what she would give him in return. She'd offered him acceptance, only that, and he doubted she ever realized how
rare a thing acceptance was. Through her, he'd had more
contact with mortals since last spring than he'd had in the
last hundred years.

Through her, two others knew his nature. Tony, an uncomplicated young man who, on occasion, shared bed and
blood, and Detective-Sergeant Michael Celluci, who was
neither young nor uncomplicated and while he hadn't come

right out and said *vampire*, he was too intelligent a man to deny the evidence of his eyes.

Henry's fingers curled against the glass, forming slowly into a fist. She was with Celluci tonight. She'd as much as warned him of it when they'd last spoken. All right. Maybe he was getting a bit possessive. *It was easier in the old days.* She'd have been his then, no one else would have had a claim on her. How *dared* she be with someone else when he needed her?

The sun burned down in memory, an all-seeing yellow eye.

He frowned down at the city. He was not used to dealing with fear, so he fed the dream to his anger and allowed, almost forced, the Hunger to rise. He *did not* need her. He would hunt.

Below him, a thousand points of light glowed like a thousand tiny suns.

Reid Ellis preferred the museum at night. He liked being left alone to do his work, without scientists or historians or other staff members asking him stupid questions. "You'd think," he often proclaimed to his colleagues, "that a guy with four degrees would know when a floor was wet."

Although he didn't mind working the public galleries, he preferred the long lengths of hall linking offices and workrooms. Within the assigned section, he was his own boss; no nosy supervisor hanging over his shoulder checking up on him; free to get the job done properly, his way. Free to consider the workrooms his own private little museums where the storage shelves were often a hell of a lot more interesting than the stuff laid out for the paying customers.

He rolled his cart out onto the fifth floor, patted one of the temple lions for luck, and hesitated with his hand on the glass door to the Far East Department. Maybe he should do Egyptology first? They usually had some pretty interesting things on the go.

Maybe he should do their workroom first. Now.

Nah, that'd leave the heelmarks on the floor outside Von Thorne's office for end of shift and I'm not up to that. He pulled out his passkey and maneuvered his cart through the door. *As my sainted mother used to say, get your thumb out*

of your butt and get to work. I'll save the good stuff for last.
Whatever they've got out isn't going anywhere.

The ka pulled free of his tenuous grasp and began to move
away. He was still pitiably weak, too weak to hold it, too
weak to draw it closer. Had he been able to move, hunger
would have driven him to desperate measures, but bound as
he was, he could only wait and pray that his god would
send him a life.

On a Sunday night in Toronto the good, the streets were
almost deserted, municipal laws against Sunday shopping
forcing the inhabitants of the city to find other amusements.

Black leather trench coat billowing out behind him, Henry
made his way quickly down Church Street, ignoring the
occasional clusters of humanity. He wanted more than just
a chance to feed, his anger needed slaking as much as his
Hunger. At Church and College, he paused.

"Hey, faggot!"

Henry smiled, turned his head slightly, and tested the
breeze. Three of them. Young. Healthy. Perfect.

"What's the matter, faggot, you deaf?"

"Maybe he's got someone's pecker stuffed in his ear."

Hands in his pockets, he pivoted slowly on one heel.
They were leaning against the huge yellow bulk of Maple
Leaf Gardens, suburban boys in lace-up boots and strate-
gically ripped jeans downtown for a little excitement. With
odds of three to one, they'd probably be after him anyway,
but just to be certain . . . the smile he sent them was deliberately provocative, impossible to ignore.

"Fuckin' faggot!"

They followed him east, yelling insults, getting braver
and coming closer when he didn't respond. When he crossed
College at Jarvis Street, they were right on his heels and,
without even considering why he might be leading them
there, they followed him into Allen Gardens Park.

"Faggot's walking like he's still got a prick shoved up his
ass."

There were lights scattered throughout the small park, but
there were also deep pockets of shadow that would provide
enough darkness for his needs. Hunger rising, Henry led
them away from the road and possible discovery, fallen

leaves making soft, wet noises under his feet. Finally, he stopped and turned.

The three young men were barely an arm's length away. The night would never be the same for them again.

They moved to surround him.

He allowed it.

"So, why aren't you fucking dead like the rest of the fucking queers?" Their leader, for all packs have a leader of sorts, reached out to shove a slender shoulder, the first move in the night's entertainment. He looked surprised when he missed. Then he looked startled as Henry smiled. Then he looked frightened.

A heartbeat later, he looked terrified.

The double doors to the Egyptology workroom had been painted bright orange. As Reid Ellis put his passkey into the lock, he wondered, not for the first time, why. All the doors in this part of the hallway had been painted yellow or orange and while he supposed it looked cheerful it didn't exactly look dignified. Not that the folks in the Egyptology Department were exactly sticklers for dignity. Three months ago, when the Blue Jays had lost six ball games in a row he'd gone in to find one of the mummified heads set up on the table with a baseball cap perched jauntily on its desiccated brow.

Now that baseball season was over, he wondered if anyone in the department owned a hockey helmet, *rest in peace* being the kindest epitaph one could give the Leafs even this early in the season.

"And what've you got for me tonight?" he asked as he hooked one of the doors open to make way for his cart—they weren't actually scheduled to have the floors done, but he liked to keep up with the high traffic areas by the desk and the sink—then he turned and got his first look at the new addition to the room. "Holy shit."

Palms suddenly wet, mouth suddenly dry, Reid stood and stared. The head had been unreal, like a special effect in a movie, evoking a shudder but easy to laugh at and dismiss. A coffin though, with a body in it, was another thing altogether. This was a person, a dead person, lying there shrouded in plastic and waiting for him.

Waiting for me? His nervous laugh went no further than

his lips, doing nothing to displace the silence that filled the huge room like fog. *Maybe I should just go, come back another night.* But he stepped forward; one pace, two. He'd forgotten to turn on the lights and now the switch was behind him. He'd have to turn his back on the coffin to reach it and he couldn't, he just couldn't. The spill of light from the hall would have to be enough even though it barely chased the shadows from around the body.

The breeze created by his approach stirred the edges of the plastic sheet, setting it fluttering in anticipation.

"Jesus, this is too weird. I'm out of here."

But he kept walking toward the coffin. Eyes wide, he watched his fingers grab the plastic and drag it off the artifact.

Man, I am going to be in deep shit. Maybe if he put the plastic back the way it had been, no one would ever know that he . . . that he . . . *What the fuck am I doing?*

He was bending over the coffin, breath slamming faster and faster against the back of his throat. His eyes stung. He couldn't blink. His mouth opened. He couldn't scream.

And then it started.

He lost his most recent self first: the night's work, all the other nights of work before it, his wife, their daughter, her birth, red-faced and screaming—*"Honestly, Doc, is she supposed to look like that? I mean, she's beautiful but she's kind of squashed . . ."*—the wedding where he'd gotten pissed and almost fallen over while dancing with an elderly aunt. He lost nights drinking with his buddies, cruising up and down Yonge Street—*"Lookit the melons on that one!"*—The Grateful Dead blaring out of the car speakers, the smell of beer and grass and sweat soaking into the upholstery.

He lost his high school graduation, a ceremony he'd made by the skin of his teeth—*"Think maybe now you can get off your ass and get a job? Now you got your fancy piece of paper with your name on it?" "I think so, Dad."* He lost the humiliation of not making the basketball team—*They're not going to call my name. I'm the only guy who tried out they didn't want. Oh, God, I wish I could sink through the floor.*—and he lost the pain when football broke his nose. He tasted again his first kiss and felt again for the first time the explosive results of masturbation, which did not grow hair on his palms or make him blind. And then he lost them.

In quick succession he lost his mother, his father, too many siblings, the house he'd grown up in, the smell of a winter's worth of dog turds melting on the lawn in the spring, a teddy bear with all the fur chewed off, the sweet taste of a nipple clutched between frantically working lips.

He lost his first step, his first word, his first breath.

His life.

Yes.

With iron control, Henry drew his mouth back from the soft skin of the young man's wrist and laid the arm down almost gently, pulling the jacket cuff forward until it covered the small wound. Although he preferred to feed from desire—it had natural parameters for the Hunger that anger lacked—it was, on occasion, good to remember his strength. He rose slowly to his feet, brushing at the decayed leaves on his coat. The coagulant in his saliva would ensure that the bleeding had stopped and all three would regain consciousness momentarily, before the damp and cold had time to do any damage.

He glanced down to where they sprawled in the darker shadow of a yew hedge and licked a drop of blood from the corner of his mouth. As well as the bruises, he'd given them a reason to fear the night, a reminder that the dark hid other, more powerful hunters and that they, too, could be prey. He was in no danger of discovery for their memories of the incident would be of essence, not appearance, and intensely personal. Whether or not he'd changed their attitudes or opinions, he neither knew nor cared.

I am vampire. The night is mine.

His mood broke under the weight of that pronouncement and he left the quiet oasis of the park, smiling at the newsreel quality of the voice in his head—*And thanks to the vampire vigilante, the streets are safe to walk again*—the dream and his earlier disquiet washed away by the blood.

Celluci sighed and stuffed the parking ticket into his jacket pocket. From midnight to seven the street outside Vicki's apartment building was permit parking only. The time on the ticket said five thirty-three; if he'd gotten up five minutes earlier, he could have avoided a twenty dollar fine.

It had been hard to drag himself away. He must've lain in the darkness for a good twenty minutes listening to her breathe. Wondering if she was dreaming. Wondering if she was dreaming about him. Or about Henry. Or if it mattered.

"What I mean, Celluci, is no commitments beyond friendship."

"We're going to be buddies?"

"That's right."

"You don't ball your buddies, Vicki."

She'd snorted and run a bare foot up his inner thigh until she could grab the soft skin of his scrotum with her toes. "Wanna bet?"

So it had been from the beginning. . . .

He scratched at his stubble and got into the car. Their friendship was solid, he knew that, the scars they'd both inflicted when she'd left the force had faded into memory. The sex was still terrific. But lately, things had gotten complicated.

"Henry's not competition, Mike. Whatever happens between him and me, doesn't affect us. You're my best friend."

He'd believed her then, he believed her now. But he still thought Henry Fitzroy was a dangerous man for her to get involved with. Not only was he physically dangerous, and that had been proven last August beyond a doubt, but he had the kind of personal power it would be easy to get lost in. *Christ, I could get lost in it.* No one with that kind of power should be, could be, trusted.

He trusted Vicki. He didn't trust Henry. That's what it came down to. Henry Fitzroy made up the rules as he went along, and for Detective-Sergeant Michael Celluci that was the sticking point. More than supposedly supernatural, undead, powers of darkness. There were a number of very definite rules surrounding his and Vicki's relationship, and Celluci knew damned well Fitzroy wouldn't honor them.

Except he had so far . . .

"Maybe what it all comes down to," he mused, maneuvering through the maze of one-way streets south of College, "is that I'm ready to settle down."

It took a few seconds for the implications of that to sink in, and he had a sudden vision of what Vicki's response would be if he brought up marriage. He couldn't stop himself from ducking. The woman was more commitment shy than any man he'd ever met.

He frowned as he guided the car around the Queen's Park circle. It was too early in the morning for deep philosophical questions on the nature of his relationship with Vicki Nelson—things were going well, he shouldn't fuck with that. Gratefully noticing the ambulance and the police car pulled up in front of the museum, he made a U-turn across the empty six-lane road and dumped the problems of his love life for more immediate concerns.

"Detective-Sergeant Celluci, homicide." He flipped his badge at the approaching constable as he got out of the car, forestalling a confrontation about the less than legal U-turn. "What's going on?"

The young woman snapped her mouth shut around what she'd been about to say and managed, "Constable Trembley, sir. They sent homicide? I don't understand."

"No one sent me, I was just driving past." The attendants were loading a body into the ambulance, face covered. Obviously D.O.A. "Thought I'd stop and see if there was anything I could do."

"Nothing I can think of, Sergeant. Paramedics say it was a heart attack. They figure it was because of the mummy."

A year ago, eight months ago even, Celluci would have repeated the word mummy, sounding intrigued or amused or both, but after having busted his ass last April tracking down a minion of hell and part of August associating with a pack of werewolves, not to mention time spent with Mr. Henry Fitzroy, his reaction was a little more extreme. He no longer took reality for granted.

"Mummy?" he growled.

"It was, uh, in the Egyptology workroom." Constable Trembley took a step back, wondering why the detective had gone for his gun. "Just laying there in its coffin. Too much for one of the janitors apparently." He still looked weirdly suspicious. "It *had* been dead for a long time." She tried a grin. "I don't think they'll need you on that case either . . ."

The joke fell flat, but the grin worked and Celluci let his hand fall to his side. Of course a museum would have a mummy. He felt like a fool. "If you're sure there's nothing I can do . . ."

"No, sir."

"Fine." Muttering under his breath, he headed back to his car. What he really needed was a hot shower, a large breakfast, and a nice simple murder.

Snapping his occurrence book closed, Trembley's partner wandered over to her side. "Who was that?" he asked.

"Detective-Sergeant Celluci. Homicide. He was driving by, stopped to see if he could help."

"Yeah? He looked like he could use some more sleep. What was he muttering as he walked away?"

"It sounded like," PC Trembley frowned, "lions, and tigers, and bears. Oh, my."

Three

"Hi, Mom."

"Good morning, dear. How did you know it was me?"

Vicki sighed and hiked the towel up more securely under her arms. "I'd just gotten into the shower. Who else could it be?" Her mother had an absolute genius for calling at the worst possible times. Henry had almost died once because of it or, conversely, she'd just missed getting killed because of that same call—Vicki had never quite settled the question to her own satisfaction.

"It's twenty to nine, dear, don't tell me you're just getting up?"

"All right."

There was a long pause while Vicki waited for her mother to work that last comment through. She heard her sigh and then she heard, faintly in the background, the staccato sound of her nails against the desk.

"You're working for yourself now, Vicki, and that doesn't mean you can lie about all day."

"What if I was up all night on a case?"

"Were you?"

"Actually, no." Vicki put her bare foot up on one of the kitchen chairs and massaged her calf with the heel of one hand. Yesterday's climb up the tower had begun to make itself felt. "Now, as I was home two weeks ago for Thanksgiving . . ." *Which is going to have to hold you until Christmas.* ". . . to what do I owe the pleasure of this call?"

"Do I have to have a reason to call my only daughter?"

"No, but you usually do."

"Well, no one else is in the office yet . . ."

"Mom, some day the Life Sciences Department is going to expect you to start paying for these long distance calls."

"Nonsense, Vicki. Queens University has lots of money

and it's not like it costs a fortune to call from Kingston to
Toronto, so I thought I'd take the opportunity to see how
your visit to the eye doctor went.''

"Retinitis pigmentosa doesn't get any better, Mom. I still
have no night sight and bugger all in the way of peripheral
vision. What difference does it make how the visit to the
eye doctor went?''

"Victoria!''

Vicki sighed and pushed her glasses up her nose. "Sorry.
Nothing's changed.''

"Then it hasn't gotten any worse.'' Her mother's tone
acknowledged the apology and agreed to drop the subject.
"Have you managed to line up any work?''

She'd finished an insurance fraud case the last week of
September. There hadn't been anything since. If she were
a better liar . . . "Nothing yet, Mom.''

"Well, what about Michael Celluci? He's still on the
force. Can't he find you something?''

"Mother!''

"Or that nice Henry Fitzroy.'' He'd answered the phone
once when she called and she'd been very impressed. "He
found you something last summer.''

"Mother! I don't need them to find me work. I don't need
anyone to find me work. I am *perfectly* capable of finding
work on my own.

"Don't grind your teeth, dear. And I know you're perfectly capable of finding work, but . . . oops, Dr. Burke
just walked in, so I should go. Remember you can always
come live with me if you need to.''

Vicki managed to hang up without giving in to the urge
for violence but only because she knew it would be her
phone that suffered and she couldn't afford to buy another
new one right now. Her mother could be so . . . so . . .
*Well, I suppose it could be worse. She has a career and a
life of her own and she* could *be after me for grandchildren.*
She wandered back to the shower, shaking her head at the
thought; motherhood had never been a part of her plans.

She'd been ten when her father left, old enough to decide
that motherhood had caused most of the problems between
her parents. While other children of divorce blamed themselves, she laid the blame squarely where she felt it belonged. Motherhood had turned the young and exciting

woman her father had married into someone who had no
time for him, and after he left, the need to provide for a
child had governed all her choices. Vicki had grown up as
fast as she could, her independence granting a mutual independence for her mother—which had never quite been accepted in the spirit in which it was offered.

Vicki sometimes wondered if her mother wouldn't prefer
a pink and lacy sort of a daughter who wouldn't mind being
fussed over, but she didn't lose any sleep worrying about
it, given that her decidedly non-pink and non-lacy attitudes
had no effect on her mother's fussing as it was. While proud
of the work that Vicki did, she fretted over potential dangers, public opinion, the men in Vicki's life, her eating habits, her eyes, and her caseload.

"Not that my caseload doesn't need fussing over," Vicki
admitted, working up a lather on her hair. Money was beginning to get tight and if something didn't turn up
soon. . . .

"Something'll turn up." She rinsed and turned the water
off. "Something always does."

"This is absolutely ridiculous! I won't stand for it!" Dr.
Rax threw himself down into his desk chair, slamming the
upper edge back into the wall. "How dare they keep us
out!"

"Calm down, Elias, you'll give yourself an ulcer." Dr.
Shane stood in the office doorway, arms crossed. "It's only
until the autopsy comes back and we know for sure it was
a heart attack that killed that poor janitor."

"Of course it was a heart attack." Dr Rax rubbed at his
eyes. Trapped in a cycle of frighteningly realistic dreams
about being buried alive, he'd welcomed the phone call that'd
freed him in the early hours of the morning. "The police
officer I talked to said you could tell just from looking at
him. Said the mummy had probably scared him to death."
He snorted, his opinion of anyone who could be scared to
death by a piece of history clear.

Dr. Shane frowned. "Mummy . . . ?"

"Oh, for God's sake, Rachel. You can't have forgotten
the baron's little souvenir."

"No, of course not . . ." Except that for a moment, she
had.

Dr. Rax rubbed at his eyes again; they felt as though bits
of sand had jammed up under the lids. "Funny thing is, I
knew young Ellis. Talked to him on a number of occasions
when I'd stayed late. He had a good mind, all things considered, but not what I'd call much of an imagination and
I'd have expected him to take anything he ran into in the
workroom in stride." He surprised himself with a dry
chuckle. "Unlike Ms. Taggart."

Although she continued to clean the department offices,
Ms. Taggart would not go into the workroom alone since
the incident last summer with the mummified head. No one
had ever admitted placing the Blue Jays cap on the artifact,
but as Dr. Rax had made no real effort to find the culprit
and had been more than vocal about the lack of depth in the
bull pen, the rest of the department had its suspicions.

"You realize this is only going to encourage her." Dr.
Shane sighed. "She'll probably transfer to Geology or
somewhere else without bone and we'll lose the best cleaning lady we've ever had. I'll never again be able to leave
papers on my desk overnight." Escorting her into the workroom was a small price to pay when measured against the
knowledge that Ms. Taggart was the only cleaning lady in
the building who *never* disturbed office work in progress.
"Speaking of papers . . ." She waved a hand at the curator's overloaded desk. "Why don't you use this time as a
chance to catch up?"

"The moment we can get back to work . . ."

"I'll let you know." She pulled the door closed behind
her and walked slowly across to her own office, brows drawn
down into a worried vee. Her memories of the mummy slid
over and around each other as though they'd been run
through a blender and she just couldn't believe that for one
moment she'd forgotten its existence entirely. *Obviously, I've
been more affected by that young man's death than I thought.*

*The ka he had taken in the night told him of wonders
greater than even Egypt in all her glory had known. The
great pyramids had been dwarfed not by monuments to the
glory of kings but by gleaming anthills of metal and glass
built for* fat-assed yuppies. *Chariots had been replaced by*
four cylinder shit-boxes with no more pickup than a sick
duck. *Although he was unclear on many of the other con-*

*cepts, beer and bureaucracy, at least, seemed to have en-
dured. He was halfway around the world from the Mother
Nile in a country that fought with sticks upon frozen water.
Its queen sat in state many leagues away, no longer Osiris
incarnate, although he who ruled for her here seemed to
think himself some kind of tin-plate, big-chinned god.*

*Most importantly, the gods he had known and who had
known him appeared to be no more. No longer would he
have to hide from the all-seeing eye of Thoth in the night
sky but, more importantly, there were none to replace the
priest-wizards who had bound him. The gods of this new
world were weak and had claimed few souls. He would go
among them as a lion among the goats, able to feed where
he willed.*

*He recognized that the one known as Reid Ellis had be-
longed to the lower classes, a common laborer, and that the
information he had absorbed was tainted by this lack of
position. That mattered little, for he had long since chosen
the one who would feed him with what he needed—the history of the time that had passed and the way to prosper in
the time that was now.*

*The life had also given him strength. Although his phys-
ical form remained bound, his ka had been able to wander
throughout the minds that knew of him.*

And how pitifully little they knew.

*With each touch, he took bits of the knowledge away; it
was knowledge of him after all and thus he could control it.
Those with the weakest wills forgot in a single passing, the
stronger lost memories a piece at a time. Soon, there would
be none who knew how to bind him again.*

*He would be released; he had not touched the one who
would ensure it, except to strengthen the bond between them,
and he left the other enough to assist. They would peel the
binding spell away and he would rise, magic restored, ready
to claim his place in this strange new world.*

He would deal with them then.

"Where is everybody?"

"Well, as no one knew when we were going to be allowed back into the workroom, I told them they might as
well finish up any paperwork and then head home."

Dr. Rax turned to stare at his assistant curator. *You told them what*? he wanted to shout. *We have the first new mummy in decades and you dismissed my staff?* But somewhere between thought and speech, the words changed. "That seems reasonable. No point in them hanging around with nothing to do." He frowned, confused.

Reaching the door to the workroom, Dr. Shane peeled off the six-inch strip of bright yellow and black police tape that has been pasted over the lock. "I'm glad you agree." She hadn't been sure he would. In fact, now that she thought about it, she wondered how she could have . . . could have . . . "And it's not like we'll need them for what we're about to do."

"No . . ." He had the strangest feeling that they were walking into deadly danger and half expected the door to creak open like a bad special effect. *We should get out of here now, while there's still time.* Then they were in the workroom with the mummy and nothing else mattered.

Together they removed the plastic shroud, bundling it carelessly to one side.

"I do feel a bit guilty about young Ellis though," Dr. Shane sighed as she pulled two pairs of cotton work gloves out of the cardboard box marked *Wear these or die!* "Heart failure might have been the cause, but our mummy certainly contributed to the effect."

"Nonsense." Dr. Rax worked his fingers into the gloves. "As dreadful as it was, as sad as it was, we are in no way responsible for that young man's fears." He picked up a pair of broad-tipped tweezers and bent over the coffin, breathing through his mouth to minimize the almost overpowering smell of cedar. Very, very gently, he caught hold of the hieroglyphic strip at the point where the winding ended on the mummy's chest. "I think we'll need some solvent. It appears to be attached to the actual wrappings."

"Cedar gum?"

"I think so."

He continued to apply a gentle pull on the ancient linen while Dr. Shane carefully moistened the end with a solvent-soaked cotton swab.

"It's amazing how little the fabric has deteriorated over the centuries," she observed. "I send a shirt to the dry cleaner twice and it begins to fall apar . . . !" The hand holding the swab jerked back.

"What is it?"

"The chest, where I touched it, it felt warm." She laughed a little nervously, knowing how ridiculous it sounded. "Even through the glove."

Dr. Rax snorted. "Probably the heat from the lights."

"They're fluorescent."

"All right, it was a by-product of the slow and continuing process of decay."

"Felt through the wrapping and the glove?"

"How about pure imagination brought on by misdirected guilt over that janitor?"

She managed a doubting smile. "I suppose I'll settle for that."

"Good. Now, can we get back to work?"

Deliberately not touching the body, Dr. Shane stroked on a little more of the solvent. "This is the damnedest funereal setup I've ever seen," she muttered. "No Osiran symbols, no tutelary goddesses, no *Ded*, no *Thet*, no hieroglyphs at all except on this strip." Her brows drew down. "Shouldn't we . . . shouldn't we be studying the strip before we remove it?"

"It'll be easier to study once it's off."

"Yes, but . . ." But what? She couldn't seem to hang onto the thought.

Suddenly Dr. Rax smiled. "It's lifting. Stand back."

He could feel the end of the linen lifting, each separate hieroglyph a weight of stone rising off his chest. The spell stretched and tore as it was pulled more and more out of alignment. Then, with a silent shriek that cut through bone and blood and sinew, it ripped apart.

He welcomed the pain. It was his first physical sensation in three millennia and a joyous agony. Nothing came without price and for his freedom, no price was too high. Had his limbs been capable of movement, he would have writhed, but movement would come slowly, over time, and so he could only endure the waves of red that raced the length of his body pushing all else before them, pounding all else beneath them. He only wished that he could scream.

Finally, the last wave began to ebb, leaving behind it a stinging of nettles in his flesh and the red glow of two eyes in the darkness.

My lord? *He should have known that if he survived his god would have survived as well.*

The eyes grew brighter until by their light his ka could see the birdlike head of his god.

The others are dead, *it said.*

This confirmed what the taste of the laborer's ka had told him.

There are gods, but not the ones we knew. *Its beak wasn't built for smiling, but it cocked its head to one side and he remembered that meant it was pleased.* I was wise when I created you; through you I survived. The new gods have been strong in the past, but they are not now. Few souls are sworn. Build me a temple, gather me acolytes until I am strong enough to make others like you. We can do what we wish with this world.

Then he was alone again in the darkness.

Nothing held him now except millennia-old fabric already beginning to rot under the pressure of accumulated time, but he would remain for a little longer where he was. His ka had one more short journey to make and then he would gather his strength before he confronted his . . . savior.

Build a temple. Gather acolytes. We can do what we wish with this world. *Indeed.*

He had not really planned beyond gaining his freedom, but it seemed he would have much to do.

Rachel Shane stepped out of the elevator on the ground floor, the rubber soles of her shoes making very little sound against the tile floor. She was worried about Elias. He'd always been an intense man, determined to make the Egyptology Department at the ROM one of the best in the world despite budgets and bureaucrats, but in all the years she'd known him—*and they were a good many years,* she admitted silently to herself—she'd never seen him this obsessed.

She paused just inside the security door to pull her trench coat closed. Although the looming bulk of the planetarium limited the lines of sight from the staff entrance, water glistened on the pavement between the two buildings. If it wasn't raining at this moment, it had been in the recent past.

Recent past . . . She thought back to the workroom and the almost dreamlike way they'd unwrapped the linen strip from around the mummy. No documentation. No photographs. Not even a notation of the hieroglyphs. It was very stra . . .

The sudden pain snapped her head forward and exploded red lights behind her eyes. She sagged against the security door, the smooth glass pulling against the damp skin of her cheek as she fought to stay on her feet. *Is it a stroke?* And with that thought came a terrifying vision of complete and utter helplessness, so much worse than death. *Oh, God, I'm too young.* She couldn't catch her breath, couldn't remember how her lungs worked, couldn't remember anything but the pain.

As if from a great distance, she saw the guard run for the other side of the door and manage to open it without throwing her to the ground. He slipped an arm around her waist and half guided, half carried her over to a chair.

"Dr. Shane? Dr. Shane, are you all right?"

She grabbed desperately onto the sound of her name. The pain began to recede, leaving her feeling as though she'd been scoured from within by a wire brush. Nerve endings throbbed and for just an instant a great golden sun blotted out the security area, the guard, everything.

"Dr. Shane?"

Then it was gone and the pain was gone as if it had never been. She rubbed at her temples, trying to remember how it had felt, and couldn't.

"Should I call an ambulance, Dr. Shane?"

An ambulance? That penetrated. "No, thank you, Andrew. I'm fine. Really. Just a little faint."

He frowned. "You sure?"

"Positive." She took a deep breath and stood. The world remained as it always had been. The tension went out of her shoulders.

"Well, if you're sure. . . ." He still looked a little dubious. "I guess you must've been working too hard, what with the cops keeping you away from your stuff until this afternoon." He went back behind his desk, still watching her with a wary eye. "So, they gonna take the mummy away?"

"Mummy?"

"Yeah. They say Reid Ellis bumped into a mummy up there in the dark and it scared him to death."

"Oh, *that* mummy . . ." It was amazing how rumors got started. She smiled and shook her head. With the police in and out of the workroom there was no real point in the department keeping quiet to save face. They'd just have to convince the scientific community that they'd meant to buy an empty sarcophagus. "There never was a mummy, Andrew. Just an empty coffin. Which I suppose is frightening enough in the middle of the night."

Andrew looked a little disappointed. "No mummy?"

"No."

He sighed. "Well, that certainly makes the story less interesting."

"Sorry." Dr. Shane paused with one hand on the outside door and fixed the security guard with a look she kept just on the edge of intimidating. "I'd appreciate you spreading the *real* story around."

He sighed again. "Sure thing, Dr. Shane. There never was a mummy. . . ."

His fingers had torn through the bottom sheet and his heartbeat echoed off the walls of the bedroom. He'd woken again to the memory of a brilliant white-gold sun centered in an azure sky.

"I don't want to die!"

But then, why the sun?

One night he could force himself to ignore; wash it away in the hunt, in blood. Two nights made it real.

He fought himself free of the sheet and sat up on the edge of the bed, hands turned up on his thighs. His palms were moist. He stared at them for a moment, then frantically scrubbed them dry, trying to remember if in over four hundred and fifty years he'd ever sweated.

The stink of his fear filled the room. He had to get away from it.

Naked, he padded out into the condo and over to the plate glass window that looked down on Toronto. Pressing palms and forehead against the cool glass, he forced himself to take long, slow breaths until he calmed. He traced the flow of traffic down Jarvis Street; marked the blaze of glory a few streets over that was Yonge; flicked his gaze over the bands of gold in nearby office towers marking where conscientious employees worked late; knew that as dusk deep-

ened to full dark, the other, still human, children of the
night would emerge. This was his city.

Then he found himself wondering how it would look with
dawn reflected rose and yellow in the glass towers, the in-
terlacing ribbons of asphalt pearly gray instead of black, the
fall colors of the trees like gems scattered across the city
under the arcing dome of a brilliant blue sky . . . and wondering how long he would last, how much he would see,
before the golden circle or the sun ignited his flesh and he
died for the second and very final time.

"Jesu, Lord of Hosts, protect me."

He jerked himself back off the glass and sketched a sign
of the cross with trembling fingers.

"I don't *want* to die." But he couldn't get that image of
the sun out of his head. He reached for the phone.

"Nelson."

"Vicki, I . . ." He what? He was having hallucinations?
He was losing his mind?

"Henry? Are you all right?"

I need to talk to you. But he suddenly couldn't get the
words out.

Apparently, she heard them anyway. "I'm on my way
over." Her tone left no room for argument. "You're at
home?"

"Yes."

"Then stay put. I'll grab a taxi. I'll be right there. Whatever it is, we can work it out."

Her certainty leeched some of the tension out of his white-
knuckled grip on the phone and his mouth twisted up into
a parody of a smile. "No hurry," he told her, attempting
to regain some control, "we've got until dawn."

Although guilt was a part of the reason that Dr. Rax remained at his desk plugging away at the despised paperwork
long after Dr. Shane had gone home—he *had* let the pile
achieve mammoth proportions—it was more a vague sense
of something left unfinished that kept him in his office, almost anxiously waiting for the other shoe to drop. He
scrawled his initials at the bottom of a budget report,
slammed the folder closed, and tossed it into his out basket.
Then he sighed and began to doodle aimlessly on his desk

calendar. *If only it wasn't so damned hard to concentrate. . . .*

Suddenly, he frowned, realizing his doodle hadn't been that aimless. Under the day and date—Monday, October 19th—he'd sketched a griffinlike animal with the body of an antelope and the head of a bird crowned with three uraei and three sets of wings. He'd sketched the creature who had been watching his dreams.

"And now that I think of it," he pushed his chair back so that he could reach the bookcase behind the desk, "you look awfully familiar. Yes . . . here we are . . ." His drawing matched the illustration almost line for line. "Amazing what the subconscious remembers." Ignoring a cold feeling of dread, he skimmed the text. "Akhekh, a predynastic god of upper Egypt absorbed into the conqueror's religion to become a form of the evil god Set . . ." The book slid out of hands gone limp and crashed to the floor. The eyes of Akhekh, eyes printed in black, had, for an instant, burned red.

Heart in his throat, Dr. Rax bent forward and gingerly picked up the book. It had closed as it fell and he had no desire to open it again.

Elias. Come. It is time.

"Time for what?" he called before he realized the voice he answered was in his head.

He carefully put the book on the desk then rubbed at his temples with trembling fingers. "Right. First I'm seeing things. Now I'm hearing things. I think it's time I went home and had a large Scotch and a long sleep."

The weakness in his legs surprised him when he stood. He held onto the back of his chair until he was sure he could walk without his knees buckling, then made his way slowly across the room. At the door, he grabbed his jacket and flicked off the light, trying not to think of two eyes glowing red in the darkness behind him as he made his way across the outer office.

"This is ridiculous." He squared his shoulders and took a deep breath as he started down the hallway to the elevators. "I'm a scientist, not some superstitious old fool frightened of the dark. I've just been working too hard." The dim quiet of the hall laid balm on his jangled nerves and by the time he reached the door to the workroom his heartbeat and breathing had almost returned to normal.

Elias. Come.

He turned and faced the door, unable to stop himself. From a distance, he felt his hand go into his pocket for his keys, saw them turn in the lock, heard the quiet movement of air as the door opened, smelled the cedar that had been filling the room with its scent since they'd opened the coffin, tasted fear. His legs carried him forward.

The plastic over the coffin had been thrown aside.

The coffin itself was empty save for a pile of linen wrappings already beginning to decay.

The physical compulsion left him and he sagged against the ancient wood. A man stooped with age, eyes deep sunk over ax blade cheekbones, flesh clinging to bone and skin stretched tight, walked out of the shadows. Somehow, he had known that it would come to this and that knowledge kept the terror just barely at bay. From the moment he had first seen the seal, he had felt this moment approaching.

"Des . . . troy those." The voice creaked like two pieces of old wood rubbing together.

Dr. Rax looked down at the linen wrappings and then up at the man who had so recently worn them that the marks still showed imprinted on his skin. "Do what?"

"There must be . . . no evi . . . dence."

"Evidence? Of what?"

"Of me."

"But *you're* evidence of you."

"Des . . . troy them."

"No." Dr. Rax shook his head. "You may be . . ." And then it hit him, finally broke through the cocoon of fate or destiny or whatever had been insulating him from what was actually going on. This man, this creature, had been entombed in the Eighteenth Dynasty, over three thousand years ago. Only his white-knuckled grip on the coffin kept him standing. "How . . . ?"

Something that might have been a smile twisted the ancient mouth. "Magic."

"There's no such . . ." Except obviously there was, so he let the protest die.

The smile flattened into an expression much more unpleasant. "Des . . . troy them."

As he had been while opening the workroom door, Dr.
Rax found himself shunted off into an enclosed section of
his mind while his body obeyed another's will. Only this
time, he was conscious of it. The fog was gone.

He watched himself gather up the linen wrappings and
carry them over to the sink.

"That . . . too."

Fighting to stop himself, he lifted the strip of hieroglyphs
from the worktable and added it to the rest. When he went
into the darkroom, he knew the creature was using his
mind—fire would have been an Eighteenth Dynasty solution, chemicals were not. A bottle of concentrated ascorbic
acid dissolved the rotting fabric sufficiently to wash the entire mess down the drain and although his hands trembled,
he couldn't prevent them from pouring it. His heart ached
at the destruction of the artifacts and the anger gave him
strength.

Slowly he jerked his body around and met eyes so dark
there was no telling where the pupil ended and the iris began. "That wasn't necessary," he managed to gasp.

The eyes narrowed, then widened. "A good thing for me
. . . your god has not recognized . . . its power."

"What the hell . . ." He had to stop to breathe. *We sound
like a couple of badly tuned transistor radios.* ". . . are you
talking about. My god?"

"Science." The ancient voice grew stronger. "Still only
an aspect. Not strong enough . . . to save your ass."

Dr. Rax frowned, his thoughts tumbling over themselves
in an attempt to pull order out of the impossible—that was
not a phrase a dynastic Egyptian would use. "You speak
English. But English didn't exist when you were . . ."

"Alive?"

"If you like." *The son of a bitch is enjoying this. He's
allowing *me* to talk to him.*

"I learn from the ka I take."

"From the ka . . . ?"

"So many questions, Dr. Rax."

"Yes . . ." A hundred, a thousand questions, each fighting to be first. Perhaps the loss of the artifacts could be
made up. He began to shake with barely suppressed excitement. Perhaps the holes in history could be filled. "There's
so much you can tell me."

"Yes." Just for an instant, something very like regret passed over the ancient face. "I'd enjoy . . . shooting shit with you. But, unfortun . . . ately, I need what you can tell . . . me."

Dr. Rax started as an ancient hand wrapped around his wrist, the grip almost painfully tight. *I learn from the ka I take.* And the ka was the soul and a young man had died this morning and English hadn't existed . . . "No!" He began to slide into the black depths of ebony eyes. "But I freed you!" *There's still so much I don't know!* And that gave him the strength to fight.

The grip tightened.

His free arm flailed, slamming his elbow into the cupboards, knocking the empty bottle off the counter, accomplishing nothing.

But he fought all the way down.

He lost the fight question by question.

How and why and where and what? And finally, who?

"I don't think you're crazy."

"But how can you know?"

Vicki shrugged. "Because I know crazy and I know you."

Henry threw himself down beside her on the couch and caught up both her hands in his. "Then why do I keep dreaming of the sun?"

"I don't know, Henry." He desperately wanted reassurance, but she didn't know how much she had to give; this was going to take more than a "poor sweet baby" and a kiss on the nose. He looked, not frightened exactly, but vulnerable and his expression sat in a knot at the base of her throat, making it hard to swallow, hard to breathe. The only comfort she had to offer was the knowledge that he wouldn't face whatever this turned out to be, alone. "But I do know this, we aren't going down without a fight."

"We?"

"You asked me for help, remember?"

He nodded.

"So." She traced a pattern on the back of his hand with her thumb. "You said this has happened to others of your kind . . . ?"

"There've been stories."

"Stories?"

"We hunt alone, Vicki. Except for during the time of changing we almost never associate with other vampires. But you hear stories. . . ."

"Vampiric gossip?"

He shrugged, a little self-consciously. "If you like."

"And these stories say that . . . ?"

"That sometimes when we get too old, when the weight of all those centuries becomes too much to bear, we get so we can no longer stand the night and finally give ourselves to the sun."

"And before that happens, the dreams come?"

"I don't know."

She closed her hand around his. "All right. Let's take this one step at a time. Have you gotten tired of living?"

"No." That, at least, he was sure of and the reason for it stared at him intently from less than an arm's length away. "But, Vicki, as much as I have changed, the body, the mind is still basically human. Perhaps . . ."

"Perhaps the equipment is wearing out?" she interrupted, tightening her grip. "Planned obsolescence? You start heading toward your fifth century and the system starts breaking down?" Her brows drew in and her glasses slid down her nose. "I don't believe that."

Henry reached over and pushed her glasses back into place. "You can't disbelieve the dreams," he said softly.

"No," she admitted, "I can't." She sighed deeply and one side of her mouth quirked up. "It'd be useful if you lot did a little more communicating, so we weren't approaching this blind—maybe put out a newsletter or something." He smiled at that, as she knew he would, and he relaxed a little. "Henry, less than a year ago I didn't believe in vampires or demons or werewolves or myself. Now I know better. You *aren't* crazy. You *don't* want to die. You are therefore *not* going to give yourself to the sun. Q.E.D."

He had to believe her. Her no-nonsense mortal attitude slapped aside the specter of madness. "Stay till morning?" he asked. For a moment he couldn't believe the words had come from his mouth. He might as well have said, *"Stay until I'm helpless."* It meant the same thing. Did he trust her that much? He saw that she understood and by her hesitation gave him time to take back the request. He suddenly realized he didn't want to take it back. That he did, indeed, trust her that much.

Four hundred and fifty years ago he'd asked, *"Can we love?"*

"Can you doubt it?" had been the answer.

The silence stretched. He had to break it before it pulled them apart; pulled her apart, forced her to hear what he knew she wasn't ready to hear. "You can tie me to the bed if I start to do anything stupid."

"My definition of stupid or yours?" Her voice was tight.

In for a penny in for a pound. "Yours." He smiled, planted a kiss on her palm, and turned to face the window. If Vicki thought him sane, then he had to think so, too. Perhaps why he dreamed of the sun was of less immediate concern than how he dealt with the dreams. "More things in heaven and earth . . ." he mused.

Vicki sagged back against the sofa cushions. "Christ, I'm getting tired of that quote."

Four

Vicki had seen a thousand dawns and seen none of them the way she saw this one.

"Can you feel it?"

"Feel what?" Half asleep, she lifted her head off Henry's lap.

"The sun."

A sudden shot of adrenaline snapped her awake and she jerked forward, peering into his face. He looked very intent, brows drawn down, eyes narrowed. She glanced at the window. Although it faced south, not east, the sky had definitely begun to lighten. "Henry?"

He blinked, focused, and shook his head when he saw her expression, his smile both reassuring and slightly embarrassed. "It's all right, this happens every morning. It's like a warning." His voice took on the mechanical tones of a dozen science fiction movie computers. "You have fifteen minutes to reach minimum safe darkness."

"Fine." Vicki stood, still holding his wrist. "Fifteen minutes. Let's go."

"I was making a joke," he protested as she pulled him to his feet. "As warnings go, it's not really that definite. It's just a feeling."

Vicki sighed and shot an anxious glance out the window at the streaks of pink she was sure she could see touching the edges of the city. "Okay. It's just a feeling. What do you usually do when you feel it?"

"Go to bed."

"Well?"

He studied her face for a moment—his intent expression back—sighed in turn, and nodded. "You're right." Then he pulled his hands free, spun on his heel, and walked across the living room.

"Henry?"

Although he stopped, he didn't turn, merely looked back over his shoulder.

I don't have to stay if you're sure you're all right. Except he wasn't sure. That was why she was there. And while he might be regretting making the offer—she recognized second thoughts in his hesitation—the reason he'd made it still existed. It seemed that if they were to both get through sunrise, she'd have to treat this like any other job. *The client fears that under certain conditions he may attempt suicide. I'm here to stop him.* With a start, she realized he was still waiting for her to say something. "Uh, how do you feel?"

Henry watched the parade of emotions cross Vicki's face. *This isn't any easier for you, is it?* he thought. "I feel the sun," he said softly and held out his hand.

She took it with what he'd come to recognize as her working expression and together they made their way to the bedroom.

The first time Vicki had seen Henry's bed, she'd been irrationally disappointed. By that time she'd known he didn't spend the day locked in a coffin atop a pile of his native earth, but she'd been secretly hoping for something a little exotic. A king-size bed—*"I bet your father would have loved to have one of those . . ."*—with white cotton sheets and a dark blue blanket was just too definitively normal looking.

This morning, she shook free of his hand and stopped just inside the closed door. The soft circle of light from the lamp on the bedside table left her effectively blind, but she knew, because he'd told her on that first visit, that the heavy blue velvet drapery over the window covered a layer of plywood painted black and caulked around the edges. Another curtain just inside the glass hid the wood from the prying eyes of the world. It was a barrier designed to keep the sun safely at bay and a barrier, Vicki knew, that Henry could rip down in seconds if he chose. Her body became the barrier before the door.

Standing by the bed, Henry hesitated, fingers on shirt buttons, surprised to find himself uncomfortable about undressing in front of a woman he'd been making love to—and feeding from—for months. *This is ridiculous. She probably can't even see you from there, the light's so dim.*

Shaking his head, he stripped quickly, reflecting that help-lessness brought with it a much greater intimacy than sex.

He could feel the sun more strongly now, more strongly than he could remember feeling it before. *You're sensitive to it this morning. That's all.* God, he hoped it was all.

For Vicki, watching the flicker of pale skin as Henry moved in and out of the circle of light, standing guard at the door suddenly made less than no sense. "Henry? What the hell am I doing here?" She walked forward until his face swam into focus and then reached out and laid her hand gently on his bare chest, halting his movement. "I can't stop you . . ." She scowled, recognizing the words as inadequate. "I can't even slow you down."

"I know." He covered her fingers with his, marveling as he always did at the heat of her, at the feel of her blood pulsing just under the skin.

"Great." She rolled her eyes. "So what am I supposed to do if you make a run for the sun?"

"Be there."

"And watch you die?"

"No one, not even a vampire, wants to die alone."

It could have sounded facetious. It didn't. Hadn't she realized only hours before that was all she had to give him? But she hadn't realized, not then, that it might come to this.

Breathing a little heavily, wishing the light was strong enough for her to see his expression, Vicki managed not to yank her hand free. *Be there.* Bottom line, it was no more than Celluci had ever asked of her. Only the circumstances were different. "Jesus H. Christ, Henry." It took an effort, but she kept her voice steady, "You're not going to fucking die, okay? Just get your jammies on—or your tuxedo or whatever it is the undead sleep in—and get into bed."

He released her and spread his arms, his meaning plain.

"Fine." She pointed at the bed and glared at him while he did as he was told. Then, pushing her glasses hard against the bridge of her nose, she perched on the edge of the mattress. If she squinted, she could make out his features. "Are you okay?"

"Are you daring me not to be?"

"Henry!"

"I can feel the sun trembling on the horizon, but the only thing in my mind is you."

"You're just a bundle of clichés this morning." But the relief in his voice had made it sound like truth. "What's going to happen? I mean to you?"

He shrugged, his shoulders whispering against the sheets. "From your side, I don't know. From mine, I go away until sunset. No dreams, no physical sensation." His voice began to slow under the weight of dawn. "Nothingness."

"What should I do?"

He smiled. "Kiss me . . . good-bye."

Her lips were on his when the sun rose. She felt the day claim him. Slowly, she pushed herself back up into a sitting position.

"Henry?"

He looked so dreadfully young. So dreadfully vulnerable. She grabbed his shoulders and shook him, hard.

"Henry!"

His heart had always beat slowly; now, her ear pressed tight against his chest, she couldn't hear it beat at all.

He couldn't stop her from doing whatever she wanted to him. He had just put himself completely and absolutely in her hands.

Be there. Bottom line, that was all Celluci had ever asked of her. Bottom line, that was all she'd ever asked of Celluci in return.

Be there. Bottom line, it meant a lot more when Henry Fitzroy asked it.

"Henry, you shit." She shoved her glasses out of the way and scrubbed her knuckles across her eyes. "What the hell can I give you to match this?"

A few moments later, she pulled herself together with a more prosaic question. "Now what? Do I leave? Or do I stay and keep watch over you all day?" A massive yawn threatened to dislocate her jaw; she hadn't gotten much sleep during the long wait for morning. "Or do I climb in with you?"

She ran one finger lightly down his cheek. The skin felt cool and dry. It always had, but with the night to give it animation it had never felt so . . . unalive. "All right, scratch that last idea." Not even as tired as she was could she sleep next to the body—to the absence of Henry—that the day had created. Scooping his discarded pants off the floor, she rummaged in the pockets for his keys.

"I'm going home," she said, needing to hear herself just to offset his absolute stillness. "I'll get some sleep and be back before dark. Don't worry, I'll lock up on my way out. You'll be safe."

The lamp by the bed switched off at the door. Vicki took one look back then extinguished the pale island of light, plunging the room into complete and utter darkness.

She had her hand on the knob and had actually begun to turn it when a sudden realization stopped her cold. "How the hell do I get out of here?" Her fingers traced the rubber seals that edged the door, blocking any possible intrusion of light. Could she leave without destroying Henry? *This is just great.* The door boomed a hollow counterpoint to her thoughts as she beat her head gently against it. *I stay to save him from suicide and end up committing murder.*

Go or stay?

There'd be light spilling into the hall through the open door of his office and if she opened this door here . . . How direct did the sun have to be? How diffuse?

We should have covered this earlier, Henry. She couldn't believe that neither of them had considered anything past sunrise. Of course, they'd both been dealing with other things.

She couldn't risk it. The entrance door to the condo had been locked and the security chain fastened. He was as safe in here as he ever was. He just had company.

Eyes closed—voluntary lack of sight seemed to help—she stumbled back to the bed and lay down on top of the covers as far from Henry's inert body as she could get.

All her senses told her she was alone. Except she knew she wasn't. The entire room had become a coffin of sorts. She could feel the darkness pressing against her, becoming a six by three by one foot box, and tried not to think of Edgar Allan Poe and premature burials.

"How did he die?"

"His heart stopped." The assistant coroner peeled off his gloves. "Which, in fact, is what kills us all in the end. You want to know why he died, ask me after I've had him on the table for a couple of hours."

"Thank you, Dr. Singh."

He smiled, completely unaffected by the sarcasm. "I live

to serve. Don't keep him too long.'' He paused on his way out the door and threw back, ''Offhand, given the position, I'd say he was dead before he hit the floor.''

Waving an acknowledgment that he'd heard, Mike Celluci knelt by the body and frowned.

His partner, Dave Graham, leaned over his shoulder and whistled through his teeth. ''Someone's got quite the grip.''

Celluci grunted in agreement. Purple and green bruises circled the left wrist, brilliantly delineating the marks of four fingers and a thumb. The left arm lay stretching away from the body.

''He got dropped when he died,'' Dave said quietly.

''That'd be my guess. Check out the face.''

''No expression.''

''Right first time. No fear; no pain; no surprise; no nothing. No record of the last few minutes of life at all.''

''Drugs?''

''Maybe. Nice jacket.'' Celluci got to his feet. ''Wonder why it wasn't taken with the shoes.''

Stepping back out of the way, Dave shrugged. ''Who the hell can tell these days? They took the cash but not the credit cards or ID. Even left him his transit pass.''

Carefully stepping around both the chalk lines and the bits of broken glass on the floor, the two men made their way over to the sink. Where the stainless steel had been previously scored, the acid poured into it had eaten into the metal. A vague ammonia smell still drifted up from the drain.

''No sign of what he dumped . . .''

Celluci snorted. ''Or of who dumped it. Kevin!'' The ident man looked up from his position at the side of the corpse. ''I want prints lifted off the glass.''

''Off the glass?'' Only the base and the section of the neck protected by the screw-on cap had survived in anything large enough to even be considered pieces. ''Shall I cure the common cold while I'm at it?''

''Suit yourself, but I want those prints first. Harper!''

The constable who'd been staring into the coffin started and jerked around. ''Detective?''

''Get someone in here to drain the trap . . . the curved pipe under the sink,'' he added when Harper looked blank. ''There's water in it, maybe enough to dilute the acid and give us some indication of what was dumped. Where's the guy who found the body?''

"Uh, in the departmental offices. His name's . . .'' Harper frowned and glanced down at his notes. ". . . Raymond Thompson. He's a researcher, been here about a year and a half. Some of the rest of the staff have arrived and they're in there, too. My partner's with them.''

"The offices are?''

"End of the hall on the right.''

Celluci nodded and started for the door. "We're finished with the body. As soon as all and sundry have got their pound of flesh, you can get it out of here.''

"Charming as always,'' Dave murmured, grinning. He followed his partner out into the hall and asked, "How come you know so much about plumbing?''

"My father was a plumber.''

"Yeah? You bastard, you never told me you were independently wealthy.''

"Didn't want you borrowing money.'' Celluci jerked his head back toward the workroom. "What do you think?''

"The good doctor interrupted an intruder?''

"And the janitor they pulled out of here yesterday?''

"I thought you said he saw a mummy and had a heart attack.''

"So what happened to the mummy?''

Dave's forehead furrowed. The coffin had definitely been empty and, while the workroom was crowded with all kinds of ancient junk, he'd bet his last loonie that there hadn't been a body tucked into a back corner. "The intruder walked off with it? Dr. Rax broke it into chunks, poured acid over it and washed it down the sink? It came to life and is lurching about the city?'' He caught sight of Celluci's expression and laughed. "You've been working too hard, buddy.''

"Maybe.'' Celluci pushed open the door marked Department of Egyptology a little more forcefully than necessary. *Maybe not.*

Besides the uniformed police constable, there were half a dozen people sitting in the large outer office, all exhibiting various forms of shock and/or disbelief. Two of them were crying quietly, a half empty box of tissues on the desk between them. Two were arguing, their voices a constant background drone. One sat, his head buried in his hands. Dr. Shane, her expression wavering between grief and anger, stood as the detectives came into the room and walked toward them.

"I'm Dr. Rachel Shane, the assistant curator. What's going on? No, wait . . ." Her hand went up before either of them could speak. "That's a stupid question. I know what's going on." She took a deep breath. "What's going to happen now?"

Celluci showed her his badge—from the corner of his eye he saw Dave do the same—and continued to hold it out while she focused first on it and then back on him. "Detective-Sergeant Celluci. My partner, Detective-Sergeant Graham. We'd like to ask Raymond Thompson a few questions."

The young man with his head in his hands jerked erect, eyes wide and face pale.

"We'd like to leave Dr. Rax's office as it is for the moment," Celluci continued, carefully using the matter-of-fact tones most people found calming. "Dr. Shane . . . ?"

"Yes, yes, of course. Use mine." She gestured at the door, then laced her fingers together so tightly the tips darkened under the pressure.

"Thank you."

She started a little at the warmth in his voice, then visibly relaxed. Not for the first time, Dave marveled at Celluci's ability to load *"I know you're hurting, but we're counting on you. If you fall apart, they'll all go."* onto two small words.

Raymond Thompson was a tall, thin, intense man who couldn't seem to hold still; he kept a foot or a hand or his head constantly moving. He'd come in early to do catch up on a little of the work the sarcophagus had disrupted and found Dr. Rax sprawled on the floor of the workroom. "I didn't touch him or anything else except the phone. I called 911, said I'd found a body, and went into the hall to wait. Christ, this is so . . . so . . . I mean, hell, did somebody kill him?"

"We don't know yet, Mr. Thompson." Dave Graham perched on the edge of the desk, one foot swinging lazily. "We'd appreciate it if you could remember how the work-

room looked. Did it appear to be the way you'd last seen
it?''

"I didn't really look at it. I mean, jeez, my boss was
lying dead on the floor!"

"But after you saw the body, you must have taken a quick
look around. Just to make sure there was no one else there."

"Well, yeah . . ."

"And the workroom . . . ?"

The younger man bit his lip, trying to remember, trying to
see past the sprawled corpse of a man he'd both liked and
respected. "There was glass on the floor," he said slowly,
"and the plastic had been pulled off the new coffin—looks
like Eighteenth Dynasty in a Sixteenth Dynasty sarcophagus,
really strange—but nothing seemed to be missing. I mean,
we had a pretty valuable faience and gold pectoral out on the
counter being restored and it was still there."

Dave raised a brow. "Faience? Pectoral?"

"Faience is, well, a kind of ceramic and a pectoral is
a . . ." long fingers sketched incomprehensible designs in
the air. "Well, I guess you could think of it as a fat necklace."

"More than historically valuable?"

Ray Thompson shrugged. "More than half of it is better
than eighteen karat gold."

Celluci turned from the window where he'd been watching traffic go by on Queen's Park Road, content to let his
partner ask the questions. Whatever the reasons were behind
the death of Dr. Rax, he was willing to bet robbery hadn't
been a motive. "What about the mummy?"

"There never was one."

"Oh?" He took a step forward. "I talked to one of the
officers on the scene yesterday morning as they were carrying
that janitor out of the building. She told me he'd seen a
mummy and had a heart attack. Essentially, died of fright."

"*Thought* he saw a mummy. Someone had popped an
empty coffin back into a stone box and resealed it. We
thought we were getting a new piece of history and all we
got was air." Ray's laugh was short and bitter. "Maybe
that's what killed Dr. Rax; scientific disappointment."

"So there wasn't a mummy?"

"No."

"You're sure?"

"Trust me, Detective, I'd have noticed."

Celluci caught a speaking glance from his partner and, scowling, closed his lips around what he'd been about to say. For the moment, he was willing to believe he'd misunderstood Trembley's explanation.

The rest of the department had even less to offer. They'd all liked Dr. Rax. Sure, occasionally he disagreed with his colleagues, but get twelve Egyptologists in a room and they'd have a dozen different opinions. No, there never had been a mummy. Professional jealousy?

Dr. Shane sighed and pushed her hair back off her forehead. "He was the curator of an underfunded department in a provincial museum. A good job, even a prestigious job compared to many but not one worth killing over."

"I suppose as his assistant curator you're next in line for the position." The words were an observation only, carefully nonweighted.

"I suppose I am. Damn him anyway, I'm the only person I can think of who hates paperwork more than he did." She pressed her fists against her mouth and squeezed her eyes tightly shut. "Oh, God . . ." A moment later she looked up, lashes in damp clumps. "I'm sorry. I'm not usually a watering pot."

"It's been an unusual kind of a day," Celluci said gently, handing her a tissue. "Dave, why don't you tell the others that anyone who wants to go home, can. But point out that once the lab people are done, we'll need a complete inventory of that workroom. Maybe some'll stay. The sooner we know for sure if anything's missing the better."

Dr. Shane blew her nose as Dave left. "You're pretty high-handed with my staff, Detective."

"Sorry. If you'd rather tell them yourself . . . ?"

"No, that's all right. You're doing fine." *I bet when he was eighteen he looked like Michelangelo's David.* She closed her eyes again. *God, I don't believe this. Elias is dead and I'm sitting here thinking about how good-looking this cop is.*

"Dr. Shane? Are you all right?"

"I'm fine." She opened her eyes again and managed a watery smile. "Really."

Celluci nodded. He couldn't help but notice that Dr. Rachel Shane had a very attractive smile, even twisted as it was with grief. He wondered how it would look when she actually had something to smile about.

"So." She tossed the soggy tissue in the wastebasket. "You've taken care of my staff, what do you have planned for me?"

For no good reason, Celluci could feel his ears turning red. He cleared his throat and gave thanks he hadn't gone in for that haircut. "If you could check Dr. Rax's office? You'd be in the best position to know if anything's been disturbed."

The curator's office was on the other side of the large common room. When PC Harper motioned him over to the hall door, Celluci waved Dr. Shane on alone.

"What?"

"It's the press."

"Yeah. So?"

"Shouldn't somebody make a statement; just to keep them from breaking the doors down?"

Celluci snorted. "I'll give them a statement."

As he watched the detective stride off down the corridor, shoulders up and fingers curled into fists, PC Harper wondered if maybe he should've waited for Sergeant Graham to finish with those staff members he'd taken off to the workroom. He had a feeling the press were about to get a statement they wouldn't be able to print.

A number of the reporters milling about in the security lobby recognized the detective as a museum guard let him through the door.

"Oh, great," muttered one. "It's homicide's Mr. Congeniality."

Questions flew thick and fast. Celluci waited, glaring the pack into silence. When the noise subsided enough so that he could be heard, he cleared his throat and began, his tone making his opinion of his audience plain. "In the early hours of this morning, a male Caucasian was found dead of causes unknown in the Department of Egyptology's workroom. Obviously we suspect foul play; I wouldn't be here if we didn't. You want anything else, you'll have to wait for it."

"What about the mummy?" A reporter near the front of the crowd shoved a microphone forward. "We heard there was talk of a mummy being involved."

Yes, what about the mummy? Although still uneasy about its accuracy, Celluci repeated the party line. "There never was a mummy, only an empty coffin being studied by the Department of Egyptology."

"Is there any possibility that the coffin could have caused both the recent deaths in the museum?"

"And how would it do that?" Celluci asked dryly. "Fall on them?"

"What about some kind of an ancient curse?"

Ancient Curse Kills Two. He could see the headlines now. "Don't be an asshole."

The reporter snatched the microphone to safety just in time and, smiling pleasantly, asked, "Can I quote you on that, Detective?"

Celluci's smile was just as sincere. "You can tattoo it on your chest."

Back upstairs, he found Dr. Shane and his partner standing just outside Dr. Rax's office.

Dave turned as he came in. "The doctor's got something for us, Mike."

Dr. Shane pushed her hair back off her face and rubbed at her forehead. "It might not be anything . . ." She looked over at Celluci, who nodded reassuringly, and went on. "It's just that Elias always kept a suit in his office, for board meetings and official business. He won't wear . . ." She paused, closed her eyes briefly, then continued. "*Wouldn't* wear one any longer than he had to. Anyway, when I left yesterday evening, his gray suit, a white shirt, and a burgundy silk tie were all hanging on the door. They're gone."

The two detectives exchanged identical looks. Celluci spoke first. "What about extra shoes?"

"No, he used to say that anywhere you couldn't get to in a pair of loafers wasn't worth going to in the first place." Her lower lip began to tremble but with a visible effort she maintained control. "Damn, but I'm really going to miss him."

"If you want to go home now, Dr. Shane . . . ?"

"Thanks, but I think I'd rather be doing something useful. If you don't need me any longer, I'll go help with the inventory." Head high, she walked across the room, paused at the door, and said, "When you catch the son of a bitch who did this, I hope you rip out his living heart and feed it to the crocodiles."

"We don't, uh, do that anymore, Doctor."

"Pity."

When they were alone, Dave sighed deeply and perched on a corner of the closest desk. "The lab'll have to go over that office. This case is getting weirder all the time." He tugged at his beard. "It's beginning to look like Dr. Rax interrupted a *naked* intruder. What kind of a nut case wanders around a museum starkers?"

Deep in thought, Celluci ignored him. He was remembering a pentagram and the human-seeming creature it had contained; remembering a man who stripped and changed and went for his throat with a wolf's fangs in a wolf's body; remembering Henry Fitzroy who wasn't human now even if he had been once. Remembering that things weren't always as they seemed.

Wondering what kind of a creature would emerge after centuries spent in darkness, locked immobile inside a box.

Except, there never had been a mummy.

He had twisted the mind of the guard so that she'd opened the outer door for him and wished him a good morning without ever wondering why an elderly man in an ill-fitting suit was leaving the museum hours before it opened. Once outside, he had turned, smiled, and brushed away her memory of the entire incident. Then he had crossed the street and lowered himself onto a bench, resting and rejoicing in the amount of space around him and his ability to move; waiting until the memories he absorbed told him it was time.

The first ka he had devoured had served to reanimate him and cover his tracks. The second had provided vital knowledge but little life force as the years remaining to Dr. Rax would have been barely a third of those he had already lived. To restore his youth and replenish his power, he needed a young ka with an almost unrealized potential.

Moving carefully, for this new country was bitterly cold and he had used a great deal of power just remaining warm while he waited, he descended underground into what both sets of stolen memories referred to as *morning rush hour*. He paid the fare, more for novelty than necessity, and moved out onto the subway platform. Which was when the walls started closing in. His heart slammed up against his chest and he thrust up a hand to stop the ceiling from falling. He would have run if he'd been able, but his bones had turned to water and he could only endure. Three trains passed before he calmed, realizing the space was not so small as he had first assumed, that if such monstrous metal beasts could move about freely, there would be room for him to move about as well.

One more train passed while he watched it in amazement—the memories of men used to such things had not done credit to the size or the speed or noise or the sheer presence of the machine—and a second followed before he found what he wanted. He almost balked at the door to the car when he saw how little space remained, but the need for more power was stronger than his fear and, at the last moment, he squeezed himself in.

The schoolboys wearing identical uniforms under fall coats were jammed so tightly up against each other by the crowds that the jerk and sway of the train couldn't move them. They were laughing and talking, even those able to reach a support not bothering to hang on, secure in the knowledge that it was impossible to fall.

He got as close as he could and began to search frantically for the youngest. He didn't know how much longer he could take being so confined.

To his surprise, one of the boys carried a protection that slapped his ka back and caused him to gasp in pain. Murmuring a spell under his breath, he stared in annoyance at the nimbus of golden light. The gods of this new age might be weak but one of them had touched this child—even if the child himself was not yet aware of the vocation—and he would not be permitted to feed.

No matter. There were plenty of others who lived with no protection at all.

It took a very long moment for him to meet the gray/blue eyes of the boy he finally chose; his gaze kept jumping around, looking for a way out. The boy, seeing only a harmless old man who looked distressed, smiled, a little confused but willing enough to be friendly. The smile remained until the end and was the last bit of life lost.

The surrounding mass of people would keep the body upright until he was long away.

At the next stop, he allowed himself to be caught up in the surging crowd and swept from the train, the power from this new ka burning away his fear with his age as he strode across the platform. Those who saw the outward changes— back straightening, hair darkening—refused to believe and he marveled at how everything outside a narrow perception of "possible" simply slid from the surface of their minds. From these people, these malleable bits of breathing clay, he would build an empire that would overshadow all empires of the past.

As he had for the last two nights, Henry awoke with the image of a great golden sun seared into his mind. But for the first time, it didn't bring the fear of madness; the blood scent lay so heavily in his sanctuary that madness became an inconsequential thing beside the Hunger.

'Well, thank God, you're awake at last.''

It took a moment for coherent thought to break through. "Vicki?'' Her voice had a tight, strained edge to it that made it difficult to recognize. He sat up, saw her for a moment, back pressed up against the door, then had to shield his eyes from the sudden glare as she switched on the light.

When he could see again, the door was open and she was gone. He followed the blood trail to the living room and found her leaning on the back of the couch, fingers dug deep into the upholstery. All the lights that she'd passed had been switched on. The Hunger thrummed in time to her heartbeat.

She looked up as he started toward her. "Henry, don't.''

Had he been younger, he might not have been able to stop, but four hundred and fifty years had taught him control if nothing else. "What's wrong?''

"I spent the day locked in that room with you, that's what's wrong!''

"You what?''

"How could I leave? I couldn't open the door without letting at least a little sunlight in and as I was supposed to be preventing you from incinerating yourself, it would definitely defeat the purpose if I fried you instead. So I was stuck.'' Her laugh sounded ragged. "At least you've got a master bathroom.''

"Vicki, I'm sorry . . .'' He stepped forward, but she

raised both hands and he stopped again although the blood moving under the delicate skin of her wrists beckoned him closer.

"Look, it's not your fault. It's something we both should've considered." She took a deep breath and settled her glasses more firmly on the bridge of her nose. "I can't stay with you tonight. I've got to get out of here."

He needed to feed and he knew he could convince her to stay; convince her in such a way that she'd think it was her idea. Although he didn't really understand, he took hold of the Hunger and nodded. "Go, then."

Vicki snatched up her jacket and purse and almost ran for the door, then she paused one hand on the knob and turned back to face him, managing a shaky smile. "I'll give you two things as a bed partner, Fitzroy; you don't snore and you don't steal the covers." Then she was gone.

As the day had claimed him and all he could feel was the press of her lips and the life behind them, Henry had envisioned how this new intimacy would change things between them.

Reality hadn't even come close.

Vicki sagged against the stainless steel wall of the elevator and closed her eyes. She felt like such a git. *Running away's a big help to Henry, isn't it?* But she just couldn't stay.

Exhaustion had kept her asleep until mid-afternoon, but the hours between waking and sunset had been some of the longest she'd lived through. Henry had been more alien to her, lying there, completely empty, than he'd ever been while drinking her blood. A hundred times she'd made her way to the door, and a hundred times she'd decided against opening it. *It's a bedroom on Bloor Street*, she'd kept telling herself. But a trembling streak of imagination she hadn't known existed kept answering, *It's a crypt.*

When the elevator reached the ground floor, she straightened and strode across the lobby as though overstretched nerves didn't twang with every movement. She nodded at the security guard as she passed his station and for the first time in over a year went gladly into a night she couldn't see.

"Yo, Victory!"

Some things she didn't need to see. "Hi, Tony. Good night, Tony." She felt him touch her arm and she stopped. Squinting, she could just make out the pale oval of his face under the streetlight.

He clicked his tongue. "Whoa, you look like shit. What happened?"

"Long day." She sighed. "What are you doing around here?"

"Well, uh . . ." He cleared his throat, sounding embarrassed. "I got this feeling that Henry needs me, so . . ."

In order to be here now, he had to have gotten the feeling before Henry had the need. Wonderful. Prescient ex-street punks. Just what *she* needed to make the day's experience complete. "And if Henry needs you, you come running?" Even to her own ears her voice appeared sharp, and she was embarrassed in turn to realize that its edge sounded very much like jealousy. Henry had needed her and she'd left.

"Hey, Victory, don't sweat it." As though he'd read her mind, Tony's voice softened. "It's easier for me. I didn't really have a life till he showed up. He can remake me any way he wants. You've been you for a long time. It makes it harder to fit the two of you together."

You've been you for a long time. She felt some of the tension begin to leave her shoulders. If anyone could understand *that,* it would be Henry Fitzroy. "Thanks, Tony."

"No problem." The cocky tone returned. "You want me to nail you a cab?"

"No."

"Then I better get upstairs."

"Before you split your jeans?"

"Jeez, Victory," she could hear the grin in his voice, "I thought you couldn't see in the dark."

She listened to him walk away, heard the door to the building open and close behind him, then made her way carefully out to the sidewalk. In the distance, she could make out the glow of Yonge and Bloor and decided to walk. City streets had enough light for her to maneuver, even if she couldn't exactly see and at the moment she didn't think she could handle being enclosed in another dark space.

A dozen steps away from the building she stopped. She'd been so caught up in getting out of Henry's apartment that she hadn't even asked him about the dream. For a moment she considered going back, then she grinned and shook her head, willing to bet that he'd be incapable of thinking coherently, let alone worrying, for the rest of the night. Tony had picked up a number of interesting skills during his years on the street, not the least of those being distraction.

Five

He gazed over the breakfast table—a bowl of strawberries and melon, three eggs over easy, six slices of rare roast beef, corn muffins, a chilled glass of apricot nectar, and a pot of fresh brewed coffee—nodded a satisfied dismissal at the young woman who delivered it, and snapped open his copy of the national paper. While he'd had the morning editions of all three Toronto papers delivered, it had been easy to tell which he should read first. Only one had more text than pictures.

After devouring the child's ka, he had spent the rest of the day acquiring suitable garments and a place to stay. The shopkeepers in the small and very exclusive men's wear stores along Bloor Street West had been so concerned with status that they'd been almost embarrassingly easy to enchant and later the manager of the Park Plaza Hotel had responded so well to appearance and arrogance that he'd barely needed to use power at all.

He had registered as Anwar Tawfik, a name he'd pulled from the ka of Elias Rax. Not since the time of Meri-nar, the first Pharaoh, had he used his true name and by the time the priests of Thoth trapped and bound him, he'd been called so many things that they could place only what he was, not who, on their binding spell. If they'd had his true name, he'd not have gotten free so easily.

He'd chosen the Park Plaza because it overlooked both the museum and, a little farther south, the provincial seat of government. He could, in fact, see both from the windows of his corner suite. The museum held only a certain amount of sentimental significance. Queen's Park, he would take as his own.

In the old days, when those who had held secular power had also wielded religious might, when there had been no division between the two and the Pharaoh had been the living Horus, he had had to build his power structure from the bottom up, from the disenfranchised and the discontented. In this age, Church and State were kept forcibly separate and that left the State ripe for his plucking.

Often in those days, he found only enough unsworn ka to extend his own life and had hoarded what power he had lest he and his god ultimately perish. Now, with so few sworn, he had no need to conserve power. He could use what magic he wished, bend the mighty to his will, knowing that a multitude existed for him to feed from.

Akhekh, he knew, would not properly appreciate the situation. His lord had . . . simple tastes. A temple, a few acolytes, and a little generated despair kept Akhekh happy.

Folding the paper into quarters, he poured himself a cup of coffee and sat back, allowing the October sun to brush warmth across his face. He had awoken in a cold, gray land where leaves the color of blood lay damply underfoot. He missed the clean golden lines of the desert, the presence of the Nile, the smell of spice and sweat but, as the world he missed no longer existed, he would make this world his own.

And frankly, he didn't see how anyone could stop him.

"Homicide. Detective-Sergeant Celluci. You sure? Caused by what?"

Dave Graham watched his partner scowl and took bets with himself as to who was on the other end of the phone. There were a number of reports still outstanding although they had already received the photographs and an analysis from the lab on the contents of the trap.

"You're sure there's nothing else?" Celluci drummed on the desktop with his fingertips. "Yeah. Yeah, thanks." Although obviously annoyed, he hung up the phone with exaggerated care—the department had refused to replace any more receivers. "Dr. Rax died because his heart stopped."

Ah, the coroner. He owed himself a quarter. "And why did the good doctor's heart stop?"

Celluci snorted. "They don't know." He picked up his coffee, swirled it around to break the scum that had formed over the last two hours, and drank. "Apparently, it just stopped."

"Drugs? Disease?"

"Nada. There were signs of a struggle, but no evidence of a blow to the chest. He'd had a sandwich, a glass of milk, and a piece of blueberry pie about four hours before he died. He was, according to fatigue buildup in the muscles, a bit tired." Celluci shoved an overly long curl of hair back off his forehead. "Dr. Rax was a healthy fifty-two-year-old. He caught a naked intruder in the Egyptology workroom and his heart stopped."

"Well," Dave shrugged. "I suppose it happens."

"*What* happens?"

"Hearts stop."

"Bullshit." Celluci crumbled his cup and tossed it at the garbage basket. It hit the rim, sprayed a few drops of coffee on the side of the desk, and dropped in. "Two deaths by unexplained heart failure in the same room in less than twenty-four hours is . . ."

"A gruesome coincidence." Dave shook his head at his partner's expression. "This is a high stress world we live in, Mike. Any little extra can tip you over. Ellis saw something that frightened him, his heart couldn't take it, he died. Dr. Rax interrupted an intruder, they fought, his heart couldn't take it, *he* died. As I said, it happens. Cardiovascular failure, occurring not as a direct result of violence, doesn't come under our jurisdiction."

"Big words," Celluci grunted.

"Well, *I'm* ready to conclude this wasn't a homicide and toss it over to the B and E boys."

Celluci swung his legs off the desk and stood. "I'm not."

"*Why* not?"

He thought about it for a moment and finally shrugged. He couldn't really come up with a reason, even for himself. "Call it a hunch."

Dave sighed. He hated police work based solely on intuition, but Celluci's arrest record was certainly good enough to allow him to ride a hunch or two. He surrendered. "So, where're you going?"

"Lab."

Watching his partner stride away, Dave considered phoning the lab and warning them. His hand was on the receiver when he changed his mind. "Nah." He settled back in his chair and grinned. "Why should I have all the fun?"

* * *

"*This* is a piece of linen?" Celluci stared into the mylar envelope and decided to take Doreen's word for it. "What's it off of?"

"An ancient Egyptian ceremonial robe, probably a size sixteen extra long. It had an empire waist, pleated sleeves, and how the blazes should I know?" Doreen Chui folded her arms and stared up at the detective. "You bring me twenty-two milliliters of sludge that's just had an acid bath and I pull out a square millimeter of linen. More miracles than that you shouldn't ask for."

Celluci took a step back. Small women always made him feel vaguely intimidated. "Sorry. What *can* you tell me about it?"

"Two things. One, it's old." She raised a cautionary hand. "I don't know *how* old. Two, there's a bit of pigment on one of the fibers that's about fifty/fifty blood and a type of vegetable paint. Also old. Nothing to do with last night's body. At least not as far as precious bodily fluids are concerned."

He took a closer look at the fleck of grayish-brown substance. Raymond Thompson had said that the coffin was Eighteenth Dynasty. He wasn't sure when exactly that was, but if the bit of linen could be placed in the same time period . . . he'd be building a case against a mummy that everyone insisted didn't exist. That should go over like a visit from a civil rights lawyer. "You couldn't find out how old this is, could you?"

"You want me to carbon date it?"

"Well, yes."

"Drop dead, Celluci. You want that kind of an analysis done—provided I had a big enough sample which I don't—you get the city to stop cutting my budget so I can get the equipment and the staff." She slapped her palm down on the desk. "Until them, you got a scrap of linen with a bloody paint stain on it. Capesh?"

"So, you're finished with it?"

Doreen sighed. "Don't make me explain it to you again, Detective. I've had a hard morning."

"Right." He carefully slid the envelope into his inside jacket pocket, and tried an apologetic smile. "Thanks."

"You really want to thank me," she muttered, turning

back to her work, the smile apparently having no effect,
"put a moratorium on murder until I take care of my back-
log."

Dr. Shane held the mylar envelope up to the light, then,
shaking her head, laid it back down on the desk. "If you
say that's a piece of linen, Detective, I believe you, but I'm
afraid I can't tell you what it's from or how old it is. When
we get the inventory finished and find out what's missing,
well, maybe we'll know what went down the sink . . ."

"It had to be something that the intruder felt would give
him away," Celluci mused.

"Why?" The detective had a very penetrating gaze, Dr.
Shane realized as he turned it on her. And very attractive
brown eyes with the sort of long, thick lashes most women
would kill for. With an effort she got her train of thought
back on track. "I mean, why couldn't it have just been
senseless vandalism?"

"No, too specific and too neat. A vandal might have
dumped acid on some of your artifacts, but they wouldn't
have rinsed down the sink afterward. And," he sighed and
brushed the curl of hair back off his forehead, "they
wouldn't have started with that. They'd have knocked a few
things over first. What about the blood/paint mixture?"

"Well, that's unusual." Dr. Shane frowned down at the
linen. "Are you sure that the blood was actually mixed with
the pigment and hadn't just been splashed on at some later
date?"

"I'm sure." He sat forward in his chair and leaned his
forearms across his knees, then had to shift as his holster
jabbed him in the small of the back. "Our lab is very good
with blood. They get a lot of practice."

"Yes, I suppose they do." She sighed and pushed the
sample toward him. "Well, then, the only historical explanation that comes to mind is that this is a piece of a spell."
She settled back and steepled her fingers, her voice taking
on a lecturing tone. "Most Egyptian priests were also wizards and their spells were not only chanted but written on
strips of linen or papyrus when the matter was deemed serious enough to need physical representation. Occasionally,
when very powerful spells were needed, the wizard would

mix his blood with the paint in order to tie his life force to the magic.''

Celluci laid his hand down on the envelope. "So this is a part of a very powerful spell.''

"It seems that way, yes.''

Powerful enough to keep a mummy locked in its coffin? he wondered. He decided not to ask. The last thing he wanted was Dr. Shane thinking he was some kind of a nut case who'd gotten his training from old Boris Karloff movies. *That* would definitely slow down the investigation. He slid the envelope back into his jacket pocket. "They mentioned carbon dating at the lab . . . ?''

Dr. Shane shook her head. "Too small a sample; they need at least two square inches. It's why the Church objected to dating the Shroud of Turin for so long.'' Her gaze focused somewhere in memory, then she shook her head and smiled. "It's one of the reasons anyway.''

"Dr. Shane?'' The tapping on the door and the entry were pretty much simultaneous. "Sorry to disturb you, but you said you wanted that inventory the moment we finished.'' At the assistant curator's nod, Doris crossed the room and laid a stack of papers on the desk. "Nothing's missing, nothing even looks disturbed, but we did find a whole pile of useless film in the darkroom. Every single frame's been overexposed on about thirty rolls and we've got a stack of video tapes that show nothing but basic black.''

"Do you know what was on them?'' Celluci asked getting to his feet.

Doris looked chagrined. "Actually, I haven't the faintest. I've accounted for everything I've shot over the last little while.''

"If you could put them to one side, I'll have someone come and pick them up.''

"I'll leave them where they are, then.'' Doris paused on her way out the door and glanced back at the police officer. "If they're still usable though, I'd like them back. Video tape doesn't grow on trees.''

"I'll do my best,'' he assured her. When the door had closed behind her, he turned back to Dr. Shane. "Budget cuts?''

She laughed humorlessly. "When isn't it? I just wish I

had more for you. I went over Dr. Rax's office again after your people left and I couldn't find anything missing except that suit.''

Which at least gave them the relative size of the intruder—if there had even been an intruder. The ROM had excellent security and there'd been no evidence of anyone entering or leaving. It could have been an inside job; a friend of the dead janitor maybe, up poking around, who'd panicked when Dr. Rax had his heart attack. The name Dr. Von Thorne had come up a couple of times during yesterday's questioning as one of Dr. Rax's least favorite people. Maybe he'd been poking around and panicked—except that they'd already questioned Dr. Von Thorne and he had an airtight alibi, not to mention an extremely protective wife. Still, there were a number of possibilities that had nothing to do with an apparently nonexistent mummy.

While various theories were chasing each other's tails in Celluci's head, part of him watched appreciatively as Dr. Shane came around from behind her desk.

''You mentioned on the phone that you wanted to see the sarcophagus?'' she said, heading for the door.

He followed her out. ''I'd like to, yes.''

''It wasn't in the workroom, you know. We'd already moved it across the hall.''

''To the storage room.'' He could feel the stare of the departmental secretary as they crossed the outer office. *''What are you doing hanging around here?''* it said. *''Why aren't you out catching the one who did this?''* It was a stare he could identify at fifty paces just by the way it impacted with his back. Over the years, he'd learned to ignore it. Mostly.

''You'll find it's just a little large to maneuver around.'' Dr. Shane stopped across from the workroom and pulled out her keys. ''That's why we moved it.''

While the workroom doors were bright yellow, the storeroom doors bordered on day-glo orange.

''What's with the color scheme?'' Celluci asked.

Dr. Shane's head swiveled between the two sets of doors. ''I haven't,'' she said at last, forehead slightly puckered, ''the faintest idea.''

To Celluci's eyes the sarcophagus looked like a rectangular box of black rock. He had to actually run his fingers along the edge before he could find the seam where the top had been fitted into the sides. "How can you tell that something like this is Sixteenth Dynasty?" he asked, crouching down and peering in the open end.

"Mostly because the only other one ever found in this particular style was very definitely dated Sixteenth."

"But the coffin was Eighteenth?" He could see faint marks where the coffin had rested.

"No doubt about it."

"Is that unusual? Mixing time periods?"

Dr. Shane leaned on the sarcophagus and crossed her arms. "Well, we've never run into it before, but that may be because we've run into very few undisturbed grave sites. Usually, if we find a sarcophagus, the coffin is missing entirely."

"Hard to run away with one of these," Celluci muttered, straightening and having a look at the end panel. "Any theories?"

"On why this one was mixed?" Dr. Shane shrugged. "Maybe the family of the deceased was saving money."

Celluci looked up and smiled. "Got a good deal on it secondhand?"

Dr. Shane found herself smiling back. "Perhaps."

Moving the sliding panel into its grooves, Celluci let it gently down, then just as gently eased it up again. There was a three-inch lip on the inside that blocked the bottom edge. He frowned.

"What's the matter?" Dr. Shane asked, leaning forward a little anxiously. Pretty much indestructible or not, this was still a three-thousand-year-old artifact.

"They might also have chosen this style because once inside, it'd be the next thing to impossible to get out. There's no way to get a grip on this door and because it slides, brute force would do bugger all."

"Yes. But that's usually not a factor . . ."

"No, of course not." He released the panel and stepped back. Maybe Dave was right. Maybe he was fixating on this nonexistent mummy. "Just a random observation. You, uh, get used to throwing strange details together in this job."

"In my job, too."

She really did have a terrific smile. And she smelled great. He recognized Chanel No. 5, the same cologne Vicki used. "Look, it's . . ." He checked his watch. ". . . eleven forty-five. How about lunch?"

"Lunch?"

"You do eat, don't you?"

She thought about it for a moment, then she laughed. "Yes, I do."

"Then it's lunch?"

"I guess it is, Detective."

"Mike."

"Rachel."

His grandmother had always said food was the fastest way to friendship. Of course, his grandmother was old country Italian and believed in no less than four courses for breakfast while what he had in mind was a little closer to a burger and fries. Still, he could ask Dr. Shane—Rachel—her opinion on the undead while they ate.

The second time Celluci left the museum that day, he headed for the corner and a phone. Lunch had been . . . interesting. Dr. Rachel Shane was a fascinating woman; brilliant, self-assured, with a velvet glove over an iron core. *Which made a nice change,* he observed dryly to himself, *because with Vicki the gloves were usually off.* He liked her wry sense of humor; he enjoyed watching her hands sketch possibilities in the air while she talked. He'd gotten her to tell him about Elias Rax, about his often single-minded pursuit of an idea, about his dedication to the museum. She'd touched on his rivalry with Dr. Von Thorne and Celluci made a mental note to look into it. He hadn't brought up the mummy.

The closest they'd actually gotten to an analysis of the undead had been an animated discussion of old horror films. Her opinion of those had decided him against mentioning, in even a theoretical way, the idea that seemed to have possessed him.

Possessed . . . He shoved his hands deep into his jacket pockets and hunched his shoulders against the chill wind. *Let's come up with another word, shall we. . . .*

When it came right down to it, there was only one person he could tell who'd listen to everything he had to say before she told him that he'd lost his mind.

* * *

"Nelson. Private investigations."

"Christ, Vicki, it's one seventeen in the afternoon. Don't tell me you're still asleep."

"You know, Celluci . . ." She yawned audibly and stretched into a more comfortable position in the recliner. ". . . you're beginning to sound like my mother."

She heard him snort. "You spend the night with Fitzroy?"

"Not exactly." When she'd finally gone to bed, having slept most of the day, she'd had to leave the bedroom light on. Lying there in the dark, she couldn't shake the feeling that he was beside her again, lifeless and empty. What sleep she'd managed to eventually get, had been fitful and dream filled. Just before dawn, she'd called Henry. Although he'd convinced her—and at the same time, she suspected, himself—that this morning at least he had no intention of giving his life to the sun, guilt about not actually being there had kept her awake until long after sunrise. She'd been dozing off and on all day.

"Look, Vicki," Celluci took a deep breath, audible over the phone lines, "what do you know about mummies?"

"Well, mine's a pain in the butt." The silence didn't sound all that amused, so she continued. "The ancient embalmed Egyptian kind or the monster movie matinee kind?"

"Both."

Vicki frowned at the receiver. Missing from that single word had been the arrogant self-confidence that usually colored everything Mike Celluci said. "You're on the ROM case." She knew he was; all three papers had mentioned him as the investigating officer.

"Yeah."

"You want to tell me about it?" Even at the height of their competitiveness, they'd bounced ideas off each other, arguing them down to bare essentials, then rebuilding the case from the ground up.

"I think . . ." He sighed and her frown deepened. ". . . I'm going to need to see your face."

"Now?"

"No. *I* still work for a living. How about dinner? I'll buy."

Shit, this is *serious.* She pushed her glasses up on her nose. "Champion House at six?"

"Five thirty. I'll meet you there."

Vicki sat for a moment, staring down at the phone. She'd never heard Celluci sound so out of his depth. "Mummies . . ." she said at last and headed for the pile of "to be recycled" newspapers in her office. Spreading them out on her weight bench, she scanned the articles on the recent deaths at the museum. Forty minutes later, she picked up a hand weight and absently began doing biceps curls. Her memory hadn't been faulty; according to Detective-Sergeant Michael Celluci, *there was no mummy.*

It was cold and it was raining as he walked from Queen's Park back to his hotel, but then, it was October and it was Toronto. According to the ka of Dr. Rax, when the latter conditions were met, the former naturally followed. He decided that, for now, he would treat it as a new experience to be examined and endured, but that later, when his god had acquired more power, perhaps something could be done about the weather.

It had been a most productive day and the day was not yet over.

He had spent the morning sitting and weighing the currents of power eddying about the large room full of shouting men and women. Question period they called it. The name seemed apt, for although there were plenty of questions there seemed to be very few answers. He had been pleased to see that government—and those who sought positions in it—had not changed significantly in millennia. The provinces of Egypt had been very like the provinces of this new land, essentially autonomous and only nominally under the control of the central government. It was a system he understood and could work with.

Amazed at how little both adult ka he had devoured knew of politics, he had convinced a scribe—now called a press secretary—to join him for food. After using barely enough power to ripple the surface of the man's mind, he had sat and listened to an outpouring of information, both professional and personal, about the Members of the Provincial Parliament that lasted almost two and a half hours. Taking the man's ka would have been faster, but until he consolidated his power he had no wish to leave a trail of bodies behind him. While he couldn't be stopped, neither did he wish to be delayed.

Later this afternoon, he would meet with the man now called the Solicitor General. The Solicitor General controlled the police. The police were essentially a standing army. He would prepare the necessary spells and begin his empire from a position of strength.

And then, having set the future in motion, there were loose ends that needed tying off; two ka still carried thoughts of him that must be erased.

Vicki pushed a congealing mushroom around her plate and squinted at Celluci. The light levels in the restaurant were just barely high enough for her to see his face but nowhere near high enough if she actually wanted to pick up nuances of expression. She should have thought of that when she suggested the place and it infuriated her that she hadn't. *Next time it's MacDonalds, right under the biggest block of fluorescent lights I can find.*

He'd told her about the case while they ate, laying out the facts without opinions to color them; the groundwork had been laid and now it was time to cut to the chase.

She watched him play with his teacup for a moment longer, the ceramic bowl looking absurdly small in his hand, then reached across the table and smacked him on the knuckle with one of her chopsticks. "Shit or get off the pot," she suggested.

Celluci grabbed for the chopstick and missed. "And they say after dinner conversation is dead," he muttered, wiping sesame-lemon sauce off his hand. He stared down at the crumpled napkin, then up at her.

It might have been the lack of light, but Vicki could've sworn he looked tentative, and as far as she knew, Michael Celluci had never looked tentative in his life. When he started to speak, he even sounded tentative and Vicki got a cold feeling in the pit of her stomach.

"I told you how PC Trembley said there'd been a mummy when I talked to her that morning?"

"Yeah." Vicki wasn't sure she liked where this was heading. "But everyone else said there wasn't, so she must've been wrong."

"I don't think she was." He squared his shoulders and laid both palms flat on the table. "I think she did see a mummy, and I think that it's responsible for both of the deaths at the museum.''

A mummy? Lurching around downtown Toronto, trailing rotting bandages and inducing heart attacks? In this day and age the entire concept was ludicrous. Of course, so was a nerd with a pentagram in his living room, a family of were-wolves raising sheep outside London, and, when you got right down to it, so was the concept of Henry Fitzroy, bastard son of Henry the VIII, vampire and romance writer. Vicki adjusted her glasses and leaned forward, elbows propped, chin on hands. Life used to be so much simpler. ''Tell me,'' she sighed.

Celluci began ticking points off on his fingers. ''Everyone we talked to, and I mean everyone, was surprised that an empty sarcophagus had been resealed. The only item that the intruder destroyed has been identified as part of a powerful spell. The only items stolen were a suit of clothes and a pair of shoes.'' He took a deep breath. ''I don't think the sarcophagus was empty. I think Reid Ellis was poking around where he shouldn't have, woke something up, and died for it. I think the creature took a little time to regain its strength and then got up out of the coffin and destroyed its wrapping and the spell that had held it. I think Dr. Rax interrupted, was overpowered, and killed. I think that the naked mummy then dressed itself in the doctor's suit and shoes and left the building. I think I'm losing my mind and I want you to tell me I'm not.''

Vicki sat back, caught their waiter's attention, and indicated they wanted the bill. Then she adjusted her glasses again although they didn't really need it. ''I think,'' she said slowly, fighting a strong sense of déjà vu—it had to be coincidence that *both* of the men in her life currently thought they were going crazy, ''that you're one of the sanest people I've ever met. But are you positive that your recent . . . experiences aren't causing you to jump to supernatural conclusions?''

''I don't know.''

''Why doesn't anyone at the museum remember a mummy?''

''I don't know.''

''And if there *is* a mummy, how and why is it killing people?''

"Goddamnit, Vicki! How the hell am I supposed to know that?" He scowled down at the bill, threw two twenties on the table, and stood. The waiter beat a hasty retreat. "I'm working on a gut feeling, circumstantial evidence, and I don't know what the fuck to do."

At least he didn't sound tentative anymore. "Talk to Trembley."

He blinked. "What?"

Vicki grinned and got to her feet. "Talk to Trembley," she repeated. "Go down to 52 Division and see if she actually saw a mummy. If she did, then you've got yourself a case. Although," she added after a moment's thought, "God only knows where you're going to go with it." She tucked her hand in the crook of his elbow, less for togetherness than because she needed a guide out of the dimly lit restaurant.

"Talk to Trembley." Shaking his head, he steered her around a Peking duck and toward the door. "I can't believe I didn't think of that."

"And if *she* says she didn't see a mummy, check her occurrence reports. Even if this thing of yours is playing nine ball with memories, it probably knows bugger all about police and procedure."

"And if the report's negative?" he asked as they went out onto Dundas Street.

"Mike." Vicki dragged him to a stop, the perpetual Chinatown crowds breaking and swirling around them. "You sound like you *want* to believe there's a mummy loose in the city." She slapped him gently on the face with her free hand. "Now we both know better than to deny the possibility but sometimes, Sigmund, a cigar is just a cigar."

"What the hell are you talking about?"

"Maybe it's a mummy, maybe it's a slight Oedipal complex."

He caught her hand and dragged her back into motion. "I don't know why I even brought it up. . . ."

"I don't know why you didn't think of talking to PC Trembley."

"You're going to be smug about that for a while, aren't you?"

She smiled up at him. "You bet your ass I am."

Six

"Did you have the dream?"

Henry nodded, his expression bleak. "A yellow sun blazing in a bright blue sky. No change." He leaned back against the window, hands shoved deep into the front pockets of his jeans.

"Still no voice-over?"

"No what?"

"Voice-over." Vicki dropped her purse and a bulging shopping bag on the floor and then flopped down onto the couch. "You know, some kind of narrative that explains what's going on."

"I don't think it works that way."

Vicki snorted. "I don't see why it shouldn't." She could tell from his tone that he wasn't amused and she sighed. So much for easing stress with humor. "Well, it still seems essentially harmless. I mean, it's not actually compelling you to do anything."

She didn't see him move. One moment he was at the window, the next leaning on the arm of the couch, his face inches from hers.

"For over four hundred and fifty years I have not seen the sun. Now I see it in my mind every night when I wake."

She didn't exactly meet his eyes; she knew better than to hand him that much power when he was in a mood to use it. "Look, I sympathize. It's like a recovering alcoholic waking every morning with the knowledge that there'll be an open bottle of booze on the doorstep that evening and having to live all day wondering if he'll be strong enough not to end the day with a drink. I think *you're* strong enough."

"And if I'm not?"

"Well, you can stop with the fucking defeatist attitude

for starters." She heard the arm of the couch creak under his grip, and kept going before he could speak. "You told me you didn't want to die. Fine, you're not going to."

Slowly, he straightened.

"I wasn't here for you this morning and I'm sorry about that, but I spent most of the day thinking about this whole thing." Celluci's phone call had given her confidence a boost when it had needed it most. She'd always managed to keep up her half of *that* relationship and she'd be damned if *this* one would defeat her. *And in return for your trust, Henry, I'm going to give you your life.* She pulled her purse up onto her lap and dug a hammer and a handful of u-shaped nails out of its depths. "I've got a blackout curtain in here." She prodded the shopping bag with the toe of her shoe. "I bought it this afternoon from a theatrical supply house. We'll hang it over the door to the bedroom. After you go out, I leave. The curtain will block the sunlight coming in from the hall. From now on, until your personal little sun sets, I tuck you in every morning and if the time comes when you can't stop yourself from heading for the pyre, I stop you."

"How?"

Vicki reached into the shopping bag. "If you go for the window," she said, "I figure I've got about a minute, maybe two, before you get through the barrier. You proved rather definitively last summer that though you heal quickly you can be hurt."

"And if I should try for the door?"

She smacked the aluminum baseball bat against the palm of her left hand. "Than I'm afraid it's a frontal assault."

Henry stared at the bat for a moment, brows drawn down into a deep vee, then he raised his head and gazed intently at Vicki's face. "You're serious," he said at last.

She met his eyes then. "Never more so."

A muscle jumped in his jaw and his brow smoothed out. Then the corners of his mouth began to twitch. "I think," he told her, "that the solution is as dangerous as the problem."

"That's the whole idea."

He smiled then, a softer smile than she'd ever seen him use. It made him look absurdly young and it made her feel strong, protective, necessary. "Thank you."

She felt her own lips curve and the knots of tension slip out of her shoulders. ''You're welcome.''

Henry set the points of the last nail against the curtain and pushed it into the wall without bothering to use the hammer. Behind him, he heard Vicki mutter, ''Show-off.'' The curtain was an inspired idea. He wasn't so sure about the baseball bat although clubbing him senseless had a certain brutal simplicity to it he could appreciate in the abstract. When it came right down to it, he still felt Vicki's presence would be enough to remind him that he didn't want to die.

Stepping down off the chair, he twitched the edge of the curtain into place. It extended about three feet past the door, similar, in form at least, to the tapestries that used to hang in his bedchamber at Sheriffhuton to block the drafts. Hopefully, it would be more effective.

Vicki had laid the bat on the bureau where it gleamed dully against the dark wood like a modern mace awaiting the hand of a twenty-first century warrior. There had been a lord at his father's court, a Scot if memory served, whose preferred weapon had been a mace. Just after his investiture as the Duke of Richmond, he had watched in open-mouthed awe as the man—who mostly certainly *had* to have been a Scot—reduced a wooden door to kindling and then defeated the three men behind it with identical strokes. Even his majesty had been impressed, clapping a beefy hand on his bastard's slender shoulder and declaring heartily, *''You can't do that with a sword, boy!''*

His royal father and that half-remembered lord had long since returned to dust. Although the mace quite probably still hung over a lowland mantel between the stag heads and the claymores, it no doubt had been centuries since it had been lifted in battle. Henry ran one finger down the smooth, cool length of aluminum.

''Penny for your thoughts?''

He could feel Vicki's unease in spite of her matter-of-fact tone. He could almost hear her thinking, *What do I do if he decides to get rid of the bat?* Or more likely, knowing Vicki, *Would a kidney punch break his grip if he decides to hold on?* ''I was just considering,'' he told her, turning slowly, ''how battle has become a stylized ritual with forms that change to fit the seasons.''

Both her brows arced above the upper edge of her glasses. "Oh, there's still plenty of real battles going on," she drawled.

"I know that." Henry spread his hands, searching for the words that would help her to understand the difference. "But all the honor and the glory seem to have been taken from reality and given to games."

"Well, I'll admit there's very little honor and less glory in having your head bashed in by some biker with a length of chain or having a junkie in an alley go for you with a knife or even in having to take your nightstick to some drunk trying to do you first, but you're going to have to go a long way to convince me that honor and glory ever went along with violence of any kind."

"It wasn't the violence," he protested, "it was the . . ."

"Victory?"

"Not exactly, but at least you used to know when you won."

"Maybe that's why they've given the honor and glory to games—you can fight for victory without leaving an unsightly mound of bodies behind."

He frowned. "I hadn't actually thought of it like that."

"I know." She ducked under the curtain and out into the hall. "Honor and glory mean bugger all to the losers. Prince, vampire; you've always been on the winning side."

"And what side are you on?" he asked a little testily as he followed her. She hadn't so much missed the point of what he'd been trying to say as completely changed its direction.

"The side of truth, justice, and the Canadian way."

"Which is?"

"Compromise, for the most part."

"Funny, I've never thought of you as a person who compromises well."

"I don't."

He reached out and took hold of her wrist, pulling her to a stop and then around to face him. "Vicki, if I said I was tired, that I've lived six times longer than the natural human span and I've had enough, would you let me walk out into the sun?"

Not bloody likely. She bit back the immediate emotional response. He'd asked her the question seriously, she could hear that in his voice and see it in his face, and it deserved more than a gut reaction. She'd always believed that a person's life was his own and that what he did with it was his business, no one else's. That worked fine in general, but would she let *Henry* choose to walk out into the sun? Friendship meant responsibility or it didn't mean much and, come to think of it, they'd settled that once already tonight. "If you want me to let you kill yourself, you'd damn well better be able to convince me that dying does more for you than living."

She'd gotten angry just thinking about it. He heard her heart speed up, saw muscles tense beneath clothes and skin. "*Could* I convince you?"

"I doubt it."

He lifted her hand and placed a kiss gently on the palm. "Has anyone ever told you that you're a very pushy person?" he murmured against the soft skin at the base of her thumb, inhaling the blood-rich scent of her flesh.

"Frequently." Vicki snatched her hand away and rubbed it against the front of her sweatshirt. Great, just what she needed, more stimulus. "There's no point in starting something you're not going to finish," she muttered a little shakily. "You fed last night from Tony."

"True."

"You don't *need* to feed tonight."

"True."

It always annoyed her that he could read her physical reaction so easily, that he always *knew* and she could only guess. Occasionally, however, the question became moot.

"I am too old for frenzied fucking in the hall," she informed him a moment later. "Stop that." Walking backward, she towed him toward the bedroom.

Henry's eyes widened. "Vicki, be careful . . ."

She tightened her grip and grinned. "After four hundred and fifty years, you should know that it won't pull off."

"I had dinner with Mike Celluci tonight."

Henry sighed, and lightly traced the shadow of a vein in the soft hollow below Vicki's ear. Although he'd taken only a few mouthfuls of blood he felt replete and lazy. "Do we have to talk about him now?"

"He thinks there's a mummy walking around Toronto."

"Lots of mummies," Henry murmured against her neck. "Daddies, too."

"Henry!" She caught him just under the solar plexus with an elbow. He decided to pay attention. "Celluci seriously believes that an ancient Egyptian has risen from his coffin and killed two people at the museum."

"The two people who died of heart attacks?"

"That's right."

"And you *believe* him?"

"Look, if Mike Celluci called me up and told me aliens had him trapped in his house, I might not believe him, but I'd show up with a flamethrower just in case. And as you're the closest thing to an expert on rising from the dead I know, I'm asking you. Is this possible?"

"Let me get this straight." Henry rolled over on his back and laced his fingers behind his head. "Detective-Sergeant Michael Celluci came to you and said, *There's a mummy loose in Toronto, murdering janitors and Egyptologists.* And let me guess, he can't tell anyone else because no one else will believe him."

"Essentially."

"Are you sure this isn't just an elaborate April Fool's prank?"

"Too complicated. Celluci's a salt in the sugar bowl kind of guy, and besides, it's October."

"Good point. I assume he gave you his reasoning behind this stu . . . ouch, unusual idea."

"He did." Tapping out the points on Henry's chest, Vicki repeated everything Celluci had told her.

"And if PC Trembley confirms that there was a mummy, what then?"

She wound a short, red-gold curl around her finger. "I was hoping you could tell me."

"We help him stop it?"

"How?"

"I haven't the faintest idea." He heard her sigh, felt her breath against his chest, and lightly kissed the top of her head. "Did he ask you to speak to me about it?"

"No. But he said he didn't mind if I did." He'd actually said, *Use a ghoul to find a ghoul? Why not?* But under his sneer there'd been a sense of relief and Vicki had gotten the feeling that he'd been waiting all evening for her to ask,

unwilling to bring it up himself. "He had to go to a hockey
practice or I'd have suggested he tell you all this firsthand."

"That *would* have been a fun evening."

Vicki grinned. Celluci's reaction would have been louder
and more profane but essentially similar.

Henry sat down at his desk and turned on his computer.
Over the hum of the fan he could hear deep, slow breathing
coming from the living room and, under that, the measured
beat of a heart at rest.

"Don't expect me to stay around every night," Vicki had
warned him, yawning. *"I expect most of the time I'll show
up just before dawn to tuck you in. But, as long as I'm here,
you might as well do some writing and I might as well get
some sleep."* She'd led the way out of the bedroom, pillow
tucked under one arm, blanket under the other. *"I'll sack
out on the couch. The airflow's better out there and you
won't have to sleep surrounded by blood scent."*

It was a plausible, even a considerate reason, but Henry
didn't believe it. He'd seen the lines of tension smooth out
of her back as they'd left the room. He listened to her sleep
for a moment longer, then shook his head and turned his
attention to the monitor. The book was due the first of De-
cember and he figured he was still a chapter away from
happily ever after.

*Veronica paced the length of her room in the Governor's
mansion, silk skirts whipping around her shapely ankles.
Captain Roxborough would hang on the morrow unless she
could find some way to prevent it. She* knew *he wasn't a
pirate but, even though the Governor had been more than
kind, would her word mean anything once everyone discovered that she'd made her way to the islands disguised as a
cabin boy? That Captain Roxborough had discovered her
and that he'd . . .*

*She stopped pacing and raised slender fingers to cover
her heated cheeks. None of that mattered now.* "He must
not die," *she vowed.*

"I can't seem to get away from dying at dawn," Henry
muttered, pushing back from the desk.

Last spring, the dawn had caught him away from safety
and he'd raced the sun for his life. He still bore the puckered
scar on the back of his hand where the day had marked him.

Would it happen as quickly as that had, he wondered, or more slowly? Would it be instantaneous as his flesh ignited and turned to ash, or would he burn slowly in agony, screaming his way to the final death?

He forced his mind away from the thought, listening to the even tempo of Vicki's breathing until he calmed. There had to be something else he could think about.

"Celluci seriously believes that an ancient Egyptian has risen from his coffin and killed two people at the museum."

He'd been to Egypt once; just after the turn of the century; just after the death of Dr. O'Mara when England had seemed tainted and he'd had to get away. He hadn't stayed long.

He'd met Lady Wallington on the terrace at Shepheard's. She'd been sitting alone, drinking tea and watching the crowds of Egyptians making their way up Ibrahim Pasha Street when she'd felt his gaze and called him over. A recent widow in her early forties, she had no objection to keeping company with an attractive, well-bred young man. Henry, for his part, had found her candor refreshing. *"Don't be ridiculous,"* she'd told him, when he'd expressed his sympathy on her loss, *"the nicest thing his Lordship ever did for me was to drop dead before I was too old to enjoy my freedom."* And then she'd stroked the inside of his thigh under the cover of the damask tablecloth.

Publicly, they were as discreet as the society of 1903 demanded. Privately, she was just what Henry needed after the incident with the grimoire. He never told her what he was and she accepted the time he spent away from her with the same aplomb as the time he spent with her. He rather suspected she had another lover for the daylight hours and found himself admiring her stamina.

On the nights he had to feed from others, he stayed away from the English and American tourists and slipped into the dark and twisting streets of old Cairo where sloe-eyed young men never knew they paid for their pleasure with blood.

And then he began to feel watched. Although he could identify no obvious threat—dark eyes watched all the visitors and certainly seemed to watch him no more than the rest—the skin between his shoulder blades continued to crawl. He began to take more care moving to and from his sanctuary.

A moonlight climb to the top of the Great Pyramid had become "the thing to do" and it took little pleading for Henry to agree to accompany Lady Wallington on her expedition. The city had started to feel like it was closing around him, as if it were some large and complicated trap. Perhaps a few hours away from it would clear his head.

They stepped out of the carriage onto moon-silvered sand that drifted up against the base of the monuments like new fallen snow, its purity broken by the pits that marked vandalized tombs or sunken shrines. The light had erased the patina of age from the pyramids and they in turn cast dark bands of shadow across the features of the Sphinx so that he looked both more and less human as he gazed enigmatically down on the night. Unfortunately, flaring torches and crawling bodies marred the pale sides of the Great Pyramid and the sounds of their progress carried clearly on the desert air.

"Hot damn, ain't we there yet?"

"While I admire Americans as a breed," Lady Wallington sighed, tucking her hand in the crook of Henry's elbow, "there are a few individuals I could gladly do without."

As they approached the pyramid, they braced themselves for the charge of self-styled guides, antiquities peddlers, and assorted beggars who stood clustered around the base waiting for the chance to part foreigners from their money.

"How strange," Lady Wallington murmured, as the men remained where they were, peering out at them from under their turbans and muttering to themselves in Arabic. "Although, I suppose we can manage quite well without them." But she looked rather dubiously at the monument as she spoke, for in full evening dress the three to three and a half foot steps would not be easy to navigate without assistance. Most of the women already climbing had two men pulling from above and another pushing from below.

Henry frowned. Under the scent of dirt and sweat and spice, he could smell fear. As he leapt up onto the first block and reached down for Lady Wallington's hand, one of them made the sign against the evil eye.

Lady Wallington followed his gaze and laughed. "Don't mind that," she explained as he lifted her easily up onto the next level, "it's just that in the torchlight your hair looks redder than it generally does and red hair is the mark of Set, the Egyptian version of the devil."

"Then I won't mind it," he reassured her with a smile. But the smile would have meant more if he hadn't seen the knot of men melt away the moment he'd climbed beyond the range of a normal man's vision.

Over the years, the top of the pyramid had been removed, leaving a flat area about thirty feet square at the summit. Breathing a little heavily, Lady Wallington collapsed onto one of the scattered blocks and was immediately surrounded by natives who tried to sell her everything from bad reproductions of papyrus scrolls, guaranteed genuine, to the finger of a mummy, undeniably genuine. Henry, they ignored. He left her to her purchases and wandered closer to the eastern edge where, past the obsidian ribbon that was the Nile, he could see the twinkling lights of Cairo.

They came from upwind, moving so quietly that mortal ears would not have heard them. Henry caught the sound of hearts pounding in a half dozen chests and turned long before they were ready.

One man moaned, grimy fist shoved up to cover his mouth. Another stepped back, whites showing all around his eyes. The remaining four only froze where they stood and over the stronger stink of fear, Henry caught the smell of steel and saw moonlight glint on edged weapons.

"An open place for thieves," he remarked conversationally, hoping he wouldn't have to kill them.

"We are not here to steal from you, *afreet*," their leader said softly, his voice pitched so that none of the other foreigners on the pyramid would hear, "but to give you a warning. We know what you are. We know what you do in the night."

"I don't know what you're talking about." The protest was purely instinctive; Henry didn't expect to be believed. Even as he spoke, he realized from their bearing that they did know what he was and what he did and that the only option left was to find out what they intended to do about it.

"Please, *afreet* . . ." The leader spread his hands, his meaning plain.

Henry nodded, once, and allowed the persona of slightly

vapid Englishman to drift away. "What do you want?" he asked, the weight of centuries giving his voice an edge.

The leader stroked his beard with fingers that trembled slightly and all six carefully kept from meeting Henry's gaze. "We want only to warn you. Leave. Now."

"And if I don't?" The edge became more pronounced.

"Then we will find where you hide from the day, and we will kill you."

He meant it. In spite of his fear, and the greater fear of the men behind him, Henry had no doubt they would do exactly as they said. "Why warn me?"

"You have proven yourself to be a neutral *afreet*," one of the other men spoke up. "We do not wish to make you angry, so we try a neutral path to be rid of you."

"Besides," the leader added dryly, "our young men insisted."

Henry frowned. "I gave them dreams . . ."

"Our people had a civilization when these people were savages." A wave of his hand indicated the tourists, Lady Wallington among them, still haggling over souvenirs. "We have forgotten more than they have yet learned. Dreams will not hide your nature, *afreet*. Will you take our warning and go?"

Henry studied their faces for a moment and saw, under the dirt and malnutrition, a remnant of the race that had built the pyramids and ruled an empire that had included most of northern Africa. To that remnant he bowed, the bow of a Prince receiving an ambassador from a distant, powerful land, and said, "I will go."

We have forgotten more than they have yet learned.
Henry drummed his fingers on the edge of his desk. Somehow he doubted that much more had been learned in the ninety odd years since. If Celluci was right and a mummy did walk the streets of Toronto, a mummy who brought with it the power of ancient Egypt, then they were all in a great deal of danger.

"Slumming, Detective?"

"Just seeing how the other half lives." Celluci leaned on the counter at 52 Division and scowled at the woman on the other side. "Trembley and her partner in yet? I need to talk to them."

"Good God, don't tell me one of you boys from homicide is actually working at six fifty in the a.m.? Just let me circle the date . . ."

"Bruton . . ." It wasn't quite a warning. "Trembley?"

"Jee-zus, take a man out of uniform and he loses his sense of humor. Not," she reflected, "that you ever had much of one. And you always were a son of a bitch in the morning. Come to think of it, you were a son of a bitch in the evening, too." Staff-Sergeant Heather Bruton had shared a car with Celluci for a memorable six months back when they'd both been constables, but the department had wisely separated them before any permanent damage had been done. "Trembley's not in yet. You want to wait or you want me to have her give you a shout?"

"I'll wait."

"Be still my beating heart." She blew him a sarcastic kiss and returned to her paperwork.

Celluci sighed and wondered if Vicki had known who'd be on duty when she suggested he talk to Trembley. Just the sort of thing she'd think was funny. . . .

". . . so then she says, 'Aren't you going to arrest him, Mommy?' "

Trembley's partner laughed. "How old is Kate now?"

"Just about three. Her birthday's November." She turned from Harbord Street onto Queen's Park Circle. "And can you believe it, for Halloween she wants . . . oh, fuck!"

"What?"

"The accelerator, it's stuck!"

The patrol car sped over the bridge and into the curve, picking up speed. Trembley swerved around a tiny import, fighting to keep control. She pumped the brakes once, twice, and then the pressure was gone.

"Shit!"

She stamped the emergency brake into the floor. Abused metal shrieked under the car.

Trembley's partner, the fingers of one hand dug deep into the dash, grabbed for the radio. "This is 5239! The car . . . Jesus, Trembley!"

"I see it! I see it!"

She yanked the wheel hard to the left. Tires squealed against asphalt. They passed behind the College streetcar with only a prayer between them.

"Throw it into reverse!"

"That'll fuse the engine!"

"So?"

The world slowed as PC Trembley suddenly realized that the car was not going where she steered it. The wheels had turned, but the car, drawing dark lines of rubber behind it, continued to head for the concrete memorial at the corner of the Toronto General Hospital.

The world resumed its normal speed just before they hit. Trembley's last feelings were relief. She didn't think she could stand dying in slow motion.

Upwind from the clouds of greasy black smoke, Celluci stared at the wreck of the patrol car, the heat from the fire lapping at his face. If by any miracle either officer had survived the impact, the explosion when the engine ignited would have finished them off. The blaze was so intense that the fire department could only let the flames burn out, concentrating on keeping them contained.

In spite of the early hour, a small crowd had gathered and the flower seller, who had been just about to set up on that corner, was having strong hysterics under the care of two paramedics.

"Funny thing," rasped a voice by Celluci's shoulder.

He turned and glared down at the filthy man swaying beside him. Even over the smell of the accident, he stank.

"I seen it," the man continued. "Told the cops. They don't believe me."

"Told them what?" Celluci growled.

"I am *not* drunk!" He staggered and clutched at Celluci's jacket. "But if you could spare some change . . ."

"Told them what?" Celluci repeated in a tone honed over the years to cut through alcoholic haze.

"What I seen." Still holding the jacket, he turned and pointed a filthy finger at the car. "Wheels was goin' one way. Car was goin' 'nuther way."

"It's barely light now, how could you have seen that then?"

"Was layin' in the park. Had a wheels-eye view."

It wasn't much of a park, more a garden planted on the median strip, but the trail of black rubber scorched onto the road passed right by it. Celluci followed the line to the wreck and then followed the smoke until it became a part of the overcast sky, spreading over the entire city.

The wheels were going one way.

The car was going another.

With a cold hand closing around his heart, Celluci ran for his car. It had suddenly become very important he see Trembley's occurrence reports for Monday morning.

"Jesus Christ, Celluci," Staff-Sergeant Bruton snapped, phone receiver cradled under her chin and three people clambering for her attention, "this is *not* the time to bother me with a missing fucking occurrence report, you . . . What?" She turned her attention back to the phone. "No. I don't want to call back. I want you to find him! Do *not* put me on ho . . . damnit!" She scrawled her signature on a preferred form, glared through the chaos and shouted, "Takahashi! Get that other line! Now then," she jabbed a finger in Celluci's direction, "if you need that report for a case, you call later. You hear me? Later."

"Sarge?" PC Takahashi held out the phone, his hand tightly over the mouthpiece. "It's Trembley's husband."

The hieroglyphs that had been etched into the paint of the toy police car had been completely obliterated and the small piece of paper folded three times toward the heart and then slipped into the front seat was no more than ash. He slid a magazine under the smoldering remains and lifted it out of the tub with a trembling hand. It had been a very long time since he'd worked that spell and, as burning down the hotel had not been part of his intention, he'd carefully set it up so that any random power would be contained. Because he'd forgotten that the fuel these cars relied upon was highly flammable, his foresight proved fortunate. As it was, the shower curtain appeared a little singed. He would have to have it replaced.

Dumping the nearly unidentifiable bit of metal into a crystal ashtray in the living room of the suite, he collapsed, exhausted, into a chair. Although there existed easier and less draining ways to accomplish the same purpose, the morning's work had, while removing the last two memories of his mummified form, proven that all his old skills were still intact. A quick trip to the station and a short chat with the young man on the desk had taken care of the written records last night.

In the old days, he wouldn't have dared to take his power as low as he had this morning. But in the old days with the gods gathering up souls almost at birth, he wouldn't have been able to feed with the ease he now could. Later, perhaps around lunch, he'd take a walk. According to Dr. Rax's ka, there was a school of sorts for very young children not so far away.

"You're late."

"I was down at 52 when the accident call came in." Celluci shrugged out of his jacket and dropped into his chair. The accident had happened at College and University, three short blocks from Headquarters; everyone in the building knew about it; half of the arriving day shift had been there.

"Was it as bad as they say?"

"Worse."

"Jesus. What do you think happened?"

Celluci glared across the desk at his partner. "The team who died in that crash were the uniforms on the scene Monday morning at the museum."

"Christ, Mike!" Dave leaned forward and lowered his voice. "We are not in some bad monster movie here! There never was a mummy, but if there had been it wouldn't be getting up and killing people and it sure as shit wouldn't be causing car accidents. I don't know where you're coming from with this, but could you just drop the bullshit so we can get on with our work?"

"Look, you don't know . . ."

"Know what? That there's a lot of strange things going on in this city? Sure I know, I've arrested some of them. But there's plenty of perfectly normal, human slime out there so don't go borrowing trouble." He studied Celluci's expression and shook his head. "Like money through a whore's hands . . . You haven't listened to a thing I said."

"I heard you," Celluci growled. He realized that nothing he said in turn could convince the other man that another world existed outside—or more frighteningly, inside—the boundaries he'd lived with all his life.

"Hey, you two; Cantree wants to see you in his office."

"Why?" Celluci scowled at the messenger even as Dave was getting to his feet.

She shrugged. "How the hell should I know? He's the Inspector, I'm just a detective." She skipped back out of the way as Celluci stood. "Maybe he just got a look at your last expense report. I told you that you should've kept receipts."

Inspector Cantree glanced up as the two detectives came in and indicated with a jerk of his head that they were to close the door. "It's about those deaths at the museum," he said without preamble. "I've looked at the reports. I've had a talk with the Chief. Leave it."

"Leave it?" Celluci took a step forward.

"You heard me. A heart attack isn't a homicide. Leave it to the B & E team. I want you helping Lackey and Dixon on the Griffin case."

Celluci felt his hands curl into fists, but because it was Cantree, probably the one cop in the city he respected without reservation—and *that* carried a lot more weight than the man's rank or position as his immediate superior—he kept a tight hold on his temper. "I have a hunch about this . . ." he began, but the Inspector interrupted.

"I don't care. It isn't a homicide, therefore it isn't any business of yours. Or your hunches."

"But I think it *is* a homicide."

Cantree sighed. "All right. Why? Give me some facts."

Celluci's lips narrowed. "No facts," he muttered, while Dave stared at the ceiling, his expression carefully neutral. "Just a feeling."

"All right." Cantree pulled a pile of folders across his desk. "I'll give *you* some facts. We've had seventy-seven homicides in this city so far this year. A teenage girl found dismembered in the lake. A man knifed behind a bar. A doctor killed in the stairwell of her apartment building. Two women bludgeoned to death in a parking garage in middle of the fucking afternoon!" His voice rose and he surged up out of his seat, slamming his palm down on the folders. "I don't need you making murders where there aren't any. As far as you are concerned, the case is closed. Do I make myself clear?''

''Perfectly,'' Celluci told him through clenched teeth.

''As a bell,'' Dave added, pulling his partner toward the door and keeping a tight grip on his elbow until they were back in the outer office. ''Well, I guess that's that,'' he said, caught sight of Celluci's face, and rolled his eyes. ''Or maybe not . . .''

''Nelson. Investigations.''

''Cantree pulled me off the case.''

Vicki dropped her bag and, balancing the receiver under her chin, shrugged out of her jacket. She'd barely gotten in the door when the phone rang. ''Did he say why?''

''He said, and I quote, *'I've looked at the reports. I've had a talk with the Chief. A heart attack isn't a homicide.'* ''

''And you said?''

''What the hell could I say? If I told him I thought there was a mummy involved, he'd think I was crazy. My partner *already* thinks I'm crazy.''

In her mind's eye she could see him shoving the curl of hair back off his forehead and forcing his fingers up through his hair. ''You still think there's a mummy involved?''

''Trembley's occurrence report for Monday morning is missing.''

''And Trembley?''

''Is dead.''

Vicki sat down. ''How?''

''Car accident on the way back to the station this morning.''

''I passed the site coming home, but I had no idea Trembley was . . . involved.'' Emergency teams had just managed to get close to the slag. The bodies had been burned beyond even retrieval. ''I talked to a couple of the uniforms. They said the car went out of control.''

''I have a witness who saw the wheels pointing one way while the car continued to go another.'' Celluci took a deep breath and she could hear the tension in it humming over the wires. ''I want to hire you.''

''You what?''

"Cantree tied my hands. You don't work for him anymore. Find that mummy."

She recognized the obsession in his voice. She'd heard it there before and as often in her own. Obsession made a good cop. It had also broken a few. "All right. I'll find it."

"Keep me informed every step of the way."

"I will."

"Be careful."

She saw again the melted remains of Trembley's car. "You, too."

Hanging up the phone, she frowned, remembering. *I've looked at the reports and I've had a talk with the Chief.* "Now why," she asked of the empty apartment, "would Inspector Cantree have talked to the Chief about a departmental matter?"

Seven

". . . no one is available to take your call at this moment. If you leave a message after the tone, I'll get back to you as soon as possible. Please don't assume I can remember where I put your phone number."

"Henry? Vicki. I want to check out that workroom tonight. The Department of Egyptology is on the fifth floor at the south end of the museum; meet me there as soon as you can." She thought for a second, then added, "There'll be a single guard on the desk. I assume you can get in without any trouble." Brow furrowed, Vicki put down the receiver. As it was still a couple of hours to sunset, she hadn't actually expected to speak to Henry, but she suddenly doubted the wisdom of putting that message on the machine.

"You're being ridiculous," she sneered at herself. "The odds of Celluci's alleged mummy randomly tapping phone lines or gaining access to Henry's answering machine are about as likely as . . ." She sighed and redialed Henry's number. ". . . as it existing at all."

"Henry? Vicki. Erase this tape once you've listened to it."

"I'm probably just being paranoid," she told a piece of cold pizza a moment later, picking a slice of salami off the congealed cheese. But as four people were already dead and they had no idea of the enemy's strength or its capabilities, she had no intention of being body number five or setting Henry up as number six.

It took less than fifteen minutes to walk to the Royal Ontario Museum from Vicki's apartment, but by the time she ducked down the alley between the McLaughlin Planetarium and the museum's main building, she was wishing she'd taken a cab. Everything below the angle of the umbrella had gotten soaked and the wind had blown cold rain up into her face at every opportunity.

"I hate October," she muttered, using the narrow band of shelter under the second floor walkway to shake some of the excess water off the bottom of her trench coat. As she straightened, a cold dribble ran off her chin, down the inside of her collar, along the side of her neck, and into the hollow of her collarbone where it finally surrendered and was soaked up by her shirt. "On second thought, I can live with October, I hate *rain.*"

At the staff entrance, she paused and peered through the outer set of glass doors. The only way to the inner set, and then into the museum, passed by a manned security station. A large sign instructed staff that security badges *must* be worn at all times and that visitors *must* check in at the desk.

Vicki smiled, peeled off her leather gloves and stuffed them in her pockets, then opened the door.

"Hello." She extended her smile to include the guard and he willingly returned it. Her clothing said, respectable and her attitude said, nice person—just the sort security guards preferred to deal with. "My name's Celluci. I'm here to see Dr. Rachel Shane in Egyptology." She figured it was the one name guaranteed to get her upstairs and if the guard recognized it, she'd merely use the same story she planned on giving Dr. Shane.

"Is Dr. Shane expecting you?"

"Not at this precise moment, no."

"I'll have to call up."

"Oh, yes, of course."

A moment later she was in the elevator, a small pink badge pinned to her trench coat with *Celluci* and the number forty-two written on it. To her surprise, an attractive dark-haired woman met the elevator on the fifth floor.

"Mike. Is it . . ." she began, stepping forward as the doors opened. Then she stopped, flushed, and stepped back as Vicki moved out into the hall. "I'm sorry. I thought you were someone else."

"Detective-Sergeant Celluci?" Vicki guessed. She had a pretty good idea of who this must be from Celluci's description, but she wondered just how much, exactly, the detective in question *hadn't* told her about the good doctor. Why would she be coming to meet him at the elevator?

"That's right, but . . ."

"You must be Dr. Shane."

"Yes. However . . ." Then she managed to read the name on the badge and her cheeks darkened. "You're not his wife are you?"

Vicki felt herself flush in turn. "Not hardly." Dr. Shane looked relieved but still embarrassed and again Vicki found herself wondering what Mike hadn't told her. And whether she really wanted to know. "I'm his cousin," she continued. "He thought he left some papers here and, as I just work around the corner on Bloor Street, he asked me to come by."

"Papers? Oh." Dr. Shane turned and started down the hall. "Well, if he left them, the departmental secretary Ms. Gilbert will know. I don't think she's left for the day."

As they walked down the hall, Vicki noted doorways, locks, lines of sight, and Dr. Rachel Shane. Celluci could, of course, eat lunch with anyone he chose—their relationship had always been nonexclusive—but Vicki had to admit to being curious. He'd been so completely neutral when talking about the assistant curator that she'd known right away he was interested. Celluci wasn't that neutral about anything. Cursory observation showed Rachel Shane to be above average in height, attractive, self-assured, pleasant, polite . . . *And obviously intelligent or she couldn't do her job. Christ, the perfect woman of the 90s. What do you want to bet she cooks, composts, and reads nonfiction?* A muscle jumped in her jaw and, surprised, Vicki unclenched her teeth.

"So why didn't Detective Celluci come himself?"

"I don't know." Dr. Shane's question had been asked in a tone as aggressively noncommittal as any Vicki had ever heard. *That must've been some lunch, Celluci.*

There were, of course, no papers to find, although Ms. Gilbert, tying a plastic rain hat over permed hair, promised to keep an eye out.

"Thanks for looking." As the older woman hurried out of the office, Vicki glanced down at her watch. Time for her to be leaving as well. This next bit had to be tightly choreographed. She held out her hand. "I appreciate you taking the time to see me, Dr. Shane."

"I'm just sorry we couldn't find the detective's papers."

She had a firm handshake and a dry palm. Another two
points in her favor. "Time he started remembering where
he leaves things anyway. But if they do turn up, will you
call him?"

"Yes, of course I will."

I'll bet. All of a sudden it was an effort to sound pleasant.
"Did he give you his home number?"

"Yes, he did."

And just what does that Mona Lisa smile mean? "Well,
thanks again. I'll find my own way back to the elevator. I
mean, it's a straight length of hall, I can hardly get lost."

Back on the first floor, a steady stream of staff members
moved through the security area, leaving for the day. Vicki,
with one eye on the clock, made sure the guard noticed her
sign out and return her badge. Shift change would be in two
minutes.

"Oh, blast, I left my umbrella upstairs." She shot a panicked look at the outer doors where sheets of rain were
slapping against the glass, then turned to the guard. "Mind
if I run up and get it?"

"Nah, go ahead." He shot a disgusted look of his own
at the rain.

The best lie isn't a lie at all, Vicki mused retrieving her
umbrella from behind one of the temple dogs at the door to
the Far East Department. She hurried down the hall to a
small supply cupboard, just past the photocopy machine.
The door had been open earlier and it had seemed like the
perfect hiding place. Unfortunately, the door was now
locked and she'd be in plain sight of anyone approaching
from either direction while she worked on it.

"Damn."

The open orange doors had to belong to the workroom;
Vicki could hear Dr. Shane discussing the restoration of a
mural. The double yellow doors across from them were ajar.
Vicki slipped inside as the voices from the workroom grew
louder.

". . . so we'll take another look at that plaster patch tomorrow."

They were in the hall now.

Vicki turned. Obviously, she was in the storeroom; the
black stone sarcophagus Celluci had mentioned sat barely
an arm's length away. Just as obviously, someone would be

arriving momentarily to turn off the lights and lock the door. After a quick glance at the lock—being trapped inside was low on her list of useful ways to spend the night—Vicki scanned the room for a hiding place. Unfortunately, the sheer volume of stuff made quiet movement impossible and the sarcophagus stood so close to the door that hiding behind it would be useless.

But in it?

She scrambled inside seconds before the storeroom door opened.

"Did you hear something, Ray?"

"Not a thing, Dr. Shane."

"Must've been my imagination . . ."

She didn't sound convinced and Vicki held her breath. A moment later, there was a soft click and the lights went out, then the door closed and Vicki heard keys in the lock.

The interior of the sarcophagus was actually quite roomy, having been built to hold a full-sized coffin, but Vicki had no intention of remaining inside. She crawled out and set both bag and umbrella on the top of the stone box. As far as the new guard knew, she'd signed out and was gone. The odds were slim to none that the old guard had told him she'd gone back inside. If the mummy was messing with people's heads—and as no one remembered it, it certainly looked like it was—there was nothing in anyone's head to incriminate her.

She was actually quite proud of the way she'd gotten past security. With the paranoia caused by two deaths, plain old sneaking in would have been impossible. That what she had done—and was doing—was illegal, bothered her a little, but as she wasn't going to hurt anything, or even disturb anything, her conscience would just have to roll with the punches. Actually, it had gotten pretty good at that since meeting Henry.

She fished her flashlight out of her bag by touch and checked her watch. Sunset would be in fifteen minutes. She'd give Henry half an hour to clear his head and get over to the museum, then she'd start working on the lock.

"Meanwhile," she turned the tight beam on the sarcophagus, "let's see what I can find out here."

Henry stood for a moment watching Vicki work. Although emergency lights put the hall in twilight rather than true darkness, he knew that for Vicki they were one and the same. She could no more see the lock, inches in front of her face, than she could see him, yet her touch was sure as she probed at the mechanism. Silently, he moved a little closer and smiled as he realized her eyes were tightly shut.

"Well done," he said softly as, with a sound only he could hear, the lock disengaged.

Heart pounding, Vicki fought the urge to leap to her feet and spin around. "Thank you very much, Henry," she muttered, aware that no matter how low her voice he could pick it up, "you've just cost me a good six years of my life and almost made me shit my drawers." Running her hand lightly up the door so as not to become disoriented, she stood. "Now, if we could get out of the hall before someone comes along . . ."

He reached past her, turned the knob, and pulled one of the double doors partway open. Before he had a chance to act as guide, Vicki slipped through the narrow space and into the room beyond. Puzzled, he followed, pulling the door shut behind him. "Can you see?" he asked.

"Not a damn thing." Although still bitter about her night blindness, a certain amount of pride colored her voice. "But I could feel the difference in the air where the door wasn't. Now then, be useful and find the lights. The doors fit tightly enough, there'll be no spill into the hall. Or not much anyway," she amended as the multiple banks of fluorescents came on. Eyes streaming from the sudden glare, she turned to face Henry and found him slipping on a pair of dark glasses.

She grinned. "You look like a spy." The black leather trench coat and sunglasses made an exotic contrast with the red-gold hair and pale skin.

His brows rose. "Isn't that what we're doing? Spying?"

"Not really. If we get caught, it's breaking and entering."

Henry sighed. "Wonderful. Vicki, why are we here? All the evidence has certainly been cleared away."

"Maybe. Maybe not. I wanted to get a look at the scene of the crime." Taking one final swipe at her eyes, Vicki glanced around the workroom. It had to be at least fifty feet square, perhaps larger; the high beige walls tended to draw

the eye up. Rows of chest-high wooden cabinets covered
half the room and floor-to-ceiling metal shelves—filled with
stone, and pottery, and sculpture—the other half. They stood
in an area obviously used for paperwork beside a buried
desk and a number of laden bookshelfs. To their left, a
camera stood on a tripod before a neutral background and
to their right a small kitchenette—fridge, counter, cupboards, and sink—ran along one wall. A lime green door
just at the end of the counter led to the darkroom. Two
padded sawhorses stood between the desk and the cabinets
in the only open space of any size. Resting on them was the
coffin, its lid on the closest cabinet. "Besides, I wanted you
to take a look at that."

Henry sighed again. He was willing to help, but he honestly didn't see how this . . . excursion . . . was going to
do any good. "Are you sure that's the right coffin?"

Vicki's mouth twisted as she studied the artifact. Even
without Celluci's description, she would have recognized it.
The hair on the back of her neck rose and although she
shrugged the feeling away, she was beginning to see why
Celluci had been so willing to believe in his mummy. "I'm
sure."

Hands shoved deep in his pockets, Henry walked over to
the coffin. His dark lenses somehow gave it an unreal appearance and painted the snakes covering it the color of
blood. Very ominous—but he had no idea what he was supposed to be looking for. His nose twitched at the still overpowering smell of cedar, then he frowned and lowered his
head toward the cavity. So faintly that only one of his kind
could pick it up, he caught the scent of a life.

Eyes closed, he breathed in the signature of centuries.
Not merely flesh and blood but terror, pain, and despair . . .

*Not stone above him, but rough wood embracing him so
closely that the rise and fall of his chest brushed against the
boards. All around the smell of earth. Screaming until his
throat was raw, he twisted and thrashed through the little
movement he had . . .*

His eyes snapped open and Henry jerked back, away from
the coffin, away from the memory of his own burial, trembling fingers sketching the sign of the cross. He turned to

find Vicki watching him, her expression saying clearly that his reaction had been observed.

"Well?" she asked.

"Something spent a long time trapped in there."

"Something human?"

He shrugged, more affected by the experience than he wanted to admit. "It was when they closed the lid. If it was aware for all those years, only God knows what it is now."

Vicki nodded thoughtfully and Henry realized that his reaction had not only been observed but anticipated. "That was why you wanted me here." He'd told her of his burial the night he'd told her of his creation.

She nodded again, not noticing his rising anger. "You keep going on about how your senses are more acute, so I figured if there'd been something, someone, in there for three thousand years you'd be able to tell."

"You used me."

Vicki's jaw dropped at the fury in his voice and she took an involuntary step back. "What are you talking about?" She forced the words past a sudden throat tightening rush of fear. "I just assumed you'd be able to sense . . ." Then she remembered.

"You know there's a very good reason most vampires come from the nobility, a crypt is a lot easier to get out of. I'd been buried good and deep and it took Christina three days to find me and dig me free."

She wet her lips and in spite of every instinct that told her to run as he advanced, she held her ground. "Henry, I didn't even think about you being buried. I didn't want an emotional reaction, just a physical one. Jesus Christ, Henry!" She brought her hands up and laid them flat against his chest, beginning to grow angry herself. "I wouldn't mess with my worst enemy's mind that way, let alone a friend's!"

The words penetrated through the red haze and he found he had to believe her. He was left shaken, aghast at how close he had come to loosing the beast. "Vicki . . . I'm sorry."

"It's okay." His cheek felt smooth and cool under her palm. He looked as though he'd frightened himself as much as he had frightened her. "We've all got triggers that cause us to act without thinking."

"And what are yours?" he asked, firmly jamming a civilized mask and a patina of control back into place.

"We haven't got time to go into *that* right now," Vicki snorted. "People'll be coming back in about twelve hours." She jerked her head toward the door, remembering the strain he was under lately, willing to forget the whole incident and go on. "We'd better go check out the offices. This place has told us everything it can."

Henry stood by the office window and looked down at the traffic. He should have known that Vicki would never use him in such a way—use his abilities, yes, but not his fears. Waking every evening to an image of the sun had him on edge and it seemed that the reminder of his burial had shoved him over. How many other reminders would there be, he wondered. Four hundred and fifty odd years of life supplied a great many things to be reminded of.

Perhaps the image *was* an indication that his time had run out, an invitation to a cleaner end than one of gradual loss of self. And if it came to a choice, he would take the fire.

"Ouch! Son of a bitch!"

Henry hid a smile as Vicki careened off a corner of Dr. Rax's desk, thoughts of death temporarily banished by the current condition of his life. As Vicki flicked on the desk lamp, he moved away from the window. "Are you sure that's safe."

"Of course I'm sure," Vicki told him, rubbing the front of her thigh and blinking owlishly. "If anyone sees the light they'll assume someone's working late, but if they see the flashlight beam," she snapped it off and dropped it into the cavernous depths of her purse as she spoke, "they'll assume a break-in."

"They teach you that at the police academy?"

"Not likely. Back when I was in uniform, a habitual criminal named Weasel took it on himself to further my education."

"Isn't that a little counterproductive on his part?" Henry asked, walking over to the desk. "Letting the cops know his secrets?"

"Oh, Weasel wasn't a bad fellow. His definition of personal property was just a bit loose." She sat down and scanned the desktop. "Now then, what have we here . . ."

"What are you looking for?"

"I'll tell you when I . . . hello." The large book sitting half on and half off the blotter had a number of pages crumpled and folded under as though the book had been dropped and then hastily shut without any regard for its condition. *"Ancient Egyptian Gods and Goddesses, Third Edition."* She opened it to the folds and pulled it directly under the pool of light, scowling at the unpronounceable names. "I wonder if Dr. Rax was looking something up the night he died."

"Is there an illustration in there that looks like this?" Henry handed her the desk calendar. The top page still read Monday, October 19th. Dr. Rax hadn't seen October 20th.

Vicki squinted at the sketch under the date. It looked like some weird combination of a deer's body and a bird's head. Then she turned back to the book.

"Here it is. Pretty good likeness, too, if he was doing it from memory. Akhekh? This guy needs another vowel . . ." She rubbed a hand over the back of her neck and found herself looking up at Henry for reassurance. She felt like a fool when she realized he stood beyond her severely limited range of vision and bent her head to continue reading. "Akhekh, a predynastic god of upper Egypt absorbed into the conqueror's religion to become a form of the evil god Se . . . Fuck!" Slamming the book closed she sat panting, eyes wide, staring at something Henry couldn't see.

"Vicki?" He grabbed her shoulders and shook her, hard enough to break through the blank expression. "What happened?"

She blinked, frowned, and checked to make sure she could still move her head. "Whiplash, I think."

"Vicki!" He shook her again, not as hard but a little more emphatically.

Wetting her lips, she shot a glance at the book. "The eyes on the diagram, they were red. Glowing. They looked right at me."

He moved his shoulders under the silk shirt and smiled at his reflection. The feeling pleased him. This century had much to offer those with the ability to appreciate it. When he finished his restructuring, it would truly be a paradise.

Missing the institution of slavery, and its simplicity of

service, he had effectively enslaved the hotel manager and two of his assistants. Their ka had submitted so completely to his, they had very little independence left. It was only a small beginning, but he had plenty of time.

The Solicitor General, with whom he had spent another productive afternoon, was under a similar depth of control. As it was necessary—at least for a time—that the man be able to function independently without arousing suspicion, the application of that control worked on a number of very subtle levels and responded to a myriad of external clues. He was to provide the men and women who would be sworn to Akhekh, their ka going to build power in the heavens even as they gathered power on Earth.

He saw the red glow in the mirror a heartbeat before his reflection faded and he stared instead at the image of his god.

High priest of my new order, it said.

Arms crossed over his breast, he bowed, centuries of practice keeping his distaste from showing. "My lord?"

Open your ka to me. I have marked the first of those who will provide me with sustenance.

Vicki ducked out from behind the blackout curtain and pulled the bedroom door closed, suppressing a shudder as she thought of Henry, stretched out immobile on the bed. Although she wasn't usually inclined to dwell on the past, the afternoon spent waiting for him to wake had made an impression that showed no signs of fading. He seemed to show no desire to immolate himself this morning, but she recognized—last night's little adventure had forced her to recognize—that his nerves were stretched to the breaking point.

"Vampires shouldn't have nerves," she muttered, stepping into the living room and lifting her face to the dawn. It infuriated her that she could do nothing for him but watch and wait.

Yawning, she pulled off her glasses and rubbed at her eyes. Getting out of the museum had been a lot less complicated than getting in; Henry had simply caught the guard's eye, then the two of them had walked right on by. Vicki hadn't been able to stop herself from muttering, *"These are not the droids you're looking for."* Unfortunately, she hadn't managed much sleep after they got back to Henry's condo. Dreams of ancient Egyptian gods and human sacrifice kept jerking her awake. Promising herself a good long nap later in the day, she collapsed into a red velvet armchair and reached for the phone. If Celluci wasn't awake by now, he should be.

He answered on the second ring.

"Celluci."

"Morning, Detective. You awake enough to hear some news?"

She heard him swallow and in her mind's eye could see him standing rumpled and unshaven in the tiny kitchen of his house in Downsview. "Good news or bad?"

"I got both. Which do you want first?"

"Give me the good news, I could use some."

"You aren't crazy. There *was* a mummy in that coffin and it now seems to be roaming around Toronto."

"Great." He swallowed again. "And the bad news?"

"There was a *mummy* in that coffin and it now seems to be roaming around Toronto."

"Very funny. When I want to know who's on first, I'll ask. How are you going to find it?"

Vicki sighed. "I don't know," she admitted. "But I'll think of something. Maybe I should find a reason for Trembley and her partner being killed when the staff at the ROM were only . . . uh, mind-wiped."

"Maybe I should have another talk with Dr. Shane."

"Well, why not. She already seems to be mistakenly impressed." *Idiot! I don't believe I said that.* Vicki smacked herself in the head with her free hand. *Brain first, mouth second!*

She could hear his eyebrows rise. "When did you meet Dr. Shane?"

"Yesterday at the museum." Not telling him would only cause him to jump to the asinine conclusion she'd been checking up on him. "During my investigation of your mummy."

"Right."

The smile in his voice set her teeth on edge. "Fuck off, Celluci. It's too early in the morning for that shit. Call me if she has anything useful to say." She hung up before he could answer.

"He thinks I'm jealous," she told her reflection in the glossy black side of Henry's stereo cabinet. "Why should I be jealous of Rachel Shane when I haven't been jealous of any of the busty bimbets he's bounced over the years?"

"Because Dr. Shane is a lot like you?" her reflection suggested.

She flipped it the finger and dragged herself up out of the chair. "It is *really* too early in the morning for this."

It had stopped raining, but the sky looked low enough to touch and a cold west wind had chased Vicki all the way down College Street to Police Headquarters. After a long nap and a leisurely breakfast of canned ravioli, she'd realized that Inspector Cantree's speaking to the Chief about a routine departmental matter still bothered her.

"And it's not like I have any other leads," she reminded herself, waiting for the light at Bay. Across the street, Headquarters loomed like an art deco Lego set. A number of people hated it, but Vicki thought it looked cheerful and had always appreciated the image/reality contrast.

She paused for a moment on the steps. Although she'd been back a couple of times in the fourteen months since she'd left the force, it had always been to one of the safe areas, like the morgue or forensics, never to homicide. To get to Inspector Cantree's office, she'd have to run the gauntlet through the entire homicide department. Where someone else would be using her desk. Where old friends and colleagues would still be fighting to keep the city from going down the sewer.

Where none of them can do the job you're doing now against a threat just as real. That helped. She glanced at her watch—twelve twenty-seven. "Oh, hell." She squared her shoulders and reached for the door. "Maybe they'll all be out for lunch."

They weren't, but the big office was empty enough that Vicki, her visitor's pass hanging off her lapel like a scarlet letter, only saw two people she knew—and one of them barely had time to call a greeting before he had to turn his attention back to the phone. Unfortunately, person number two had time on his hands.

"Well, well, well. If it isn't Victory Nelson, returning to the fold."

"Hey, Sid." Although a number of the other women on the force had complained that he was a bit of a tomcat, Vicki had nothing personal against Detective Sidney Austen. Professionally, she thought he didn't take his job seriously enough and was a little surprised to see him still in homicide. "How's it going?"

He perched on the edge of his desk and grinned at her. "You know the drill; overworked and underpaid." She saw him noting the thickness of her glasses, wondering how much she could see. "So, what did you do with your seeing eye dog?"

"I made stew."

His shout of laughter drowned out the grinding of her teeth. "Seriously, Victory, how's life as a private investigator?"

"Not so bad."

"Yeah? Celluci says you're doing pretty good."

Trust Celluci to issue bulletins. "I'm managing."

"I hear a couple of the others have tossed a few cases your way, too." He recognized her expression and hurriedly spread his hands. "Hey, I didn't mean that the way it sounded."

"I'm sure you didn't." Her smile felt tight.

Sid shook his head. "Jesus. It doesn't seem like you've been gone more than a year. You could come back right now and it'd be like you were never away. Speaking of which," he pulled his brows down in an exaggerated frown, "how come you haven't been back more often? You know, just dropping in and touching base?"

Because it sticks a knife in my heart and twists it, you asshole. But she couldn't say that to him. Instead, she shrugged and asked, "If you got out of this shithole, would you come back?" knowing he'd misunderstand the edge on her voice. "I've got to go. The Inspector's expecting me."

Stepping into Inspector Cantree's office was like stepping into the past. How many times had she gone through that door? A hundred? A thousand? A hundred thousand? The last time, just before she left, they'd both been painfully polite. The memory hurt but not so much as she'd feared. She had a new life now and the place where they'd amputated the old had pretty much scarred over.

"Welcome back, Nelson." Cantree covered the mouthpiece of the phone and jerked his head toward the coffee maker on the filing cabinet. "Get yourself something to drink, I'll be with you in a minute."

The coffee had the thick, black, iridescent look of an oil slick. Vicki half-filled a pressed cardboard cup and added two large spoonfuls of powdered whitener, past experience having taught her that after the first couple of mouthfuls her taste buds would surrender and she'd be able to get the rest down without gagging. Someone had suggested once that offering the Inspector's coffee to suspects might convince them to confess, but the idea had to be abandoned as a potential human rights violation.

"So." Cantree hung up the phone as Vicki pulled a chair closer to the desk and sat down. "It's good to see you again, Nelson." He sounded like he meant it. "I've been following your new career when I can. You've been responsible for a couple of nice convictions along with the lost dogs and cheating husbands. I'm sorry we had to lose you."

"Not as sorry as I was to be lost." She managed a wry smile as she said it.

The Inspector nodded acknowledgment, of both the statement and the delivery. "How *are* the eyes?"

"Still in my head." But as he was one of the four people in the world who she felt was owed an honest answer, she continued, "Piss useless after dark but fully functional in bright light, as long as I'm willing to face the world square on. Peripheral's closed in another twenty-five percent in the last year."

"Could be worse."

"Could be raining!" she snapped and savagely swallowed a mouthful of coffee but, after it seared a trail the length of her esophagus, the pressure of his gaze forced her to add, "All right, it could be worse."

Cantree smiled. "You know you're welcome back any time, but as this is the first you've darkened my door since you turned in your badge, I assume there's a reason for the visit."

"I've been hired to look into the deaths at the ROM and I wondered what you could tell me about them."

"Hired by who?"

Vicki smiled in turn. "I can't tell you that."

"All right, tell me this: Why aren't you picking Celluci's brain."

"Picked clean. And, as he tells me you've taken him off the case, I just wondered why."

"You've never *just wondered* anything in your life, Nelson, but, in view of past services and because I'm a nice guy, I'll tell you what I told him . . ."

As he spoke, Vicki hid a frown. He was telling her *exactly* what he told Celluci, word for word, as though it were something he'd memorized and now repeated by rote. And try as she would, she couldn't get him to expand on it. Finally, she gave up and stood. "Well, thanks for the time and the coffee, but I've got to be . . ." A thick cream-colored envelope, its return address done in embossed gold ink caught her eye. "You going to a wedding?" she asked, picking it up.

"I'm going to a Halloween party at the Solicitor General's." Cantree snatched it out of her hand and Vicki stared at him.

"You're bullshitting me?"

"Wouldn't dream of it." He slapped the envelope down on his blotter. "Apparently the Honorable Member's got some hot new adviser he wants everyone from department heads on up to meet."

"Who?"

"How should I know? I haven't met him yet. Some new guy in town with a lot of big ideas no doubt."

Vicki reached down and twitched the invitation free. "The thirty-first. Next Saturday. Halloween. How nice, it's a costume party." She had an image of Inspector Cantree—who did look remarkably like James Earl Jones—dressed as Thulsa Doom, the villain of the first Conan movie, and hid a smile.

"Sure, nice for you, you haven't been ordered to attend." He grimaced and Vicki barely managed to save her fingers as he swept both invitation and envelope into the top drawer of his desk. "The Chief says we're going, no excuses, and I hear the local OPP boys'll be there as well. Not to mention the goddamned Solicitor General's entire goddamned department." The grimace hardened into a scowl. "Just the way I look forward to spending a Saturday night, talking shop with a bunch of politicians and political cops."

"And very powerful people . . ." She caught the Inspector's expression and grinned, masking a sudden rush of apprehension. "I see you at least got enough notice to get your loins properly girded."

"You leave my loins out of this. And the damn thing came by special courier this morning."

"Special courier? Don't you find that a little strange?"

He snorted. "Ours is not to reason why . . ." The rest of the quote got lost in the shrilling of the phone and she mouthed, *I'll see myself out,* as she backed toward the door.

Out on the street, Vicki looked back at Headquarters and shook her head. *I've got a bad feeling about this.*

Sometimes, only a cliché seemed adequate.

Eight

"Did you ever find those papers you misplaced?"

"Papers?" Celluci asked, holding open the restaurant door.

"The papers your cousin came over to the museum for." Dr. Shane shook her head at his blank expression. "You called her yesterday, asked her to check for them at the museum after work . . . ?"

All at once, Celluci understood. "Oh, that cousin. Those papers." He wondered if Vicki had left him in the dark on purpose or if it just hadn't occurred to her to fill him in on their new relationship. "They turned up this afternoon at the office. I guess I should've called to let you know." He tried a charming smile and made a mental note to take care of Vicki later. "I *did* call to ask you to dinner."

"So you did."

She didn't appear particularly charmed, but neither did she appear completely immune.

Celluci was having a little trouble deciding how to approach the evening. Rachel Shane could have information that would help them find and capture the mummy, which meant he'd have to question her and, to complicate matters, he couldn't question her directly or she'd want to know why. He couldn't *tell* her why.

"Look, this is where things stand: the mummy that killed Dr. Rax is now rampaging through the city and we need your knowledge to catch it."

"And where did this mummy come from?"

"The sarcophagus in your workroom."

"But I told you that was empty."

"The mummy messed with your mind."

"Excuse me, waiter, could you call 911? I'm having dinner with a crazy man."

No. Telling her would merely cut off the only source of information they had. A scientist trained to pull knowledge out of bits of old bone and pottery simply wouldn't believe that a few of those old bones got up and committed murder on the say-so of a homicide detective, a smart-mouthed PI, and a . . . a romance writer. She'd need proof and he simply didn't have any.

Telling her would also ensure that he'd never see her again, but with four people dead what she thought of him personally became significantly less important.

When it came right down to it, he needed the information and he'd have to use her interest in him—or, more exactly, her perception of his interest in her—to get it. He'd once watched Vicki pump a man dry by spending two hours batting her eyelashes and interjecting a breathless "Oh really?" into every pause in the conversation. He wouldn't have to sink that low, but even so, Rachel Shane deserved better. God willing, he'd get a chance to make it up to her another time.

As dinner progressed, he had no trouble getting her to talk about herself and her work. The police had long since learned to exploit the human fondness for self-exposure and an amazing number of crimes were solved every year when the perpetrator just couldn't keep quiet any longer and told all. Nor was it difficult to steer the conversation sideways into ancient Egypt.

"I have the feeling," she said as the waiter set desert and coffee on the table, "that I should only have given you my name, rank, and serial number. I haven't been so thoroughly interrogated since I defended my thesis."

Celluci pushed the curl of hair back off his forehead and searched for something to say. He had, perhaps, been probing a little deeply. And he had, perhaps, not been as subtle as he could have been. The desire to be honest kept fighting with the need to be devious. "It's just that it's a relief not to be talking about police work," he told her at last.

A chestnut brow rose. "Now, why don't I believe that," she mused, stirring cream into her coffee. "You're trying to find something out, something important to you." Lifting her chin, she looked him squarely in the eye. "You'd find out a lot faster, if you'd come right out and asked me. And then you wouldn't have wasted an evening."

"I don't consider the evening to be a waste," he protested.

"Ah. Then you found out what you needed to know."

"Damnit, Vicki, don't twist my words!"

Both brows rose, their movement cutting the silence to shreds. "Vicki?"

He *did* say Vicki. Oh, shit. "She's an old colleague. We argue a lot. It just seems natural that a protest like that would have her name attached."

The brows remained up.

Celluci sighed and spread his hands in surrender. "Rachel, I'm sorry. You were right, I did need information, but I can't tell you why."

"Why not?" The brows were down, but the tone was decidedly cool.

"It would put you in too much danger." He waited for her protest, and when it didn't come he realized he was waiting for Vicki's protest.

"Does this have anything to do with Dr. Rax's death?"

"Only indirectly."

"I thought you were taken off the case."

He shrugged. Anything he said at this point could give her ideas and telling her about hiring Vicki—not to mention Vicki's supernatural sidekick—would only complicate things further.

"You know I'll help in any way I can."

Most of the people Celluci met divided the man and the cop into two very neat and separate packages. Certain subtle differences in tone and bearing indicated Rachel Shane had just closed the first package and opened the second.

She kept him in police officer mode for the rest of the evening, and when he dropped her off at her condo he had to admit that, although he felt like he'd just finished Archaeology 101, as far as dates went, it hadn't been exactly a success. She obviously had no intention of inviting him in.

"Thank you for dinner, Mike."

"You're welcome. Can I call you again?"

"Well, I tell you what." She looked up at him, her expression speculative. "You decide you want to see me and not the Assistant Curator of the Royal Ontario Museum's Department of Egyptology *and* you dump the hidden agen-

das and I'll think about it." Tossing a half smile back over
her shoulder, she went into the building.

Celluci shook his head and slid back into his car. In a
number of ways Rachel reminded him of Vicki. Only not
quite so . . . so . . .

"So Vicki," he decided at last, pulling out of the driveway and turning east toward Huron Street without really
thinking. It wasn't until he was searching for a parking
space, which was, as usual, in short supply around Vicki's
apartment, that he wondered what the hell he was doing.

He drove twice more around the block before a space
opened up and he decided he didn't need an excuse for being here; he didn't even particularly need a reason.

When Vicki heard the key in the lock, she knew it had to
be Celluci and, for one brief moment, she entertained two
completely opposing reactions. By the time he got the door
open, she'd managed to force order on the mental chaos and
was ready for him.

*If he thinks he's going to get sympathy after Dr. Shane
dumped him early, he can think again.* "What the hell are
you doing here?"

"Why?" He threw his jacket over the brass hook in the
hall. "Are you expecting Fitzroy?"

"What's it to *you*?" She pushed up her glasses and rubbed
at her eyes. "As a matter of fact, I'm not. He's writing
tonight."

"Good for him. How long has this coffee been sitting
here?"

"About an hour." Settling her glasses back on her nose,
she watched him fill a mug and rummage in the fridge for
cream. He seemed, well, if she had to put a name to it,
she'd say melancholy came closest. *Christ, maybe Dr. Shane
broke his heart.* Her own heart gave a curious twist. She
ignored it. "So. How went the date?"

He took a swallow of coffee. Two strides brought him
across the tiny kitchen and up against the back of Vicki's
chair. "It went. What's with all the books?"

"Research. Believe it or not, a history degree is appall-
ingly short on coverage of ancient Egypt."

Behind her, Celluci snorted. "You're not going to find
much help from historians."

Vicki tilted her head back and smiled smugly up at him. "That's why I'm researching myths and legends. So, uh, Dr. Shane didn't respond to the celebrated Celluci charm? Guaranteed to get a confession at fifty paces?"

He pushed her head forward, put down the coffee cup, and dug his fingers into her shoulders. "I didn't turn it on."

She sucked in a sudden breath; part pain, part pleasure. "Why not?" *This is kind of like picking a scab,* she decided. *Once you get started, it's hard to stop.*

"Because she deserved better. Bad enough I spent the evening under false pretenses. I had no intention of compounding it. Christ, you're tense."

"It's not tension, it's muscle tone. What do you mean, she deserved better? You've got a lot of faults, Celluci, but I never thought false modesty was—ouch—one of them."

"She deserved honesty. She deserved to have me thinking of her, not of how much she could tell me."

Well, as my mother always says, if you don't want to know, don't ask. "You liked her."

"Don't be an ass, Vicki. I wouldn't have asked her out to dinner if I didn't like her—I could have picked her brains in her office a hell of a lot more cheaply. I find her attractive, intelligent, self-confident . . ."

Of course, the trouble with picking scabs is when you get deep enough they start to bleed.

". . . and, as a result, I found I spent most of the evening thinking about you." He gave her shoulders a final dig, picked up his coffee, and went into the living room.

Vicki opened her mouth, closed it, and tried to sort out some kind of response. From the beginning, they'd never talked about their relationship; they'd accepted it; they'd left it alone. When they got back together last spring, it had been under those same parameters. *That son of a bitch is changing the rules* . . . But beneath the protest she recognized a surge of relief. *He spent most of the evening thinking about me.* And beneath the relief, a hint of panic. *Now what?*

He was waiting for her to say something but she didn't know what to say. *Oh, God, please, send a distraction!*

The knock on the door jerked her around so fast her glasses slid down her nose. "Come in."

"I asked for a distraction, not a disaster," she muttered a moment later.

Celluci snapped the recliner forward. "I thought you were supposed to be writing tonight," he growled, standing and scowling down the hall.

Henry smiled, deliberately provoking. He had known Celluci was in the apartment before he knocked; he could hear his voice, his movements, his heartbeat. But the mortal had the days; he would not have the darkness as well. "I was writing. I finished."

"Another book?" The word book came out as if it were something that turned up on the soles of shoes after a brisk walk through a barnyard.

"No." He hung his trench coat up beside Celluci's jacket. "But I finished the work I intended to do tonight."

"Must be nice as it isn't quite midnight. Still, it's not like it's real work."

"Well, I'm sure it's not as strenuous as taking someone out to dinner, then maintaining the illusion that you're interested in her when you're really only interested in what she knows."

Celluci shot a furious look at Vicki, who winced and said hurriedly, "Low blow, Henry. Mike had to do that, he didn't want to."

Henry moved into the kitchen, which put the two men, although in separate rooms, less than ten feet apart with Vicki, still sitting at the table, squarely between them. He inclined his head graciously. "You're quite right. It was a low blow. And I apologize."

"The fuck you do."

"Are you calling me a liar?" Henry's voice had gone deceptively soft; the voice of a man who had been raised to command, the voice of a man with centuries of experience behind him.

Celluci couldn't help but respond. His anger didn't have a snowflake's chance in hell of making an impression against the other man and he knew it. "No," he forced the words out through clenched teeth, "I'm not calling you a liar."

Vicki looked from one to the other and had a strong desire to go out for pizza. The currents running between the two were so strong that when the phone rang she felt she had to fight against their pull to answer it.

"Hi, honey. It's after eleven and the rates are down so I thought I'd give you a call before I turned in."

Just what the evening needed. "Bad timing, Mom."

"Why? What's wrong?"

"I've, uh, got company."

"Oh." While not exactly disapproving, the two letters carried a disproportionate amount of conversational weight. "Michael or Henry, dear?"

"Uh . . ." Vicki knew the moment she paused that it was a mistake. Her mother excelled at reading silence.

"*Both* of them?"

"Trust me, Mom, it wasn't my idea." She frowned. "Are you laughing?"

"I wouldn't think of it."

"You *are* laughing."

"I'll call you tomorrow, dear. I can't wait to hear how this comes out."

"Mother, don't hang . . ." Vicki glared at the receiver, then slammed it back down onto the phone. "Well, I hope you're happy." She shot up out of the chair and kicked it back out of her way. "I'm going to be hearing about this for the rest of my life." Glaring from Celluci to Henry and back, she raised her voice an octave. "*Don't say I didn't warn you, dear. Well, what do you expect when you're seeing two young men* . . . I'll tell you what I expect, I expect you both to act like intelligent humans beings and not like two dogs squabbling over a bone. I can't see any reason why all three of us can't get along!"

"You can't?" Henry asked, mildly incredulous.

Vicki, recognizing sarcasm, turned on him and snapped, "Shut up, Henry!"

"She always was a lousy liar," Celluci muttered.

"And you can shut up, too!" She took a deep breath and shoved her glasses up her nose. "Now then, seeing as we're all here together, I think we should be discussing the case. Do either of you have any problems with that?"

Celluci snorted. "I wouldn't dare."

Henry spread his hands, his meaning plain.

They moved into the living room, all three of them aware this was only a postponement. That was fine with Vicki; if they had things to work out between them, they could do it without her in the line of fire.

* * *

". . . so there's no obvious reason why it murdered Trembley and her partner but only mind-wiped the people at the museum." Celluci took another swallow of coffee, grimaced at the taste, and continued. "The only difference between the two cases is that the people at the museum spent three days close to it while Trembley saw it for maybe three minutes."

"So maybe it takes time and proximity to mess with someone's head." Vicki chewed thoughtfully on the end of her pencil for a moment then spit it out and added, "I wonder why it killed that custodian?"

Celluci shrugged. "Because it could? Maybe it was just flexing its muscles after being cooped up for so long."

"Maybe it was hungry." Henry leaned forward to make his point. "The custodian just happened to be closest when it came fully awake."

"Then what did it eat?" Celluci sneered. "There wasn't a mark on that body and there sure as shit wasn't anything missing."

Henry sat back and let the shadows in the corner of the living room cover him again. "That's not quite accurate. When the custodian was found, he was missing his life."

"And you think this mummy *ate* it?"

"Mortals have always had legends of those who extend their own lives by devouring the lives of others."

"Yeah, and those are *legends*."

The shadows couldn't hide Henry's pointed smile. "So am I. So, for that matter, are mummies who walk. And demons. And werewolves . . ."

"All right, all right! I get the idea." Celluci shoved one hand up through his hair. He really hated all this supernatural bullshit. Why him? Why not Detective Henderson? Henderson wore a crystal on a leather thong, for Christ's sake. And how come before Vicki got mixed up with Fitzroy the closest thing to a supernatural occurrence in the city was when the Leafs managed to win two in a row? *Just because* you *don't see something doesn't mean it's not there.* Okay, so he knew the answer to that one. He sighed and wondered how many previously unsolved crimes could be attributed to ghoulies and ghosties and things that went bump in the night. As much as he might want to, he couldn't blame this whole mess on Fitzroy. "So, why did it kill Dr. Rax?"

"It was stil hungry and Dr. Rax came into the workroom alone."

"But it must've known that two bodies dying in the same place the same way would start an investigation. Why go to all the trouble to hide its tracks and then do something so stupid?"

"Dr. Rax discovered it as it was leaving and it overreacted."

"Oh, great," Vicki rolled her eyes, "an impulsive mummy." She yawned and resettled her glasses with the end of her pencil. "At least we know it can make mistakes. Unfortunately, it looks like its god survived as well."

Celluci's brows climbed for his hairline. "And how do we know that?"

"Last night at the museum . . ."

"Wait a minute," Celluci held up his hand. "You went to the museum last night? After closing? You broke into the Royal Ontario Museum. . . . *He* might not be aware of this," Celluci jabbed a finger at Henry then swung around to glare at Vicki, "but *you* know damn well that's against the law."

Vicki sighed. "Look, we didn't break in anywhere; we didn't disturb anything; we had a quick look around. It's late, I'm tired. If you're not going to arrest me, just drop it." She paused, knowing there wasn't a thing Celluci could do but accept it, smiled, and continued. "We found a sketch on Dr. Rax's desk, then found a corresponding illustration in a book of ancient gods and goddesses, also on Dr. Rax's desk.

"So?"

"The illustration looked at me." She swallowed and tucked the pencil behind an ear so she could wipe palms gone suddenly damp on her jeans. "Its eyes glowed red and it looked at me."

Celluci snorted. "How much light was in the room?"

"I know what I saw, Mike." Her eyes narrowed. "And RP does *not* cause hallucinations."

He studied her face for a moment, then he nodded. "Does this god have a name?"

"Yeah. Akh . . ."

Henry's hand was tightly clamped over her mouth before either of them saw him move. "When you call the gods by name," he said softly, "you attract their attention. *Not* a good idea."

He dropped his hand and Celluci waited for the explosion; Vicki, more than most, didn't take well to being summarily silenced. When no explosion occurred, he could only assume that she felt Fitzroy's action justified and a shiver of disquiet ran down his spine. If this ancient god had Victory Nelson spooked, he didn't want to run into it.

Vicki, her fingers still wrapped around Henry's wrist, wet her lips and tried not to think of those burning eyes taking a longer look. After a moment, she let go. "I think we can safely assume, that . . . this god and the mummy are connected."

"The mummy is probably the god's high priest," Celluci suggested. When Vicki and Henry both turned to stare, he shrugged. "Hey, I watch horror movies."

"Not exactly a credible source for research," Henry pointed out as he returned to his chair in the shadows.

"Yeah, well, we don't all have Count Dracula as a close personal friend."

"Gentlemen, it's going on two in the morning; can we get on with this before I fall over?" Vicki yawned and leaned back in the recliner. "As it happens, I think Celluci's right."

"Oh, joyous day," he muttered.

She ignored him. "The wheels on Trembley's car were turned, but the car continued to move in a straight line. That only happens if some outside force is applied. There *was* no visible outside force. According to the books I've been reading, priests of ancient Egypt were also wizards."

"You're saying the mummy killed Trembley with magic?" Celluci asked incredulously.

"All the pieces fit."

In the silence that followed, the sound of the kitchen tap dripping away the seconds could be clearly heard.

"Oh, what the hell," Celluci sighed. "I've already believed seven impossible things before breakfast, what's one more."

"So," Vicki ticked the points off on her fingers as she listed them, "what we're trying to find is the reanimated wizard-priest of a god who may or may not live on the life force of others, who can twist the minds of those near to it, and who can magically kill at a distance."

"Great." Celluci yawned into his fist. "And in this corner, the Three Stooges."

"Nyuk, nyuk, nyuk," Henry agreed.

Vicki jerked forward and stared at Henry in horror while Celluci gave him something close to a nod of approval. "I don't believe this," she muttered. Vicki had a theory that the Three Stooges did sex-linked comedy as she'd never known a woman who thought they were funny. This just proved her theory as Y chromosomes were about the only thing Henry and Celluci had in common. *Vampires are supposed to have more taste!* "If we could get back on topic, maybe you two would like to hear the rest of it."

Celluci, who dearly wanted to do one routine just to provoke a reaction from Vicki, decided against it when he realized who he'd have to do the routine with. The Stooges were something you did with your buddies, not with . . . romance writers. "Go on," he growled.

Henry merely nodded. He no more wanted something in common with Celluci than Celluci wanted with him. *Except, of course, the one thing that neither of us is willing to give up . . .*

"Okay . . ." A yawn cut her off and, although she'd slept for a while in the early evening, Vicki knew that if she didn't fall over soon there'd be no way she'd be conscious for dawn. *Let's wrap this up fast and get to bed.* "Okay, ignoring the wizard aspect for the moment, what is it that priests want? Congregations. Because their gods want followers. And I think I know the congregation this god's trying for." While Celluci's face grew dark, she outlined her meeting with Inspector Cantree. "It's after the police force, not just in Toronto but across the province. Its own private little army and the perfect start to a secular power base."

"Why would a god have any interest in acquiring a secular power base?" Henry asked.

Vicki snorted. "Don't ask me, ask the Catholic Church. Look, the god wants the congregation, the *priest* wants the power base—somehow, all things considered, I can't see this guy as altruistic—and the police provide both."

"Then why across the province? Why not begin with just the city?"

"Cities aren't autonomous enough, they're too tightly controlled by higher levels of government. But if you control a province, you control a country within a country. Look at Quebec . . ."

"Weak, Vicki, very weak," Celluci snarled, finally giving his anger voice, unsure which infuriated him more, that the mummy would dare to subvert the police or that Vicki thought it could be done. "You have no proof that this new adviser is the mummy."

"I have a hunch," Vicki told him, her voice edged. "That's what you started with and look where it's gotten us. Cantree's repeating messages from the Chief like they were holy writ. You know that's not like him." They locked gazes. When Celluci looked away, Vicki continued. "One of us has to go to the Solicitor General's party on Saturday."

"One of us?" Henry asked quietly.

"All right, you." Snapping the recliner upright, Vicki laid her forearms across her knees. "Over half the people there would know Mike or me, so neither of us can do it. Besides, it's invitation only and you're good at getting past . . ."

"Social obstacles," he supplied when she paused. "You're right. I'll have to do it."

"What if Vicki's wrong and the mummy isn't there?"

Henry shrugged. "Then I'll leave early, no harm done."

"And if she's right?"

Henry smiled. "Then I'll take care of it."

Celluci remembered a dark barn and pale fingers closing around the throat of a man with only seconds to live. He averted his eyes from the smile. "You think you're up to this wizard-priest?"

Actually, he had no idea, but he wasn't about to let Celluci know that. "I am not without resources."

"Then it's settled." Vicki stood and stretched, snapping the kinks out of her spine. "This little session has been very useful. We'll all get together after the party and talk again. Thank you both for coming. Go home." She made it pretty obvious who she meant.

"I'll be there just before dawn," she told Henry at the

door, dropping her voice too low for Celluci to hear. "Don't start without me."

He lifted her hand and lightly kissed the inside of her wrist. "I wouldn't dream of it," he told her softly and was gone.

Celluci came out of the bathroom and reached for his jacket. "I'm on stakeout for the next few nights, so I won't be around, but when this is over you and I have to talk."

"What about?"

He reached over and with one finger, gently slid her glasses up her nose. "What do you think?" The same finger dropped down to trace the line of her jaw.

"Mike, you know . . ."

"I know." He moved out into the hall. "But we're still going to talk."

The door closed behind him and Vicki collapsed against it, fumbling for the lock. For the next few hours, all she wanted was a chance to sleep. For the next few days, she'd concentrate on stopping the mummy. And after that . . .

"Oh, hell," she stumbled into the bedroom, yanking her sweatshirt off over her head. "After that, maybe something'll come up . . ."

He wanted the dawns he remembered where a great golden disk rose into an azure sky, burning the shadows away from the desert until each individual grain of sand blazed with light. He wanted to feel the heat lapping against his shoulders and the stone still cool from the darkness against the soles of his feet. This northern dawn was a pallid imitation, a pale circle of a sun barely showing through a leaden sky. He shivered and walked in off the balcony.

Soon he would have to deal with the woman his god had chosen. Over the next few days he would use the key to her ka that he had been given and lift the manner of her despair off the surface of her mind.

His lord never demanded death, feeding instead on the lesser, self-perpetuating energies generated by the darker aspects of life. In time, of course, the chosen ones usually prayed for an ending. Occasionally, they achieved it.

Nine

Those outside of political circles who thought about the Ontario government at all, thought only of Queen's Park, the massive red sandstone, copper-roofed building anchoring the north end of University Avenue. Although it *was* the building where the provincial parliament actually sat, the real work got done in the blocks of office towers to the east. At 25 Grosvenor Street, between Bay and Yonge, the Office of the Solicitor General was about as far east as the government went.

Vicki squinted up at the building with distaste. It wasn't that she disliked the pink concrete tower—even though from the east or west it looked like it had been extruded from a Play-Doh modern architecture toy set—it was just that the three extra blocks from Queen's Park, while not far enough to take transit, had been long enough for her right foot to find a puddle and get soaked.

"Toronto in October. Christ. Any mummy in its right mind would hop the first Air Egyptian flight home." She sighed as she passed the sculpture outside the main entrance. It looked like a set of giant, aluminum prison bars, bent out of shape, and she'd never understood the symbolism.

Nodding at the special constable on duty at the information desk, she crossed the lobby to the cul de sac that held the elevators. Of the half dozen spotlights in the ceiling, only two were working, dropping the area into an amber-hued twilight. As far as Vicki was concerned, they might as well all have been off.

Some fair-haired wunderkind probably thought this up as a way of saving money—just before his monthly raise. She dragged her hand along the marble facing on the wall, across the stainless steel door, and finally to the plastic plate that held the call button. *Let's hope they left the lights on inside the cars or I'll never know when one arrives.*

They had. Although her eyes watered violently in the sudden glare, the reaction was preferable to groping her way into an elevator shaft. Besides, after a ten-block walk in pissing rain, she was already wet.

The Solicitor General's suite was on the eleventh floor and, as government offices went, bordered on palatial. Power colors and a conservative/modern design were intended to both offend the least number of voters and impress the most. Vicki recognized symbolic decorating when she saw it and knew full well that behind closed doors on this floor and others, utilitarian cubicles carried the workload.

"Can I help?"

The young woman at the desk served the same function as the decor—to impress and reassure. Vicki, who hated being pleasant to strangers, wouldn't have had her job for twice the money. "I hope so. My name is Nelson, I have an appointment with Mr. Zottie at one-thirty." She checked her watch. "I'm a little early."

"No problem, Ms. Nelson. Please, go on in."

She's good, Vicki mused, passing through the indicated double doors. *Even watching for it, I barely saw her check the list.*

The woman at the inner desk, while still impressive, was not the least bit reassuring. "Mr. Zottie will see you in a moment, Ms. Nelson. Please, have a seat."

It was considerably more than a moment before the door to the Solicitor General's office opened. Vicki tried not to fidget while she waited. The weekend had passed as a non-event, their only leads unavailable. Each morning she'd tucked Henry in—unsure if she should worry that the dream continued or be grateful that it remained only a dream and he still showed no sign of seeking the sun—then went home and did laundry, a little grocery shopping, called her mother, and marked time. First thing this morning, she'd pulled a few strings to get this appointment.

"Ms. Nelson?" Solicitor General George Zottie was a not very tall, not very slim, middle-aged man with a full head of dark hair, heavy dark brows, and long dark eyelashes. "Sorry to keep you waiting."

He had the firm, quick handshake of someone who'd spent

time out from behind a desk and Vicki, who despised politicians on principle, considered him to be one of the best.
A combination of personal integrity and a sincere respect
from the combined police forces he was responsible for had
kept him in this top cabinet position for his last two terms
of office. If the current government won the next election,
which seemed certain, his third term was pretty much assured.

Vicki had met him three times while she'd been on the
force, the last occasion only eight months before her failing
eyesight forced her to quit. They'd spoken for a few moments after the presentation ceremony and that conversation
had given Vicki the idea that had gotten her in to see him
today; a plan to raise the profile of the police force in both
elementary and high schools. In fact, it was such a good
idea that she was half convinced to pursue it once the
mummy threat had been taken care of. Provided, of course,
that the good guys won.

That conversation would also give her a basis for judging
his—stability? reality? For judging how much of a hold the
mummy already had. Or if it had any kind of a hold at all.
Anything she found out today would help to arm Henry for
Saturday night.

Following the Solicitor General into his office, she had a
quick look around. With next to no peripheral vision she
couldn't be subtle about it, but she figured he should be
used to first time visitors rubbernecking. Unfortunately, if
the mummy had been visiting, it had left no easily discern-
ible signs. No bits of rotting bandage, no little piles of sand,
not even a statue of the sphinx with a clock in its tummy.

"Now then," he settled himself behind his desk and
waved her into a chair, "about this proposal of yours . . ."

Vicki pulled a pair of file folders out of her bag and
handed him one. As she spoke she watched his eyes, his
hands, his overall bearing, trying to spot some indication
that he was being influenced, if not controlled, by a
millennia-old wizard-priest. He didn't seem nervous. If
anything, he seemed calmer than he had at the police reception where he'd spent the evening twitching at the collar
of his jacket.

I suppose giving up your conscious will might calm you

down, she allowed as she finished up the presentation. *But then, so would cutting back the caffeine.*

"Very interesting." The Solicitor General nodded thoughtfully and made a quick notation across the top of the first page. Vicki's eyes weren't up to reading his reversed handwriting although she squinted down at it while he continued. "Have you discussed this with public relations?"

"No, sir. I thought I'd try to get your support first."

"Well," he stood and came around the desk, "I'll have a look at your written proposal and get back to you say, late next week?"

"That would be fine, sir." Vicki stood as well and slid her own copy back into her bag. *Let's just hope we haven't all had our lives sucked out our noses by then.* "Thank you for taking the time to listen."

"Always willing to listen to a good idea." He paused at the door to smile up at her. "And that *was* a good idea. A little visible law and order at an early age might tarnish the appeal of petty crime. I'm very interested in raising the police profile in the province's schools."

"Yes, sir, I know." She slipped past him. "That's why I'm here."

His smile broadened. "It was a pity you had to leave the force, Ms. Nelson, you were one of the best. How many citations was it? Two?"

"No, sir. Three."

"Yes, good job. I can't imagine civilian life suits you as well."

"Not as well, no." She adjusted her glasses and forced the corners of her mouth up. "But it's been . . . interesting."

"Glad to hear it."

Vicki let the closing door cut off her smile and, shrugging her bag onto her shoulder, she crossed the outer office, conscious of disapproving eyes on her back. *Give it a break, lady,* she thought upon safely reaching the reception area, *before I forget which side I'm on and stuff my white hat up your nose.*

The visit could pretty much be considered a wasted effort; if George Zottie *was* being controlled by the mummy, she couldn't see it. *Which may mean nothing more than it's a subtle son of a bitch. God, what I wouldn't give for a nice simple divorce case right about now, one where you start out with a photograph of the bad guy . . .*

The elevator chimed and she hurried to catch it before someone called it away. At first, she thought the man who pushed his way out as the doors opened was drunk, but an instant later she realized he was actually unwell. His skin had a grayish cast, sweat beaded his upper lip and forehead. One long-fingered, exquisitely manicured hand crushed his cashmere overcoat toward his stomach, the other groped blindly at the air.

Vicki ducked under the moving arm and deftly guided him toward a chair. Fortunately he wasn't much larger than she was as, during the moment between standing and sitting, his entire weight came down on her shoulders. He murmured something in a language she didn't know, but as his looks placed his ethnic background in north Africa, Vicki assumed it was Arabic.

Recognizing his condition could be adding years to her estimate, she placed his age at somewhere between thirty and forty. His facial features were uninspiring—two eyes, a nose, and a rather thin-lipped mouth in the usual arrangement—but even sick and unfocused as he was, he had a perceptible force of personality.

Attempting to hold him steady, Vicki jerked around at an unfamiliar noise behind her and saw that the receptionist had just finished pulling back the thick maroon curtains that covered a wall of windows. With a convulsive shudder, the stranger fixed his gaze on the view—gray skies, the Coroner's Building, made of more pink extruded concrete, and a little farther on Police Headquarters—and seemed to relax.

Frowning, Vicki let the receptionist adroitly take her place as ministering angel. As far as she could see, there wasn't anything especially comforting out the . . . Then she had it. "He's claustrophobic, isn't he?"

"Very." The young woman had undone the top two buttons of the overcoat. "The elevator is sheer terror for him."

"Yet he still uses it . . ."

"He's *very* brave." Her expression grew slightly misty.

"That will be enough, Ms. Evans." The older woman from the inner office advanced purposefully across the dark gray carpet, lowered brows demanding to know what Vicki was doing so close to such an important visitor. "Please, Mr. Tawfik, allow *me*."

Vicki left before she threw up. *Although,* she mused, as she rode down in an elevator that suddenly seemed a lot smaller than it had, *if this thing causes that violent a reaction and he keeps using it, he is very brave. Or moderately masochistic.* While she had no idea of what sort of diplomatic position the stranger held, she wasn't surprised at the reactions he'd evoked. Something about him, in spite of his condition, reminded her of Henry.

"Is there *anything* I can get you, Mr. Tawfik."

"No. Thank you." Keeping his gaze firmly locked on the window and the space beyond it, he forced his breathing to calm. Gradually his heartbeat slowed and the spasms that twisted his gut into knots eased and finally stopped. He pulled a linen handkerchief from the pocket of his suit, fingers still slightly trembling, and wiped the sweat from his face.

Then he frowned at the two women hovering an arm's length away. "There was a third . . ."

"Merely a visitor, Mr. Tawfik. No one for *you* to concern yourself about."

"I shall be the judge of that." Even in his distress her ka had held a certain familiarity. A flavor he had not quite been able to identify. "Her name?"

"Nelson," the younger woman offered. "Victoria Nelson. Mr. Zottie knew her from when she was on the police force."

No. Her name meant nothing to him. But he couldn't shake the feeling that he had touched her ka before.

"May I inform Mr. Zottie that you've arrived?"

"You may." He had made it very clear, right from the beginning, that the Solicitor General was not to be called until he had completely recovered. Control must come from strength and a personal weakness would weaken the whole. The women of this culture were trained to nurture weakness, not despise it, and, while in theory he disapproved, he would, in practice, use the attitude. By the time George Zottie had hurried out to the reception area, anxious to escort his newest adviser into the inner sanctum, he had all

but recovered from the effects of the elevator. The mild
nausea that remained could not be seen, so it did not matter.

Leading the way toward the double doors, he could feel
the heat of the younger woman's gaze. She had created her
desire from the merest brush across her ka, intended only
to ensure her loyalty; he had not placed it there nor did he
welcome it. If truth be told, he found the whole concept
vaguely distasteful and had found it so for centuries before
he'd been interred. The older woman had responded to a
show of power—*that* he understood.

His plans for the Solicitor General had required a more
thorough remaking.

Once they were alone inside the office with the doors
tightly closed behind them, he held out his hand. Zottie,
with remarkable grace for a man of his bulk, dropped to
one knee and touched his lips to the knuckles. When he
rose again, his expression had become almost beatifically
calm.

The scribe—the press secretary—had given him the key
to Zottie and fifteen hundred years of dealing with bureaucracy had enabled him to use it. He had gone to their first
meeting with a spell of confusion ready on his palm. He
had passed it through the ceremonial touching, activated it,
and with it gained access to the ka. In the past, a man with
this much power would have had powerful protections,
would have most likely kept a wizard in his employ solely
to prevent exactly this sort of manipulation. At times, he
still found it difficult to believe that it could be so easy.

There wasn't much of George Zottie left.

With Zottie, he could go one by one to the others he
needed to build a base for his power but, with Zottie, that
was no longer necessary; they would come to him.

"Has it been done?"

"As you commanded." The Solicitor General lifted a
handwritten list off his desk and offered it with a slight bow.
"These are the ones who will be in attendance. In spite of
the short notice, most of those invited have agreed to come.
Shall I *reinvite* the others?"

"No. I can acquire them later." He scanned the list. Only
a few of the titles were familiar. That would not do.

"I need a man, an elderly man, one who has spent his
life in government but not as a politician. One who knows

not only the rules and regulations, but one who knows . . .''
The first ka he had taken supplied a phrase and he smiled
as he used it. ''. . . where the bodies are buried.''

''Then you need Brian Morton. There isn't anything or
anyone around Queen's Park he doesn't know.''

''Take me to him.''

''. . . an unfortunate occurrence at Queen's Park this afternoon as senior official Brian Morton was found dead at
his desk of a heart attack. Morton had been employed by
the Ontario Government for forty-two years. Solicitor General George Zottie, in whose ministry Morton was serving
at the time of his death, said that he had been an inspiration
to younger men and that his knowledge and experience will
be missed. Morton's widow expressed the belief that her
husband had not been looking forward to his retirement in
less than a year and, if given a choice, he would have preferred to die, as he did, with his boots on. Funeral services
will be held Monday at Our Lady of the Redeemer Church
in Scarborough.

And now, here's Elaine with the weather.''

Vicki frowned and switched off the television. Reid Ellis
and Dr. Rax had died of heart failure at the museum. The
mummy had come from the museum. Brian Morton died of
a heart attack while in the employ of the Solicitor General.
She believed the mummy was using the Solicitor General to
gain control of the police and build its own private army.
Morton was an older man, his death could be coincidence.
She didn't think so.

Henry thought the mummy might be feeding. It had been
free for a week now; how often did it have to feed?

She pulled the papers for the last week off the ''to be
recycled'' pile to the left of her desk and sat down on her
weight bench to read them. *Sudden deaths in public places
. . . makes sense to check the tabloid first.*

It took her less than ten minutes to find the first article.
Two inches square on the bottom right-hand corner of page
twenty-two, it would have been easy to miss except for the
headline. ''BOY DIES MYSTERIOUSLY ON SUBWAY.''
The body had been removed from the University Subway
line at Osgoode Station, Queen Street, and had been pronounced dead on arrival at Sick Children's Hospital. Cause

of death, heart failure. Osgoode was three stops south of
Museum. The date was October 20th. The time, nine forty-
five. Only hours after Dr. Rax had died and everyone began
declaring that the coffin was and always had been empty.

Vicki's hands closed into fists and her fingers punched
through the newsprint. The boy had been twelve years old.
Teeth clenched, she clipped the article, then slowly and me-
thodically ripped the paper into a thousand tiny pieces.

It was almost three a.m. before she found the second
death buried in a story about child care facilities under investigation. On Thursday, October 22nd, a three-year-old
had plunged off the top of a play structure at the Sunnyview
Co-op Daycare and, according to the autopsy, had been dead
before hitting the ground. Only one long block along Bloor
Street separated the Sunnyview Co-op Daycare from the
museum.

Tuesday afternoon, after seeing Henry safely into the day
and catching a few hours of sleep, Vicki stood with one
hand resting on the chain link fence that surrounded the
Daycare Center where the second child had died. *Not much
of a barrier,* she thought, rubbing at a wire pebbled with
rust. *Not when you add a reanimated evil to all the other
dangers of the city.* Although the sky was gray and heavy
with moisture, no rain fell and the playground seethed with
small people. Here, half a dozen assaulted a tower made of
wood and tires and rope while its four defenders shrieked
defiance. There, two used the empty cement wading pool
as the perfect racetrack. Here, one squatted in rapt contem-
plation of a puddle. There, three argued the rights of a slide.
And through it all, in the spaces between the scenes where
Vicki's limited vision couldn't take her, children ran and
jumped and played.

There should be one more. She followed the fence up the
driveway and, lips tight, entered the building.

"". . . all right, the death of a child under her care might
drive the rest of the day out of her mind—I'll give her that,
I've seen it happen before—but it's the *way* she didn't remember things, Henry. It just didn't ring true."

Henry looked up from the pair of clippings, his face ex-
pressionless. "So what do you think happened?"

"She was in the playground, not ten feet from where the

child fell. I think she saw it. I think she saw it and it wiped the memory from her mind, just like it did at the museum.''

"By *it* you mean . . . ?''

"The mummy, Henry.'' Vicki finished stamping down another length of the living room and whirled around to start back. "I mean the goddamned mummy!''

"Don't you think you're jumping to conclusions?'' He asked the question as neutrally as he could, but even so, it brought her shoulders up and her brows down.

"What the hell do you mean?''

"I mean, children die. For all sorts of reasons. It's sad and it's horrible, but it happens. I was the only one of my mother's children to make it out of early childhood.''

"That was the fifteenth century!''

"And in this century children have stopped dying?''

She sighed and her shoulders dropped. "No. Of course not. But Henry . . .'' A half dozen quick strides took her across the room to his chair where she dropped to her knees and laid her hands over his. ". . . these two were taken by the mummy. I know that. I don't know how I know it, but I know. Look, cops are trained to observe. We, they, do it all the time, everywhere. They may not consciously recognize everything they see or hear as important, but the subconscious is constantly filtering information until all the bits and pieces add up to a whole.'' She tightened her grip and lifted her eyes to meet his. "I *know* the mummy took out these two kids.''

He held her gaze until her eyes began to water. She felt naked, vulnerable—worth the price if he believed her.

"Perhaps,'' Henry said thoughtfully at last, finally allowing her to look away, "there are those few who take observing one step further, who can see to the truth. . . .''

"Oh, Christ, Henry.'' She retrieved the newpaper clippings and stood. "Don't give me any of that New Age metaphysical bullshit. It's training and practice, nothing more.''

"If you wish.'' Over the centuries he'd seen a number of things that "training and practice'' couldn't have accounted for, but as he doubted Vicki would react well to a discussion of those experiences, he let it drop. "So if you're right about the mummy and the children,'' he spread his hands, "what difference does it make? We're no closer to finding it."

"Wrong." She jabbed the word into the air with a finger. "We know it's staying around the museum and Queen's Park. That gives us an area in which to concentrate a search. We know it's continuing to kill, not just to protect itself from discovery but for other reasons. Feeding, if you wish. We know it's killing children. And that," she snarled, "gives us an incentive to find it and stop it. Quickly."

"Are you going to tell all this to the detective?"

"To Celluci? No." Vicki leaned her forehead against the glass and stared down at the city. She couldn't see a damned thing but darkness; since she'd entered Henry's building, the city might as well have disappeared. "It's my case now. This'll only upset him."

"Very considerate," Henry said dryly. He saw a muscle in her cheek move and the corner of her mouth twitch up a fraction. Her inability to lie to herself was one of the traits he liked best about her. "What do you want me to do?"

"Find it."

"How?"

Vicki turned from the window and spread her arms. "We *know* what area to search. You're the hunter. I thought you got its scent from the coffin."

"Not one I could use." The stink of terror and despair had all but obscured any physical signature. Henry hurriedly pushed the memory, and the shadows that flocked behind it, away. "I'm a vampire, Vicki. Not a bloodhound."

"Well, it's a magician. Can't you track power surges and stuff?"

"If I am nearby when it happens, I'll sense it, yes, as I sensed the demonic summonings last spring. But," he raised a cautioning hand, "if you'll remember, I couldn't track them back to their source either."

Vicki frowned and began to pace again. "Look," she said after a moment, "would you know it if you saw it?"

"Would I recognize a creature of ancient Egypt reanimated after being entombed alive for millennia? I think so." He sighed. "You want me to stake out the area around the museum, don't you? Just in case it wanders by."

She stopped pacing and turned to face him. "Yes."

'If you're so sure it'll be at this party on Saturday night, why can't we wait until then?''

''Because today's Tuesday, and in four days who knows how many more children may die.''

Henry shoved his hands deep into the pockets of his leather overcoat and sat down on one of the wood and cement benches scattered out in front of the museum. A cold, damp wind skirted the building, dead leaves rising up and performing a dance macabre in the gusts and eddies. The occasional car appeared to be scurrying for cover, fragile contents barely barricaded against the night.

This wasn't going to work. The odds of him running into the mummy, even in Vicki's limited search area, because it just happened to be casting a spell as he wandered by were astronomical. He pulled a hand free and checked his watch. Three twelve. He'd still be able to get in a good three hours of writing if he went home now.

Then a wandering breeze brought a familiar scent. He stood and had anyone been watching it would have seemed he disappeared.

A lone figure walked east on Bloor, jacket collar turned up against the cold, chin and elbows tucked in tight, eyes half closed. Ignoring the red light at Queen's Park Road, he started across the intersection, following the silver plume of his breath.

''Good morning, Tony.''

''Jesus Christ, man.'' Tony scrambled to regain his footing as his purely instinctive sideways dive was jerked into a non-event by Henry's precautionary grip on his arm. ''Don't do that!''

''Sorry. You're out late.''

''Nah, I'm out early. You're out late.'' They reached the curb and Tony turned to peer at Henry's face. ''You hunting?''

''Not exactly. I'm waiting for a series of incredible co-incidences to occur so I can be a hero.''

''This Victory's idea?''

Henry smiled at the younger man. ''How could you tell?''

''Are you kidding?'' Tony snickered. ''It has Victory written all over it. You've got to watch her, Henry. Give her a chance, give any cop a chance—or any ex-cop," he amended, "and they'll try to run your life."

"My life?" Henry asked, allowing the civilized mask to slip a little.

Tony wet his lips, but he didn't back down. "Yeah," he said huskily, "your life, too."

Henry played with the Hunger a little, allowing it to rise as he traced the line of jaw, then forcing it back down again as he admitted he had no real desire to feed. "You should get some sleep," he suggested over the wild pounding of Tony's heart. "I think you've already had enough excitement for one night."

"Wha . . . ?"

"I can smell him all over you." Henry heard the blood rush up into Tony's face, saw the smooth curve of cheek flush darkly. "It's all right." He smiled. "No one else can."

"He wasn't like you . . ."

"I should certainly hope not."

"I mean, he wasn't . . . it wasn't . . . well, it was but . . . I mean . . ."

"I know what you mean." He made the smile a promise and held it until he saw that Tony understood. "I'd walk you home, but I have an assignment to complete."

"Yeah." Tony sighed, tugged at his jeans, and began to walk away. A few paces down the road, he turned. "Hey, Henry. Those crazy ideas that Victory gets? Well, most times they turn out not to be so crazy after all."

It was Henry's turn to sigh as he spread his arms. "I'm still out here."

". . . leave a message after the tone."

"Vicki? Celluci. It's four o'clock, Wednesday afternoon. One of the uniforms just told me they saw you poking around the drains behind the museum this morning. What the fuck do you think you're doing? You're looking for a mummy, not a goddamned Ninja Turtle.

"By the way, if you find anything—and I mean anything—and you don't immediately let me know, I'm going to kick your ass from here to Christmas."

The house and garden looked vaguely familiar, like a childhood memory too far in the past to put a name or a

*place to. Remaining a cautious distance away, she walked
around to the back, knowing before she saw them that there'd
be hollyhocks by the kitchen door, that the patio would be
made of irregular gray flagstones, that the roses would be
in bloom. It was sunny and warm and the lawn smelled like
it had just been mowed—in fact, there against the garage
was the old push lawn mower that she'd used every Monday
evening on their handkerchief-sized lawn in Kingston.*

*The baseball glove she'd inherited from an older cousin
lay by the back step, the lacing she'd repaired standing out
against the battered leather in a way she didn't think it
really had. Her fringed denim jacket, the last thing her father bought her before he left, swayed from the clothesline.*

*The garden seemed to go on forever. She began to ex-
plore, moving slowly at first, then faster and faster, suddenly aware that something followed close behind. She
circled the house, raced up the front path, leapt up onto the
porch, and came to a full stop with her hand on the doorknob.*

"No."

It wanted her to go in.

*The knob began to turn and her hand turned with it. She
could see her reflection in the door's window. It had to be
her reflection, although for a moment she thought she saw
herself inside the house looking out.*

*Whatever had been following her in the garden came up
onto the porch. She could feel the worn boards move under
its tread and in the window she saw the reflected gleam of
glowing red eyes.*

"No!"

*She dragged her fingers off the doorknob and, almost in-
capacitated by fear, forced herself to turn around.*

Vicki shoved her glasses at her face and peered at the
clock. Two forty-six.

"I don't have time for this," she muttered, settling back
against the pillows, heart still slamming against her ribs. In
barely two hours she'd be heading over to Henry's which
made sleep the priority of the moment. Although that incident at the museum had obviously spooked her more than
she'd thought, dream analysis would just have to wait. She
dropped her glasses back where they belonged, stretched up

a long arm, and switched off the light. "I'm going to blacken the next set of glowing red eyes that wakes me up," she promised her subconscious.

A few moments later, lying awake in the dark, she frowned. She hadn't thought of that jacket in years.

Thursday night, the house stood alone on a gray plain and the dream began by the front door. The compulsion to open it was too strong to resist and she walked in, closely followed. She caught just a glimpse of the contents of the first room when the light dimmed and she fought to hold it down.

It wanted to see what was in the house. Well, it could just take a flying fuck.

Although her head felt as if it had been slammed repeatedly between two large rocks, Vicki woke feeling smug.

She was giving him more of a fight than he'd anticipated. His lord would not be pleased. As she had no protecting gods, merely a strongly developed sense of self, the failure would be perceived as being his.

Akhekh did not tolerate failure and his punishments were such that anything became preferable to facing them.

He needed more power.

In spite of the the cold and the damp, a Friday afternoon spent in the park beat the hell out of a Friday afternoon spent with the Riel Rebellion and grade ten chemistry. Brian tightened his grip across Louise's shoulders and turned her face up to meet his.

Now this is what I call getting an education! he thought as her lips parted and she flicked at his tongue with hers. *I wonder if she'll let me slip my hand up under her . . . ouch. Guess not.*

He opened his eyes, just to see what another person looked like from that angle, and frowned as he saw a well-dressed man watching them from no more than five feet away. *Oh, great. A pervert. Or a cop. Maybe we should . . . we should . . .*

"Brian?" Louise pulled back as he went limp. "Cut it

out.'' His head flopped forward onto her shoulder. "I mean it, Brian. You're scaring me. Brian?

"Oh, my God.''

He settled back on the bed, throwing the bags of feathers to the floor. Someday soon he'd have a proper headrest made.

It was eleven forty-three—this culture's preoccupation with the division of time into ridiculously small units never failed to amuse him—and she would be asleep by now, her ka at its most vulnerable. Tonight she would not be able to stand against him; he would throw all the power from the ka he had absorbed this afternoon at her defenses.

He closed his eyes and sent his ka forth, following the path his lord had laid out, entering through the image of his lord's eyes.

It was as if something held her elbow and walked her through the house, observing, discarding, searching. She couldn't shake free. She couldn't dim the lights.

She couldn't let it find what it needed.

Except she had no idea of what that was.

They climbed a staircase and started down a long corridor with a multitude of doors off to either side. As they reached for the knob of the second door, she saw the pencil lines and the dates, realized who waited within, and thought—or spoke, she wasn't sure—"Not the third door, anything but the third door," and tried to push them forward.

It stopped her, turned her, walked her down the hall, and into the third room. When they came out, it moved her on. It never came back to the second room.

Obviously, it had never read Aesop's fables.

She managed to protect her mother, Celluci, and Henry. It found everything else.

Everything.

He knew how she would suffer. It would take a while to arrange, even with some of the necessary influences already in place, but his lord could not help but be pleased with the result.

* * *

"You don't look so good. Are you all right?"

Vicki shifted her grip on the aluminum baseball bat and managed a smile. "I'm okay. I'm just a little tired."

"I'm sorry I haven't turned up any leads these last couple of nights but, to be honest, I never expected to."

"That's all right. It was a long shot. Henry . . ." She sat down on the edge of the bed and with one finger stroked the patch of red gold hair in the center of his chest. ". . . are you still dreaming?"

Henry pulled the sheet aside to expose a ragged clutch of multiple holes in the mattress. "I drove my fingers through here this morning," he said dryly. He flicked the sheet back, then covered her hand with his. "If I hadn't caught a hint of your scent on the pillow, I don't know how much more damage I might have done." She looked away and he decided not to say the rest, not to tell her that she gave him reason to hold onto his sanity. Instead, he asked, "Why?"

"I just wondered if they were getting worse."

"They haven't changed. You getting tired of standing guard?"

"No. I just . . ." She couldn't tell him. The dream had seemed so important while it was going on, but now, faced with Henry's basic terror, it seemed stupidly abstract and meaningless.

"You just?" Henry prodded, knowing full well from her expression that she wasn't going to tell him.

"Nothing."

"Look at the bright side." He brought her hand to his mouth and kissed the scars on the inside of her wrist. "Tonight's the night of the party. One way or another, something's bound to . . ."

". . . happen." Vicki drew her hand away and straightened Henry's arm. Sliding her glasses back up her nose, she leaned the bat against the end of the bed. "One way or another."

Ten

"Oh, my God."

"What's wrong?"

Vicki wet her lips. "Absolutely nothing. You look . . . uh, good." Henry's costume had been made traditional in a score of movies—turn-of-the-century formal wear with a broad scarlet ribbon cutting diagonally across the black and a full-length opera cloak falling in graceful folds to the floor. The effect was amazing. And it wasn't the contrast between the black and the white and the sculptured pale planes of face and the sudden red/gold brilliance that was Henry's hair. No, Vicki decided, the attraction was in the way he wore it. Few men would have the self-assurance, the well-bred arrogance to look comfortable in such an outfit; Henry looked like, well, like a vampire. *The kind you'd like to run into in a dark alley. Several times.* "In fact, you look better than good. You look amazing."

"Thank you." Henry smiled and smoothed the sleeve of his jacket down until only a quarter inch of white cuff showed. A heavy gold ring gleamed on his right hand. "I'm glad you approve."

He could feel the years settling on him with the clothing, feel the Henry Fitzroy who wrote romance novels and was occasionally permitted to play detective submerge into the greater whole. Tonight, he would walk among mortals; a shadow amid their bright lights and gaiety, a hunter in the night. *Good lord, I'm beginning to sound as melodramatic as one of my own books.*

"I still think you've got a lot of chutzpah going to this party as a vampire. Aren't you taking a big chance?"

"And what chance is that? Discovery?" He draped the cloak over his arm and peered at her in the classic Hammer Films Dracula pose. "What you're looking at here is the

purloined letter trick; hiding in plain sight.'' Dropping the
pose, he smiled down at her. ''And it isn't the first time
I've done it. Think of it as a smoke screen. Halloween calls
for a disguise. If Henry Fitzroy is a vampire on Halloween,
then obviously he isn't the rest of the year.''

Vicki draped one leg over the arm of the chair and smoth-
ered a yawn. ''I'm not sure about that logic,'' she muttered.
Early mornings and late nights were beginning to take their
toll and a four-hour nap in the afternoon hadn't done much
beyond throwing her internal clock even further out of
whack. Barely more than a year away from the twenty-four
hour aspect of police work, she was amazed at how quickly
she'd lost her ability to adapt. The evening spent with her
weights had gotten the blood flowing a little, washing away
some of the fatigue. Henry's appearance had started things
moving faster yet.

Henry's nose twitched as he picked up the sudden inten-
sifying of her scent and he lifted one eyebrow, murmuring
softly, ''I know what you're thinking.''

She felt herself flush but managed to keep her voice tol-
erably casual even as she shifted position in the chair and
crossed her legs. ''Don't start anything you can't finish,
Henry. You've already eaten.''

The Hunger had been blunted earlier, a necessity if he
was to spend the evening in close proximity to mortals and
be able to think of anything except the life that flowed beneath clothes and skin, but Vicki's interest had resharpened
an edge or two. ''I haven't started anything,'' he pointed
out, not bothering to hide his smile. ''I'm not the one
squirming in my . . .''

''Henry!''

''. . . seat,'' he finished quietly as the phone rang. ''Excuse me a moment. Good evening. Henry Fitzroy speaking.
Oh, hello, Caroline. Yes, it *has* been a while. Working on
my latest book for the most part.''

Caroline. Vicki recognized the name. While Henry was
no more her exclusive possession than she was his, she
couldn't help but feel . . . well, smug. She not only shared
Henry's bed, which the other woman no longer did, but she
shared the mysteries of Henry's nature, which the other
woman never had.

"Unfortunately, I have plans for tonight, but thank you for asking. Yes. Perhaps. No, I'll call you."

As he hung up the phone, Vicki shook her head. "You know, of course, that there's a special circle in hell for those people who make promises to call, then don't."

"They'll probably run out of room long before my time." Henry's voice trailed off. *And then again, maybe not.* While he continued to dream of the sun, every dawn might be his last. For the first time, he looked beyond the possibility of his death to all the things it would leave undone. He stood quietly for a moment, hand resting lightly on the phone, then came to a decision.

Vicki watched him curiously as he came around and knelt, capturing her hands, opera cloak pooling around his legs. While she had no objection to having handsome men at her feet, she had an uneasy feeling that the situation was about to get uncomfortable.

"You're right, I'm not going to call," he began. "But I think you need to know why. I can feed from a chance encounter with a stranger and not feel I'm betraying anything, but when I feed from Caroline I feel I'm betraying you both. Her, because I can give her so little of what I am and you because I have given you all of me."

Suddenly more frightened than smug, Vicki tried to pull her hands free. "Don't . . ."

Henry let them go but stayed where he was. "Why not? Tomorrow's dawn might be the one I've been waiting for."

"Well, it isn't!"

"You don't know that." At this moment, his death had become less important than what he had to say. "What will it change if I say it?"

"Everything. Nothing. I don't know." She took a deep breath and wished the light were dimmer, so she couldn't see his face so clearly. So he couldn't see hers. "Henry, I can sleep with you. I can feed you. I can be your friend and your guardian, but I can't . . ."

"Love me? Don't you?"

Did she?

"Is it because of how you feel about Mike?"

"Celluci?" Vicki snorted. "Don't be a fool. Mike Celluci is my best friend and, yes, I love him. But I don't *love* him and I don't *love* you."

"Don't you? Not either of us? Or both of us?"

Both of them . . . ?

"I'm not asking you to choose, Vicki. I'm not even asking you to admit the way you feel." Henry stood and twitched the cloak back over his shoulders. "I just thought you should know that I love you."

It almost hurt to breathe, everything felt so tight. "I know. I've known since last Thursday. Here." She touched herself lightly on the chest. "You gave yourself to me completely, with no strings. If that's not love, it's a damned close approximation." She got to her feet, moved a careful distance away, then turned to face him. "I can't do that. I come with too many strings. If I cut them all, I'll—I'll fall apart."

He spread his hands. "I'm not demanding a commitment. I just wanted to tell you while I could."

"You have an eternity, Henry."

"The dream of the sun . . ."

"You told me you've almost gotten used to it." If the effects had gotten stronger and he hadn't told her, she was going to wring his neck.

"I'm sure Damocles got used to the sword, but it's still only a matter of time."

"Time! Jesus Christ, look at the time! That party started half an hour ago. We'd better get moving." Vicki grabbed up her bag and headed for the door.

Henry arrived long before she did, teetering between anger and amusement at her sudden change of subject as he blocked the exit with a swirl of satin. "We?"

"Yeah, we. I'll be waiting in the car as backup."

"No, you won't."

"Yes, I will. Get out of the way."

"Vicki, in case you've forgotten, it's dark out there and you can't see anything."

"So?" Her brows drew down and her tone grew heated. "I can hear. I can smell. I can sit in the fucking car for hours and not do anything. But I'm coming with you. *You* are not trained in this sort of thing."

"I am not *trained* in this sort of thing?" Henry repeated slowly. "For hundreds of years I have fit myself into society, been the unseen hunter in their midst." As he spoke, he allowed the civilized mask to slip. "And you *dare* to tell me I am not trained in this sort of thing."

Vicki wet her lips, unable to look away, unable to move away. She thought she'd become used to what Henry was; she realized, now, she seldom saw it. A trickle of sweat ran down her side and she suddenly, desperately, had to go to the bathroom. *Right. Vampire. I keep forgetting.* Half of her mind wanted to run like hell and the other half wanted to kick his feet out from under him and beat him to the floor. *Oh, for Chrissakes, Vicki, get your goddamned hormones under control.*

"All right," her voice shook only a little, "you've had more training than I could ever hope to have. Your point. But I'm still going to go with you and wait in the car." She managed to raise a cautionary hand as he opened his mouth. "And *don't* tell me it's too dangerous," she warned. "I won't face anything tonight that's more dangerous than what I'm facing right now."

Henry blinked, then started to laugh. After four hundred and fifty years, he could recognize when he'd been outmaneuvered.

"This is good. This is very good." He looked out into the room filled with powerful men and women and in his mind's eyes saw them bowing before the altar of Akhekh, giving their power and those it commanded into the hands of his god.

George Zottie bowed his head, pleased that his master was pleased.

"I will move amongst them for a time. You may introduce me as you see fit. Later, when they hold thoughts of me and I can touch their ka, you will bring them to the room I have prepared, so I may speak with them one at a time."

Henry had no need to use any persuasion to get into the Solicitor General's large house on Summerside Drive nor did he expect to have to use much to stay. Arrival at this type of party implied the right to attend. He nodded at the young man who opened the door and swept past him toward the greatest concentration of sound. Servants did not require an explanation, something modern society tended to forget.

The huge formal living/dining room had been decorated in subdued Halloween. Black and orange candles glowed in a pair of antique silver candelabra, the table had been covered by a brilliant orange cloth, the flowers both in vases and in the large centerpiece were black roses and the wine glasses were black crystal—Henry assumed the wine had not been colored orange. Even the waiters, who moved gracefully among the crowd with trays of canapes or drinks, wore orange and black plaid cummerbunds and ties.

He took a glass of mineral water, smiled in a way that set the server's pulse pounding, and moved further into the room. Many of the women wore floor-length gowns from a variety of periods and just for an instant he saw his father's court at Windsor, the palace of the Sun King at Versailles, the Prince Regent's ballroom in Brighton. Smoothing a nonexistent wrinkle from the front of his jacket, he wondered if perhaps he shouldn't have taken the opportunity to indulge in the peacock colors this age normally denied to men.

The costumes on the men ranged from flamboyant to minor variations on street wear—unless the brown tweed suit stood for something or someone Henry didn't recognize. Two additional vampires glared at each other across the broad shoulders of a Keystone Cop. Having joined their various police departments before the height requirements had been relaxed, all the police present were large, usually tall and burly both. A couple, after years of patrolling a desk, had added an insulating layer of fat. The politicians scattered throughout the crowd were easily spotted by their lack of functional bulk.

Henry was not only the shortest man in the room, by some inches, but he also appeared to be the youngest. Neither mattered. These were people who recognized power, height and age came a distant second.

"Hello, I'm Sue Zottie."

The Solicitor General's wife was a tiny woman with luminous dark eyes, and a coil of chestnut hair piled regally upon her head. Her dark green velvet Tudor gown added majesty to what had been labeled more than once in society pages as a quiet beauty. Instinct took over and Henry raised the offered hand to his lips. She didn't seem to mind.

"Henry Fitzroy."

"Have—have we met before?"

He smiled and her breathing grew a little ragged. "No, we haven't."

"Oh." She meant to ask him what police force he was with or if, perhaps, he was a junior member of her husband's staff, but the questions got lost in his eyes. "George is in the library with Mr. Tawfik, if you need to speak with him. The two of them have been in there for most of the evening."

"Thank you."

She'd never felt quite so completely thanked before and walked away wondering why George had never invited that lovely young man over for dinner.

Henry took a sip of his mineral water. Tawfik. His quarry, it seemed, was in the library.

It was cold in the car with the window open, but sightless, Vicki couldn't afford to block off her other senses. The wind smelled of woodsmoke and decaying leaves and expensive perfume—she supposed the latter was endemic to the neighborhood—and brought her the noise of distant traffic; a door, fairly close, opening and closing; a phone, either very close or beside an open window, demanding to be answered; a late trick-or-treater imploring his mother to cover just one more block. Two teenaged girls, too old for candy, reviewed the day as they walked down the other side of the street. As her eyes got steadily worse, her hearing seemed to be getting better—or maybe she just had to pay more attention to what she heard.

Vicki had no doubt that based on sound alone, she'd be able to pick these girls out of a lineup. One pair of flats, one pair of heels; the soft shirk, shirk of polyester sleeves rubbing against the body of a polyester jacket; the almost musical chime of tiny, metal bangles, chiming in counterpoint so they each must be wearing a set. One sounded as if she had a mouth full of gum, the other as if she had a mouth full of braces.

". . . and like she was just pressing her breasts up against him."

"You mean she was pressing her padding up against him."

"No!"

"Uh-huh, and then she has the nerve to say she really loves *Bradley* . . ."

And what do you children know about love? Vicki wondered, as they moved out of earshot. *Henry Fitzroy, the bastard son of Henry VIII, the Duke of Richmond, says he loves me. What do you think of that?* She sighed. *What do I think of that?*

She dragged her fingernail against the vents in the dashboard of the BMW, then sighed again. *Okay, so he's afraid of dying, I can understand that. When you've lived in darkness for over four hundred years and then start dreaming about daylight . . .* A sudden thought struck her. *Jesus, maybe he's afraid of dying tonight. Maybe he thinks he can't deal with the mummy.* She fumbled for the door handle but stopped herself before she actually got the door open. *Don't be ridiculous, Vicki. He's a vampire, a predator, a proven survivor. A friend. And he loves me.*

And I'm going to drag up that goddamned non sequitur every goddamned time I think about him from now on. She raised her eyes to the heavens she couldn't see. *First Celluci and his wanting to have a "talk" and now Henry and his declarations. It isn't enough we have a mummy rampaging around the city? Do I need this?*

It's just like a man to want to complicate a perfectly good relationship.

Sliding down on the leather seat until her head was even with the lower edge of the window, she closed her eyes and settled down to wait. But only because there wasn't anything else she could do.

With the lights in the hall turned down to a dim orange glow—extending the Halloween motif out of the actual party area—the curve of the stairs threw a pool of deep shadow just outside the library door. Shrouded by the pocket of darkness, Henry wrapped himself in his cloak and leaned back against the raw silk wallpaper to consider his next move.

According to Sue Zottie, the Solicitor General and Mr. Tawfik were in the library—but he could sense three lives on the other side of the wall and there was nothing to suggest that any of the three had just broken free after millennia of confinement. All three hearts beat to the same rhythm and . . .

No. To an *identical* rhythm.

The hair rose on the back of Henry's neck as he pressed himself farther away from the light. Hearts did not beat so completely in sync by accident. He had, in fact, heard it happen only once before, in 1537 when, faint and dizzy with loss of blood, he had pressed his mouth to the wound in Christina's breast and drunk, conscious of nothing save the heat of her touch and the painful throbbing of his heart in time with hers.

What was happening in that room?

For the first time, Henry felt a faint unease at the thought of actually facing the creature who had been so long entombed. The time of change had been the most powerful, all encompassing experience in his life, not only in the seventeen years before but in the four hundred and fifty-three years since, and if the mummy could call that kind of power to its control . . .

"You think you're up to this wizard-priest?" Celluci had asked.

His answer had been scornful. *"I am not without resources."*

He had defeated wizards in the past, relying on strength and speed and force of will, but they had followed rules he recognized and had not come with their own dark god.

"You think you're up to this wizard-priest?"

The voice of memory had grown sarcastic and Henry's brows drew down. He certainly wasn't going to give Celluci the pleasure of seeing him give up without a fight.

The three hearts paused, then two began again in tandem and one beat to a rhythm all its own.

He had to get into that library. Perhaps through the gardens . . .

Then the single heartbeat approached the door and Henry froze. The knob turned, the door opened, and a woman with close-cropped salt-and-pepper hair stepped out into the hall. Henry recognized the Chief Justice of the Supreme Court of Ontario from a recent newspaper photograph although the picture had not managed to capture either her very obvious self-assurance or her sense of humor. The cavalier costume she wore suited both.

As Henry watched, she brushed the feather in her hat against the floor in a credible bow and said, "You'll have my complete support in this, George. Mr. Tawfik. I'll see you both at the ceremony and I'll tell Inspector Cantree you want to see him now." Then, grinning, she replaced the hat and headed down the hall toward the party. She didn't appear to be enchanted.

There were now only two heartbeats sounding in the library—Tawfik's and the Solicitor General's—and they sounded as one. Through the open door, Henry heard a low voice ask thoughtfully, "And what is Inspector Frank Cantree like?"

"He won't be easy to convince."

"Good. We prefer, my lord and I, to work with the strong; they last longer."

"Cantree believes that independence yields greater results than conformity."

"Does he now."

"They say he's incorruptible."

"That in itself can be used."

Used for what? Henry wondered. There was something in the tone that reminded Henry of his father. He didn't find that at all comforting. His father had been a cruel and Machiavellian prince who could play tennis with a courtier in the morning and have him executed for treason before sunset. Still motionless, he frowned as he watched a large man in a pirate costume walk down the hall on the balls of his feet, carrying himself as though he were perpetually ready for a fight, his expression just to one side of suspicious. Bearing and attitude both said "Cop" so strongly that Henry doubted the man had ever been of any use undercover.

The newcomer paused in the doorway, one beefy hand dropping to the pommel of the plastic cutlass that hung at his hip. Instinct seemed to be warning him of a threat within the room and his tone was carefully, aggressively neutral. "Mr. Zottie? You wanted to speak with me?"

"Ah, Inspector Cantree. Please, come in."

As Cantree stepped over the threshold, Henry raced forward, letting the heavy folds of the cape slip from his shoulders to the floor. Over short distances, he could move almost faster than mortal eyes could register but not while dragging meters of fabric behind him. Sliding between the burly Inspector and the door, he sped shadow silent into the room, along a book-covered wall, and behind a floor-to-ceiling barrier of heavy curtain.

Convenient, he thought, his back pressed against glass, his feet turned to either side so as not to protrude, his entire body motionless again. Over the sound of three heartbeats, he heard the door close, the hardwood floor contract beneath the Inspector's weight, but no hue and cry. His entry had gone unnoticed.

He felt something. It brushed against his ka with all the innocent strength of a desert storm, almost dragging him from the light trance he'd been maintaining for most of the evening. Before he could begin to react, the barrier wards, set up more from old habit than perceived necessity, diverted the touch and only by lowering them could he hope to find it again.

For an instant, he weighed what he did tonight against such tantalizing potential and, regretfully, left the wards in place. His lord perceived this evening as the initial gathering of a core of acolytes—which it was, in addition to an initial gathering of a more secular power—and his lord would not look kindly upon personal indulgences during such a time.

The touch had been undirected, accidental, therefore it would have to wait.

But the glorious memory of it lingered in the back of his mind and he vowed it would not have to wait long.

"Inspector Frank Cantree, Mr. Anwar Tawfik."

Henry slid the curtains apart a centimeter, movement masked by the quiet sound of flesh touching flesh.

"Please take a seat, Inspector. Mr. Tawfik has a proposal that I think you'll find very interesting."

He watched the Inspector lower himself onto an expensive leather sofa and saw Solicitor General Zottie move across the room to stand beside a wing chair, its high back barely a meter from his hiding place, completely hiding Anwar Tawfik from Henry's line of sight.

This is beginning to feel like some cheap horror movie, Henry mused, *where the creature rises out of the chair to*

*face the camera at the end of the scene. I guess I wait for
my cue.* He'd make his move after Cantree left the room and
before another high ranking official took the Inspector's
place. Zottie was merely mortal and could be quickly dealt
with. As for the mummy—if Tawfik *was* the mummy—it had
proven itself to be a taker of innocent lives. Henry didn't
particularly care what its reasons were. The time for it to
die was millennia past.

From where he stood, he could see Cantree's gaze flick-
ing constantly over the room, observing, noting, remembering. It was apparently a habit all police officers acquired,
for Henry had seen both Vicki and Celluci perform variations on the theme.

Then Tawfik began to talk, his voice low and intense. To
Henry it sounded like law and order generalities, but obviously Cantree heard something more. The movement of his
gaze began to slow until it locked on the man—on the creature—in the chair. Certain words began to be repeated and
after each the Inspector nodded and his expression grew
blank. A rivulet of sweat—the library was at least ten degrees warmer than the rest of the house—ran unnoticed down
his face.

Unease danced icy fingers along Henry's spine as Tawfik's cadence grew more and more hypnotic and the key
words occurred more and more frequently. It was magic,
Henry could sense that, however much it looked like something less arcane, but magic completely outside his understanding. A working for good or evil he could have sensed,
but this was neither. It just was.

When all three hearts beat to an identical rhythm, Tawfik
paused, then said, "His ka is open.

"Frank Cantree. Can you hear me?"

"Yes."

"From this moment on, your primary concern is to obey
me. Do you understand?"

"Yes."

"You will protect my interests above all else. Do you
understand?"

"Yes."

"You will protect me. Do you understand?"

"Yes." But this time after the single syllable of assent,
Cantree's mouth continued to work.

"What is it?"

Although independent movement should have been impossible under the conditions of the spell, Cantree's lips curled slightly as he answered. "There is someone standing behind the curtains behind your chair."

For a heartbeat, the scene hung in limbo, then Henry threw the curtains aside, charged forward, came face-to-face with the creature rising from the chair, and froze.

He got a jumbled impression of gold leather sandals, a linen kilt, a wide belt, a necklace of heavy beads that half covered a naked chest, hair too thick and black to be real, and then the kohl-circled eyes under the wig caught his and all he saw was a great golden sun centered in an azure sky.

In blind panic, he wrenched his gaze away, turned, and dove through the window.

Although she knew it was impossible, that the night for her was as dark as it would ever get, Vicki suddenly felt that it had grown darker still; as if a cloud had covered the moon she couldn't see and the shadows had thickened. Senses straining, she slowly got out of the car, allowing the door to close but not to latch. A quick tug would turn on the interior light and enable her to at least find her way back again.

They pay high enough taxes in this neighborhood, you'd think they could manage a few more streetlights.

The night seemed to be waiting, so Vicki waited with it. Then, from not so far away, came the sound of breaking glass, the violent snapping of small branches, and, approaching more quickly than possible, leather soles slapping out a panicked flight against concrete.

There was no time to think, to weigh her move. Vicki stepped away from the car directly into the path of the sound.

They both went down.

The impact drove the breath out of her lungs and her jaw slammed up with enough force so every tooth in her head shuddered with the impact. She took a moment to thank any gods who might be listening that her tongue had been tucked safely out of the way even as she grabbed onto what felt like expensive lapels. During the landing, her head bounced off the pavement, the glancing blow creating an impressive fireworks display on the inside of her lids. Somehow she managed to keep her grip. Not until cold hands grabbed her wrists and yanked them effortlessly away did she realize who she held. Or more accurately, had held.

"Henry? Damnit, it's me, Vicki!"

Sanctuary. The sun was rising. He must reach sanctuary.

Vicki twisted and, barely in time, wrapped herself around Henry's right leg. If she couldn't stop him, maybe she could slow him down.

"Henry!"

A weight clung to his leg, impeding his flight. He bent to rip it free and a familiar scent washed over him, masking the stink of his own fear.
Vicki.
She said she would be there when the dawn reached out to take him. She would fight with him. For him. Would not let him burn.
Sanctuary.

The tension went out of his muscles and his fingers loosened where they crushed her shoulder. Tentatively, she let him go, ready to launch herself forward should he start to run again.

"The car's just back here." Actually, she'd kind of lost track of where the car was but hoped Henry would turn and see it. "Come on. Can you drive?"

"I—I think so."

"Good." Other questions could wait. Not only did the echoes of her skull hitting the sidewalk make it difficult to hear the answers, but from the sounds that had preceded his flight, Henry had just left a house full of police officers by way of a closed window. They'd be playing the chase scene any second and that would lead into a whole new lot of questions there were no answers for.

Ms. Nelson, can you tell us why your friend turned into a smoldering pile of ash in the holding cell at dawn?

One hand held tightly to his jacket as Henry surged toward the car, continuing to grasp it until her other hand touched familiar metal. She scrambled to get into her own seat the moment she figured out where it was, then watched him anxiously—or rather watched his shadow against the lights of the dash—as he started the engine and pulled carefully out of the parking space. She had no idea why people weren't boiling out of the Solicitor General's house like wasps out of a disturbed nest, but she certainly wasn't going to complain about a clean getaway.

"Henry . . . ?"

"No." Most of the raw terror had faded, but even Vicki's presence wasn't enough to completely banish the fear. *I can feel the sun. It's hours to dawn and I can feel the sun.* "Let me get home first. Maybe then . . ."

"When you're ready. I can wait." Her voice was deliberately soothing even though she really wanted to grab him, and shake him, and demand to know what had happened in there. *If this is Henry's reaction to the mummy, we're in a lot more trouble than we thought.*

"Do I go after him, Master?"

"No. You are tied into the spell and the spell is not yet finished." He spat the words out, the power of his anger crackling almost visibly around him.

"But the others . . ."

"They can hear nothing that happens within this room. They did not hear the window break. They will not interrupt." With an effort, he forced his attention back to the multilayered spell of coercion he had been in the middle of evoking. "When I have finished with the Inspector, then you may search the grounds. Not before."

Inspector Cantree tossed his head and sweat began to soak through the armpits of his costume. His eyes rolled back and the muscles of his throat worked to produce a moan.

"It didn't hurt the others, Master."

"I know."

The ka that had touched him earlier with its magnificent, unending potential for power, had been within his grasp and he had been forced by circumstance to let it get away.

That did not please him.

But now he knew of its existence, and, more importantly, it knew of him. He would be able to find it again.

That pleased him very much.

* * *

When Vicki finally saw Henry's face in the harsh fluorescent glare of the elevator lights, it gave nothing away. Absolutely nothing. He might as well have been carved from alabaster for all the expression he wore. *This isn't good . . .*

Three teenagers—in what might or might not have been costumes—got on in the lobby, took one look at Henry and stood quietly in their corner, not a word, not a giggle until they got off on five.

And every cloud has a silver lining, Vicki mused as they filed silently out.

The last, finding courage in leaving, paused in the doorway and stage-whispered back. "What's he supposed to be?"

Why not?

"A vampire."

Hennaed curls bounced on sequined shoulders. "Not even close," was the disdainful judgment as the elevator door slid closed.

Vicki used her keys to let them into the condo, then followed close on Henry's heels as he strode down the hall and into the bedroom. She flicked on the light as he flung himself on the bed.

"I can feel the sun," he said softly.

"But it's hours until dawn."

"I know."

"Colonel Mustard, in the library, with a mummy. . . ."

Henry glared at her from under knotted brows. "What are you talking about?"

"Huh?" Vicki started and lowered her arm. She'd been doing a painful fingertip investigation of the goose egg on the back of her head. Fortunately, it appeared that her little meeting with the pavement outside the Solicitor General's house had done no lasting damage. *And a concussion would be just what I need right now.* "Oh. Nothing. Just thinking out loud." The party had put them ahead only in that they now *knew* what they'd only suspected before; the mummy was ensorcelling the people who controlled the police forces of Ontario, acquiring its own private army. No doubt it intended to set up its own state with its own state religion. It had, after all, brought its god along.

They had a name, Anwar Tawfik, the man she'd helped

out of the elevator at the Solicitor General's office. She couldn't prevent a twinge of sympathy, after three thousand years in a coffin, she'd be violently claustrophobic, too. *Still, I should've dropped the son of a bitch down the elevator shaft when I had the chance.*

She banged her fist against her thigh. "I don't think it can succeed at what it's attempting, but a lot of people are going to die proving that. And no one's going to believe us until it makes its move."

"Or a good while after it makes its move."

"What do you mean?"

"Who does the average citizen call when there's trouble?" Henry pointed out.

"The police."

"The police," Henry agreed.

"And it controls the police. Shit, shit, shit, shit."

"*Very* articulate."

Vicki's smile was closer to a snarl as she shifted position on the edge of the bed. "It looks like it's up to us."

Henry threw his forearm up over his eyes. "A lot of help I'll be."

"Look, you've been dreaming about the sun for weeks now and you're still functioning fine."

"Fine? Diving through that library window wasn't what I'd call fine."

"At least now you know you're not going crazy."

"No. I'm being cursed."

Vicki pulled his arm off his face and leaned over. The spill of light from the lamp just barely reached his eyes but, in spite of the masking shadows, she thought they looked as mortal as she'd ever seen them. "Do you want to quit?"

"What?" His laugh had a hint of bitter hysteria. "Life?"

"No, you idiot." She wrapped one hand around his jaw and rocked his head from side to side, hoping he couldn't read through her touch how frightened she was for him. "Do you want to quit the case?"

"I don't know."

Eleven

The absence of shadows against the wall told him he had slept late, his body trying vainly to regain some of the energy spent on spell-casting the night before. His tongue felt thick, his skin tight, and his bones as though they had been rough cast in lead. *Soon, a slave will wait at my bedside, a glass of chilled juice ready upon my awakening.* But *soon*, unfortunately, did him no good at the moment. He looked over at the clock—eleven fifty-six, oh three, oh four, oh five—and then tore his glance away before it could trap him further in the progression of time. Only half the day remained for him to feed and find the ka that burned so brightly.

Moving stiffly, he swung out of bed and made his way to the shower. The late Dr. Rax, who over the course of a varied career had been familiar with the sanitary facilities, or lack thereof, along the banks of the Nile, had considered North American plumbing to be the eighth wonder of the world. As gallons of hot water pounded the knots from his shoulders, he was inclined to agree.

By the time he finished a large breakfast and was lingering over a cup of coffee—an addiction every adult ka he had absorbed seemed to share—he no longer felt the weight of his age and was ready to face the day.

For a change, a cloudless blue sky arced up over the city, and, although the pale November sun appeared to shed little warmth, it was still a welcome sight. He took his cup to the wall of windows that prevented the other, more solid walls from closing in around him and looked down at the street. In spite of laws that forced most businesses to remain closed on the day known as Sunday, a number of people were taking advantage of the weather and spending time outside. A number of those people had small children in hand.

The series of individually tailored spells he had worked last night, each with its own complicated layering of controls, had drained him and the power he had remaining would barely be enough to keep him warm as he chose the child whose ka would replenish his. He was using power in a way he would never have dared when unsworn souls were few and even slaves had basic protections but, with nothing to stand in the way of his feeding, he saw no reason to hold back. Not one of the deaths could be traced to him—necessity had taught him millennia ago to take the mundane into account—and very shortly even that would cease to be a consideration. When the police and their political masters gave themselves to Akhekh, he, as High Priest, would be inviolate.

He had no idea how many sworn acolytes his lord needed in order to gain the strength to create another such as he. Forty-three had been the greatest number he had ever been able to gather in the past but, as that had been just before Thoth's priests had been instructed to intervene, he suspected that forty-four or forty-five would be enough. That the thirty ka to be gathered up in this time had been coerced would make only a minimal difference. He had used the smallest pieces of their ka necessary to convince them—in two cases those had been very small pieces indeed—and enough truth had been spoken during the spellbinding that their pledges would hold. The thirty coerced would be equivalent to no less than twenty free; a respectable beginning.

After the ceremony, he would not need to be as magically involved and would, therefore, need to feed less often.

"And when I find you, my bright and shining one . . ." He placed his empty cup down with the rest of the breakfast dishes and scooped up the opera cloak the Solicitor General had found outside the library door. ". . . I may never need to feed again." As the satin folds slid across his fingers, he basked in the remembered glow. This ka would stand out like a blaze of glory against the others in this city; now that he had touched it, it would not be able to hide from him. He was mildly curious about what kind of a man—for it had been only a man, there had been no mark of god or wizard about the presence—would carry such a ka, but curiosity paled beside his desire.

The opera cloak pooled about his feet. Perhaps he would return the young man's forgotten garment, and as their fingers touched he would look into his eyes and . . .

With such power at his command there would be nothing he could not do.

Tony wasn't sure what had driven him from his basement room this morning, but something had nagged him up out of sleep and onto the street. Two coffees and a double chocolate chip muffin in Druxy's had brought him no closer to an answer.

Hands shoved deep into the pockets of his jacket, he stood on the corner of Yonge and Bloor and waited for the light, effortlessly eavesdropping on the conversations around him, filtering out the yuppie concerns, paying close attention to a cluster of street kids complaining about the cold. At this time of the year, those who lived in parks and bus shelters worried first about surviving the coming winter and then about their next meal, their next smoke, their next bit of cash. They talked about the best places to panhandle, to turn tricks, what doorways were safe, what cop would cut a little slack, who'd been picked up, who'd died. Tony had survived on the street for almost five years and knew what talk had substance behind it and what talk was just wind. No one seemed to be saying anything that would clue him into whatever it was that had him so jumpy.

He walked west on Bloor, thin shoulders hunched high. The new jacket he wore, bought with money from a real honest-to-God steady job, kept him plenty warm enough, but old habits took time to break. Even after two months, he was still a little unsure about the job, afraid that it would vanish as suddenly as it had appeared and with it the room, the warmth, the regular meals . . . and Henry.

Henry trusted him, believed in him. Tony didn't know why, didn't really care why. The trust and the belief were enough. Henry had become his anchor. He didn't think it had anything to do with Henry being a vampire—although he had to admit that was pretty fucking awesome and it certainly didn't hurt that the sex was the best he'd ever had and just remembering it made him hot—he thought it had more to do with Henry just being a . . . well, being Henry.

The feeling that had driven him out and onto the street

had nothing to do with Henry, not specifically at least. Henry feelings, he could always recongize.

Dropping down onto the low wall in front of the Manulife Center, Tony rubbed at his temples and wished the feeling would go away. He had better things to do with his Sunday afternoon than wander about trying to find where the ants between his ears came from.

He kicked his heels against the concrete and watched the parade of people pass by. A baby in a backpack, barely visible under a hat and mittens and a scarf and a snowsuit, caught his attention and he grinned up at it, wondering if it could even move. *Jeez, the kid's gonna spend the first few years of its life only seeing where it's been. Probably grow up to be a politician.*

The baby appeared to be gazing in happy fascination at the man who walked along behind its parents although, as far as Tony could tell, he wasn't doing anything to attract its attention. He wasn't a bad looking man either; quite a bit of gray in the hair and a nose that hooked out into tomorrow but with a certain something that Tony found attractive.

Guess he likes kids. Sure is staring at that . . . that . . . Jesus, no.

Under the pale blue hat with its row of square-headed yellow ducks, the baby's face had gone suddenly slack. The bulk of its clothing held it upright, arms reaching out over the carrier but Tony knew, without the shadow of a doubt, that the baby was dead.

Cold fingers closed around his heart and squeezed. There was now no gray in the hair of the man who followed.

He killed it. Tony was more certain of that than he'd ever been of anything in his life. He didn't know how it had been done, nor did he care. *Jesus God, he killed it.*

And then the man turned, looked right at him, and smiled.

Tony ran, instinct guiding his feet. Horns sounded. A voice yelled protest after a soft collision. He ignored it all and ran on.

When even terror could no longer keep him moving, he collapsed in a shadowed doorway and forced great lungfuls of air past the taste of iron in the back of his throat. His whole body trembled and every breath drove a knife blade, barbed and razor sharp, up under his ribs. Exhaustion wrapped itself shroudlike around what he'd seen, dulling the immediacy, allowing him the distance to look at it again.

That man, or whatever he was, had killed the baby just by looking at it.

And then he turned and looked at me. But I'm safe. He can't find me here. I'm safe. No footsteps sounded in the alley, nothing threatened, but his scalp prickled and the flesh between his shoulder blades twisted into knots. *He didn't need to follow. He's waiting for me. Oh, God. Oh, Jesus. I don't want to die.*

The baby was dead.

They'll think the baby's asleep. They'll laugh about the way babies sleep through anything. Then they'll get home and they'll take it out and it won't be sleeping. Their baby will be dead and they won't know when or how or why it happened.

He scrubbed his palms across his cheeks.

But I know.

And he knows I know.

Henry.

Henry'll protect me.

Except that sunset wouldn't be for hours and he couldn't stop thinking of the baby's parents arriving home and finding . . . He couldn't just let that happen. He had to tell someone.

The card he pulled from his pocket had seen better days. Limp and stained, the name and number on it barely legible, it had been for years his link to another world. Clutching it tightly in a sweaty hand, Tony moved cautiously from his hidey-hole and went looking for a pay phone. Victory would know what to do. Victory always knew what to do.

"Nelson Investigations. No one is available to take your call, but if you leave your name and number, as well as a brief reason for your call, after the tone, I'll get back to you as soon as possible. Thank you."

"Shit." Tony slammed the receiver down and laid his forehead against the cool plastic of the phone. "Now what?" There was always the number scrawled on the back of the card, but somehow Tony doubted that Detective-Sergeant Michael Celluci would appreciate having this kind of thing dumped in his lap. "Whatever kind of thing it is. Jesus, Victory, where are you when I need you?"

He shoved the card back in his pocket and, after a cautious examination of the passing crowds, slipped out of the phone booth. Squinting at the sky, he began making his way back to Yonge and Bloor. He knew where Henry was and the hours between now and sunset would only seem like they were taking up the rest of his life. With any luck.

The boy had seen him feed; or been aware, at least, that he had fed. Apparently, there *were* a few in this age who had not built barriers of disbelief around their lives. The incident was of interest but placed him in no danger. Who would the boy tell? Who would believe him? Perhaps later he would search him out and, if he could not be used, he was young enough still that his life would be an adequate source of power.

At the moment, he had all the power he needed. He felt wonderful. An infant's life, so very nearly entirely unrealized potential, was a pleasure to absorb. Occasionally, in the past, when his fortunes were high, he would buy a female slave, have her impregnated by an acolyte, and devour the life of the child at the moment of its birth. The slave's birth pains and then the despair at the loss of her child became a sacrifice to Akhekh. Such nourishment took careful purchasing and then constant monitoring, however, as the children of some women could be claimed by the gods while still in the womb. Perhaps, with so few gods active, when Akhekh's temple had been built anew, he would be able to feed in such a way as a matter of course.

He raised his personal temperature another two degrees just because he had the power to spare. It was too lovely a day to return to the enclosure of his hotel room. He would walk to the park, ward a small area, and *soak up a few rays* while he searched for the ka that blazed so brightly.

"Mike, it's Vicki. It's about two-ten, Sunday afternoon. Call me when you've got time to talk." She hung up the phone and reached for her jacket. Now that they *knew* high-ranking police officers were involved and, given those same officers had already pulled him off the case, a tap on Celluci's phone line was a possibility; a slim one, granted, but

Vicki saw no reason to discount it just because the odds were ridiculously high. After all, they were hunting down an ancient Egyptian mummy and who'd want to figure the odds on that.

"An ancient Egyptian mummy named Anwar Tawfik." She hoisted her shoulder bag up into position. "How much do you want to bet that's not its real name." Still, it was the only name they had, so she planned on spending the afternoon checking the hotels clustered around the Royal Ontario Museum. Everything pointed to it having remained in that area and, from what Henry had to say, Mr. Tawfik apparently preferred to travel first class. She wondered briefly how it paid for such a lifestyle and muttered, "Maybe it has a platinum Egyptian Express card. Don't be entombed without it."

Henry.

Henry wanted to get as far away from this creature and its visions of the sun as was humanly possible. He didn't have to say it, it was painfully obvious. She doubted he'd be willing, or even able, to face the mummy again.

"So I guess that means it's up to me." Her glasses slid forward and she settled them firmly back on the bridge of her nose. "Just the way I like it best."

The vague, empty feeling, she ignored.

His ka swept over the city and found no trace of the life he had touched so briefly the night before. A ka with such potential should shine like a beacon and searching for it should only be a matter of following the blaze of light. He knew it existed. He had seen it, felt it. It should not be able to hide from him!

Where was it?

The connection between them had lasted less than a searing, glorious instant before the young man threw himself backward through the library window and away but even such a slight touch would enable him to gain access into the young man's ka. If he could find it.

Had the young man died in the night? Had he taken one of the miraculous traveling devices of this age and flown far away? His frustration grew as he brushed over a thousand kas that together burned less brightly than the one he desired.

And then he felt his own ka gripped by a greater power and, for a moment knew a sudden, all-encompassing fear. Recognition lessened the fear only slightly.

Why have you not given me the suffering of the one I claimed?

Lord, I . . . He had walked through the woman's ka and gathered all the information he needed for his lord's pleasure. He had intended to set it in motion the night before. Had he done so, the suffering would have begun. The touch of the intruder's ka had driven it right out of his mind.

No excuses.

It made no difference that the pain existed on the spiritual level only. His ka screamed.

"Are you all right?"

He felt strong hands around his arm, lifting him back into a sitting position, and knew the wards had broken. Slowly, because it hurt, he opened his eyes.

At first, while he fought his way free of the webs of pain, he thought the young man standing so solicitously by resembled the young man who had escaped him; who had been responsible for the delay in the working of his god's desire. Who had been responsible for the agony his god had seen fit to twist around him. A moment later, he saw the hair was lighter, the skin darker, the eyes gray rather than pale brown, but by then it didn't matter.

"You tipped over." The young man smiled tentatively. "Is there anything I can do?"

"Yes." He forced his throbbing head up enough to meet the other's gaze. "You can throw yourself in front of a subway."

Eyes widened and face muscles spasmed.

"Your last word must be Akhekh."

"Yes." Legs moved jerkily away. Body language screamed no.

He felt better. There had been nothing subtle about the coercion, but there had been no need. The young man would live such a short time that laying on an appearance of normalcy would be a waste. He could feel his lord following close behind, drinking in the despair and panic. The young man knew what he was about to do, he just couldn't stop himself from doing it.

Hopefully, his lord would be appeased until the chosen one could be delivered.

Vicki paused outside the Park Plaza Hotel and looked down at what she was wearing. Sensible shoes, gray cords, and a navy blue duffle coat were fine for most places in this city, but she had a feeling that when she walked through the door and into the lobby she was going to feel underdressed. The hotels she usually searched for suspects did not have a doorman; if someone was stationed out front, he was there as a lookout in case the police arrived. Adjoining shops sold cigarettes and condoms, not seven thousand dollar diamond and emerald necklaces. The windows would be opaque because of plywood, not because the glass had been impregnated with gold.

And I am not *being intimidated by a building.* The Park Plaza was directly across Bloor Street from the museum and therefore the logical place to begin a search for Anwar Tawfik. She strode past the doorman, swung through the revolving door at a speed that would have swept any other occupants off their feet, and paused again in the echoing quiet of the green marble lobby.

Some things, however, were universal to hotels. The registration desk had two harried clerks behind it and eleven people—eleven very well-dressed people, Vicki noted—attempting to check in. She sighed silently and got into line, mourning the loss of the badge that would have made waiting unnecessary.

His stride had nearly steadied by the time he reached the hotel. The vast amount of power he had absorbed from the infant's ka had acted as a buffer between the anger of his lord and any lasting damage. There had been times in the past when he had crawled away from such an encounter on his belly and it had taken days of pain and fear to recover his strength. Thankfully, the new acolytes would soon be sworn and his lord's attention would not then be directed so exclusively at him.

Akhekh, while not one of the more powerful gods, was still very conscious of services owed in return for immortality.

The liveried doorman scurried to open the door and he

swept past the tinted glass and into the lobby, stopping abruptly at the touch of a familiar ka.

She looked much as she perceived herself although in truth was a little less tall, a little less blonde, and rather more determined of jaw. What was his lord's chosen doing here, however? He reached out and gently stroked the surface of her thoughts. After the nights he had spent mapping it, her ka could hold no secrets from him.

He frowned as he uncovered the reason for her presence. She searched for him? She was no wizard to be aware of his wandering in her . . . ah, she searched at the request of another. Apparently, he had not been as thorough at the museum as he had thought. No matter. He smiled. His lord would have twice the pleasure for the plans he had made for the suffering of Ms. Nelson could be adapted to include Detective-Sergeant Michael Celluci as well, without even the need to search the detective's ka.

But, in the meantime, it would not do for the chosen one to disrupt his sanctuary. Without so much as touching her awareness, he laid a false memory over the parameters of her search.

What am I doing back in line? Vicki wondered, shaking her head and turning for the door. *They're not going to have any more information now than they did a moment ago.* Computer listings could be changed, Anwar Tawfik might not be the name he was registered under, and if the manager had never heard of him, there wasn't much else she could do but check the rest of the hotels in the area.

Maybe she'd think of another angle to hit later.

"Yes, it was a very pleasant evening, Mrs. Zottie. Thank you. Now, if I could speak with your husband . . ." He looked out over the city as he waited for the Solicitor General to pick up the phone. When he stood close to the wall of windows, the rest of the suite seemed less enclosing.

"You wished to speak with me, Master?"

"I assume you are alone?"

"Yes, Master. I took the call in my study."

"Good." It had become necessary to ask for the effect of the control spell had Zottie's mental abilities deteriorating at an unanticipated pace. Fortunately, his assistance would be necessary only until the others were pledged.

"Pay attention, there's something important I want you to arrange . . ."

Henry had faced enemies before, faced them and conquered them, but his nature denied him the ability to face the sun. Vicki had offered him a chance to leave—she'd understand if he ran from this creature he had no chance of defeating.

She'd understand. But would I?

Forcing his muscles to respond, he swung his legs off the bed and sat up, golden afterimages of the sun still dancing across the periphery of his vision.

When I face this wizard-priest, I face the sun. When I face the sun, I face death. So when I face him, I face death. I've faced death before.

Except he hadn't. Not when he truly thought he was going to die. Deep in his heart he had always known he was stronger and faster. He was the hunter. He was Vampire. He was immortal.

This time, for the first time in over four hundred and fifty years, he faced a death he believed in.

"And the question becomes, what am I going to do about it?"

It was one thing to endure the dreams when he had no knowledge of how or why they came, it was another to let them continue knowing they were sent. *He must have become aware of me from the moment he woke at the museum.* But even knowing who, the question of why still haunted him. Perhaps the dream of the blazing sun was a warning, a shot fired across his bow saying, *"This is what I can do to you if I choose. Do not interfere in what I plan."*

"So it all returns to running. Do I let him have his way or do I face him again?" He leapt to his feet and strode across the room, head high, eyes blazing. "I am the son of a King! I am Vampire! I do not run!"

With a loud crack, the closet door ripped off in his hands. Henry stared at it for a moment, then slowly let the pieces fall. In the end, the anger and the fine words meant nothing. He didn't think he could face Tawfik again, not knowing he had to face the sun as well.

The sudden ringing of the phone slammed his heart against his chest in a very mortal reaction.

* * *

"All right, Mr. Fitzroy says you can go up."

Tony nodded, brushed his hair back off his face with a hand that still trembled, and hurried for the inner door. The old security guard disapproved of him, could see the street kid lurking just below the surface; thought thief, and addict, and bum. Tony didn't give a rat's ass what the old guy thought, especially not tonight. All he wanted was to get to Henry.

Henry would make it better.

Greg watched the boy run for the elevator and frowned. He'd fought in two wars and he knew bone-deep terror when he saw it. He didn't approve of the boy—part of his job as security guard included keeping that type out of the building—nor did he approve of his relationship, whatever it was, with Mr. Fitzroy, but he wouldn't wish that kind of fear on anyone.

Henry could smell the fear stink from across the apartment and when Tony launched himself into his arms it became almost overwhelming. Keeping a tight grip on the Hunger that had risen with a body so vulnerably presented, he set his own fears aside and held the younger man silently until he felt muscles relax and the trembling stop. When he thought he'd get an answer, he pushed Tony gently an arm's length away and asked, "What is it?"

Tony rubbed his palm across lashes spiked with moisture, too frightened to deny there had been tears. The skin around his eyes looked bruised and he had to swallow, once, twice, before he could speak.

"I saw, this afternoon, a baby . . . he just . . ." The shudder ran the length of his body, Henry's presence finally allowing him release. "And now, he'll . . . I mean I saw him kill the baby!"

Henry's mouth tightened at the suggestion that someone would threaten one of his. He pulled Tony, unresisting, over to the couch and sat him down. "I will not allow you to be harmed," he said in such a tone Tony had no choice but to believe it. "Tell me what happened. From the beginning."

As Tony spoke, slowly at first, then faster as though he were racing his fear to the end of the story, Henry had to turn away. He walked to the window, spread one hand against the glass, and looked out over the city. He knew the dark-haired, dark-eyed man.

"*He's killing children,*" Vicki told him.

"*He'll come for me,*" cried Tony.

"*Because we're all there is.*" Even Mike Celluci had a voice in his head.

I feel the sun. It's hours to dawn and I feel the sun.

"Henry?"

Slowly, he turned. "I'll go to where you saw him last, and try to track him." He had no doubt he would recognize the scent, pick it out of a hundred scents laid across concrete on a November afternoon. And if he found the creature's lair, what then? He didn't know. He didn't want to know.

Tony sighed. He knew Henry wouldn't let him down. "Can I stay here? Until you come back?"

Henry nodded and repeated, "Until I come back," as if it were some sort of mantra that would ensure his return.

"Do you, do you need to eat before you go?"

He didn't think he could; not eat, not . . . "No. But thank you."

Brushing his hair back off his face, Tony managed a shaky grin and the shadow of a shrug. "Hey, it's not like I mind or anything."

Because he could do no less than this mortal boy, Henry drew up a smile in return. "Good."

The shrilling of the phone snapped both heads around wearing almost identical expressions of panic. Henry quickly slid a mask in place so that when Tony glanced over at him and asked, "You want me to get it?" he appeared under control and could calmly answer, "No. I'll take care of it."

He lifted the receiver before the second ring had quite finished sounding, having moved from the window to the phone in the space between one heartbeat and the next. It took him almost as long to find his voice.

"Hello? Henry?"

Vicki. No mistaking the tone split equally between worry and annoyance. He didn't know what he'd expected. No, that wasn't true; he knew exactly what he'd expected, he just didn't know why. If Anwar Tawfik decided to contact him, he would *not* be using the phone.

"Henry?"

"Vicki. Hello."

"Is something wrong?" The words had been given a professional shading that told him she knew something was wrong and he might as well tell her what.

"Nothing's wrong. Tony's here." Behind him, he heard Tony shift his weight on the couch.

"What's wrong with *Tony*?"

The obvious conclusion; he should've known she'd jump to it. "He has a problem. But I'm going to take care of it for him. Tonight."

"What kind of problem?"

"Just a minute." He covered the mouthpiece, half turned, and raised a questioning eyebrow.

Tony emphatically shook his head, fingers digging deep into a cushion. "Don't tell her, man. You know what Victory's like; she'll forget she's only human, just charge out there and challenge the guy and the next thing we'll know, she's history."

Henry nodded. *And I am not only human. I am the night. I am Vampire. I want her with me. I don't want to face this creature alone.* "Vicki? He doesn't want me to tell you. It's uh, trouble with a man."

"Oh." He didn't dare read anything into the pause that followed. "Well, *I* want to spend some time with Mike this evening; fill him in on what we know is happening. Warn him." Again the pause. "If you don't need me . . ."

What did she sense? The half lie? His fear? "Will you be here for the dawn?" Regardless of what happened tonight, if he was to have another dawn, he wanted her there for it.

"I will." It had the sound of a pledge.

"Then give my regards to the detective."

Vicki snorted. "Not likely." Her voice softened. "Henry? Be careful." And she was gone.

A little of the horror lost its effect. It was amazing how much *"be careful"* could sound like *"I love you."* Holding her words—her tone—like a talisman, he went over the location with Tony one more time, shrugged into his coat, and went out into the night. He took dubious comfort in the knowledge that now, at least, he could be sure he wasn't going crazy.

* * *

Many of the spells he had spent long years learning would have to be adapted to this new time and place. Unfortunately, as he now found himself in a culture that held few things sacred, finding substitutions would not be easy. The ibex had been revered to the extent that sacred had become a part of its name and that made beak and blood and bone very powerful agents for magic. Somehow he doubted that rendering up a Canada goose would have the same effect.

Suddenly he sat bolt upright in the chair and twisted to face the windows. It was out there. And it was close. He scrambled to his feet and began to throw on street clothes. His ka would not need to search again, simple awareness of the young man would be enough to find him.

He didn't know how that glorious light had been hidden during the day, although he expected he'd soon find out. One way or another.

Henry had traced the scent to the southeast corner of Bloor and Queen's Park Road where it split, one track going north, the other south. Slowly he stood, brushed off the knee that had been resting on the concrete, and considered what he should do next. He knew what he wanted to do, he wanted to go back to Tony, say he couldn't find the creature, and deal with the younger man's fear instead of his own.

Except that wasn't the way it worked. He had made Tony his responsibility. Honor had driven him out onto the streets and honor would not let him return.

Night had followed day, cold and clear, the kind of weather where the scent clung to the ground and the hunt rode out behind the hounds.

His best friend, the brother of his heart, Henry Howard, the Earl of Surrey, rode beside him, their geldings tearing across the frozen turf neck and neck. Ahead, the staghounds bayed and just barely ahead of the pack the quarry raced in a desperate attempt to outrun the death that closed upon its heels. Henry didn't see the exact moment the dogs closed in, but there was a scream of almost human pain and terror and then the stag thrashed on the ground.

He pulled up well back from the seething mass of snarling dogs who darted past striking hooves and tossing antlers to worry at the great beast, but Surrey took his horse as close as it would go, leaning forward in the stirrups, eyes on the knife and the throat and the hot spurt of blood that steamed in the bitter November air.

"Why?" he asked Surrey later, when the hall was filled with the smell of roasting venison and they were sitting bootless, warm before the fire.

Surrey frowned, the elegant line of his black brows dipping in toward the bridge of his nose. "I didn't want the death of such a splendid animal to be wasted. I thought I might find a poem . . ."

His voice trailed off so Henry prodded, "Did you?"

"Yes." The frown grew thoughtful. "But a poem too red for me I think. I will write the hunt and keep the stag alive."

Four hundred and fifty odd years later, Henry answered as he had then. "But there is always death at the end of a hunt."

The track to the south had almost been buried beneath the other footsteps of the day. The track to the north seemed better defined, as though it had been taken more than once; to and from a hotel room perhaps. Henry crossed Bloor, drew even with the church on the corner, and froze so completely motionless that the stream of Sunday night pedestrians flowed seamlessly around him.

He knew the dark-haired, dark-eyed man approaching.

Twelve

Henry waited, motionless, while the other man drew closer. He felt like a rabbit caught in headlights, fully aware that death and destruction bore down on him but unable to move. The sun grew brighter and brighter behind his eyes until he struggled to see around it.

I have no way to fight this. . . .

And then, suddenly, he recognized what he faced. His kind could sense the lives around them, not only through scent and sound but also with an awareness peculiar to those who hunted the night. What he felt approaching was a life, ancient, unlike any life he had ever felt before, and the sun only a symbol created to deal with it.

I have been aware of his life from the moment he awoke, most aware in the times I am most vulnerable. Blessed Christ, he has driven me almost to death just by existing.

Brows down and teeth clenched, he fought to drive this life from the foreground of his mind, finally managing to push it back and dim the light although he could not banish it entirely. It existed now as a background to all he did, but at least it no longer blinded him.

The night returned, Henry blinked, and found himself sinking into irises so deep a brown they looked black. Just before this darkness closed over him, he snarled and pulled free.

"I will not go unresisting like a lamb to the slaughter!"

Force of will slammed at the spell of absorption and shattered it. In all the centuries since his god had changed him, he had never felt such raw power.

He should have known it would not be so easy and he would not have even made the attempt had he not been blinded by the glory of the other's ka. This one had protections; not only personal strength but also strong ties to the one God who had swept the old ways down. Each alone might be enough to stop him from taking what he so deeply desired, together they were very nearly an impenetrable barrier.

But I will *have this ka. I must.*

He touched only the very outermost edges of the other's thoughts. In them, he could feel himself and he could feel fear. Both would give him, if not a way through, a way around. He probed for other weaknesses but saw only the blaze of unlimited potential.

"What are you?"

Henry, muscles twisted into knots across his shoulders, hands clenched so tightly into fists that his nails cut crescents into his palms, saw no reason not to answer. He pitched his voice so that it traveled across the distance between them but no further and threw it like a challenge.

"I am Vampire."

The ka he had absorbed since awakening gave him a confusing pastiche of images not many of which seemed to have much to do with the young man standing before him. He sifted through the information until he recognized what he faced. His people had called them by another name.

No wonder the young man's ka burned so brightly; as long as the Nightwalkers fed on the blood of the living, they were immortal. As immortal as he was himself. Did his own ka burn like a beacon? A pity he would never know, for it was the one ka he could not see.

What power would be his if he fed on the ka of an immortal being! It would no longer be necessary to work through pitiful human tools. He would rule from the beginning in his own name.

Perhaps . . . perhaps a seat in the council of the gods would not be beyond him. He saw himself surrounded by glory, no longer the servant of a petty minor deity but a master in his own name. Quickly, as much as he thrilled to it, he buried the thought deep. It would not do for Akhekh to find it.

But to devour an immortal ka—he had been so blinded by the life remaining, he had never even looked at the life lived, never even noticed it was far longer than the normal human span. He was, he discovered, the elder by a good many centuries, even discounting the millennia he had spent imprisoned. Still, he would have to move carefully, for if he was to finally feast, the Nightwalker's protections must be lowered. He did not have the power to break them down, even considering the fear woven through them.

Why do you fear me, Nightwalker?

Although it was an emotion he would use, it was a question he could not ask. So he asked another.

"Why do you search me out, Nightwalker?"

Why indeed?

"You hunt in my territory."

Ambiguous enough to hide a multitude of motives and also, Henry discovered as he spoke, the truth.

Again he attempted to read the other's ka, to enter past the surface, but he got no further this time than he had before.

"I would talk with you, Nightwalker. Shall we walk together for a time?"

Henry wanted to say no, torn between a desire to run and a desire to rip out the creature's throat and drink deeply of the blood he could hear surging beneath the smooth column of throat. The first would bring him no closer to a solution. The second . . . well, even if he could get past the defenses all wizards wore, which he doubted, it was Sunday evening at a major intersection in downtown Toronto and committing a violent murder in front of hundreds of witnesses, while it would be a solution of sorts, would not be one he himself would likely survive.

So, because it seemed the best, if not the only choice, he turned and fell into step at the other's side, trying to ignore the sun that continued to blaze in one corner of his mind.

They walked south down Queen's Park Road and the power that walked with them turned more than a few heads as they went.

"What shall I call you?" Henry asked at last.

"I use the name Anwar Tawfik. You may call me that."

"That's not the name you were born with."

"Of course not." He laughed gently, an elder chiding an errant pupil. "I took the name upon awakening. I am not likely to give you the power of my birth name." He had not heard his birth name spoken since before the joining of Egypt into a single country. "And I am to call you . . . ?"

"Richmond." Although he had answered to it in the past it had been a title, not a name, and so should be safe from whatever magics could be wrapped around it.

They walked a short distance further, until the sounds of Bloor Street faded and then, in mutual agreement, crossed over to the park. After dark on a November evening, they walked alone on paths damp with fallen leaves, under trees nearly bare. No one would overhear the words to be spoken; no one would have to die because they had heard.

The scattering of lights pushed back the darkness only in isolated areas; in the rest of the park the night stretched unbroken from infinity to the ground. Little light of any kind reached the bench they chose and as Henry watched Tawfik lower himself carefully down, he realized that the other had no better than mortal vision.

So I hold the advantage of sight. For all the good it will do.

Tawfik smelled of excitement, not fear, and his heart beat only a fraction faster than human norm. The movement of his blood called to the Hunger even as the weight of his life overwhelmed any desire Henry had to feed. Henry could smell the fear on himself and his own heart, while still ponderously slow by mortal measuring, beat faster and harder than it had in years.

Tawfik spoke first, his voice sounding mildly amused. "You have a hundred questions, why not begin?"

Why not? But where? Perhaps with the question he himself had answered. "What are you?"

"I am the last remaining priest of the god Akhekh."

"What are you doing here?"

"Do you mean how do I come to be here, in this century, in this place? Or do you mean what am I doing now I am here?"

"Both."

Tawfik shifted on the bench. "Well, that is, as they say, a long story and as you have only until dawn . . ." He saw no reason to lie to the Nightwalker about how and what he was and, although he would chose his words carefully, he was also willing to speak of his plans. After all, he wanted to win young Richmond's trust.

Fortunately, Dr. Rax provided him with a twentieth century framework to hang his story on.

"I was born about 3250 BC, in Upper Egypt just before Meri-nar, who had been King of Lower Egypt, created one empire that stretched the length of the Nile. I was, at the time of the conquest, a high-ranking priest of Set—not the Set that common history remembers, he was then a benevolent god, unfortunately on the losing side. After the conquest, Horus the elder, the highest of the gods of Lower Egypt, cast Set down and declared him unclean. Set, still very powerful, merely worked his way into the new pantheon.'' Tawfik's tone grew slightly dry. "Egyptian gods were, if nothing else, flexible.

"I, as a ranking priest, had been cast down with my god, stripped and scourged and thrown out of my temple. Only mortal and already middle-aged, I hadn't the luxury of concerning myself with Set's long-term plans. I wanted immediate revenge and I was willing to do . . .'' He paused and Henry saw him frown as he remembered. "I was willing to do anything to regain the power and prestige I had lost.

"To me came Akhekh, a minor and dark deity, who in the confusion of the heavens had managed to get hold of more power than usual. *'Swear to me,'* said Akhekh, *'dedicate your life to my service, and I will give you the time you need for your revenge. I will make you more powerful than you have ever been. Become my priest and I will give you the power to destroy the ka of your enemies. You will feed on their souls and with such nourishment live forever.'* ''

Tawfik turned to face Henry and smiled tightly. "Now do not for a moment think that Akhekh made this offer out of regard for me. The gods exist only as long as belief exists. A change in those who believe, means a change in the gods. When no one believes any longer, the gods lose definition, their sense of self if you will, and are absorbed back into the whole.'' He caught a powerful negative flare from the Nightwalker's ka and inclined his head politely toward the other man. "You wanted to say . . . ?''

Henry hadn't intended to say anything, but he found that when challenged he couldn't hold back. *I will not be like Peter and deny my lord.* "There is only one God."

"Richmond, please." Tawfik didn't bother to keep the amusement out of his voice. "You, at least, should know better. Perhaps there may someday be only one god, when all people dream and desire alike, and there are certainly less gods now than there were before I was entombed. But one god? No. I can . . . introduce you to my god, if you wish."

The night seemed to grow a little darker.

"No." Henry ground the word through clenched teeth.

Tawfik shrugged. "As you wish. Now then, where was I? Oh, yes. Of course, I accepted Akhekh's offer; that it came from a dark god meant little to me under the circumstances. I discovered that not only could I extend my life and power my magics with the life remaining in the ka I absorbed, but I also gained the life knowledge that ka held. An invaluable resource for those necessary moves between cultures that occur over a long, a very long life."

"So when you killed Dr. Rax . . ."

"I absorbed the power of his remaining life and came to know everything he knew. The younger the life the less knowledge but the greater potential for power."

"Then the infant you killed earlier today . . ."

That jerked Tawfik out of his relaxed posture. "How did you know?" he demanded and knew the answer before the question had quite left his mouth. The young man who had been watching, fully aware of what had occurred—the young man who had fled in terror—must have fled to the protection of the Nightwalker. He had heard they sometimes gathered mortals about them, a ready food source when hunting became unsure. *So, another pawn has entered the game.* Tawfik let nothing but the question show on his face or in his voice. If the Nightwalker thought he had forgotten the young man, his protection would be less extreme and easier to circumvent.

Henry heard Tawfik's heart speed up, but the wizard-priest made no mention of Tony. Perhaps Tony had been wrong and he hadn't been spotted. Given Tony's terror, that seemed unlikely. Perhaps Tawfik played a deeper game and had no wish to tip his hand. Tawfik no doubt had his own reasons for denying a witness; Henry's were simple, he would not betray a friend. He let the beast show in his voice as he repeated, "You've been hunting in my territory."

Tawfik recognized the threat, and countered with one of his own, playing on the Nightwalker's barely controlled fear of him. "As you were about to observe, the infant I killed earlier today made me *very* powerful." Stalemate again. "Now then, if I may continue with my history . . . ?"

"Go on."

"Thank you." Akhekh's offer had come with a condition; he could not devour the ka of one already sworn. For the first hundred years after the conquest, while the pantheon settled, the unsworn were easy to find and he had risen in power—which he discovered he desired much more than revenge—and the cult of Akhekh had grown strong. But the more stable and prosperous Egypt was, the more the people were content with their gods and the fewer unattached ka were available, so his power and Akhekh's—waxed and waned in counterpoint to Egypt's. *This* age had a decadence he recognized and had every intention of exploiting—they were ripe for rituals Akhekh had to offer. Tawfik saw no reason to mention any of that to the Nightwalker.

"Because of me, my lord, in spite of his relatively subordinate position in the pantheon, was never absorbed into the greater gods like so many of the lesser deities had been and so in every age, in a thousand places along the Nile, I raised a temple to Akhekh." Occasionally, he was the only worshiper, but no need to mention that either. "Now and then, other priests objected to my having stepped out of the cycle of life, but the centuries had made me a skilled wizard—*And had taught me when to cut my losses and leave town.*—so they could not take me down. As I only destroyed those who had no allegiance to a god, the other gods refused to get involved."

"But you were taken down, in the end."

"Yes. Well, I made a slight error in judgment. It could have happened to anyone." In the darkness, Tawfik smiled. "Shall I tell you what it was? It is completely irrelevant to this time and place so even if you wished to, you couldn't use it against me. During what you now call the Eighteenth Dynasty, although things were extremely prosperous for Egypt, most nobles had very large families which meant that a number of the younger nobility had nothing to do. In such a social climate, the temple of Akhekh grew and flourished. My lord had more sworn acolytes than at any time since the conquest. Unfortunately, although I didn't see it as unfortunate at the time, two of the Pharoah's younger sons joined our number. This finally attracted the attention of the greater gods."

He paused, sighed, and shook his head. When he began to speak again, his voice had lost its lecturing tone and had become only the voice of a man sharing painful memories.

"The sons of the Pharoah were the sons of Osiris reborn and Osiris would not have them corrupted by what he termed an abomination. So Thoth, god of wisdom, came to one of his priests in a dream and told them how I might be overcome. My protections were shattered and once again I was dragged from my temple. The first time, I was left alive because my life had no meaning. This time, they were afraid to kill me because my life had gone on for so long. Even the gods were wary of what might happen should my ka be released into Akhekh's keeping with so many acolytes still performing the rituals. I was not to be slain, I was to be entombed alive. All this I was told as the priests of Thoth prepared me for burial.

"Three thousand years later, my prison was brought here to this city and I was freed."

"And you destroyed the man who gave you your freedom."

"Destroying him gave me my freedom. I needed his knowledge."

"And the other. The custodian."

"I needed his life. I had been entombed for three thousand years, Nightwalker. I had to feed. Would you have done any differently?"

Henry remembered the three days he had spent beneath the earth, hunger clawing at him until hunger became all he was. "No," he admitted, as much to himself as to Tawfik, "I would have fed. But," he shook free of the memory, "I would not have killed those others, not the children."

Tawfik shrugged. "I needed their power."

"So you took their lives."

"Yes." He shifted on the bench, linking his fingers together and leaning his forearms across his thighs. "I told you all this, Nightwalker, so you would learn you cannot

stop me. You are no wizard. Thoth and Osiris are long dead
and cannot help you. Your god does not interfere.''

First the stick. ''If you oppose me, I will be forced to
destroy you.''

And then the carrot. ''As I see it, you have two choices;
live and let live, as *I* am willing to do with you, or join
me.''

''Join you.'' Henry was not quite in control of the repe-
tition.

''Yes. We have much in common, you and I.''

''We have nothing in common.''

Tawfik lifted his brows. ''Of course we don't.'' The sarcasm had a razor edge. ''This city has many more immortal
beings.''

''You murder the innocent.''

''And you have never killed to survive?''

''Yes, but . . .''

''Killed for power?''

''Not the innocent.''

''And who declared them guilty?''

''They did, by their own actions.''

''And who appointed you as judge and jury and execu-
tioner? Have I not as much right to appoint myself to the
position as you did?''

''I have never destroyed the innocent!'' Henry held tightly
to that while the sun grew brighter behind his eyes.

''There are no innocents. Or do you deny your church's
position on original sin?''

''You argue like a Jesuit!''

''Thank you. I am as immortal as you are, Richmond. I
will never grow old, I will never die, I will never leave you.
Not even another Nightwalker can promise you that.''

Vampires were solitary hunters. Humans were pack ani-
mals. In order to survive in a human world, the vampire
could not surrender all humanity—those who did were
quickly destroyed by the terror they evoked—and this double nature found itself constantly at war with itself. But to
find a companion, one who would neither cause instinctive
bloody battles over territory nor die just when he had become an intrinsic part of life. . . .

''No!'' Henry leapt to his feet and flung himself forward
into the darkness, trying to outdistance the sun. Halfway

across the park, he managed to stop himself and, fingers dug deep into the living bark of a tree, old and gnarled and half his age, he fought back.

"I have lived, knowing I was immortal, for thousands of years." Tawfik continued to speak, sure that the Nightwalker could hear him. He watched the reaction of the other's ka and chose his words accordingly. "I am perhaps the only man you will ever meet who can understand you, who can know what you go through. Who can accept you entirely for what you are. I, too, have seen the ones I love grow old and die."

Listening, in spite of himself, Henry saw the years take Vicki from him as the years had taken the others.

"I am asking you to stand by my side, Nightwalker. A man should not go alone through the centuries; neither of us need ever stand alone again. You need not go blindly forward. I have lived the years you will live, I can be there to guide you." Tawfik couldn't quite hide the gasp as the Nightwalker was suddenly, silently, beside him again.

"You never told me what you plan to do now." The answer wasn't as important as shutting off the words, banishing the specter of isolation they invoked. He couldn't just walk away, so he had to change the subject.

"I plan to build a temple, as I have always done when I start a new life, and I will gather acolytes to serve my god. This is my only concern at this time, Nightwalker, for the acolytes should be sworn as soon as possible—a god deserves worshipers, rituals, all the little things that make being a deity worthwhile."

"Then why try to control the police and the justice system?"

"New religions are often prosecuted. I have a way to prevent that and so I do. With no need to hide, I will shout AKHEKH from the top of the highest mountain. And once the temple is large enough to provide me with the power I need, your innocents will be safe." Tawfik stood and held out his hand. "You live like a mortal, searching for immediate solutions, immediate answers. Why not plan for eternity? Why not plan with me?" He now had enough of a key to the Nightwalker's ka that if Richmond would just voluntarily reach out and take his hand, that act of trust would plant hooks that the younger man would never shake loose.

In time those hooks would pull him closer and, in time, he would feed.

Scent and sound told Henry that Tawfik had not lied once since he began to speak.

Henry felt young, confused, afraid. For the seventeen years he had lived as a mortal he had fought to gain his father's love and approval. Tawfik—older, wiser, incontestably in control—made him feel the way his father had. Four hundred and fifty years hunting the night alone should have erased the bastard who only wanted to belong. It hadn't. He didn't know what to think. He stared down at the offered hand and wondered how it would feel to be able to plan for more than just a part of one mortal lifetime. To be part of a greater whole. But if Tawfik hadn't lied . . .

"Your god is a dark god. I want no part of him."

"You need have nothing to do with my god. Akhekh asks nothing of you. *I* ask for your companionship. Your friendship."

"*You* are more dangerous than your god!" On the last word, Henry launched himself forward. Red lines flared and he found himself flat on his back two meters away.

Tawfik let his hand drop slowly to his side. "Foolish child," he said softly. "I will not destroy you now as I could, nor will I take back the offer. If you grow tired of an eternity alone, come to the corner where we met tonight and I will find you." He felt the Nightwalker's gaze on him as he turned and walked away, not entirely displeased with the evening's work. The surface of the other's ka boiled with emotions too tangled for even millennia of experience to sort out but all of them, eventually, came back to him.

The evening mass was nearly over when Henry slipped into the church and settled into one of the empty pews at the back. Confused and frightened, he had come to the one place that had, through all the years and all the changes, stayed the same. Well, almost the same. He still missed the cadences, the grandeur of the Latin and occasionally murmured his responses in the language of the past.

The Inquisition had driven him from the church for a time but needing, at the very least, the continuity of worship, he had returned. Sometimes he saw the church as an immortal being in its own right, living much as he did during carefully prescribed hours, surviving on the blood of the mortals who surrounded it. And often the blood was less than metaphorical, for more had been shed in the name of a god of love . . .

He stood with the rest, hands lightly holding the warm wood of the pew in front of him.

Over the centuries there had been compromises, of course. The church declared he had no soul. He disagreed. He had seen men and women without souls—for a soul can be given up to despair or hatred or rage—but did not count himself among them. Confession had been a trial in the beginning, until he realized that the sins the priests would understand, gluttony, anger, lust, sloth applied as much to him as to mortals and that the specific actions were unimportant. He did the penance prescribed. He came away feeling part of a greater whole.

Except that he could not, since his change, take communion.

So once again I am set to one side, different from the closest thing to community I have known.

He found it interesting that Tawfik—the only other immortal being he had met since Christina and he had parted—came complete with a god of his own. Perhaps immortals *needed* that kind of continuity outside themselves. He found himself thinking of discussing the theory with Tawfik and thrust the thought away.

The pew back groaned under his grip and he hurriedly forced his hands to relax.

If not for the promises he had made to Tony, he would have run before he had the chance to be tempted. And if not for Vicki, the temptation would not have been so great. Vicki offered him friendship, perhaps even love, although she seemed to be frightened of what that implied, but her mortality sounded in the song of her blood and every beat of her heart took her one heartbeat closer to death. In time, in a very short time relative to the time he had already lived, she would be gone and soon after her, Tony, and then the loneliness would return.

Tawfik promised an end to the loneliness, a place to belong for longer than the length of a mortal life.

Why not *plan for eternity?*

The sun blazed up behind his eyes. It seemed he could no longer be completely unaware of Tawfik's existence.

If I die, I would have the eternity the church promises. It would be so easy to take that way out, come the dawn. *Except that suicide is a sin.*

The greater sin would be the pain he would leave behind. If he wanted to take that way out, he would have to wait. With a sudden lightening of his heart, he realized that for the first time in weeks, for the first time since the dreams had started, he could face the dawn without fear. The sun that Tawfik pushed at him could no longer push him in that direction. Whatever else happened—desire and fear and identity were still a tangled mess he could not sort—that would not.

The priest lifted one hand, his eyes nearly shut above the curves of his cheeks. "Go in peace," he said softly, and it sounded as though he meant it.

The mass over, the congregation of mostly elderly immigrants began to file out. Henry hung behind, waiting, while the priest greeted each of them at the door. When the last black-clad body was on its way down the path, he stepped forward and captured the priest's gaze.

"Father, I need to talk to you."

More than vocation made it impossible for the priest to refuse that request.

It was seven ten when he got back to the condo, barely eighteen minutes before sunrise. Vicki met him at the door, grabbed his hands, and practically dragged him inside.

"Where the hell have you been," she snarled, worry twisting into anger now he was safe.

"I had an encounter with our mummy."

The flatness of his tone penetrated. *You can deal with this only if you deny the effect it had.* Over the years Vicki had seen enough of the effects of major trauma to recognize this particular defense mechanism in her sleep. With an effort, she damped her own emotions to suit. "So you found it. Tony called me about midnight, he was afraid the creature had sucked up your life the way it had the baby's. Mike drove me over. I'll have to call him after sunrise and let him know what happened." *Provided* you *let me know what happened.*

Henry could hear a slow and quiet heartbeat coming from the living room.

"Tony finally fell asleep on the couch about four," she continued. "I'll get him out of here after I've got you safe."

The grip that pulled him purposefully through the apartment would have been painfully tight around a mortal's hand; even Henry found it a bit uncomfortable. He made no effort to break it though; it was a welcome anchor.

Not until they reached the bedroom and the door had been closed behind him and the blackout curtain drawn, did Vicki release him. Leaving him standing in the middle of the room, she sat down on the end of the bed and slid her glasses back up the bridge of her nose.

"If you had died out there," she said slowly, because if she didn't speak she was going to explode, "you would have left a hole in my life impossible to fill. I've always hated the thought of putting conditions on . . ." She wet her lips. ". . . on love but if you ever go off to face an enemy whose strengths we don't know, who we know can kill with a look, who just the night before sent you running from him in panic, and don't come back looking at least a little the worse for wear . . ." Her head jerked up and she met his eyes. ". . . I'm going to wring your fucking vampiric neck. Do I make myself clear?"

"I think so. You went through hell, so I better have?" He sat down beside her on the bed. "If it makes you feel any better, I did."

"Fuck off, Henry, that's not what I meant." She wiped viciously at the tear that traced a line down her cheek. "I was scared spitless you'd taken on more than you could handle . . ."

"I had." He raised a hand to cut her off. "But not because I had to prove something after last night. I grew out of stupid displays of machismo three centuries ago. I went because Tony needed me to."

Vicki took a deep breath, and her shoulders straightened as though a weight had lifted. God knows, she'd taken impossible risks in her time, and, thank God, he'd had a reason she could live with. "You are such an idiot."

Henry leaned forward and drew the flavor of her mouth deep into his. "And you have such interesting ways of saying *I love you*," he murmured against her lips. He realized

just how frightened for him she'd been when she made no
protest, merely returned his embrace with an intensity that
held a hint of desperation. When she finally drew back, he
got to his feet and began to strip off his shirt. If he didn't
hurry, he'd be spending the day in his clothes.

She watched him, the soft, anxious expression she'd worn
for a moment hardening into something a little closer to,
All right, let's get on with this. "Are you okay?"

"Well, to begin, I didn't find him, he found me." He
tossed the shirt to the floor. "And I discovered that the sun
that I've been dreaming about has been nothing more than
a manifestation of his life-energy."

"What?"

"Apparently there were times I was more susceptible than
others. And now I've met him, I can't completely tune him
out."

"You can always see the sun?"

"It hovers on the edge of my consciousness."

"Jesus Christ, Henry!"

"He frightens me, Vicki. I can't see any way we can beat
him."

Her brows drew down. "What did he do to you?"

"He talked." Henry flipped the covers back and got into
the bed. The sun, the other sun, trembled on the horizon.
"He twisted me into knots and left me to sort myself out."

She shifted around until she faced him again. "Did you?"

"I think so. I don't know." *I won't know until I face him
again.* "I spent the night trying to redefine myself. The
church. The hunt." He reached out and laid two fingers
against her wrist. "You."

*I'm worried sick and he's out having a prayer, a snack,
and a fuck?* The smell of sex that clung to him was faint
but unmistakable now she'd been made aware of it. *Calm
down. Everyone deals with trauma his own way. At least he
made it home.* "And what about you do I define?"

"My heart."

She laid her palm gently on his bare chest, stroking the
soft red-gold curls with her thumb. "I really hate this mushy
stuff."

"I know." He almost smiled, then quickly sobered again.
"I tried to attack him. I couldn't even get close. He's dangerous, Vicki."

He obviously wasn't referring to the deaths that had occurred since the mummy disentombed itself and the faint shadow of pain that slipped into his voice was far more disturbing than out and out panic would have been. "Why?"

"Because I can't reject his offer out of hand."

"His offer?" Vicki's brows snapped down so hard that her glasses trembled on the very tip of her nose. "What offer? Tell me!"

He began to shake his head . . .

. . . then the motion slowed . . .

. . . then the day took him.

"When he wakes up, I'm going to grab him and shake him and he's going to tell me everything he knows and we're going to go over what happened second by second." Vicki stuffed another handful of cheese balls into her mouth. "This is what comes of letting your hormones interfere with your caseload," she muttered savagely, but indistinctly to an uninterested pigeon. Because she'd been so worried about Henry, first she'd babbled then she'd let him babble and nothing, absolutely nothing of any use had been passed on before he'd passed out.

"If I'd ever done anything half so stupid with a witness while I was on the force I'd have been up on charges of gross incompetence." Sucking the virulent orange stain from her fingers, she shook her head, growling around them, "And they wonder why I won't get mushy romantic." All right, that was unfair. Neither of them wondered. Celluci understood and Henry accepted. This screwup she could lay at no one's door but her own.

"Good lord. Celluci." She shoved the half-eaten package of cheese balls into her shoulder bag and checked her watch. He'd be going into headquarters for eleven and he'd told her to call him before he left. Vicki figured she owed him that much; not, given her lack of relevant information, that she was looking forward to it. To her surprise it was only eight fifty-three. Why did she feel like it should be later? *Time flies when you're having fits.* . . .

With Henry safely and infuriatingly tucked away, she'd roused Tony, reassured him, and popped him onto a subway heading toward his current job site, shoving five bucks into his hand so he could buy breakfast when he got there. Then

she'd taken transit in the other direction, paused only long
enough to pick up a snack and a short lecture on nutrition
from Mrs. Kopolous at the store, and had just rounded the
corner onto Huron Street and home. They left Henry's condo
at ten to eight, it was now ten to nine. An hour seemed
about right . . .

"Daylight savings time. My body thinks it's ten to ten."
She sighed. "My body is an idiot. My emotional state is
completely unreliable. Damn, but it's a good thing I'm so
smart."

The legal side of Huron Street was, as usual, parked solid,
so Vicki paid less than no attention to the brown sedan that
had pulled over illegally in front of her building. She moved
onto the walk, heard a car door open behind her, and froze
when a familiar voice called out, "Good morning, Nelson."

"Good morning, Staff-Sergeant Gowan." She pivoted
around to face him, the smile she wore completely uncon-
vincing. Staff-Sergeant Gowan had resented everything
about her while she'd been on the force, his resentment
growing with every promotion, every citation, every bit of
praise she got until it had festered into hate. To be fair, she
despised him in turn. "Oh, and I see you brought Constable
Mallard." She'd once turned Mallard into the Police Re-
view Board for conduct unbecoming a human being. As far
as she was concerned, the uniform meant responsibility; it
didn't excuse the lack of it.

Her palms began to sweat. They were both out of uniform. Whatever was going to happen, it didn't look good.

"So, what unexpected pleasure brings you two out so
early in the morning?"

Gowan's smile spread all over his face. It was the happiest
she'd ever seen him. "Oh, a pleasure indeed. . . . We have
a warrant for your arrest, Nelson."

"A what?"

"I knew if I waited long enough, you'd go one step too
far and piss off the wrong person."

She backed away as Mallard approached.

"Looks like resisting arrest to me," he murmured and
swung out with the nightstick he'd been holding, hidden,
behind his leg.

The blow came too fast to avoid. It hit her hard across

the solar plexus and she folded, gasping for breath. *He always was a fucking hotshot with that thing.* Each man
grabbed an arm and the next thing she knew, she'd been
tossed across the back seat of the car. Mallard climbed in
with her. Gowan scurried around to the front.

The whole operation, from the time Gowan had first
spoke, had taken less than a minute.

Vicki, her face pressed hard against musty upholstery,
struggled to breathe. As the car began to move, Mallard
yanked her arms back and forced the cuffs around her wrists,
closing them so tightly the metal edges dug into the bone. The
pain jerked her head up and his fist slammed it down.

"Go ahead, fight." He snickered and she felt him drive
his forearm across the small of her back, immobilizing her
with his weight.

Her glasses were hanging off one ear and losing them
frightened her more than anything Mallard or Gowan could
do. Although it wasn't going to be fun . . . she'd seen prisoners both men had released into holding cells. Apparently,
they'd fallen down a lot.

When he started fumbling with the waistband of her jeans,
she got one leg free and attempted to drive the heel of her
sneaker through his ear. He grabbed her foot and twisted.

Goddamned, fucking, son of a bitch!

The pain gave her something new to think about for a few
seconds and the lesser pain of the needle almost got lost in
it.

Needle?

Oh, shit . . .

The drug worked quickly.

Thirteen

"Nelson Investigations. No one is available to take your call, but if you leave your name and number as well as a brief outline of your problem . . ."

"*You're* my problem, Nelson," Celluci growled as he dropped the receiver back into the cradle. He glared at the clock on the kitchen wall. Ten twenty-five. Even at this hour of the morning, theoretically well past rush hour, driving from Downsview to the center of town was going to take just about all of that thirty-five minutes. He couldn't afford to wait any longer; Cantree had an understandable objection to his detectives wandering in to work when it suited them.

Of course, there was another number he could call. Fitzroy himself would have long ago crawled back into his coffin for the day, but Vicki might still be at his apartment.

Celluci snorted. "No, at his *condominium.*" God, that was such a yuppie word. People who lived in condominiums ate raw fish, drank lite beer, and collected baseball cards for their investment potential. Granted Fitzroy did none of those things, but he still played at the lifestyle. And romance novels? Bad enough for a man to write the asinine things but for a . . . a . . . for what Fitzroy was . . .

No. He wasn't calling Fitzroy's place. It was a big city, Vicki could be anywhere. Very likely she was taking young Tony home and tucking him in. The thought of Vicki in such a maternal role brought a sardonic smile and the thought that followed lifted his eyebrows almost to his hairline.

Tucking Tony in?

No. Celluci shook his head emphatically. Thinking about Fitzroy was driving his mind right into the gutter. He shrugged into his jacket, grabbed his keys up off the kitchen table, and headed for the door. Vicki no doubt had a good reason for not calling. He trusted her. Maybe Tony's fears hadn't been completely unfounded—Fitzroy *had* been hurt facing the mummy, and she'd taken him wherever one took a hurt . . . romance writer. He trusted her innate good sense not to have used the information Fitzroy may have brought back and gone out after the mummy herself. . . .

"And if there isn't a message waiting for me at the office, I'm going to take her innate good sense and beat her to death with it."

The phone rang.

"Great timing, Vicki, I was just on my way out the door. And where the hell have you been anyway? I told you to call me first thing!"

"Celluci, shut up for a minute and listen."

Celluci blinked. "Dave?" His partner didn't sound like a happy man. "What's wrong. It's not the baby, is it?"

"No, no, she's fine." On the other end of the line, Dave Graham took a deep breath. "Look, Mike, you're going to have to lay low for a while. Cantree wants you picked up and brought in."

"Say what?"

"He's got a warrant for your arrest."

"On what charge?"

"There doesn't appear to be one. It's a special . . ."

"It's a fucking setup." Celluci grinned, suddenly relieved. "You didn't actually believe it, did you?"

"Yeah. I believed it. And you'd better, too." Something in Dave's voice wiped the grin off his face. "I don't know what's going on around here today, but they've shuffled a couple of departments around, no warning, and that warrant'll stand. I've never seen Cantree so serious about anything."

"Shit." It was more of an observation than an expletive.

"You can say that again, buddy-boy. I'm not sure I should ask, but just what have you done?"

"I was in the wrong place at the wrong time and I found out something I shouldn't have." Celluci considered what Vicki had told him about the Solicitor General's Halloween party. *Cantree. God damn it! The son of a bitch has subverted one of the few honest cops in the city*. He had to assume that Fitzroy had been an accurate witness, but the thought of Cantree, of all people, blindly dancing to another man's tune made him feel physically ill. *And he's dancing*

*right over me. The next time I think there's a mummy on the
rampage in Toronto, I'll keep my fucking mouth shut.* "Are
you calling from headquarters?"

"Do I look like an idiot?" Dave's voice was dry. "I'm
at the Taco Bell around on Yonge Street."

"Good. Look, Dave, this is bigger than just me. Watch
your back and, for the next little while, keep a very, very
low profile."

"Hey, you don't need to tell me. There's something ma-
jorly weird going down around here and I've never been
keen on being strip searched. How do I stay in touch?"

"Uh . . . good question." He could access messages off
his machine by remote and as long as the messages were
short enough there wouldn't be time to trace the line back;
but they'd be monitoring and that would put Dave right in
the toilet with him. Odds were good they'd also be monitoring Vicki's line. Cantree was well aware how close the
two of them had been and how close they'd stayed. Best to
keep away from Vicki's place completely and that included
keeping Dave away from Vicki's answering machine.

"You could call me."

"No. Even if they don't suspect you warned me, they'll
be monitoring your lines. You're the logical person for me
to call. Damn it all to hell anyway!" He slapped his palm
against the table and stared at the scrap of pink memo paper
that fluttered down to the floor. Fitzroy? Why not. "I've
got a number you can leave a message at. I can't guarantee
I'll get it until after dark, but it should be safe. Memorize
it, don't write it down, and use . . ."

"A public phone line. Mike, I know the drill." Dave
repeated the number three times to be sure he had it, then
warned, "You better get out of there. Cantree might not
have wanted to wait until you came in. He may have sent a
car up."

"I'm gone. And Dave? Thanks." Partners who could be
depended on when the chips were down—or sideways—had
saved the lives of more cops than a thousand fancy pieces
of equipment. "I owe you one."

"One? You still owe me for a half a dozen meals, not to
mention getting that asswipe from accounting off your back.
Anyway, be careful." He hung up before Celluci could re-
ply.

Be careful. Right.

Accompanied by a fine libretto of Italian swearing, Celluci threw a few clothes, some papers, and a box of ammunition in a cheap Blue Jays' gym bag. He had no time to change out of his suit, but the moment he could he'd ditch it for the uniform of the city—jeans and a black leather jacket worked better around Toronto than a cloak of invisibility. Not counting a pocket load of change, he had twenty-seven bucks in his wallet and another hundred in emergency money taped under the seat of the car. He'd take the money; he'd have to leave the car.

On his way out the door, he stopped and glanced back at the phone. Should he leave a message on Fitzroy's machine for Vicki? A second thought decided him against it. Cantree was likely to have a check run on all the numbers he'd called in the last couple of days and if Fitzroy's number showed up on the list . . .

"Good thing I didn't call it earlier." It appeared his ego was looking out for him.

He slipped the chain on, pulled the door closed, and heard the deadbolt click. His security system had been designed by one of the best break and enter boys in the city. Cantree would probably have the door smashed—the police were often less subtle than those they arrested—but it ought to slow the bastards down.

Very faintly, through the steel-reinforced oak, he heard the phone ring. It might be Vicki. He couldn't afford the time it would take to go back and answer it. If it *was* Vicki . . . well, Vicki had always been able to take care of herself and besides, she was safe enough for now; Cantree wanted him, not her.

The holding cell smelled of vomit and urine and cheap booze sweated out through polyester layered over years of too many desperate people and far too little money. A half dozen tired looking whores, waiting for their morning trip to court, huddled in one corner and watched Vicki forced down on the bench.

"What's she in for?" asked a tall brunette, adjusting what was either a very wide belt or a very short skirt.

"None of your damned business," grunted Mallard

struggling with the cuffs, his shoulder pressing Vicki hard against the wall.

The hooker rolled her eyes. The other nodded.

"What was that?" Gowan asked. His position outside the cage had allowed him to see the expression Mallard had missed. "You got a problem with the officer's answer?"

"No." Her voice dropped just to one side of servile. "No problem."

Gowan smiled. "Glad to hear it, ladies."

Her expression supplicating, she gave him the finger, the gesture carefully hidden behind one of her companions. Working girls learned fast that cops came in two basic varieties. Almost all of them were just regular guys doing a job, but a nasty few would like nothing more than an excuse to pull out their sticks and apply a personal judgment. If fate threw them the latter, maintaining the merchandise dictated ass-kissing as hard and as fast as necessary.

Swearing softly, Mallard yanked the cuffs around on Vicki's wrists to give him a better angle with the key. "God-damned things are stuck a . . . there." They dropped into his hands and he straightened. Without his support, Vicki sagged away from the wall and toppled sideways off the bench.

Although voluntary motor functions seemed to be under someone else's control and all the crevices of her brain had been filled with mashed potatoes, she was completely aware of everything that was going on. This was the Metro East Detention Center on Disco Road. Mallard and Gowan had tossed her bag at the Duty Sergeant and dragged her past saying, "Wait until you hear the story on this one . . ." They were now, obviously, going to leave her in the holding cell. Locked up. They said they had a warrant.

What the hell is happening?

She managed to focus on Mallard's face. The son of a bitch was smiling.

"Such a pity when a cop goes bad," he said clearly.

Cop? God damn it, don't say I'm a cop. Not here!

He reached down and pinched her cheek, hard enough for her to feel it through the drug, and gently resettled her glasses on her nose. "Wouldn't want you to miss any of this."

Don't leave me here! You can't just leave me here, you

bastard! The thought slammed around inside her head but all that made it out was a kind of stuttering moan.

"I'll always remember you like this." His smile broadened, then he turned and moved back out of her line of sight.

She couldn't turn her head fast enough to watch him go. *NO!*

Heels rang against the concrete floor and Vicki struggled to focus on the young woman now standing over her.

Oh, Christ . . .

"Fucking cop."

The toes of her boots were dangerously pointed. Fortunately, she didn't know where use them to their best advantage. Nothing broke.

Vicki made an effort to remember the face behind the garish makeup before pain squeezed her eyes shut.

"Leave her alone, Marian. She's too stoned to feel it anyway."

She could feel snot running over her upper lip. She could feel something damp soaking through her jeans where her hip pressed against the floor. She'd never felt so desperately helpless in her entire life.

Somewhere else.
Eyes glowed red and Akhekh fed.

"How long do you figure the drug will last?"

Gowan shrugged. "I dunno, a few hours. It's the same stuff the animal control people use to bring down bears. Doesn't really matter how long it lasts. After the story we spun, they're not going to believe a word she says."

"But what if she gets a lawyer?"

"Not where she's going."

"But . . ."

"Chill out, Mallard." Gowan pulled carefully out of the parking spot and waved at the driver of a wagon just coming in. "Cantree said he needed a couple of days to get the evidence to nail the bitch and we've given it to him. It's his problem now."

"And hers."

Staff Sergeant Gowan nodded. "And hers," he repeated in pleased agreement.

* * *

The whores had been taken away. Vicki didn't know
when. Time moved so slowly she might have been in the
holding cell for days.

Inch by inch, she crawled one arm up the wall far enough
for her hand to grab the edge of the bench. It took four tries
for her grip to finally hold and another three before she
could remember how to bend her elbow. Finally she was
sitting, still on the floor but a definite improvement.

The massive physical effort needed to get this far had held
panic at bay but now she could see—thank God, they hadn't
taken her glasses—it rolled over her in turgid red waves that
crashed against the backs of her eyes, receded and crashed
down again. The only coherent word in the surging tide was
NO! so she clutched at it and used it to keep from being
pulled under.

NO! I will not surrender!

A sharp slap on her right cheek gave her a new focus and
she managed to drag herself partially free.

"Hey? I said, can you walk?"

Vicki blinked. A guard. The panic receded further and
relief flooded in to take its place. They'd realized what had
happened and come to get her. She tried to smile and nod
at the same time, couldn't do both so achieved neither, and
threw everything she had into a struggle to get to her feet.

"Atta girl, upsa daisy. Christ," the guard grunted as she
ended up lifting most of Vicki's weight. "Why are the ston-
ers always so fucking big?"

The second guard, standing at the door of the cage,
shrugged. "At least this one doesn't stink. I'll take a head
over a drunk any day. Drugs don't make you puke on your
shoes."

"Or my shoes," the first guard agreed. "Okay, you're
up. Now then, left foot, right foot. *None* of us will enjoy it
if we have to carry you."

It was more of a threat than an encouragement, but Vicki
didn't notice. She could walk. It was shuffling, unsure, and
slow, but it was forward locomotion and while both guards
seemed merely satisfied, Vicki was overjoyed. She could
walk. The drug must be wearing off.

Her relief grew when they took her straight to the Duty
Sergeant and pushed her down onto a wooden chair.

I'm on my way out of here. . . .

"So," he said when the door closed and they were alone, "the two officers who brought you in suggested I book you myself."

Book me?

He patted the warrant with his fingertips. "They've left me a number to call for the official explanation. I can't wait. Cops who take advantage of their position to molest little kids don't go down very well with my people, or the inmates either for that matter. The officers seemed to think it would be better if no one else knew what you'd done."

I haven't done anything!

"Now they had no idea what drug you'd taken and I can't wait for it to wear off—if it's going to wear off—so we'll just enter your information off the warrant."

Okay. Don't panic. My name goes into the system, someone'll recognize it.

"Terri Hanover . . ."

Oh, God.

". . . age, thirty-two . . . five-foot ten . . . one hundred and forty-seven pounds . . ." He clicked his tongue. "Shaved a few pounds off there, did we?"

It's me, but it's not my name. Detectives were issued fake ID all the time and her specs were probably still on file. *What the hell is going on?*

The sound of his fingers against the keyboard began to sound like nails pounding into a cage being built around her. She couldn't just sit there and let it happen.

"I am not who they say I am!"

Except her mouth refused to form the words. Nothing came out except guttural noises and a trickle of saliva that ran off her chin to drip slowly into the hollow of her collarbone.

"Now then," he set the keyboard to one side and reached for the phone, "let's see what headquarters has to say."

"The Solicitor General's office. One moment please, he's expecting your call."

The phone on Zottie's desk buzzed but the Solicitor General just stared at it, a puzzled smile on his face.

"Pick it up," Tawfik commanded softly. The man would not last much longer. Fortunately, he wouldn't have to.

"Zottie here. Ah, yes, Sergeant Baldwin. Well, actually, it's not me you should be talking to. Hold on . . ." He passed the receiver to Tawfik, then lapsed back into semi-awareness as Tawfik began to speak.

The Solicitor General? Oh, God, then that means . . .
After his initial enthusiastic greeting, the Duty Sergeant said little. Finally, even the monosyllables faded into a blank stare.

This time the panic came with words.

The mummy put me here. Not Mallard and Gowan. The mummy. Christ. I should have remembered Cantree is under its control. But why? How? It doesn't know about me. Henry. Henry talked to it. Did Henry betray me? Without meaning to? Meaning to? Henry? Or Mike. It found out about Celluci. He was there. At the museum. It got Celluci. Took what it needed to know. I'm just another loose end. Mike? Are you dead? Are you dead? Are you dead?

She couldn't breathe. It hurt to breathe. She couldn't remember how to breathe.

The . . . mummy . . . has . . . to . . . be . . . stopped.
And if Mike Celluci was dead? His death must be avenged. *A . . . venged.* She breathed in the first syllable and breathed out the second. *A . . . venged. A . . . venged. Avenged.*

"I understand."

Understand what?

"It will be done."

Eyes wide, unable to look away, Vicki watched him hang up the phone, pick up the warrant, her warrant, and walk over to the shredder.

NO!

She'd been entered into the system and as far as the system was concerned she now belonged here until they pulled her for a court appearance. Court appearances were booked by warrant. Without a warrant, she would rot here forever.

I could jump the sergeant. Hold him hostage. Call the newspapers! Call . . . call someone. I can't just disappear! But her body still refused to obey. She felt muscles tense, and then go slack, and then she began to tremble, unable to stop it or control it.

Sergeant Baldwin looked down at the shredder, frowned,

and brushed one hand over the gray fringe of his hair. "Dickson!"

"Sarge?" The guard who had lifted Vicki to her feet back in the holding cell, opened the door and stuck her head into the office.

"I want you to search Ms. Hanover and then take her down to Special Needs."

"To the nut bars?" Dickson's brows rose. "You sure she shouldn't go to the hospital? She doesn't look so good."

The Sergeant snorted. "Neither did the kid when she got through seeing to him."

"Right."

Vicki heard the guard's voice pick up an edge; skinbeefs against children were universally despised. Strong fingers closed around her upper arm and heaved her up and out of the chair. Shoved toward the door, she struggled to remember how to walk.

"Oh, and Dickson? I want it to be a thorough search."

"Aw, come on, Sarge!" The guard's grip loosened a little as she turned to protest the order. "I had to do the last one."

"And you get to do this one, too. Here."

Vicki heard Dickson grunt as she caught something heavy and managed to get her head turned enough to see that it was her black leather shoulder bag.

The guard looked down at the huge, bulging bag in disbelief. "What am I supposed to do with this?"

"It came with her. When you've got her put away, you can enter the contents in her file."

"It'll take days."

"All the more reason to get started."

"Why me?" Dickson muttered, throwing the bag over her shoulder and dragging Vicki out of the office.

The grip on her arm had not been retightened. While going through the crowded doorway, Vicki attempted to twist free, reaching for her bag. If she could get her hands on it, it would make a decent weapon. She shouldn't be here. Anything to attract attention . . .

"Don't do that," Dickson sighed, effortlessly bouncing her off the wall and then propelling her forward. "I'm not having a very good day."

The strip search was worse than Vicki could have imag-

ined although, as she'd regained some gross motor control
on the walk down the hall, it wasn't as bad as it could have
been. Trapped inside her own head, there wasn't anything
she could do but endure. She didn't blame Dickson, the
guard was just doing her job, but when she got out of there
Gowan and Mallard were going to be having their balls for
breakfast. The image helped sustain her.

Dickson peeled off the rubber glove and tossed it into the
trash. "These things only come in two sizes," she said,
replacing the clothing Vicki had removed with jail issue.
"Too big and too small. Can you dress yourself, Hanover?"

"Yuh . . ." *My God, that was almost a word!* She tried
it again, humiliation wiped out in that one small victory
over her body. "Yuh, yuh, yuh."

"Okay, okay, I get the picture. Jesus, you're drooling
again."

With every article of clothing a small measure of control
returned. Her movements were still jerky and unsure, but
somehow she struggled into the jail blues, oblivious to the
bored stare of the guard, oblivious to anything but the battle
she fought with her body. Hands worked. Fingers didn't.
Her sense of balance was still skewed and large movements
nearly tipped her over but she leaned against the wall and
got into the underwear, the jeans, and the shoes. The T-shirt
nearly defeated her. She couldn't find the opening for her
head and began to panic. Outside hands yanked it down,
nearly taking her nose with it.

"Come on, Hanover. I haven't got all day."

The cotton overshirt with its wide v-neck was a little easier.

*The drug's wearing off. Thank God. As soon as I can talk,
someone's going to get one hell of an earful.* As carefully
as if she were threading a needle, Vicki reached for her
glasses. Dickson reached them first.

"Forget that. You'll just have to squint."

It had never occurred to her that they wouldn't let her
keep her glasses. Of course they wouldn't. Not in Special
Needs. Glasses could be used as weapons.

But I can't see without my glasses.

All the composure she'd managed to gain with the control
over her muscles fled.

I'll be blind.

It was what she'd been terrified of since the retinitis pigmentosa had been diagnosed.

Blind.

"Nuh!" Using her arm like a club, she knocked the other woman's hand away and attempted to snatch her glasses up off the pile of discarded clothing. But her fingers wouldn't close fast enough and a sharp shove from the guard sent her lurching back against the wall.

"Here, none of that! You show fight and you wear the restraints. Understand?"

You don't understand. My glasses . . .

Something of Vicki's fear must have shown on her face. Dickson frowned and said brusquely, "Look, Hanover, you convince the shrink you don't belong in Special Needs and we'll give you your glasses back."

Hope. The psychiatrist would listen to her. Probably even recognize the drug.

"Now come on, I haven't got all day. Christ, it'll probably take me the rest of the shift just to list what you've got in that bag."

The world had condensed into a fuzzy tunnel. Vicki shuffled along it, heart leaping as doors and furniture and people loomed up without warning. She cracked her knee on the edge of something and slammed her shoulder into a corner she couldn't see.

Dickson sighed as she steered her charge through the first of the locked doors and onto the range. "Maybe you'd do better if you just closed your eyes."

The noise was overwhelming; the clatter of a busy cafeteria with the volume control gone and so many women's voices that all individual sound was lost. The smell of food overpowered the smell of prison. Vicki suddenly realized that she hadn't eaten since about nine o'clock the evening before. Her mouth flooded with saliva and her stomach growled audibly.

"Great timing, Dickson," called a new voice. "We're just counting the spoons. You'll have to keep her out here until we finish and lock 'em in for cleanup."

"Oh, joy, oh, bliss," Dickson muttered. Vicki tensed as the guard pushed her back until her shoulder blades pressed against the concrete wall. "Stay there. Don't move. You've missed lunch, but considering the food in here, that might be a good thing."

Vicki could feel people staring. The bars were a hazy grid at the edge of her vision and beyond that she could make out only a shifting sea of blue.

The hair on the back of her neck rose. *You're only in there until you talk to the shrink. You don't need to see anything.*

To her right, she could hear the clatter of spoons against a plastic tray and then the new guard's voice rising above the noise. "So, what've you got?"

"Skinbeef. Brain-fried, too."

"Violent?"

"Barely mobile."

"Can she piss in the pot?"

"Probably."

"Well, thank God for small mercies. I've already got four that have to be hosed down. Where the fuck am I supposed to put her though, that's the question. I'm three down in fifteen out of eighteen cells now."

"Put her in with Lambert and Wills."

During the long pause that followed, Vicki realized the two guards were talking about her. As though she wasn't there. As though she didn't matter. Because she didn't.

"Skinbeef, eh?" The second pause had a more ominous sound. "How old was the kid?"

"Don't know."

"Well, I think Lambert and Wills will make her feel real welcome." She raised her voice. "All right, you lot, get inside, you know the drill. Oh, for Christ's sake, Naylor, take Chin with you. You know she gets lost. . . ."

Gradually the sea of blue receded, turned into separate shapes, then disappeared. Vicki heard the sound of steel doors closing.

"Shu . . . shu . . . shu . . . ?"

"What the hell are you muttering about?" Dickson's face swam into focus as she grabbed Vicki's arm above the elbow and tugged her toward the set of double doors that led into the cell block.

"Shink . . ."

"Oh, the *shrink.* Hey, Cowan, the shrink been in yet today?"

"Yeah. Came and left before lunch."

"You heard her. Looks like you're in here until Wednesday at least."

Wednesday. Monday's half over. Then Tuesday. Then Wednesday. But the shrink came in the morning. So really only two days. Half of Monday, Tuesday, and half of Wednesday. I can do two days. I can make it. Even without my glasses.

They stopped in front of one of the cells and Vicki was willing to take any odds that the two women inside were watching her suspiciously from their bunks. The cells were built for two, a third meant the beginning of crowding that often went as high as five. She intended to move quietly into the cell, but her legs froze at the threshold and the panic started to rise again.

"Come on, Hanover, move it!"

A shove in the small of her back catapulted her forward and after three wild steps she crashed to her knees.

It's okay. It's only two days. Once the drug is gone, I'll be fine. These people are crazy. I'm not. Slowly, carefully, she got to her feet. Behind her, she heard the cell door locked and Dickson moving away. *Even if the mummy got to Henry, or Celluci*—and dealing with that possibility would have to wait—*it can't have gotten to the psychiatrist. Two days. I'll be out of here in two days.*

The bunk to her right squealed a protest as the woman reclining on it swung to her feet. Hands held out from her sides, Vicki turned to face her cell mate. *Remember, she's crazy. Probably confused. Lost. You're not. Two days.*

Cropped gray hair and a tiny, whippet-thin frame. Large dark eyes in a face that seemed all points. Something familiar . . . but Vicki couldn't see well enough to determine what.

"Well, well, well. Will wonders never cease."

The voice sound low and clear and frighteningly sane.

"Isn't it amazing the people you meet in these places, Natalie?"

The grunt from the other bunk could've meant anything.

Vicki felt a dry palm and fingers wrap around her right hand. Her knuckles began to rub painfully. She tried to return the pressure without much effect.

"It's *so* nice to see you again, Detective Nelson . . ."

*Lambert. Angel Lambert. What the hell is she doing in
Special Needs?*

". . . you can't imagine."

Oh, yes, I can . . .

"Nelson Investigations. No one is available to take your
call, but . . ."

"Damn it, Vicki, where the fuck are you?" Celluci
slammed down the receiver and slammed out of the phone
booth. Vicki never used her answering machine when she
was home. So she wasn't home. So where was she? He'd
left a message on Fitzroy's machine and called Vicki's
apartment half a dozen times from half a dozen different
areas in the city.

She was probably out working; tracking the mummy,
gathering information; maybe even doing her laundry or the
grocery shopping. He had no reason to believe she might
be in danger.

*Cantree's looking for me. Dave would've mentioned it if
she'd been pulled into this as well.* Trouble was, Cantree,
not to mention a good part of the force, knew about their
relationship. And if Fitzroy had found something out about
the mummy that Vicki thought she could use, and then she
had, Cantree and the Metro Police could be the least of her
worries. *She was a good cop. One of the best. You don't get
to be one of the best without learning not to throw yourself
at a superior force.*

So that takes care of Cantree and the mummy, Celluci
told himself. *Vicki's fine. There's no reason to believe she's
in any danger just because she didn't call you when she said
she was going to.* You're *the one up shit creek without the
paddle.*

He lit a cigarette, shoved his hands back into his pockets,
and slouched down the street, trying not to inhale—a haze
of cigarette smoke made an almost impenetrable camouflage
when people thought they were looking for a non-smoker.
It had been one of Vicki's tricks for going undercover and
he suddenly realized how much he'd been counting on her
help. *Sure, she rushes right over when Fitzroy needs her,
but when my balls are in the fire where is she . . . ?*

Fourteen

There were four messages on Henry's answering machine.
Two were from Mike Celluci for Vicki. One was from
someone named Dave Graham for Celluci; apparently nothing had changed. With a growing sense of unease, Henry
wondered just what nothing referred to. The fourth message
was from Tony, for him.

*"Look, Henry, I know Victory says you're okay, but I
want to hear it from you. Call me. Please."*

He'd barely hung up after reassuring the younger man
when the phone rang.

"Fitzroy? Celluci. Have you heard from Vicki?"

Henry's grip tightened on the receiver. The plastic
groaned. "No," he said quietly, "I haven't. Why?"

"I've been trying to get her all day. When she contacts
you, warn her to lay low. Cantree's got a warrant out for
my arrest and he might have one for her."

Cantree. The man Henry had watched ensorcelled. According to Vicki, Celluci had been vocal about his belief in
the mummy around the station so it wasn't surprising Tawfik
had decided to silence him. Henry frowned. Tawfik had no
contact with Vicki though.

"What does Vicki have to do with this?" he demanded.

"Cantree knows how close we are, Vicki and I." The
emphasis was unmistakably a deliberate dig. "He won't believe for a minute that I didn't give her all the details on
something I felt that strongly about."

Henry fought his way through a wave of jealousy and
barely made it out the other side. "How do we know he
doesn't already have her?"

"I gave Dave Graham, my partner, your number. If she's
picked up, he'll let me know."

"Graham left a message. He says nothing's changed."

"Okay. Cantree doesn't have her. You stay put in case she calls. I'll stay in touch. Once we know she's safe, we can make plans."

"Do not presume, mortal . . ."

"And don't bullshit me, Fitzroy. Can you find her?"

Could he track the call of her blood, with so many other lives around? "No."

"Then stay put! Look," Henry heard the effort it took for Celluci to force reason into his voice, "if you hit the streets, we'll have no way to pull together again. Vicki can take care of herself."

"Not against Tawfik."

"God damn it, Fitzroy, she's not up against Tawfik. He's using Cantree now to . . ."

"What about Trembley?"

"He didn't have his bully boys in place then. I know how these guys work. Once they have an organization set up, they don't dirty their own hands anymore."

"Tawfik is not some petty crime boss, Detective." Henry bit the words off and spat them into the phone. "And you have no idea of how the mind of an immortal works." Ignoring anything further Celluci had to say, and that seemed to be a great deal, Henry very carefully hung up the phone. Vicki lived. He would have felt the absence of her life.

Come to the corner where we first met, Tawfik had told him. *And I will find you.*

Find me, Henry thought back at the memory, *give yourself up into my hands, and you will tell me where she is.*

The world had taken on a tint of red.

For a few hours at least, it was over. Vicki lay back on her mattress and tried to relax her muscles enough to sleep. Although she regained more control with every hour, the twisted ridges across her back refused to unknot. She didn't blame them.

Angel Lambert was pretending to have slipped a few gears in order to get out of a trip to Kingston and the Women's Penitentiary. The right diagnosis would send her to the relative comfort of a hospital and a short time later back out on the streets. Her bragging had been very explicit. Of course, the bragging had come after Lambert had assured herself that Vicki hadn't been placed on the range as a police spy.

"Maybe they figure'd that 'cause you aren't on the force no more you'd be safe." Arms crossed, Lambert had walked a slow circle around her new cell mate. Vicki tried to keep her in sight, nearly fell over, and gave up. " 'Course, druggin' you seems to be goin' just a bit far." Making sure Vicki saw what she was about to do, she lashed out, kicking Vicki hard in the calf, the toe of her sneaker sinking deep into the muscle.

Vicki tried to avoid the blow but couldn't get her leg to respond in time. She grunted in pain and made a grab for Lambert's throat.

Lambert leaned easily back out of the way. "Well, well, well. Got doped up and got yourself in trouble, eh? Heard the guard say you were in on a juvie skinbeef. You know what that means, don't you? They're not gonna care if you pick up a few bruises. In fact, they're hopin' you will. That's why you're in with us. We got us a bit of a rep for playin' rough." She leaned back against the wall and crossed her arms, scratching a little at her biceps. "I saw your eyes when you recognized me, so I know you're in there. And I know what you're thinkin'. You're thinkin' that as soon as that drug wears off you're gonna clean my clock. Not a bad plan, you're bigger than me and you got all that fancy training, but," she smiled, "I got something you don't. Natalie, come around where our new friend can see you."

At five ten, Vicki didn't look up at many women, but Natalie Wills was huge. Even slouched she had to top six feet; if she ever straightened up, she'd probably hit six six or six seven. Her frizzy halo of blonde hair emphasized the rounded curves of her face and her pale blue eyes bulged slightly out of the sockets. At some point in the past, her nose had been broken, at least once, and improperly set. Through the space between slack lips, Vicki could hear heavy adenoidal breathing. Her breasts and belly stretched the limits of the jail uniform. It looked and moved like fat but Vicki wasn't willing to give any odds that it actually was.

"Natalie's my friend," Lambert purred. "Aren't you, Natalie?"

Natalie nodded slowly, the corners of her mouth twisting up in what Vicki assumed was a smile.

"Natalie's very strong. Aren't you, Natalie?"

Natalie nodded again.

"Why don't you show our new roommate how strong you are, Natalie. Pick her up."

Enormous hands closed around Vicki's upper arms with a grip that painfully compacted muscle down onto bone. Her shoulders rose first, but the rest of her body soon followed until her feet were six inches off the floor.

Oh, great. Darth Vader in drag.

"Very good, Natalie. Now, shake her."

After the first few seconds, it seemed as though Vicki's brain had broken free of its moorings and was slamming around independently inside her skull.

"Drop her, Natalie."

The floor seemed much farther away than she knew it was. Her knees cracked painfully hard against the concrete and she fell forward, just barely managing to get an arm between her face and the floor. If she'd had anything in her stomach, she'd have lost it.

"You puking down there?" Lambert inquired, squatting down and grabbing Vicki's hair. "You puke in my cell and you lick it up."

"Uck uf." Her voice still wasn't clear, but she figured Lambert got the point when her fist twisted around, nearly removing the handful of hair.

"Once that drug wears off, you'll be out of here next time the shrink's by. That'll be Wednesday at the earliest. You and me and Natalie, we're gonna have a fun two days."

Two days. I can take two days of anything.

But lying there, listening to Natalie's moist breathing, Vicki wondered if she could. It wasn't the physical abuse—if that got too bad, the guards would intervene, even for a skinbeef, and by morning she should be in better shape to defend herself—it was the sheer hopelessness of the situation. She'd been swept up and slotted neatly into the system and the system didn't like to admit it had made a mistake. The shrink would get her out of Special Needs, but that would only land her in another cell just like this one in another part of the jail. From there she could talk all she wanted, but her court date would never come up and like Lambert said, *"Who the hell's gonna believe you? A cop gone bad; a juvie skinbeef, a doper. In here, I've got more credibility."*

It was almost as if she'd been dropped into her worst nightmare.

Two days in here, but how long until I'm out?

And what about Henry and Celluci? Had Henry betrayed her? Had Celluci been taken? Not knowing made everything worse.

Her eyes filled with moisture and she angrily blinked them dry. Then she frowned. Refracted in a tear, she seemed to see two tiny pinpoints of glowing red light. That was impossible. She couldn't see anything.

Although the cells went no darker than a gray and shadowed twilight, lights out for Vicki had meant the end of what little sight she had without her glasses. Lambert had quickly recognized the handicap and set about taking full advantage of it. Surprisingly enough, when there was no longer any point in struggling to see, Vicki found things a little easier. Sound and smell, and the movement of air currents against her skin were a lot more useful than her deteriorating vision had been although, unfortunately, not useful enough to avoid the constant attacks. Natalie could have played the game all night, but Lambert had soon gotten bored and ordered the larger woman to bed.

Natalie liked hurting people—her strength was the only power she had—and Lambert liked seeing people hurt. Vicki sighed silently. *How nice for them that they've found each other.*

She knew she needed sleep, but she didn't think she'd be able to find it; she ached in too many places, supper had congealed into a solid lump just under her ribs, the mattress seemed to be deliberately digging into her shoulders and hips, and the smell of the place coated the inside of her nose and mouth, making it hard to breathe. Mostly she didn't think she could sleep because despair kept chasing its tail around and around in her head.

Finally exhaustion claimed her and she drifted off to the sound of plastic against concrete as two cells down a woman struggled against padded shackles and banged the hockey helmet she wore over and over against the wall.

* * *

Henry's fingers tightened where they rested against the concrete light standard and under the pressure the concrete began to crumble.

Tawfik! Here I am!

"Hey, buddy, can you spare a . . ."

Who dared? He turned.

"Holy Mary, Mother of God." Under stubble and dirt, the drunk paled. His nightmares often wore that expression. One filthy arm raised to cover his eyes, he staggered away, muttering, "Forget it, man. Forget me."

He was already forgotten.

Henry had no time to spare on thoughts of mortals. He wanted Tawfik.

He could feel the Nightwalker's anger. The brilliance of his ka was aflame with it.

Find me!

He stood at the window and stared down at the street. Although the angle of the hotel cut through his line of sight, he knew exactly where young Richmond waited. His passion thrust his ka forward with such force that Tawfik barely had to reach out to touch it. Surface thoughts were still all that were open to him, but those thoughts boiled with enough raw emotion that, for tonight, the surface was entertaining enough.

"Such a small city this turns out to be," he murmured, lightly touching the glass. "So you know my lord's plaything *and* the police officer who sent her to find me—who appears to be giving my hunting dogs a good run." Tawfik suddenly remembered the doors he had been maneuvered past on his walk through the chosen one's mind and he smiled. Two of the doors had just given up their secrets. How noble that she had tried to protect those close to her. "I imagine all these little interconnections have twisted her up far worse than I ever could. My lord must be pleased." If his lord even noticed; very often subtleties were ignored in favor of blind gorging. Tawfik sighed. He had realized long, long ago that he had sworn himself to a god without grandeur.

FIND ME!

"You can rant and rave all you like, Nightwalker. I am

not going down there. You're not thinking right now, you're only reacting. Thoughts can be twisted. Reactions, especially from one with your physical power, should be avoided.''

The Nightwalker, he was amused to note, had not grown beyond the possibility of love. How foolish, to love those who were fed upon. Like a mortal declaring himself for a cow or a chicken . . .

He took one last look at the burning, brilliant ka that he so desired and then closed his mind to it, removing temptation. ''We'll straighten things out later,'' he promised softly. ''We have the time, you and I.''

''Graham. What?''

''Any word on Vicki?''

Dave Graham raised himself up on his elbow and peered at the illuminated numbers of the clock. ''Jesus Christ, Mike,'' he hissed, ''it's two o'clock in the fucking morning. Can't it wait?''

''What about Vicki?''

Curling around the receiver so as not to wake his wife, Dave surrendered. ''There's no warrant in the system. No one's got orders to pick her up. They're keeping an eye on her place, but they're watching for you.''

''Then they've already got her.''

''They who? Cantree?''

''That's who he seems to be using.''

''He?''

''Never mind.''

Dave sighed. ''Look, maybe she's got nothing to do with this. Maybe she just went to Kingston to visit her mother.''

''We were working on the same case.''

''A police case?'' Dave took the long silence that followed his question as an answer and sighed again. ''Mike, Vicki's not on the force anymore. You're not supposed to do that.''

''Have you talked to Cantree?''

''Yeah, right after I talked to you this morning.''

''And?''

''And like I said in my message, nothing's changed. He still wants you. I don't know why. He said it had something to do with internal security, that I wasn't to ask questions, and all would be made clear later on. He's got me doing scut work out in Rexdale.''

"Did he seem strange?"

"Fuck, Mike, this whole thing is strange. Maybe you should just come in and straighten it out. Cantree'll listen.''

The bark of laughter held little humor. "The only hope the whole city, maybe the whole world has is that I don't get picked up and I don't go anywhere near Frank Cantree.''

"Right." It was two o'clock in the morning; he had no intention of getting into conspiracy theories. "I'll keep ears and eyes open, but there's not much I can do.''

"Anything you see or hear . . .''

"I'll leave a message. Not that I'm likely to see or hear anything out west of God's country, I mean, we're talking Rexdale here. You'd better get going in case they've got a trace on this call . . . Mike? I was joking. Celluci? Christ . . .'' He stared down at the receiver for a moment, then shook his head, hung up and wrapped himself around the soft, warm curves of his wife.

"Who was that?" she murmured.

"Celluci."

"What time is it?"

"Just after two.''

"Oh, God . . .'' She burrowed deeper under the covers. "They catch him yet?"

"Not yet.''

"Pity.''

By breakfast, Vicki had regained most of her muscle control; arms and legs moved when and where she wanted them to although the fine-tuning still needed work. Attempting to use her fingers for more than basic gripping of utensils was chancy and stringing more than two or three words together tied her tongue in knots. Thinking beyond her present situation, trying to analyze or plan, continued to wrap her brain in cotton, and thinking *about* her present situation did no good at all.

Without her glasses, breakfast was a heap of yellow and brown at the end of a fuzzy tunnel. It tasted pretty much exactly the way it looked.

She couldn't avoid eating sandwiched between her two

cell mates, nor could she miss noticing how the other women
on the range steered well clear of them, allowing them to
move to the front of the food line as well as claim an entire
pitcher of coffee. Natalie's strength combined with Lambert's viciousness placed them firmly on the top of the peck-
ing order. The more coherent of the other inmates regarded
Vicki with something close to relief, their expressions pro-
claiming not so much *better you than me* as *at least when
it's you it isn't me*.

Protecting her food as well as herself turned out to be
more than Vicki was capable of. Egged on by Lambert,
Natalie lifted most of Vicki's breakfast and, under the cover
of the rickety picnic table—that tilted alarmingly under every
shift in weight—pinched her thigh black and blue. Natalie
thought the whole thing was pretty funny. Vicki didn't, but
the attacks came in from the side and she couldn't fight what
she couldn't see. The meal became a painful and humiliat-
ing lesson in helplessness.

Locked back in the cell during cleanup, she kept her back
against the wall and tried to force her eyes to function. Unfortunately, it didn't take Lambert long to map the limits of
her vision. Trying to duck away from the wet end of a towel
dipped in the toilet, Vicki felt a sudden kinship with those
kids in school yards whom everyone picked on just because
they could.

When they were let back out into the range, she groped
her way past the row of tables and tried to talk to the guard.
She knew where the duty desk should be even though she
couldn't actually see it.

"Hey?"

"Hey what?" The guard's voice offered nothing.

"I ne . . ."

"No. No! NO! NO!NO!NO! NOOOOOO!"

Natalie. Standing right behind her. Although she knew
what the result would be, Vicki tried again. "You go . . ."

"NO!NO!NO! NOOOOOO!"

*She didn't think of this on her own. Lambert put her up
to it.* Teeth clenched so tightly her jaw ached, Vicki was
willing to bet that the noise would go on indefinitely.

"Look!" she finally screamed, as she shoved impotently
at the woman bellowing a hundred and twenty decibel ac-
companiment to everything she said. "I don' belon' he'!"

All at once iron rods slammed up against Vicki's face as
Natalie shoved her, and for an instant the guard loomed into
focus. It wasn't Dickson. It wasn't anyone Vicki knew.

"So tell the shrink," she suggested. Her expression tee-
tered between boredom and annoyance. "And back away
from those bars."

"Mine for two days," Lambert told her as Natalie led
Vicki back to her side.

They spent the morning watching game shows. Vicki sat
in a kind of stupor, thankful, given what she could hear over
the noise of forty women in an area designed for eighteen,
that she couldn't see the televisions. Middle America rejoicing in the glory of frost free refrigerators would've
pushed her over the edge.

Lunch was a repeat of breakfast, although Natalie moved
to her other side and therefore pinched her other thigh. A
woman with a bad case of the d.t.'s threw her plate against
the bars and two others began screaming random profanity.
Someone began to howl. Vicki kept her gaze locked firmly
on her plate. Misery seasoned every mouthful.

After lunch, things quieted down as the soap operas came
on. Lambert sat enthroned by the best of the four televisions
with Natalie enforcing at least a localized silence.

"That's my husband, you know. That's my husband," an
elderly woman called pointing at the screen. "We have thirteen children and a dog and two . . ." A squawk of pain
cut off the litany.

For the moment, Vicki appeared to have been forgotten.
Moving carefully, she headed for the showers. Maybe if she
scrubbed the stink of the place off she'd feel less wretched.

The concrete barricade that separated the showers from
the common area rose from the floor to waist height and
dropped from the ceiling to just above her shoulders. Everything in between was exposed to inmates and guards.

No one's going to be looking at your tits, Vicki, she told
herself running one hand along the damp cement. *You're
just another piece of meat. No one cares.*

A number of the stalls near the entrance were already
full. In one, the flesh-colored blur separated itself out into
two people. Anything that happened below the level of the
barricades happened in as close to privacy as was available.

Stripping off shoes and pants and underwear wasn't so

bad, but the flesh on Vicki's back crawled as she shrugged out of the shirt, and pulling the T-shirt up over her head left her feeling more exposed and vulnerable than she ever had in her life. She hurried in under the minimal protection the water offered.

Lost in the heat and the pounding of the spray, she almost convinced herself that she was safe at home and just for that moment things didn't seem so hopeless.

"Good idea, Nelson, but you shouldn't be by yourself. You're still unsteady on your pins and sometimes people fall in the shower. Terrible place. So easy to get hurt."

Lambert. And, as usual, not alone.

Vicki tried to twist her arm out of Natalie's grip. Natalie's answering twist nearly dislocated her elbow. The pain shot scarlet flames up behind her eyes and burned the fog away. Despair turned suddenly to anger.

She didn't stand a chance. She didn't care.

It didn't last long.

"What the hell is going on in there?"

"Nothing, boss," Lambert purred. "My buddy fell down." Below the guard's line of sight, her foot pressed lightly on Vicki's throat.

"She okay?"

"Fine, boss."

"Then pick her up and get out of there."

Natalie giggled, reached down, and pinched Vicki's stomach. Hard.

Vicki flinched but ignored it. Her head still rang from its violent contact with the tiles, but for the first time in what seemed like centuries, she was thinking clearly. Lambert and Wills were minor annoyances, no more. Her enemy was a three-thousand-year-old mummy who'd taken the law and twisted it and trapped her in the spiral he'd created. He was going to pay for that. She didn't know who he'd hurt to find her, Henry or Celluci, but he was going to pay for that, too. In order to make him pay, she had to be free and if the system wouldn't free her, then she'd have to do it herself.

"Thank you," she muttered absently, as Natalie dragged her upright.

People had broken out of detention centers before.

* * *

"Another beautiful day in the Metro West Detention Center. Thanks, guys, we can take her from here."

The young woman fought against the shackles, hissing and spitting like a large cat. The guards ignored her, hooked their hands under her arms and dragged her away.

"Fucking pigs!" she shrieked. "You're nothing but fucking pigs and I hope I fucking knocked your goddamned tooth out!"

Dave Graham sighed and turned to face his temporary partner. "Did she?"

"Nah," Detective Carter Aiken dabbed at the corner of his mouth and winced as his palm came away covered in blood, "but she split my lip."

"Not a bad right cross."

Aiken snorted. "Easier to appreciate it from your angle. There's a crapper at the end of the hall, I'll be right back."

"What're you going to do, stick your head in the toilet?"

"Who said anything about my head?" Aiken sucked the blood off his teeth and his brows rose dramatically. "I've had to piss since we left division."

Dave laughed as the other man disappeared around the corner and leaned back against the wall. He liked Aiken. He wished they'd met under better circumstances. He wished he knew what the hell was going on.

"Well, hello, stranger."

He straightened and turned. The Auxiliary Sergeant with her arms full of computer printout looked familiar but . . . "Hania? Hania Wojotowicz? Hot damn! When did you make sergeant?"

She laughed. "Six weeks ago. Actually, six weeks, two days, four hours and," she checked her watch, nearly losing the pile of papers, "eleven minutes. But who's counting. What are you doing way out here? Where's Mike?"

Obviously, she hadn't heard about Celluci. Fine with him, he was getting tired of talking about it. "Temporary duty. You know how it is. What about you?"

"Detention's having a little trouble with the OMS. Their computer program," she continued when he looked blank, "the Offender Management System. I've come to try and straighten it out."

"If anyone can do it . . ." When they'd first met, Hania had been brought in to crunch the data gathered as part of a massive manhunt after a homicide down in Parkdale. As far as he was concerned, what she could do with a computer should be filed somewhere between magic and miracle. Even Celluci, who'd been heard to suggest that all silicon should go back to the beach where it belonged, had been favorably impressed. "How bad is it?"

Hania shrugged. "Not very. In fact, I've done my part, all that's left is for someone to enter all this," a nod of her head indicated the printouts she carried, "back into the system."

"Good lord, that'll take days."

"Not really, most of this paper is blank. It's all personal possession lists and not many people book in here with luggage. Well, there are exceptions. . . ." She flipped a page back and grinned. "Listen to this. Four pens, four pencils, a black magic marker, a plastic freezer bag containing six folded empty plastic freezer bags, a brush, a comb, a cosmetic case containing a lipstick and two tampons, seven marbles in a cotton bag, a set of lock picks in a leather folder, a magnifying glass in a protective case, three notebooks half full, one notebook empty, a package of tissues, a package of condoms, a package of birth control pills, a screwdriver, a Swiss Army knife, a fish-shaped water pistol, cotton swabs, tweezers, a pair of needlenose pliers, a pair of wrapped surgical gloves, a small bottle of ethyl alcohol, a high-powered flashlight with four extra batteries, two u-shaped nails, $12.73 in assorted change, and a half-eaten bag of cheese balls. Now I ask you, what kind of weirdo carries all that in her purse?"

It took Dave a moment to find his voice. "No ID?" he managed at last.

"Not a thing. Not so much as a Visa statement. Probably pitched it just before she got picked up. They do sometimes, but you know that."

"Yeah." They did sometimes. He didn't think they had this time. "Who do they say belongs to all this?"

"They don't. But I can find out for you." She started down the hall. "Come on, there's a terminal in here we can use."

He followed blindly. He knew exactly what kind of weirdo carried all that in her purse.

"Dave? Detective-Sergeant Graham? Are you listening to me?"

"Yeah. Sorry." Except he wasn't. He couldn't hear anything over Celluci's voice saying, *"Then they've already got her."*

"Fitzroy? Celluci. I'm assuming that if you'd managed to find Vicki last night you'd have changed your message to let me know." *And if you found her and didn't change the message,* the tone continued, *I'm going to rip your head off.* "Stay put tonight. At least until I call. I'm going to try to get into her apartment and have a look around—no one disappears without leaving some kind of evidence—but after that we need to talk. We're going to have to work together to find her." The last statement landed like a thrown gauntlet even through the tiny speaker of the answering machine.

In spite of everything, Henry smiled. *You need my help, mortal man. Time you admitted it.*

"Hi, Henry, it's Brenda. Just a reminder that we need *Love's Labor Lashed*, or whatever you've decided to name it, by the fifteenth. We've got Aliston signed to do the cover on this one and he promises no purple eye shadow. Call me."

"Celluci? Dave Graham. It's quarter after four, Tuesday, November third . . ."

It was now six twelve, eight minutes after sunset.

". . . Call me the instant you get this message; I'll be home all evening." His voice grew strained, as though he couldn't really believe what he was saying. "I think I've found her. It isn't good."

Henry's fingers closed around the chair back and with a loud crack the carved oak splintered into a half dozen pieces. He stared down at the wreckage without really seeing it. This man on the phone, this David Graham, knew where Vicki was. If he wanted the information, he would have to take the message to Michael Celluci.

The police in the unmarked car were easy to avoid. They appeared to have little interest in the job they were doing and paid the shifting shadows just back of the sidewalk no attention at all. As for getting into the apartment itself, well, he had a key. The door opened quietly before him and closed

as quietly behind. He stood silently in the entryway and
listened to the life that moved about at the end of the hall.
The heartbeat pounded faster than it should and the breath
was short and almost labored. The blood scent dominated,
but fear and anger and fatigue layered over it in equal proportions.

He walked forward and paused at the edge of the living
room. Although it was very dark, he could see the kneeling
man clearly.

"I have a message for you," he said, and took a perverse
pleasure in the sudden jump of the heartbeat.

"Jesus H. Christ," Celluci hissed, surging to his feet and
glaring down at Henry. "Don't do that! You weren't there
a second ago! And besides, I thought I told you . . ."

Henry merely looked up at him.

Celluci pushed the curl of hair back off his forehead with
a trembling hand. "All right, you have a message." His
eyes widened. "Is it from Vicki?"

"Are you ready to hear it?"

"God damn you!" Celluci grabbed the lapels of Henry's
leather trench coat and tried to drag him off his feet. He
couldn't budge the smaller man although that took a moment to sink in. "Damn you!" he swore again, anchoring
his grip more firmly in the leather. "If it's from Vicki, tell
me!"

The pain in the detective's voice got through where anger
alone wouldn't have and shame followed close behind. *What
am I doing?* Almost gently, Henry pulled Celluci's hands
off his coat. *She won't love me more for hurting you.* "The
message was from Dave Graham. He wants you to call him
at home. He says he thinks he's found her."

One breath, two, three; Celluci groped blindly for the
phone, the darkness no longer a protection but an enemy to
be fought. Henry reached out and guided his hands, then
moved quickly to the extension in the bedroom as he dialed.

"Dave? Where is she?"

Dave sighed. Henry heard the soft flesh of his lower lip
compressed between his teeth. "Metro West Detention
Center. At least, I think it's her."

"Didn't you check!"

"Yeah, I checked." From the sound of his voice,
Detective-Sergeant Graham still didn't believe what he'd

found. "I better start at the beginning. . . ." He told how
he'd run into Hania Wojotowicz and how she'd listed the
contents of the purse, how she'd called up the inmate file,
how the description had fit Vicki Nelson even though the
name had said Terri Hanover. "They picked her up on a
skinbeef, Mike, against a twelve-year-old boy. You've never
read such a crock of shit. She was on something, they don't
know what, so they stuck her in Special Needs."

"They drugged her! The bastards drugged her!"

"Yeah. *If* it's her." But he didn't sound like he had any
doubts. "Who are *they,* Mike? What the fuck is going on?"

"I can't tell you. Where is she exactly—now?"

The pause said Dave knew exactly why Celluci asked.
"She's still in Special Needs," he said at last. "D Range.
Cell three. But I didn't actually see her. They wouldn't let
me onto the range. I don't *know* it's her."

"I do."

"This has gone too far." He swallowed, once, hard. "I'm
talking to Cantree tomorrow."

"No! Dave, you talk to Cantree about any of this and
you'll be ass deep in it with the rest of us. Just keep your
mouth shut for a little while longer. Please."

"A little while longer," Dave repeated and sighed again.
"All right, partner, how long?"

"I don't know. Maybe you should take that vacation time
you've got coming."

"Yeah. Maybe I should."

The quiet click as Dave Graham hung up his end of the
line sounded through the apartment.

Henry came out of the bedroom and the two men stared
at each other.

"We have to get her out," Celluci said. He could see
only a pale oval of face in the darkness. *I'll do anything I
must to get her out no matter how little I like it. I'll even
work with you because I need your strength and speed.*

"Yes," Henry agreed. *The "detention centers" I know
are centuries in the past. I need your knowledge. My feelings
here are not important; she is.*

The silent subtext echoed so loudly between them it was
amazing it didn't alert the police watching the building and
bring them racing inside.

Fifteen

"All right, when the lights go out, you go over the wall, across the yard, in the emergency exit and . . ."

"Up three flights of stairs and through the first emergency door on my left. I remember your instructions, Detective." Henry stepped back from his BMW and looked down at Celluci who still sat in the driver's seat. "Are *you* certain you can get near enough to the generator?"

"Don't worry about me, you just be ready to move. You won't have much time. The moment the power goes off, all four guards will move to A Range to start emergency lockup. Vicki's in D; they'll do that last. You'll also have to deal with the other women on the range; it's just turned eight, so they won't be in the cells yet. . . ."

"Michael."

Celluci started. Something in the sound of his name stopped the flow of words and brought his head up. Although he knew the other man's eyes were hazel, they seemed much darker than hazel could be as if they'd absorbed some of the night.

"I want her out of there as much as you do. We will be successful. She will be freed. One way or another."

The words, the tone, the man himself, left no room for argument, no room for doubt. Celluci nodded, comforted in spite of himself and, as he had once before in a farmhouse kitchen, he thought that he would be willing to follow . . . *a romance writer. Yeah, sure.* But the protest had little force behind it. He wet his lips and dropped his gaze, aware as he did that Fitzroy had allowed it and, strangely enough, found himself not resenting the other's strength. "You won't have much time before the emergency system kicks in, so you'll have to be fast."

"I know."

He put the car into gear. "So, uh, be careful."

"I will." Henry watched the car drive away, watched until the taillights disappeared around a corner, then walked slowly across the street toward the detention center. His pants and crepe-soled shoes were black, but his turtleneck sweater was a deep, rich burgundy; no point in looking more like a second story man than necessary. He carried a dark wool cap to pull over his hair the instant he started over the wall as he'd learned early after his change that a pale-haired vampire was at a disadvantage when it came to moving through the darkness.

From not very far away came the sound of traffic, of a radio, of a baby crying; people who paid no attention to the knowledge that other people were locked in cages only a short distance from where they lived their lives. *Or perhaps they've forgotten they know.* Henry reached out and lightly touched the outer wall, sensitive eyes turned away from the harsh glare of the floodlights.

Dungeons, prisons, detention centers—there was little to choose between them. He could feel the misery, the defiance, the anger, the despair; the bricks were soaked in it. Every life that had been held here had left a dark impression. Henry had never understood the theory that torture by confinement was preferable to death.

"*They're given a chance to change,*" Vicki'd protested when a news article on capital punishment had started the argument.

"*You've been inside your country's prisons,*" he'd pointed out. "*What chance for change do they offer? I have never lived in a time that so enjoyed lying to itself.*"

"*Maybe you'd rather we followed good King Hal's example and chained prisoners to a wall until it was time to cut off their heads?*"

"*I never said the old ways were better, Vicki, but at least my father never insulted those he arrested by insisting he did it for their own good.*"

"*He did it for* his *own good,*" she'd snorted and had refused to discuss the matter further.

Having found the place he'd go over the wall, Henry moved on until he crossed the line between the floodlights and the night, then he turned and waited. He had faith in Celluci's ability to cut the power, more faith he suspected than Celluci had in his ability to go into the detention center and bring Vicki out—but then, he'd had a lot more time to learn to see around the blinkers jealousy insisted be worn.

They were very much alike, Michael Celluci and Vicki Nelson, both wrapped up in their ideas of The Law. There was one major difference Henry had noticed between them; Vicki broke The Law for ideals, Celluci broke it for her. *She*, not justice, had kept him silent last August in London. It was her personally, not injustice, that drove him tonight— however little he liked what they were about to do.

It probably wouldn't have helped, Henry reflected, if he'd told Celluci that he had attempted this sort of thing before. . . .

Henry had not been in England when Henry Howard, Earl of Surrey, had been arrested, and between the time it took for news to reach him and the complications laid on travel by his nature, he didn't arrive in London until January eighth; two days before the execution. He spent that first night frantically gathering information. An hour after sunset on the ninth, having quickly fed down by the docks, he stood and stared up at the black stone walls of the Tower.

Originally, Surrey had been given a suite overlooking the river, but an attempt to escape by climbing down the privy at low tide had ensured his removal to less congenial, interior accommodations. From where he stood, Henry could just barely see the flicker of light in Surrey's window.

"No," he murmured to the night, "I don't imagine you can sleep, you arrogant, bloody fool, not with the block awaiting you in the morning."

All things considered, he decided there was no real need to go over the wall—although he rather regretted the loss of the flamboyant gesture—and moved, a shadow within the shadows, past the guards and into the halls of the Tower. At Surrey's door, he raised the heavy iron bar and slipped silently inside, pulling the door closed behind him. Unless things had changed a great deal since his days at court, the guards would not bother them before dawn and by dawn they would be far away.

He stood for a moment drinking in the sight and scent of the dearest friend he had had in life, realizing how much he had missed him. The slight figure, dressed all in black, sat

at a crude table by the narrow window, a tallow candle his
only light, a heavy iron shackle locked around one slim
ankle and chained in turn to a bolt in floor. He had been
writing—Henry could smell the fresh ink—but he sat now
with his dark head pillowed on his arm and despair written
across the line of his shoulders. Henry felt a fist close around
his heart and he had to stop himself from rushing forward
and catching the other man up in a near hysterical embrace.

Instead, he took a single step away from the door and
softly called, "Surrey."

The dark head jerked erect. "Richmond?" The young
earl spun around, eyes wide with terror and when he saw
who stood within his cell he threw himself against the far
wall with a rattle of chain and strangled cry. "Am I so near
to death," he moaned, "that the dead come calling?"

Henry smiled. "I'm as flesh and blood as you are. More
so, you've lost a lot of weight."

"Yes, well, the cook does his poor best but it's not what
I'm used to." One long-fingered hand brushed the air with
a dismissive gesture Henry well remembered and then rose
to cover Surrey's eyes. "I'm losing my mind. I make jokes
with a ghost."

"I am no ghost."

"Prove it."

"Touch me then." Henry walked forward, hand outstretched.

"And lose my soul? I will not." Surrey sketched the sign
of the cross and squared his shoulders. "Come any closer
and I'll call for the guards."

Henry frowned, this was not going the way he'd planned.
"All right, I'll prove it without your touch." He thought a
moment. "Do you remember what you said when we
watched the execution of my father's second wife, your
cousin, Anne Boleyn? You told me that although her con-
demnation was an inevitable matter of state business, you
pitied the poor wretch and you hoped they'd let her laugh
in hell for you'd always thought her laugh more beautiful
than her face."

"Richmond's spirit would know that, for I said it while
he lived."

"All right," Henry repeated, thinking, *it's a good thing
I came early, this could take all night.* "You wrote this after

I died and, trust me, Surrey, your poems are not yet read in heaven.'' He cleared his throat and softly recited, ''The secret thoughts, imparted with such trust,/The wanton talk, the diverse change of play,/The friendship sworn, each promise kept so just,/Wherewith we passed the winter night away . . .''

'' ' . . . That place of bliss,/the graceful, gay companion, who with me shared,/the jolly woes, the hateless short debate . . .' '' Surrey stepped away from the wall, his body trembling with enough force to vibrate the chain he wore. ''I wrote that for you.''

''I know.'' He had copies of nearly everything Surrey had written; the earl's flamboyant lifestyle meant his servants often waited for their pay and were, therefore, open to earning a little extra.

'' 'Proud Windsor, where I, in just and joy/With a King's son my childish years did pass . . .' Richmond?'' Eyes welling, Surrey flung himself forward and Henry caught him up in a close embrace.

''You see,'' he murmured into the dusky curls, ''I have flesh, I live, and I've come to get you out of here.''

After an incoherent moment of mingled joy and grief, Surrey pushed away and, swiping at his cheeks with his palm, he looked his old friend up and down. ''You haven't changed,'' he said, fear touching his expression again. ''You look no different than you did when you . . . than you did at seventeen.''

''You look very little different yourself.'' Although eleven years had added flesh and he now wore the mustache and long curling beard fashionable at court, Surrey's face and manner were so little changed that Henry had no difficulty believing he'd gotten himself into the mess he had. His beloved friend had been wild, reckless, and immature at nineteen. Mere months short of thirty he was wild, reckless, and immature still. ''As to my lack of change, well, it's a long story.''

Surrey flung himself down on the bed and with difficulty lifted the shackled leg up onto the pallet. ''I'm not going anywhere,'' he pointed out with a sardonic lift of ebony brows.

And he wasn't, Henry realized, not until his curiosity was satisfied. If he wanted to save him, he'd have to tell him the truth. "You'd gone to Kenninghall, to spend time with Frances, and His Majesty sent me to Sherifhutton," he began.

"I remember."

"Well, I met a woman . . ."

Surrey laughed, and the laughter held, in spite of his outward calm, a hint of hysteria. "So I'd heard."

Henry was thankful he could no longer blush. In the past that tone had turned him scarlet. This was the first time he had told the story since his change; he'd not expected it to be as difficult as it was and he walked over to the desk so he could look out into the night as he talked, one hand shuffling the papers Surrey had left. When he finished, he turned and faced the rude bed.

Surrey was sitting on its edge, head buried in his hands. As though he felt the weight of Henry's gaze, he slowly looked up.

The force of the rage and grief that twisted his face drove Henry back a step. "Surrey?" he asked, suddenly unsure.

"Vampire?"

"Yes . . ."

Surrey stood and fought to find his tongue. "You gained immortality," he said at last, "and you let me believe you were dead."

Taken completely by surprise, Henry raised his hands as though the words were blows.

"The death you allowed me to believe in dealt me a wound that still bleeds," Surrey continued, his voice shredding under the edge of his emotion. "I loved you. How could you betray me so?"

"Betray you? How could I tell you?"

"How could you not?" His brows drew down and his tone grew suddenly bitter. "Or did you think you couldn't trust me? That *I* would betray *you?*" He read the answer on Henry's face. "You did. I called you the brother of my heart and you thought I would give your secret to the world."

"I called you the same, and I loved you just as much as you loved me, but I knew you, Surrey; this is a secret you would not have been able to keep."

"Yet after giving me eleven years of sorrow you trust me with it now?"

"I've come to get you out. I could not let you die . . ."

"Why? Because my death would cause you the same grief that I've carried for so long?" He took a deep breath and closed his eyes, his throat moving in an effort to suppress the tears that trembled on the edge of every word. After a moment he said, so softly that had Henry still been mortal he would not have heard, "I'll keep your secret. I'll carry it to my grave." Then his head came up and he added, a little louder. "Tomorrow."

"Surrey!" Nothing Henry said would change his mind. He begged; he pleaded; he went down on his knees; he even offered immortality.

Surrey ignored him.

"Dying to have revenge on me is foolishness!"

"The Richmond I knew, the boy who was my brother, died eleven years ago. I mourned him. I mourn him still. You are not here."

"I could force you," he said at last. "I have powers you can't defend against."

"If you force me," Surrey said, "I will hate you."

He had no answer to that.

He stayed and argued until the coming sun forced him away. The next night, he entered the chapel of the Tower, opened the unsealed coffin that held the severed head and trunk of Henry Howard, Earl of Surrey, kissed the pale lips, and cut free a lock of hair. His nature no longer allowed him tears. He wasn't sure he would have shed them if it had.

" '*Sat Superest,* it is enough to prevail.' " Henry shook himself free of the memories. "I should have taken Surrey's motto as my own, shoved it down his throat, and carried him out of there flung over my shoulder." Well, he was older now, more sure of himself, more certain that his way was the right way, less likely to be swayed by hysterical reactions. "I should have let him hate me, at least he'd have been alive to do it." Vicki, he knew, would not have been so foolish. Had she been in the tower in Surrey's place, first she would have worried about getting free, *then* she would have hated him.

And she was unlikely to protest against this rescue tonight.

If she were in her right mind.

As Henry tried not to think of what the drugs might have done, the floodlights went out.

Vicki had spent the afternoon using sound and touch to discover the boundaries of her confinement. Surprisingly enough, with her eyes removed from the general equation and used only to peer at specific close-ups, she seemed to get around better, not worse. She hadn't realized how much she'd come to rely on other senses over the last year until they were all she had to rely on. Without her glasses, her vision—or lack of it—had become more of a distraction than a help.

After the incident in the showers, Lambert had returned triumphant to the soap operas, but Natalie followed close on Vicki's heels, her adenoidal breathing occasionally drowning out the constant roar of the four televisions and intermittent roar of the women who watched them. Commercials seemed to have the greatest effect—Vicki wondered if maybe it was because the plots of commercials were understood by the greatest number of the inmates.

Every now and then, Natalie would reach out and viciously pinch a hunk of Vicki's flesh. Her muscle control still affected by the residue of the drug, Vicki hadn't the speed or coordination to avoid the snakelike strikes. The fifth time it happened, she slowly turned and beckoned her tormentor closer.

"The nect time you do tha'," she said, forming the words as carefully as she could, "I'm gona' grab you' wris', pull you close, and rip you' ear off. Then I'm gona' feed it to you. You understand?"

Natalie giggled, but the intervals between the pinches became longer and finally she wandered away to watch Family Feud. Vicki wasn't sure if her threat had worked or if the large woman had just become bored and moved on to another victim.

By suppertime Vicki had decided there was only one way out. Back in behind the shower there was an emergency exit; it wasn't particularly visible from the inside and most of the inmates weren't even aware it existed, but nine years spent on the police force gave Vicki an advantage. The Metro West Detention Center was the only detention center for women in the city, and while the numbers were climbing every year there were still far fewer female police officers than male. Female cops spent a disproportionate amount of time at Metro West.

Trouble was, the door opened in, there wasn't a handle or any real way to get hold of it, and the lock was a huge solid metal presence.

That any half decent cracksman could have open in a heartbeat and a half, Vicki decided after a quick fingertip examination. *Of course, lock picks and opportunity might prove a little difficult.*

After supper, during cleanup while they were locked back in the cells, Vicki sat cross-legged on her mattress and probed thoughtfully at the cotton ticking. The mattresses on the bunks were slabs of solid foam, absolutely useless for anything except as a barrier between body and boards, but the extras, the ones thrown on the floor were old army surplus issue. They weren't very thick, they weren't very comfortable, but they did appear to have metal springs. In time, she could work a piece free and . . .

Except, she didn't have time. The shrink would be doing examinations tomorrow afternoon and she'd be sent off Special Needs to one of the regular ranges—with the mummy in control she had no hope of being set free. It wouldn't be as easy to escape a regular range—or for that matter, to survive one. More of the inmates were likely to recognize her and fatal "accidents" were not unknown when cops found themselves on the other side of the system. She'd obviously have to convince the shrink she belonged right where she was.

Vicki grinned. Her playing crazy would drive Lambert crazy for sure.

"What the fuck are you grinnin' about?"

Vicki turned toward Lambert's side of the cell and her grin broadened. "I was just thinking," she said, carefully maintaining control of each word, "how in the country of the blind, the one-eyed man, or in this case, woman, is king."

"You're fuckin' crazy," Lambert growled.

"Glad you think so." She didn't see Lambert's expression, but she heard Natalie come off her bunk and felt the air shift as the large woman moved toward her. *Oh, shit . . .*

She fought the nearly overwhelming urge to scramble away. It wouldn't prevent the inevitable. *And I am not going to give Lambert the satisfac . . .* The open-handed blow flung her head back and almost knocked her over. Vicki rolled with it and came up facing the fuzzy column of blue that was Natalie, trying to ignore the ringing in her ears.

Off to her left, she heard Lambert laugh. "So she's showin' fight, eh? This is gonna be interestin'. Hurt her, Natalie."

Natalie giggled.

"All right, cleanup's over!" The cell doors opening added percussion to the guard's announcement. "Everybody out! Roberts, put your clothes back on."

"Itchy, boss."

"I don't care. Get dressed."

Natalie paused and Lambert joined her in Vicki's limited field of vision. "Later," she promised, patting a massive biceps. "You can hurt her later. Meanwhile, I think she should sit with us to watch Wheel of Fortune."

Oh, God . . . "I'd rather be beaten unconscious," Vicki growled, trying to free her arm from Natalie's sudden crushing grip.

Lambert leaned close so Vicki could see her smile. "Later," she promised again.

Billy Bob Dickey from Tulsa, Oklahoma, had just bought a vowel when the lights went out, cutting Vanna off as she turned the first of four e's. The range erupted into complete and utter pandemonium.

"Everyone just stay calm!" The bellowing of the guard could barely be heard over the sounds of terror, rage, and hysterical glee. "Get back in your cells. Now!"

Vicki had no idea how much the others could or couldn't see, but from the sound of it even those with normal night sight were nearly blind. The guards, she knew, would be racing for A Range where all four of them would be needed to coordinate a manual lockup. D Range would be unobserved for the next few minutes.

My kingdom for a set of lock picks. A God-given chance and I can't use it for anything . . . Jesus! She scrambled backward as the picnic table lurched sideways under the sudden shifting of weight across from panicked inmates. *This thing's being held together with spit and prayers.*

"And where the fuck do you think you're goin'?" Lambert demanded. "*I* say when we leave. Natalie, bring her back!"

"Can't see!" Natalie protested, wood groaning with relief as she stood.

"So what? Neither can she!"

Vicki felt the surge of air and stepped sideways out of the way. " 'Trust me, he said, and come. I followed like a child—a blind man led me home.' "

"What the fuck are you talking about?"

"It's a poem," Vicki told her, easily avoiding Natalie's next rush; the large woman displaced a tropical storm's worth of air. "By W. H. Davies. He was saying, I believe, that when everyone's blind, the people with the practice have the advantage." She smiled, bent, and used Natalie's momentum to heave her up and across her shoulders and into the air.

The crash of splintering wood told Vicki her enormous tormentor had just smashed through the abused table. "I hope . . . that . . . hurt," she panted as her knees buckled and she collapsed to the floor trying to get her breath. *Good God, she's got to weigh close to four hundred pounds; isn't it amazing what adrenaline can do.*

Her fingers brushed against a six-inch sliver of wood and, still fighting for breath, she picked it up. Given the spread of the debris, the table had been completely destroyed by the impact. *Jesus H. Christ. This thing could've killed somebody!* She sat back on her heels and tried to break the fragment across the grain. It bent but it didn't even crack. *I don't think this is pine. . . . Just like the city to buy oak picnic tables for a detention center and then let them fall apart.* Her heart suddenly began to slam against her ribs, her heartbeat drowning out the chaos around her. Oak. Hardwood. A splinter with a thin, flexible tip.

No. No way. That lock's big and clumsy, sure, but only an idiot would try to pick it with a chunk of wood. No.

Why not?'

It's not like I've got a lot of options.

As Vicki stood, she brushed up against another body

standing so close they were all but breathing the same air. Small, powerful fingers dug into her forearm.

"Natalie's going to fucking rip you apart!"

The emergency generator would be kicking in soon and Vicki knew she didn't have much time, but there were some temptations it would take a saint to resist.

"You shouldn't have come this close," she said, yanked Lambert's hand loose, twisted the arm up and around, and kicked her, hard, in the direction of her enforcer. A strangled grunt, a curse, and a cry of pain told her the target had been hit as she hurried toward the showers.

She found the concrete privacy barrier by crashing into it, and, limping a little, groped her way along its rough edge.

They're finished with A Range by now, probably well into B. So little time . . .

The area between the barrier and the wall was less than ten feet wide. Vicki launched herself across the gaping chasm it represented in the dark with no thought of caution. Preventing a few more bruises wouldn't pay for another night spent behind bars. She hit the wall with enough force to bounce back, then began searching frantically for the hidden exit.

The crash of steel doors sounded over the confusion behind her and she jumped, almost dropping her sliver of wood.

If they've already moved onto C Range . . .

Finally her fingers found the lock and she dropped to her knees in front of it.

And while I'm down here, I might as well say a prayer as I don't have a hope in hell of . . . son of a bitch. The first tumbler fell.

Christ, I could practically pick this thing with my fingernails. I get out of here and I'm going to have a long talk with someone. Those picnic tables are death traps and this lock is a joke. Odds are good the men's *detention center gets decent upkeep.*

The second tumbler fell.

This is a disgrace.

She could hear one of the guards yelling something about tranquilizers. He sounded close.

Oh, shit . . . Her hands were slick with sweat and she could feel the wood beginning to splinter.

Okay.

The guards were definitely in C Range. It suddenly got harder to breathe.

Almost.

Someone appeared to be putting up a fight.

Give 'em hell, slow them down, and . . .

That wasn't Natalie she could hear breathing behind her? No. Just the echo of her own desperate sucking in of air that tasted of shower mold.

There . . .

Although unlocked, the heavy door stayed securely closed and Vicki realized she had no way to pull it open.

"NO!" One knuckle split with the force of the blow and then she had to scramble back out of the way as the door flew open toward her.

She couldn't mistake the arm that wrapped around her and kept her from falling, nor the embrace she suddenly found herself enfolded in. With adrenaline sizzling along every nerve, she fought to get free.

"Goddamnit, Henry!" Something started her trembling violently. It felt like anger. "What the fuck took you so long?"

The sound of the shower had been going on for a long time. When it finally shut off, the two men looked at each other across the width of the living room.

"You've known her longer," Henry said softly. "Is she okay?"

"I think so."

"It's just she doesn't seem to be . . ." He spread his hands.

"Feeling anything?"

"Yes."

"It's all there. It's just all locked in behind the anger."

"She has every right to be angry."

Celluci scowled. "I didn't say she didn't have."

During the ride back to Henry's condo, Vicki had spat out the bare bones of what had happened to her. Both men had listened quietly, both recognizing that interrupting with either questions or passions would stop the flow of words completely. When she'd finished, Celluci had immediately begun making plans to take care of Gowan and Mallard, but Vicki had glared through the spare pair of glasses he'd brought for her and said, *"No. I don't know how or when, but the pay back's mine. Not yours. Mine."*

Her tone left little doubt that Gowan and Mallard would get exactly what they had coming.

And then she'd added, *"I want Tawfik,"* in such a voice that even Henry had found himself chilled by it.

They turned toward her as she limped into the living room, wet hair slicked back, the bruise that discolored one side of her face a sharp contrast to the pallor of the other cheek. The hand smoothing the front of her sweatshirt was wrapped in gauze.

I've seen holy fanatics, Henry thought, as Vicki crossed over to the window, *wearing exactly that expression.* Again, the two men exchanged worried glances. She moved, not as if she might break at any second, but as if she might explode.

"Before we begin," she said to the night, "order a pizza. I'm starving."

"But we still don't know," Celluci pointed out, waving a piece of gnawed crust for emphasis, "how Tawfik found out about Vicki."

"Once Cantree told him about you, it wouldn't have been difficult for Tawfik to have lifted the information from his mind." Henry paused in his slow pacing and looked down at Celluci. "Cantree would believe that anything you knew, you would have told Vicki and Tawfik must have decided to tie up the loose end."

"Yeah? Then why such an elaborate scenario?" Celluci tossed the crust into the box and straightened, wiping his hands. "Why not get rid of her the way he got rid of Trembley? Kapow and it's over."

"I don't know."

"It seems to me that you spent at least as much time talking with him as Cantree did. How do we know you didn't say anything?"

"Because," the pause filled with something very close to menace, "I wouldn't."

Celluci fought a nearly irresistible urge to drop his gaze

and continued, his voice beginning to rise. "We know he can mess with people's thoughts—the staff at the museum are proof of that. How do we know he didn't lift her from your mind?"

"No! I would never betray her."

Celluci's eyes narrowed as he realized the source of the pain that shadowed Henry's protest. *No, he wouldn't betray her. He loves her. He really loves her. The son of a bitch. And he's afraid he might have done it. That Tawfik might have lifted Vicki out of his head.* "Would you have even noticed him doing it?" The question needed to be asked. He wasn't just twisting the knife. At least he didn't think he was.

"No one walks uninvited through my mind, mortal." But Tawfik had touched him just by existing and Henry had no real idea what the wizard-priest might have picked up. For all his declared certainty, this showed in his voice. Celluci heard it and Henry knew he did.

"Enough." Vicki threw herself up out of the armchair, wiping grease off her mouth with the palm of her hand. "It doesn't matter how he knew about me. It's over. The only thing that matters now, and I mean the *only* thing, is finding Tawfik and taking him out. Henry, you said that the woman who left the Solicitor General's library before Cantree went in said she'd meet him at the ceremony."

"Yes."

"And Tawfik himself told you it was essential for the gathered acolytes to be sworn to his god as soon as possible."

"Yes."

"Well, since we know that his first group of acolytes have been pulled—at the very least—from the upper ranks of both the metro and the provincial police forces, we'd better stop him before this ceremony happens."

"How do we know it hasn't?"

Vicki snorted. "You tell me. I've been a little out of touch the last couple of days."

"The party was Saturday. Tawfik spoke with me Sunday." Had it only been two days ago? "Monday . . ." Was that why he hadn't come, Henry wondered. Were they already too late?

"For what it's worth," Celluci offered, "Cantree was home last night."

"How do you know?"

"I watched his house for a while."

"Why?"

"I thought I might ask him what the fuck was going on."

"Did you?"

"No."

"Why not?"

"Because I remembered what happened to Trembley and it occurred to me that lying low might be a healthier plan. All right?" Celluci threw the question at Henry, then followed it with, "Might have been more useful if you'd done as thorough an interrogation on Tawfik during your little stroll. Or were you too busy being creatures of the night together that you forgot the s.o.b.'s a killer?"

"I am as immortal as you are, Richmond. I will never grow old. I will never die. I will never leave you."

Celluci read the thought off Henry's face. He flung himself up out of the chair and across the living room. "You bastard, that's exactly what happened, isn't it?"

Henry met the rush with an outstretched hand and Celluci rocked to a halt as though he'd hit a wall. Just for a moment, Henry wanted to make him understand. And then the moment passed. "Never presume," he said, catching the other man's gaze and holding it, forcing him to stand and listen, "that you know what I do or why I do it. I am not as you are. The laws I follow are not the laws that master you. We are very, very different you and I; in two things only we are the same. Whatever Tawfik and I spoke of, whatever my reaction to him, all that has changed. He has hurt one of mine and I will not have that."

As Henry dropped his hand, Celluci staggered forward. He had the strange feeling he would have fallen had Henry not continued to hold his gaze until he steaded. "And the second thing," he demanded, stepping back and shoving the curl of hair back off his face.

"Please, Detective," Henry purposefully lowered his lids, allowing Celluci to look away if he chose, "do not attempt to convince me you have no knowledge of the other . . . interest we share."

Brown eyes stared into hazel for a moment. Finally, Celluci sighed.

"If you two have finished," Vicki snapped, leaning back against the windows and crossing her arms, "can we get on with it?"

"Finished?" Celluci snorted quietly, turning and walking back to the couch. "Something tells me we're just getting started." He pushed the pizza box out of the way and dropped down, the couch springs protesting the sudden weight. "Look, ceremonies don't usually happen on a whim. Most religions have schedules to keep."

Vicki nodded. "Good point. Henry?"

"He said, *soon.* Nothing more definite."

"Damnit, there's got to be somewhere we can find out about ancient Egyptian religious rituals." Her eyes narrowed. "Mike . . ."

"Uh-uh. The closest I ever got to ancient Egypt was doing a little overtime at the Tut exhibit. And that was years ago."

"Oh, you've been a lot closer to ancient Egypt than that." Vicki smiled. She never thought she'd be grateful he'd cultivated the woman. "What about your friend, Dr. Shane?"

"Rachel?"

"If there's anyone left in the city who'll know," Vicki pointed out, handing him the phone. "It's her."

Celluci shook his head. "I don't want to bring more civilians into this. The danger . . ."

"Tawfik is at his weakest now," Henry said quietly. "If Dr. Shane can't help us stop him before he completes his power base, then you won't be able to keep her safe, not from what's likely to come."

"Rachel? It's Mike. Mike Celluci. I need to ask you a couple of questions."

She laughed and doodled a sarcophagus in the margin of the acquisition report she'd been spending the evening with. "What? Don't I even get dinner this time?"

"Sorry, but no."

Something in his voice drew her up straight in the chair. "It's important?"

"Very. Did the ancient Egyptians have specific dates

when the priests of dark gods would perform important ceremonies?''

''Well, there were very specific dates set during the calendar year for the rites of Set.''

''No, we're not looking for their version of Christmas or Easter . . .''

''Hardly that, Set is a *dark* god.''

''Yeah. Well, it's not Set we're concerned about. If one of the lesser dark gods needed to hold an unscheduled rite, when would it happen?''

''It might help if you gave me some idea of why you needed to know.''

''I'm sorry, I can't tell you.''

Why did she know he was going to say that? ''Well, it could happen any time, I suppose, but a dark rite would most likely be held during the dark of the moon, when the eye of Thoth is out of the sky. And probably at midnight, when Ra, the sun god, has been out of the world for the longest time, and will still be gone for an equal amount of time.''

''Where?''

She blinked. ''I beg your pardon?''

''Where would the rite be held?''

''Does this god of yours not have a temple?''

''The rite involves creating a temple.''

Involves creating a temple? Present tense? Police work in Toronto was stranger than she thought. ''Then the rite would have happened wherever the priest wanted the temple to be.''

From the sound of his voice, his teeth were clenched. ''I was afraid you were going to say that. Thanks, Rachel. You've been a help.''

''Mike?'' The pause before he answered told her she'd barely caught him before he hung up. ''Will you tell me why you needed to know this when you've finished whatever you're working on?''

''Depends.''

''On?''

''On who wins.''

Rachel laughed at the melodrama as she settled the receiver back on the phone. Perhaps she should see Detective-

Sergeant Celluci again; he was certainly more interesting than academics and bureaucrats.

"Depends on who wins," she repeated, bending back over the report. "He even sounded like he meant it." The sudden chill that brushed against the fine hair on her neck, she credited to an overactive imagination.

Vicki turned to look out the window and frowned. "It's the dark of the moon tonight."

"How do you know?" Celluci asked. "Maybe the moon's behind a cloud?"

"I start my period two days after the dark of the moon. It's Tuesday. I start Thursday."

Hard to argue with. "Yeah, but the dark of the moon happens once a month," Celluci pointed out.

"Tawfik said soon." She wrapped her arms around her body and winced as the motion pulled one of her multiple bruises into a painful position. "It's tonight."

"We're in no shape to take him on tonight."

"You mean I'm not. *We* don't have a choice."

Celluci knew better than to argue with that tone. "Then we still have to find him."

"He must have told you something, Henry." The city stretched out below her, offering a thousand possibilities. "What else did he say?"

"Nothing about the location of a temple."

"Wasn't there something about a mountaintop?" Celluci asked.

"In a manner of speaking. He said, 'With no need to hide, I will shout Akhekh from the top of the highest mountain.' "

"Well, we're a little short of mountains in this part of the country. High or low."

"No." Both of Vicki's hands pressed flat against the glass as she suddenly realized what had caught her attention. "No. We aren't. Look."

Her tone pulled both men to her side without questions. Her eyes were wide, her breathing labored, and her heart beating so hard, Henry was almost afraid for her.

"What are we looking at?" he asked softly.

"The tower. Look at the tower."

The CN Tower rose at the foot of the city, a shadow

against the stars. As they watched, a section of the revolving disk lit up as though a giant flashbulb had gone off inside. It only lasted for an instant, but the light left an afterimage on the eye like a film of grease.

"It could be anything." Not even Celluci believed the protest, but he felt he had to make it. "There're often lights on the tower."

"It's him. He's up there. And I'm going to bring him down if I have to bring the whole goddamned tower down with him."

Up above the observation deck, two of the red airplane safety lights hovered strangely close together.

Almost like eyes.

Sixteen

"What the hell are you doing?"

Henry slipped the BMW into neutral. "I'm stopping at a yellow light."

"Why?"

"Detective, contrary to popular belief, a yellow light does not mean speed up, there's a red light coming."

"Yeah? Well, contrary to what you seem to believe, we haven't got all night. Rachel said this thing'll go down at midnight and it's eleven thirteen now."

"And being pulled over for a minor traffic violation with a wanted felon in the car would slow us down a lot more than obeying the rules of the road."

"Why don't I drive?"

Vicki leaned forward. "Why don't we compromise? Mike, shut up. And, Henry, speed up. Neither of you are proving a damned thing."

They left the car on Front Street and pounded up the stairs and onto the walkway that led over the railway tracks to the base of the CN Tower. Although Henry could have quickly outdistanced the two mortals, he matched his speed to Vicki's; just in case.

Without the crowds of people that filled the area during the day, the acres of concrete had a surreal, deserted look and even rubber-soled shoes echoed. Flashing their messages at empty space, neon advertisements blazed along the path to the tower—for the restaurant, for the disco, for the Tour of the Universe.

"Actually only takes you to Jupiter," Vicki panted as they passed under the last sign. "Half a solar system. Some universe." She ran with one hand touching the wall for both guidance and support and didn't bother worrying about not being able to see her feet. The path was smooth and obvious, and after what she'd been through, she wasn't going to let a little lack of light stop her.

"If he's up there," Celluci yelled as they flung themselves down the stairs at the other end of the walkway and rounded the corner to the main entrance. "I bet he's locked the elevators at the top with him."

"No bet." Vicki threw herself against a glass handle with no more effect than if she'd been the wind. "Not when the son of a bitch has locked the doors at the bottom."

Henry wrapped both hands under Vicki's and pulled. With a crack that echoed up the tower and back from the Skydome, the handle snapped off.

"Shit!" She glared at the tinted glass door and then at Henry. "Can you break through it?"

He shook his head. "Not without some kind of weapon. That's three-quarter-inch solid glass. Even I'd break bones first."

It almost seemed as though the tower designers had thought ahead to such a possibility; nothing in the immediate neighborhood could be used to shatter the door. Even the various levels were joined by solid masses of poured concrete, no metal banisters, no steel safety rails.

"Don't bother," Vicki snapped as Henry squatted and attempted to pry up a paving block. "We're wasting our time trying to get in here when Celluci's most likely right about the elevators."

Henry straightened. "We have to get him tonight, now. Before those people are sworn. We have to stop his god from gaining enough power to create more of him."

"I know. We take the stairs."

Celluci shook his head. "Vicki, that door's going to be locked, too."

"But it's a metal door with a metal handle—not likely to pull off in Henry's hand." She was moving before she finished speaking, limping around the reflecting pool and up to the back of the tower. "I am not," she snarled as they arrived at the entrance to the stairwell, "going to have this place turned into the world's tallest freestanding Egyptian fucking temple. Henry—!"

The heavy metal door bowed on his first pull, layers of paint cracking and dropping to the ground, a battleship gray avalanche of paint flakes. The second pull ripped it free of its hinges and dragged the very expensive security system out through the door frame nearly intact.

It made surprisingly little noise, all things considered.

"Why no alarms?" Celluci demanded suspiciously, frowning at the tangle of ripped wires.

"How should I know?" Muscles protesting, his strength tested to its limit, Henry leaned the door against the tower. "Perhaps Tawfik's providing burnt offerings and he doesn't want to set off the sprinkler system."

"Or it's silent and there's a fleet of patrol cars on the way."

"Also possible," Henry agreed.

"Then maybe you'd better stop wasting time talking about it." Although the ambient light did Vicki little good, it provided contrast between the concrete giant and the jagged black hole that was their only entrance. She charged toward it only to be brought to a rocking halt by Celluci's grip on her arm.

"Vicki, wait a minute."

"Let go of me." The edge on her voice threatened to remove his arm if he didn't.

He took the chance. "Look, we can't just go charging up there without a plan. You're letting your emotions do the thinking for you. Hell, *we're* letting your emotions do the thinking for *us*. Just stop and consider for a second—what happens when we get to the top?"

She glared at him and twisted free. "We take out Tawfik, that's what happens."

"Vicki . . ." Henry moved forward into her line of sight. "We probably won't be able to get close to him. He has protections."

Her eyes narrowed. "If you're still afraid of him, Henry, you can wait down here."

Henry took another step toward her, his silence nearly deafening.

"I'm sorry." She reached out and touched him lightly on the chest. "Look, how hard can it be? Mike'll shoot him from the doorway. I doubt he has a protection up against that. You *do* have your gun?"

"Yeah, but . . ."

"It does have a certain simplicity that appeals," Henry

admitted. "But I doubt he'll let us get that close. He'll have warded the temple area and the moment we cross those wards . . ." His voice trailed off.

"So you distract him and Mike shoots him," Vicki ground out through clenched teeth. "As you said, simple. And surprise is essential and *we are wasting time*!" She started for the tower again and again Celluci stopped her.

"You wait down here," he said. He'd already nearly lost her once this week. He wasn't going through that hell again.

"I *what*?"

"You're in no shape to face natural opposition let alone supernatural. I doubt you can even make it to the top; you're at the end of your resources, you're already limping, you're . . ."

"You. Just. Let. Me. Worry. About. Me." Each word emerged as a separate, barely controlled explosion.

Henry laid a hand on her shoulder. "You know he's right. I distract Tawfik and he shoots him; you didn't include yourself in your simple plan."

"*I* am going up there to watch him die."

"*You* are putting yourself at unnecessary risk," Celluci growled. "And what happens if we fail? Who's left to take a second shot?"

Vicki yanked her arm out of his hands and shoved her face up close to his. "What? Did I forget to mention plan B? If you two screw up, I'm there to pick up the pieces. Now either give me your gun and I'll shoot him myself, or get the fuck up those stairs."

"She has the right to be there," Henry said after a second that lasted several lifetimes, and it was obvious from his tone he liked it no more than Celluci did.

Vicki turned on him. "Thank you *very* much. *You* could have been at the top of the goddamned tower by now!" She stomped into the stairwell and groped for the first stair. Then the second. The emergency lights were a distraction so she closed her eyes. *Two down, one thousand, seven hundred and eighty-eight left to go.*

"Vicki?"

She hadn't heard Henry come up behind her, but she could feel his presence just back of her left shoulder. She didn't want to listen to apologies or explanations or whatever he had to say. "Just go."

"But you're going to need help getting to the top. I could carry . . ."

"You could worry about Tawfik and not about me. Get moving." Through gritted teeth, she added, "Please."

The presence moved past, touched her lightly on the wrist, just at the spot where the vein lay closest to the surface, and was gone.

"He's right. You've barely got that drug out of your system not to mention the overt physical abuse. You won't make it to the top without help."

She glared at the vaguely man-shaped bit of dark on dark. "Fuck you, too, and stop worrying about *me*."

Celluci knew better than to say anything further although she heard him snarl something under his breath as he brushed by.

She tried to match his speed, and anger actually kept her to it for a while, but the distance between them gradually grew. Finally, the sound of single footsteps blended into a staccato background to the pounding of her heart.

Ten steps and a landing. Ten steps and a landing. It was going to take her a little longer than nine minutes and fifty-four seconds this time. Her lack of vision made no difference—after establishing the pattern, her feet were well able to find their own way—but with each movement the last two days made themselves felt on her body. Everything ached.

Ten steps and a landing.

Her lungs began to burn. Each breath became purchased with greater denominations of pain.

Ten steps and a landing.

Her left knee felt as though a spike had been driven up under the bone.

Ten steps and a landing.

Lift the right leg up, pull the left leg forward. Lift the right leg up, pull the left leg forward.

She peeled out of her jacket and let it lie where it fell.

Ten steps and a landing.

Unnecessary risk, my ass.

Ten steps and a landing.

Of course I wasn't part of my plan. Did they actually think I wasn't aware of the shape I'd be in at the top of this thing? I'm going to be lucky if I can stand.

Ten steps and a landing.

"She has a right to be there." Jesus H. Christ.

Ten steps and a landing.

Damned right I'm going to be there. And I'm going to spit on Tawfik's corpse.

Ten steps and a landing.

She'd read an article once about an American Medal of Honor winner who'd been hit twenty-three times by enemy fire and still managed, despite his injuries, to run across a bridge to save another member of his unit. She'd wondered at the time what he'd been thinking of when he did it. She suspected now that she had a pretty good idea.

You can fall down when this is over, not before.

Ten steps and a landing.

Leg muscles began to tremble, then jump. Every step became an individual battle against pain and exhaustion. She stumbled, lost the rhythm, and slammed her shin into a metal fronting.

Eight, nine, ten steps, and a landing.

With so much of her weight pulled ahead by hands and arms, the gauze wrapped round her split knuckle sagged— wet with sweat or blood, she neither knew nor cared. When it became more hindrance than help, she ripped it off and dropped it.

Ten steps and a landing.

Lesser angers burned away until only the anger at Tawfik remained. He'd drugged her and jailed her, but worst of all, he'd perverted something she believed in. *That* stretched between them like the rope she'd hang him with and she dragged himself toward him on it.

Ten steps and a landing.

Henry felt the wards as he crossed them, a faint sizzle along the surface of his skin that jerked every hair on his body erect. He had no idea what information they conveyed back to Tawfik, whether general or specific, but either way time now became critical. He raced up the last two flights of stairs. Far below he could hear Celluci laboring, and below that, Vicki's crippled progress. Their heartbeats echoed in the stairwell, their breathing so loud it sounded as if the whole structure inhaled and exhaled with them. It seemed he'd be on his own for some time.

Only one in four of the fluorescents were on in the hall

that wrapped around the central pillar of the tower and
Henry, exiting out of the dim confines of the stairwell, gave
thanks. Very often the level of light that mortals preferred
placed him at a handicap and tonight he'd need every advantage.

Silently, he moved around the sweeping curve, following
the hum of chanting. The background murmur in at least a
dozen voices, consisted of nothing more than the name Akhekh repeated over and over with a kind of low-key intensity
that worked its way beneath the surface and throbbed in
bone and blood. Senses extended, Henry wasn't surprised
to hear one single, all encompassing heartbeat where there
should have been a multitude.

Rising over the chanting, a single voice spoke in a language that Henry didn't know, using cadences that sounded
strange even to ears that had heard four and a half centuries
of changes. Whatever else they were—and Henry had no
doubt they held layers of meaning wrapped around each
syllable, each tone—the words were a calling. Only the outermost edges brushed against him and he could feel himself
urged closer.

He burst through the disco's main entrance, past an arc
of empty tables. The background chanting grew louder.

Tawfik stood on the raised platform, inside an arc of padded rail where the dee jays usually sat, arms raised in the
classic high priest pose. He wore a pair of khaki colored
pants and an open necked linen shirt—not exactly the style
of ancient Egypt, but then he didn't need a costume to de-
clare what he was. Power crackled around him in an almost
visible aura.

Crowded to either side of the dance floor, gazes riveted
on Tawfik, were high-ranking officers from both the Metro
and the Ontario Provincial police, two judges, and the pub-
lisher of the most powerful of the three Toronto daily newspapers. Henry had thought he'd heard a dozen voices, now,
if he'd had to rely on hearing alone, he'd have said six although there were clearly more than twenty people involved. Individual tones and timbres were dissolving into
the chant.

The most incongruous part of the entire scene had to be
the giant silver disco ball that hung from the ceiling and

spun slowly, flinging multicolored points of light over both
Tawfik and his acolytes.

All this, Henry took in between one heartbeat and the
next. Without breaking stride, he gathered himself up to
spring forward at Tawfik's apparently unprotected back.

"AKHEKH!"

For a single voicing of the name, Tawfik joined the chant,
the points of light began to coalesce, the silver ball stopped
spinning, and Henry barely got his arm up over his eyes in
time. He staggered, almost fell, and tried to blink away the
afterimages left by the tiny fraction of the brilliance that
had actually gotten through.

The volume of the chanting rose, then fell to a nearly
subliminal murmur, almost easy to ignore, and Henry realized that the overlay of spell-casting had stopped.

"You are interfering in things you have no understanding
of, Nightwalker." The voice was cold, distant, a counterpoint to the golden sun now burning in Henry's mind, larger
and more brilliant than it had been only two days before.

Teeth clenched, Henry ignored the pain and wrapped the
sun in his anger, dimming the overpowering life of the
wizard-priest to the point where he could function. Through
dancing patterns of light he saw Tawfik frown, an elder disturbed by the actions of a youth; those actions not a threat
but merely an annoyance.

"Fortunately," Tawfik continued, still parent to child,
teacher to student, "we have reached a point in the ceremony where a short pause will not affect the final outcome.
You have time to explain your presence here before I decide
what to do about you."

For an instant, Henry felt himself sliding into the role the
wizard-priest defined. Snarling, he thrust it aside. He was
Vampire, Nightwalker. He would not be made subordinate
again by mere words. The confusion Tawfik had used and
twisted before had all been burned away in his rage at
Vicki's disappearance and the elder immortal's part in it. *He
has hurt one of mine. I will not have that.*

He'd nearly gained the edge of the platform, less than an
arm's reach away from Tawfik's throat, when red lines flared
and slammed him back against the wall of the disco.

"I told you when we first met that you couldn't destroy
me. You should have listened." The words stood out flat

and uncompromising against the background chant as Tawfik realized that the Nightwalker's relative youth could no longer be manipulated and dropped the pose of bored disdain. After the challenges he had ignored the night before, he had known this confrontation would come, but tonight, when all his attention should be focused on Akhekh, tonight was not the time he would have chosen.

Not even the ceremony of sanctification had blocked the approaching glory of the Nightwalker's ka. He wanted it, wanted it more than he had ever wanted anything in his long life, and he had known from the moment the wards were shattered that tonight, at this moment, he held enough power to take what he so desperately desired. But the power he held wasn't his and Akhekh, for all he named his lord a petty godling, had painful ways of claiming ownership. The centuries had taught caution. After the ceremony, when Akhekh would be in a mood to grant favors, there would be power to spare and no risk of angering his lord. And once he had the Nightwalker's ka, he need never fear his lord's anger again.

If words were not enough to hold the Nightwalker, then other steps had to be taken. With a curt gesture, he raised the volume of the chant a fraction and then carefully, so as not to disturb the magical structures already in place and using only his own power, he began to weave a spell of binding. The mortals, still in the stairwell, could be ignored until they arrived, then their destruction would become part of the ceremony.

Stunned and bruised, Henry struggled to his feet. He had no idea how far behind him Celluci was as the scent and sound of the acolytes blocked the scent and sound of the detective's approach.

"So you distract him and Mike shoots him. Simple."

Not so simple. Although if a physical attack had no effect, perhaps the wizard-priest could be distracted in other ways. He was fond enough of the sound of his own voice. Henry moved away from the wall. There was only one thing he was interested in hearing about. "Why did you attack Vicki Nelson?"

Tawfik smiled, fully aware of what the Nightwalker attempted, for the accumulated power gave him access to all but the deepest levels of that glorious immortal ka. It didn't

matter. In a moment he would invoke the binding spell and
the moment after begin the third and final part of the calling. And the moment after that, he would feed. Answering
the Nightwalker's question would serve to fill the time.
"Your Vicki Nelson was chosen by my lord. To use an anal-
ogy you might understand, he occasionally orders a specific
meal rather than taking what's offered on the buffet. As the
gods may not directly interfere except in the lives of those
sworn to their service, I prepare the meal for him, placing
the chosen one in a situation of optimum hopelessness and
despair. That she happened to be the mortal you cared for
was pure coincidence, I assure you. Did you go to a great
deal of trouble getting her out of jail?"

"Not really." Henry stopped at the edge of the platform,
at the point where the ambient power surrounding the
wizard-priest brushed against him, throbbing in time with
the single heartbeat of the chorus. "She'd nearly gotten herself out when I arrived."

"Almost a pity that she came along with you tonight."
The Nightwalker's ka flared and Tawfik nearly lost himself
in desire. "You didn't think I was unaware of your companions, did you? I'll have to kill her, of course."

"You'll have to kill me first."

Tawfik laughed, but Henry's expression didn't alter and
his ka burned high and steady. Slowly, he realized that the
statement, as unbelievable as it was, came from those
guarded, innermost regions of the ka and that the younger
immortal had meant exactly what he'd said. Shock and confusion destroyed his control of the binding spell. Ebony
brows drew down to meet in a painfully tight vee. "You
would lay down your immortal life for her? For one whose
entire existence should mean no more to you than a moment's nourishment?"

"Yes."

"That's insane!" With the binding spell in tatters, Tawfik
saw his options slip from his grasp. From the time the two
mortals had entered the tower, their deaths had been woven
into the ceremony of sanctification. The woman had to die.
Her death was promised to Akhekh. But in order for the
woman to die, he must kill the Nightwalker as well. If he
killed the Nightwalker, all the power of that glorious ka
would be lost.

No! I will not lose his ka! It is mine!

Henry had no idea what caused Tawfik to scowl so, but the wizard-priest certainly looked distracted. He pushed against the power barrier. It pushed back.

I could take the ka. Take it now. Use the power generated by the first two-thirds of the spell of sanctification. Use the power bled from the acolytes. Pay the price . . .

But would there be a price? Surely the devouring of an immortal life, would give him power equal to Akhekh's. Perhaps greater.

The chant began to rise in volume. The time had come to begin the third and final part of the spell of sanctification. He had no time to create another binding spell. He had no intention of losing the Nightwalker's magnificent, glorious ka.

Decision made between one heartbeat and the next, Tawfik wrapped his will around the accumulated power and threw all of it into the spell of acquisition. This would be rape, not the seduction he had initially planned, but the end result would be the same.

The sun flared white-gold behind Henry's eyes and he felt himself begin to burn. He could feel the strength that fed the flames, feel his edges consumed, feel . . . something familiar.

Hunger. He could feel Tawfik's Hunger.

Then he felt Tawfik's hands cup his face, lifting his head so their eyes met. Ebony eyes with no bottom to stop his fall.

The heartbeat of the acolytes roared in his ears. No. Not the acolytes. Not the heartbeat he had heard since he gained the top of the tower. Another heartbeat, a little faster than human norm, sound carried through the contact of skin against skin. Tawfik's heartbeat. Driving Tawfik's blood. For all his stolen centuries of life, Tawfik's scent was mortal. Had been mortal that night in the park. Was mortal now.

Henry set his own Hunger free, loosing the leash of restraint survival in a civilized world forced it to wear.

Steel fingers clamped down on Tawfik's shoulders and he cried out, forcing focus past the ecstasy to find the threat. He recognized the Hunter snarling out at him from the face between his hands.

"Nightwalker," he whispered, suddenly realizing what

he held, what the legends meant when they were not legends any longer. During the time it took him to say the name, he felt the ka he sought to devour pull almost clear of the spell and just for that instant he slid beneath the surface of hazel eyes gone agate hard.

The grip on his shoulders tightened. The bone began to give. Desperately, Tawfik sucked yet more power from the acolytes and fed it into the protection spell—so stupid to have touched him and rendered all but the most basic defense useless. If he released the spell of acquisition, he had power enough to break free, but the spell of acquisition was all he had left. There could be no turning back.

He wrenched his gaze free of the Nightwalker's and dropped his hands down to the corded column of throat. An instant later, an answering band of flesh closed tightly around his own throat, only his magic keeping the crushing thumbs from his windpipe.

I will not loose this ka! He slammed the spell of acquisition against the Nightwalker's strength.

The sun became a holocaust of flame, but the Hunger dragged Henry through it to answer the blood that called from the other side.

How the fuck am I supposed to shoot at that? Celluci leaned panting against the wall of the disco, one hand shielding his eyes from the painfully bright lights scattering off the spinning silver ball. *Goddamned son of a bitch was supposed to distract him, not fucking dance with him.*

From where he stood, Celluci could see Fitzroy's back and, just above that, long golden fingers wrapped around Fitzroy's throat. A slight shift to his right showed him that Fitzroy's fingers were in turn locked around the throat of a tall dark man; probably good-looking under more normal circumstances. Although he couldn't say why, Celluci had the strangest feeling that the attempt at mutual strangulation was merely window dressing, that the real struggle was taking place somewhere else.

Maybe I should let them throttle each other and then shoot what's left. Gun cocked, he stepped out onto the dance floor. The new angle moved the combatants into unobstructed profile. Although their upper bodies swayed back and forth barely a hand's span apart, both sets of feet were firmly planted with nearly a meter between them. *Well, I'm no Barry Wu, but I think that I can at least guarantee not to hit the wrong legs.* He took his stance, braced his service revolver with his left hand, and tried to steady his breathing. He'd probably have a better chance if he waited until his lungs stopped heaving air in and out like asthmatic bellows, but it was coming up on midnight, and if Rachel Shane was right, the world didn't have much time. *Once in the knee to get his attention and then a second round to finish him.*

In such a small, enclosed space the sound of the gunshot expanded to touch the walls then slam back. And forth. And back. The shot itself went wide.

"Shit goddamnit!"

Ears ringing, Celluci raised the gun to shoot again, but unfortunately, although he'd done no damage, he had gotten the wizard-priest's attention.

The sound nearly jerked his grip from the Nightwalker's ka and only centuries of practice kept the spell of acquisition from shattering. He tightened his grip, slammed his rage at the interruption against the younger immortal's will, and, in the instant of breathing space that bought, sucked yet more power from the acolytes in order to snarl, "Stop him!"

"Stop him?" Celluci stepped back a step and then another. "Oh, fuck." He'd been so intent on the battle between Fitzroy and the mummy that he'd completely ignored the semicircles of chanting men and women that lined both sides of the dance floor. He had, in fact, passed right through one group in order to gain his current position, their presence never even registering. *Look, it's been a long day, I've got a lot on my mind.* But that kind of inattention to detail could get a man killed. *I can't believe I did that.*

Somewhere between twenty and thirty people shuffled out of the shadows, placing their bodies between their master and the threat. Still chanting, they moved slowly toward Celluci, faces frighteningly blank.

He backed up another few steps and raised his gun. Although he recognized a number of the group as senior police officers, they didn't seem to recognize the weapon and kept advancing. In another two or three feet, he'd be at the

edge of the dance floor, his back against the wall. Fifteen
years on the force allowed him to maintain a patina of calm,
but he could feel panic beginning to lap at the edges.

Almost frantically he searched for something to shoot,
something that would get their attention, force them to ac-
knowledge that *he* was the one with the gun. Unfortunately,
the spinning disco ball, the most obvious target, was providing over half of the available light. Backing up another
step, he made his decision and squeezed the trigger.

The ceiling tile exploded, throwing compressed foam and
sound insulation down over the chanting crowd. Ignoring
the echos battering the inside of his skull, Celluci lowered
the gun.

Some instinct of self-preservation seemed to kick in
and they stopped advancing, but the living barrier between
him and Tawfik remained.

Okay. Now what?

A single man shuffled forward out of the front rank. In
spite of the bad light, Celluci had no trouble recognizing . . .

"Inspector Cantree."

His hand grew sweaty around the pistol grip as his immediate superior shuffled closer. While there were any number of high-ranking police officers Celluci could've
cheerfully shot, Cantree wasn't one of them. He'd been a
black man on the force long before affirmative action pro-
grams and, in spite of all the bullshit thrown at him, he'd
risen through the ranks with both his belief in the law and
his sense of humor intact. That Tawfik could take a decent
man, who had survived so much, and strip him of free will
and honor twisted Celluci into knots, and to his horror he
felt his eyes grow damp.

"Inspector, I don't want to shoot you."

One massive hand came up, palm outstretched, miming,
"Give me the gun," very clearly over the continuing chant.

The roaring in his ears made it nearly impossible to
think. "Inspector, don't make me do this."

Vicki heard the gunshot as she fell out of the stairwell
and onto her knees, forehead pressed against the pale gray
carpet. *Shooting should've been over ages ago. What the
hell's going on up here?*

She had very little memory of how she'd managed to climb the last few flights of stairs although she knew that every movement had been imprinted on muscle and sinew and that her body would collect payment later, with interest, for the layers of abuse. She'd fallen twice and the second time, sprawled writhing on a concrete landing, only the thought of Celluci, already at the top, had given her the strength to move again. Her howl of desperate denial still echoed up and down the length of the tower.

Teeth clenched against the agony in her calves, she crawled to the wall and inched her way along it, not bothering, not able, to stand. Having been the native guide for her mother on numerous occasions, she ignored the disco's main entrance and continued around the curve of the hall as quickly as tortured muscles and bones could take her. All she could hear was her own labored breathing—in with the taste of blood, out with the taste of defeat.

You can't have won, you antique son of a bitch. I won't allow it.

Almost a quarter of the way around the arc of the tower was a window, designed so tourists could stand and watch the gyrations inside on the dance floor. The disco side of the window had been heavily tinted—apparently the management assumed the dancers had no interest in watching the tourists.

Just beyond, a dark line of shadows advanced toward Celluci.

Backing carefully away from the window, one hand still clamped to the frame for support, Vicki jammed her glasses back onto the bridge of her nose. *Looks like it's time for plan B.*

Close by, tucked discreetly into an angle in the wall, was an emergency exit; beside it, a glass-fronted cabinet of firefighting equipment. Vicki fell toward the cabinet, hung off the latch for a heartbeat, and finally managed to get it open. Clamping the nozzle under her arm, she turned the water on full force, then let her weight drop against the bar-latch on the door. She figured she had between five and ten seconds before the water reached the end of the hose and the pressure blew her off her feet.

Three seconds to drag the door toward her far enough to let her pass.

*There's got to be a light here. You can't deal with emer-
gencies in the dark.* Two further seconds while logic actually answered and groping fingers closed on a familiar plastic
switch.

One final second for her to take in Celluci backed against
the wall, gun out; Inspector Cantree crawling on his stomach toward him, dragging blood across the parquet from a
wounded thigh; a crowd of two dozen terrifyingly blank-
faced men and women shuffling forward, fingers curled into
claws.

For the first time, she could hear the chanting over the
protests of her own body.

And then the water exploding from the nozzle nearly
jerked the hose out of her hands. Knuckles white, thrown
against the wall and held upright between the irresistible
force and the immovable object, Vicki fought to keep the
stream spraying across the dance floor, slamming Tawfik's
puppets off their feet.

The chant abruptly shut off and with it the power he pulled
from the acolytes. He felt thumbs press harder against his
windpipe and his will drawn into the trap of agate eyes. To
dissolve the spell of acquisition was no longer an option, in
order to win, in order to live, his will must prove stronger
and he must absorb the Nightwalker's ka. All or nothing.
He released his personal power into the spell.

On a platform on the far side of the dance floor, Vicki
saw Henry locked in combat with a tall, dark-haired man.
Tawfik. It had to be. She felt Celluci push up against her
side and shoved the hose into his hands, bellowing, "Keep
. . . them down." Then she staggered back out into the hall
for the fire ax.

"Vicki? Goddamnit, Vicki, what are you doing?"

She ignored him. It was all she could do to drag herself
across the dance floor using the heavy ax as a kind of wedge-
headed cane. Leg muscles had begun to spasm by the time
she reached the platform and Tawfik's hair had gone from
black to gray.

Teeth locked down on her lower lip, desperately fighting
for enough air through flared nostrils, she stepped up behind

the wizard-priest. It took her two tries to lift the ax over her head.

The sun became a burning weight, a thousand, a hundred thousand lives bearing down on him. The smell of his own flesh burning began to bury the blood scent. Ebony depths promised a cooling, an end. Henry pushed past the Hunger to reach them.

The ax went into the center of Tawfik's back with a meaty thunk and sank haft deep. Vicki'd put everything she had left into the blow. Fingers with no strength in them slid off the handle and the weight of her arms falling drove her back an involuntary step. Her hips slammed into the platform rail, her legs folded, and she dropped straight down to sit, more or less upright, against a padded support.

Tawfik's head jerked up and his mouth opened, but no sound came out. His hands released their hold on Henry's throat and groped behind him. He spun around, pulling free of Henry's grip, staggered, and fell, back arched against the pain, mouth still silently working.

Henry's shoulders straightened and his lips came up off his teeth. Now, finally, he would feed. . . .

"No, Henry!"

Snarling, he lifted his head toward the voice. Dimly, through the Hunger, he recognized Vicki, and turned to see what she stared at with such terror.

Two red eyes burned in the air at the edge of the platform. A faint crimson haze hinted at a bird's head, strangely winged, and an antelope's body.

Tawfik lifted one hand toward his god, trembling fingers spread, silently begging to be saved.

The red eyes burned brighter.

Gray hair turned white, brittle, and then fell to expose a yellowed dome of skull. Cheeks collapsed in upon themselves. Flesh melted away and skin stretched tight, tighter, gone. One by one, the tiny bones dropped from Tawfik's outstretched hand as tendons rotted and let go.

Finally, there were only clothes and the ax and a fine gray powder that might have been ash.

And the red eyes were gone.

"You guys okay?"

Henry reached across the remains and touched Vicki lightly on the cheek. In four hundred and fifty years, he had never felt the Hunger less. Vicki managed to nod. Together they turned to face Celluci.

"We're okay." Henry's throat closed around the words and they emerged with all the highs and lows scraped off. "What about you?"

Celluci snorted. "Fine. Just fine." He looked down at the powder, his movements jerky and tightly controlled. "All things considered. Why didn't . . ." The pause filled with a common memory of glowing red eyes. ". . . it save him? I mean, it made him."

Henry shook his head. "I don't know. I guess we'll never know. But I could feel Tawfik's life right until the last second. He was aware the whole time he was . . . was . . ."

"Dying. Jesus H. Christ." It was more a prayer than a profanity.

A collective moan that broke down into a babble of near hysteria drew their attention back out onto the dance floor. Most of Tawfik's ex-acolytes appeared to be in a state of shock. Most but not all.

Shirt wrapped in a makeshift bandage around his leg, supported by one of the two judges and the Deputy Chief of the OPP, Cantree dragged himself out of the crowd and scowled at the three on the platform.

"What the hell," he demanded, "has been going on here?"

"Go ahead, Mike." Vicki's head lolled back against the rail as she tried to decide whether she'd rather puke or cry, and if she had the energy to do either. "He's your boss. You tell him. . . ."

Celluci showed up at Henry's condo about an hour before dawn. He'd spent an uncomfortable two hours with Cantree in the emergency ward at St. Michael's Hospital telling him as much as he seemed willing to hear.

"You realize what this sounds like, don't you?"

"Yeah, I realize."

"I'd say you were the biggest liar of my acquaintance if it weren't for two things. I had no reason to have you arrested, yet I can remember giving the order and, just before

you shot me, kind of hovering over your head . . ." He wet his lips. *". . . I saw a pair of red glowing eyes."*

"Apparently, it feeds on despair."

Cantree shifted position on the gurney and winced. *"Nice to hear you weren't looking forward to pulling the trigger. . . ."*

Moving carefully, he crossed the living room, threw himself down on the couch, and rubbed his face with his hands. "Christ, Vicki, you stink of liniment. You should've gone to the hospital yourself." Behind her glasses her eyes narrowed in warning and he let it drop. Again. He had to believe she was too smart to allow machismo to cripple her. "So how did the rest of it go?"

Henry turned away from the city. The night was his again. He'd almost lost it, would have lost it had Vicki not used the ax when she had. For all he had meant nothing by it, Tawfik had been right when he'd said a man shouldn't travel alone through the years. *You were the one traveling alone, old man,* he told the memory of ebony eyes. *And that's what killed you in the end. I have companions on the road. I have someone to guard my back. You gave up humanity for your immortality. I only gave up the day.* There would be no more dreams of the sun.

He leaned back against the window, arms folded across his chest, his gaze caressing Vicki lightly on its way to Celluci's face. "Fortunately, the various ex-acolytes remembered enough of what they'd agreed to—including rather explicit hallucinations during the chanting that none of them wanted to talk about—that 'it's over, it never happened' seemed to be explanation enough. Your Inspector Cantree was the only one involved who wanted to know what was really going on. By morning, the rest of them will have convinced themselves that they were at a wild party that got a little out of hand."

"All except George Zottie," Vicki added from the armchair. "Tawfik had taken over so much of his mind that when Tawfik died he didn't have anything left. The doctors say it was a massive stroke and he probably won't live long."

"A massive stroke," Celluci repeated, his eyes narrowing suspiciously, and he peered across the room at Henry. "What would make them think that?"

Henry shrugged. "Well, they were hardly likely to think his brain had been magically destroyed by a three-thousand-year-old Egyptian wizard-priest trying to sanctify a temple to his god."

"Yeah? And what about that god? Tawfik's dead. Is it?"

"Of course it isn't," Vicki snapped before Henry could speak. "Or Tawfik wouldn't *be* dead."

"Look, Vicki," Celluci sighed, "pretend it's very late and that I've been up for almost forty-eight hours, which it is and I have, and explain that to me."

"Tawfik's god allowed Tawfik to die. Therefore Tawfik was no longer necessary for its survival."

"But Tawfik told me that his god only survived because of him," Henry objected. "That a god with no one to believe in it is absorbed back into good or evil."

Vicki rolled her eyes. "Tawfik's god has people who believe in it," she said slowly and distinctly. "Us. Worship isn't necessary. Only belief."

"No, Tawfik worshiped."

"Sure he did; he sold his soul for immortality and that was his part of the bargain. But he also spent a few thousand years out cold in a sarcophagus and he sure as shit wasn't worshiping then. His god seems to have survived just fine." She slid her glasses back up her nose. "So tonight, Tawfik does something to piss off his god. We don't know what. Maybe it didn't approve of the venue for the temple—although any god that feeds off hopelessness and despair should find itself right at home in that meat market—maybe it didn't like the taste of the acolytes, maybe it didn't like Tawfik's attitude. . . ."

"Tawfik wanted to be seen as all powerful," Henry said thoughtfully, remembering.

"Well, there you have it." Vicki spread her hands. "Maybe it was afraid of a temple coup. Whatever the reason, it chose to trade Tawfik in. It'd never get a better opportunity because you," she jabbed an emphatic finger in Henry's direction, "are as immortal as Tawfik was."

Celluci frowned. "Then Henry's in danger."

Vicki shrugged. "We all are. We know its name. The moment we give in to hopelessness and despair, it'll be on us like—like politicians at a free bar. It may not need worshipers to survive, but it certainly needs them to get stronger. All it has to do is convince one of us and then we tell two friends and they tell two friends and so on and so on and here we go around the mulberry bush again. It'll want Henry, he'll last longer. But it'll settle for you or me.''

"So basically what you're saying,'' Celluci sighed, ''in your own long-winded way, is that it isn't over. We've beaten Tawfik, but we've still got Tawfik's god to fight.''

To his surprise, Vicki smiled. ''We've been fighting the god of hopelessness and despair all our lives, Mike. Now, we know it has a name. So what? It's the same fight.''

Then her expression changed and Celluci, who recognized trouble, shot an anxious look at Henry who apparently recognized it, too.

"And now, I have something to say to you both.'' Her voice should've been registered as a lethal weapon. ''If either of you ever again pull the patronizing bullshit you pulled on me tonight at the base of the tower, I'm going to rip your living hearts out and feed them to you. Do I make myself clear?''

The answering silence spoke volumes.

"Good. You can spend the next few months making it up to me.''

DAW

Tanya Huff

VICTORY NELSON, INVESTIGATOR:
Otherworldly Crimes A Specialty

☐ **BLOOD PRICE: Book 1**   UE2471—$3.99
Can one ex-policewoman and a vampire defeat the magic-spawned
evil which is devastating Toronto?

☐ **BLOOD TRAIL: Book 2**   UE2502—$4.50
Someone was out to exterminate Canada's most endangered species—
the werewolf.

☐ **BLOOD LINES: Book 3**   UE2530—$4.99
Long-imprisoned by the magic of Egypt's gods, an ancient force of evil
is about to be loosed on an unsuspecting Toronto.

THE NOVELS OF CRYSTAL

When an evil wizard attempts world domination, the Elder Gods must
intervene!

☐ **CHILD OF THE GROVE: Book 1**   UE2432—$3.95
☐ **THE LAST WIZARD: Book 2**   UE2331—$3.95

OTHER NOVELS

☐ **THE FIRE'S STONE**   UE2445—$3.95
Thief, swordsman and wizardess—drawn together by a quest not of
their own choosing, would they find their true destinies in a fight
against spells, swords and betrayal?
